THE HOWLING DEMARIAN WAR CRY
FILLED THE AIR. . . .

A great figure leaped into the courtyard, metal singing a deadly song before him. The Prince of Gwyneth had joined the fray, a veil of red-gray fire surrounding him, vying with the sunlight in its brilliance.

Swinging his great broadsword, flames licking up the blade, he sliced through an enemy in one stroke. Howling with wild laughter, the Crown Prince threw himself at another. Terrified, the man gave way before him.

Their Lord in their midst, the Royal Guard rallied and charged the enemy. Forming a protective circle around him and those who'd left the building following him, they held their ground. With Hough leading the defense, they fought their way across the yard. Then a Shield Knight fell, breaking the ring of protective swords and the red veil guttered and went out. The circle faltered. Kelahnus saw a black-robed woman by the archway, her arms raised to the sky, saw Demnor's squire swept away, and the Earl's bright hair stained with blood, saw Demnor stumble as the magic of the Flame deserted him. . . .

**Be sure to read all the magnificent novels
in Fiona Patton's
tales of the Branion Realm:**

THE STONE PRINCE

THE PAINTER KNIGHT

THE GRANITE SHIELD

THE STONE PRINCE

Fiona Patton

DAW BOOKS, INC.
DONALD A. WOLLHEIM, FOUNDER
375 Hudson Street, New York, NY 10014

ELIZABETH R. WOLLHEIM
SHEILA E. GILBERT
PUBLISHERS

First Printing, April 1997

5   6   7   8   9

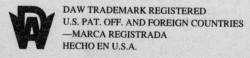

DAW TRADEMARK REGISTERED
U.S. PAT. OFF. AND FOREIGN COUNTRIES
—MARCA REGISTRADA
HECHO EN U.S.A.

PRINTED IN THE U.S.A.

For Tanya

For quiet walks and not so quiet cats

THE BRANION REALM
and Surrounding Countries 893 DR

Hereditary Branion Holding

THE COLUMBAS

DANELIND

NORDANGER

Bryholm

BJERRE SEA

STORVICHOLM

HEATHLAND

SORLANDY

Falmarnnock
Braxborough

Liddesdane

FENLAND

BACHIEM

Grimscombe

KORMANDEAUX

Linconford

ANVRE

Briery

Branion
Continental
Holdings

GALLIA

GWYNETH

Branbridge

FORNESS
ISLAND

MIST RIVER

ROLAND

AQUILLIARD

BRANION

GASPELLIER

EIRION

PANISHA

TIBERIA

N

uLaiBert '96

I. Demnor

Autumn, Mean Fhomhair, 893 DR
The Most Holy Temple of the Living Flame, Branbridge

As the new sun touched the spiral tips of the capital city an elder priest of the Most Holy Order of the Flame slipped into the temple's main sanctuary. Kneeling before the hearth, he lit his torch and paused, watching the flames crawl greedily over the knot of oil-soaked hemp. Fire was the center of his faith and as always he was caught by the power that flickered in even this tiny manifestation. The priest had seen just such a spark ignite a city. He had seen it rise in the gaze of one ruler while it faded from the eyes of another and had seen it burn in the newborn gaze of every Royal child since he himself had been a boy. He had seen it in prophecy that very night and the future it foretold made him shiver.

He returned his attention to the torch. When it burned steadily, he rose with a groan, making the sign of the Holy Triarchy across his breast. He was getting too old for this duty, he grumbled to himself. Time to pass it on to younger shoulders. Bowing before the hearth, he turned and left the sanctuary.

A chill breeze lifted the tapestry edges as he moved swiftly through the corridors. Stopping to relight a wall sconce that had been extinguished in the night, he shivered again. The autumn was beginning colder than usual and the swallows were already leaving. The signs spoke of dire changes to come.

"Harsh winds bring harsh news," the priest muttered to himself as he moved on.

At the far end of the hall a Flame Champion came to attention and opened the portal cut in the south door. After helping the priest step through, she accepted his blessing with a murmur of thanks before closing the door behind him. Descending the worn stone steps at a dignified pace, the priest paused to catch his breath, then crossed the temple's cobbled courtyard.

In the center of the courtyard a copper dish sat atop a stone pillar. Two acolytes had just finished filling it with oil and they bowed as the priest approached. Speaking the ancient words of renewal, he touched the torch to the wick and the flame took hold, burning brightly as it had every morning for almost nine hundred years. The priest turned to the open gates, his arms wide.

"The Living Flame burns for all the people of Branion. Let any who need Its blessing come and be replenished."

A small group of respectfully hushed citizens entered, each carrying one of the small lamps that the temple distributed to the poor. One by one, the acolytes filled the lamps and raised them to the Flame. In their midst an old man who'd once served at the palace before age and infirmity had ended his service awaited his turn.

His eyes straying to the great line of oak trees that separated the temple from Bran's Palace, the priest's thoughts turned to the Avatar of their Faith, the Aristok Melesandra DeMarian, fortieth Vessel of the Living Flame. All was not well in her capital this autumn. The Archpriest of the Flame, Her Grace Gwynne DeLlewellynne, had predicted dire changes to come, and the priest believed. Heathland was rumbling to the north and the Crown Prince had returned to Branion from the fighting in eastern Gallia with an unwanted marriage in the wings and war on the wind. Once before the tensions between the Aristok and her first-born son had erupted into violence. The priest had lost a sister in that year's fighting.

Drawing his cloak more tightly about his shoulders, the priest turned his back on the palace and the memories it invoked and returned to the warmth of the Temple. There were other fires to rekindle this morning and his musing had made him late, but as the Champion closed the portal behind him, his eyes were drawn inexorably back to the palace's spiral turrets. Only once before in his lifetime had the prophecy spoken of such dire changes; in 875 when a noble family had proved itself traitorous to the core and the Royal Vessels of the Flame had shown the world the strength of will that still burned within their veins. The priest prayed that the bloodshed of those days would not repeat itself in this time. He prayed, but he didn't really believe.

Spring, Mean Boaldyn 875 DR
Migard Castle gardens, Kormandeaux, Gallia

Amedeus DeMarian, Prince of Gwyneth and Heir to the Throne of Branion, walked in the castle's expansive gardens with two of his generals. Captured over one hundred and fifty years before, the small keep of Migard still retained its airy Continental architecture within its more newly constructed curtain wall. In the past it had housed musicians and artists from across the Tiberian Continent, now it held the combined troops of Kalandra, thirty-eighth DeMarian Aristok of Branion and those of her sons, Amedeus, Prince of Gwyneth and Quinton, Duke of Yorbourne.

Amedeus walked with a pronounced limp through the slumbering, spring foliage, nodding as his generals argued some point of battle. Branion was at war with Gallia and Heathland. As Heir to the Throne, Amedeus was expected to lead his troops to victory in his mother's name, despite the deep gash in his leg that had sent him to convalesce at Migard. That meant interminable hours of meetings, councils and strategy sessions. This conference in the gardens had been meant to exercise his leg as well as his authority, but the surroundings were dull this early in the spring and his generals were quarrelsome, sinking him into a mood of gloomy introspection.

One of his advisers, Albion DeSandra, Earl of Archester, coughed. When he saw he had his Lord's attention, he cocked his head toward the main keep.

Out from a side door a young child had emerged at a dead run. The sun shone off the dark auburn of his hair and flashed over the DeMarian fire-wolf crest on his dark blue tunic. Behind him, a man dressed in the uniform of the Branbridge Palace Guard tried without success to catch him before he interrupted the Prince of Gwyneth's meeting.

Amedeus grinned, his mood suddenly brightening like the sky after a storm. "Demi!"

The Heir held out his arms to accept the child's boisterous greeting. Forgotten, his advisers smiled and bowed to the youngster as Amedeus caught his greatnephew, Prince Demnor, up in a hug. Sweeping the boy into the air, Amedeus let him rest his feet against his shoulders.

"And what mischief have you been up to today, young tyrant?" he asked, looking warmly up at the boy.

"None!" Demnor glared indignantly back at him, his gray eyes flecked with the Living Flame mirroring those of his uncle. "Ask Randolf. I've been perfect all day!"

"All day! I can't believe it!

"Can it be true?" Amedeus turned to the guard who'd stopped at a respectful distance.

Unexpectedly ordered to accompany his mother to the Continent, Demnor had no troops from his own Earldom to escort him, so a contingent of the Palace Guard had been swiftly gathered as his entourage.

Most had spent their time since arriving trying unsuccessfully to keep their young charge out of mischief.

Now, the man bowed. "Yes, Your Highness. His Grace, Prince Demnor has been most attentive to his tutors today."

"Well then." Amedeus settled the child onto his shoulders. "You're fit to be introduced to noble company. Demi, this is the Earl of Archester, Albion DeSandra, one of my oldest friends, and the uncle of your friend Julian, and this is Alexander DeKathrine, Branion's most illustrious General and the Earl of Cambury. Gentlemen, this is my niece Melesandra's firstborn, Prince Demnor, Earl of Briery."

The two men bowed. Demnor gave them a regal wave of his tiny hand, then fixed the second man with a fiery gaze.

Alexander DeKathrine was a tall and handsome man with the same broad features and breadth of shoulder as the boy and his uncle. His identical dark auburn hair was as thick and unruly, but where Amedeus' and Demnor's eyes glowed with the Living Flame, this man's eyes were the smooth gray of a spring sky, and he wore dark green and black instead of the dark blue and black of the DeMarians. Demnor stared at him frankly.

"Are we related, My Lord?" he asked with grave seriousness that brought a faint smile to the men's lips.

Alexander nodded. "We are, Your Highness. Cousins in the second degree through your grandmother, my aunt, Flaira DeKathrine."

"Oh." Having ascertained their connection, the boy twisted on his great-uncle's shoulder's, indicating his desire to be put down.

Obediently, Amedeus lowered him onto a stone bench so the boy was nearer to their own height. Demnor leaned forward.

"I need to speak to you, Uncle," he said in an urgent voice. "It's *very* important."

After a searching look to ensure the boy was serious, Amedeus turned to his generals.

"Excuse us a moment, My Lords."

The two men withdrew to a disused fountain some distance away. After a pointed look from his young charge, Randolf also moved off so he could not overhear their conversation.

"So," Amedeus said to the child when they were alone. "What was so important that it couldn't wait until supper?"

Demnor regarded his uncle solemnly. "Snowfoot is lame," he said. "The grooms promised that it was only a stone, but . . ." he stopped and began to twist the red-gold threads woven into his tunic.

"But?"

"But I'm scared he might . . . die like Bracken did." The boy's voice had dropped to a whisper, and the Heir had to lean forward to hear him.

"But Bracken was very old, Demi, and Snowfoot is very young."

"I know." The thread broke free and was twisted around the boy's finger. Demnor did not look up.

Amedeus pulled him into an embrace. "Now you mustn't worry," he said. "Bracken did good service and is waiting in the Shadow Realm for you. Snowfoot will go there one day, too, but not for many years to come." He seated himself on the bench, the child beside him. "If the grooms say he'll be fine, he will be."

"Will you come and see him anyway?"

"Of course I will, but right now I have to speak with Alexander and Albion and then I have to meet with the Aristok and your grandfather. Do you want to come?"

The child pushed his face into his uncle's tunic and shook his head.

"Why not?"

The boy shrugged.

Digging him out, Amedeus placed him on his knee. "Why not?" he repeated.

Demnor looked up into his uncle's kindly face. "He doesn't like me," he answered finally.

"Now, I'm sure that's not true. Quinton is just . . . well, it's hard for him to show affection."

The boy made a disbelieving face, but did not argue the point.

Amedeus bounced him on his knee a little and Demnor smiled.

"Stop it."

"Why?" He bounced him again.

"Because I'm . . . stop it! I'm five and a half now. I'm too big to bounce."

"Oh." Amedeus pretended contrition. "I'm very sorry, Your Grace."

"It's all right," the boy answered generously. Leaning against his uncle's chest, the blue of their identical tunics blending easily together, he kicked his feet idly in the air. "What were you talking about before?" he asked.

"War."

"Oh. When I grow up, I'm going to fight in wars, too, instead of just watching. I'll have troops and be a knight and fight the Gallians and the Panishans and the Heaths and win all kinds of lands for you and Grandmother Kalandra."

"Why, thank you, Your Highness," Amedeus answered, suppressing a smile. "And what knightly order are you planning to grace with your prowess?"

Demnor plucked at the fur lining of his uncle's sleeve. "Shield," he announced, "so I can protect you."

"That's very kind of you, but don't you want to join the Sword, like your mother?"

"No."

"Why not?"

The boy looked up at his uncle, his young face serious. "Mother is like Grandfather," he said. "She doesn't like me either."

Amedeus' broad face was pained. "You must know that's not true, Demi," he said, but his voice lacked conviction.

"She has Quin now," the boy sighed, meaning his sister, the Prince Quindara, almost a year old. "Uncle?"

The softly asked question caused Amedeus to look

down with a sad expression. "Yes, Demi," he answered
gently.

"Why does my mother love Quindara, but not me?"

"Oh, Demi." His uncle gathered the boy into his
arms. "She does, really she does."

"No." Demnor's flame-touched gray eyes were sad,
but certain. "She doesn't."

His uncle just held him. The truth was far too complicated to explain to a five-year-old. The truth about
adults and royalty and the responsibilities that caused
them to marry for duty instead of for love; the truth
about an unstable and unloving father raising an
unstable and unloving daughter. Amedeus had tried to
bring Demnor into his world, the world of poetry and
music, of honor and duty carried out with love, not
with bitterness, but had met with increasing resistance
from Quinton and Melesandra. They had their own
ideas about Demnor's upbringing.

"I don't know what to tell you," he said at last.
"When you're all grown up, you'll understand, but *I*
love you."

"I know."

At that moment Albion coughed.

"Yes?"

"Excuse me, Your Highness," the Earl said, still
keeping a discreet distance. "But it's time for your
meeting with the Aristok and the Prince's man informs
me that His Grace has a strategy lesson."

Demnor made a face.

Amedeus nodded. "Thank you, My Lord Earl.
Inform Her Majesty that pressing matters of a cavalry
nature have kept me late, but that I shall come at once."

"Yes, Your Highness." The Earl of Archester bowed
and withdrew. Amedeus turned back to his nephew.

"Now, we both have duties we must attend to, but I
promise I'll visit the stables and tell you what I learn at
supper tonight."

Demnor nodded. Waving Randolf forward, he allowed
the guard to escort him back inside.

Alexander DeKathrine remained in the garden at a gesture from the Heir.

"He's a sweet child," Amedeus said when they were alone.

"He is, Highness. He doesn't remember it, but we spent some time together during last year's campaign."

"I know."

The two men began to walk slowly toward the garden's main exit. Amedeus obviously had something he wished to discuss with his DeKathrine cousin, so Alexander waited patiently without speaking.

At the door, the Heir paused.

"You know that Archpriest Gwynne DeLlewellynne has prophesied dire and violent changes to come?" he asked.

"Yes, Your Highness."

"Yes. Well, what you may not know is that her interpretation speaks of those changes affecting myself and young Prince Demnor most particularly."

He frowned, remembering her words.

I see the boy's face reflected in a gem the color of blood. There is a flaw deep within its heart. He must fight that flaw and win if he is to survive, but he will fight it alone. There are those who would aid him with the weapons of love and honor, but the boy's very nature will oppose this aid, and without it, he is lost.

Amedeus had pressed her for more details, but she'd been unable to provide them. The future was shrouded by the Flame, she'd said. They would have to wait until It chose to reveal more of Its purpose to them.

Beside him, Alexander looked troubled. "Highness?"

"I'm not deeply concerned," Amedeus said reassuringly, "Priests make their living predicting catastrophe and chaos, but just in case . . ." He paused. "I love Demnor. He's a bright and affectionate child, and I'm afraid of what might happen to his nature should anything befall me, so I want you to promise that you'll watch over him and protect him."

"But what could happen, Your Highness?"

Amedeus shrugged. "We're at war. Any one of us could fall to an enemy's blade at any time."

Alexander shifted uncomfortably. "You have my vow, of course, My Prince, but, no disrespect intended, shouldn't you be asking Albion as well?"

Amedeus shook his head. "I have my reasons for asking you alone, My Lord Earl of Cambury. Trust that I know what I'm doing and promise me that you'll carry out my wishes, telling no one of our conversation or of your vow."

"You have my word on it, My Prince." Disturbed, but obedient, Alexander bowed.

"Good." Amedeus gave a twisted smile. "Now, we must to the Aristok's hall to see what she has planned for Gallia this spring."

Together, the two men entered the keep.

Three weeks later, the impossible occurred. The DeSandra family, led by the Earl of Archester, suddenly swung its support behind Gallia. Kalandra and many of her nobles fell on the fields of Kormandeaux when the promised DeSandra troops attacked their flank with a contingent of Heathland infantry. Amedeus, watching the battle from a high vantage place with his oldest friend was struck down by treachery.

Quinton, with help from his senior commanders, Melesandra and Alexander DeKathrine, managed to hold the shattered Branion troops together and kept a rout from becoming a defeat. They retreated to defensible ground and dug in for the night. The young Prince Demnor, brought into the battle camps as was his mother's custom, was sent under guard to Migard Castle for safekeeping.

That night, in the midst of a terrible storm, the DeSandras took the castle. They fanned out, seeking the new Aristok's grandson as a hostage. They failed to take him. What Demnor DeMarian, now Heir Apparent to the Throne of Branion, saw that night, he never told another living soul.

Quinton DeMarian's rage at hearing of the attack was frightening to behold. He sent Melesandra to retake the castle, and in one bloody hour she put every member of the rebelling family within it to the sword. Quinton's troops meanwhile, scoured the countryside, killing as they went. Every home suspected of housing the Aristok's enemies was burned to the ground. He then turned his attention to the DeSandras of Branion.

The next morning, as messengers hurried back and forth between the Aristok's battle tent and the ships that would take his orders across the Anvre Strait to Branbridge, Quinton the Second turned to his daughter.

"We must summon our grandson at once," he said, his flame-washed eyes glittering in the lantern light.

"He is with Alexander." Melesandra DeMarian, now Prince of Gwyneth and Heir to the Throne, answered in a dismissive tone as she studied the map of Gallia spread out before her. Her own gaze marked the passing of the Flame with an increased red glow that nearly obliterated the green of her eyes. It gave her thin face a fevered look that matched her father's.

Quinton rose. "We must be ever vigilant at this time," he said almost to himself, staring out at the tent strewn field before him. "We must ferret out all weakness and draw it forth before it poisons our Realm again. We must replace it with the strength of the sword and the iron shield."

Melesandra merely nodded again.

"Our mother was strong, but our brother was weak and that is why the Flame let him die," Quinton mused. "It passed to me because it knew I had the strength to rule, as you do." Quinton stroked the large ring, known as the Ruby of Flame, that newly adorned his right hand. "Our grandson is the future," he continued, "but he carries that same weakness in his breast as our brother did. It must be swept away and replaced with steel so that the Realm may never again be vulnerable to its enemies. You will do this, Anda."

Melesandra turned and stared into the eyes of her Royal father. The Flame crackled in the air between them, then ebbed under the iron grip of their unwavering self-control.

"Of course," she said coldly, her husky voice as emotionless as his. "He is *my* son, and he shall be strong."

With a satisfied nod, Quinton the Second, thirty-ninth Aristok of Branion and Vessel of the Living Flame, returned his thoughts to revenge and conquest.

Autumn, Mean Fhomhair, 893 DR
Bran's Royal Palace, Branbridge

Lord Demnor DeMarian, His Most Royal Highness, Crown Prince of Gwyneth, Lord of Kraburn and Briery, Archpriest of the Knights of the Sword, Defender of the Realm, and Heir to the Blood Right of the Living Flame strode through the palace halls, his boots kicking at the faded carpet. Glimmering reflections cast by the newly installed stained glass windows made seeing difficult and he squinted as he climbed the short flight of granite stairs that marked the boundary between the west and north wings.

In the distance the last chime of the city bells faded away. He was late for the Hunt. Shifting his black-enameled helm to his other hand, he quickened his pace, falling into a rhythmic march that kept his sword and cloak from entangling his legs.

After crossing a small, overgrown courtyard, he ducked through a low doorway and turned left. He was late, he thought with a grimace, because he'd allowed himself to get entangled in yet another circular argument with his Companion Kelahnus about . . . He frowned. What had it been about?

The morning had begun as always with his servants laying out breakfast and his secretary reading off his itinerary. Today there'd been only one item, the Hunt. Kelahnus and he had begun discussing the inclusion of the Cailein family of Heathland in the day's excursion and ended up fighting about the Companion's absence yesterday . . . he thought.

Striding through a gallery lined with stone statues, he turned over the earlier conversation in his mind.

"You're jealous."

Wrapped loosely in a lavender silk robe, Kelahnus was lounging in a chair by the balcony window in Demnor's isolated west wing suite. He smiled as his words brought a glare from the Prince's flame-touched, gray eyes.

"No." Demnor banged his pipe clean on a silver tray by the bed. A small, wooden box filled with fenweed sat nearby and he studied it a moment before dropping the pipe next to it.

"Jealous," Kelahnus repeated with a smile.

Rising, the Prince crossed the room to stare out the open window. Fog still covered the rich lawns of Collin's Park to the south and pooled over the grounds of the Flame Temple to the west. The air was chill. Dressed only in breeches, Demnor shivered and reached for the latch. A gust of wind splattered him with rain and knocked his dark, auburn hair into his eyes before he got the window closed. He flicked the hair away impatiently and turned to the other man.

"Do I have reason to be?"

Kelahnus gazed up at him with a gentle smile. "Would you believe me if I said you didn't."

"I would, if you said it."

"Then you don't." The Companion rose and caught the other man's hand, pressing his lips to the palm in a warm, lingering kiss. "All the world is a cold and pale comparison to Your Most Passionate Highness."

"You're being purposely provoking." Demnor disengaged his hand, but his accompanying frown carried no force behind it.

"And you're being totally unreasonable." With a throaty laugh the Companion twined his arms about the other man.

Demnor tried to pull away, then surrendered to the

moment. His own arms went around the Companion's waist, stroking him through the cool silk of his robe. The other man's hair enveloped them and Demnor breathed in the faint scent of lilacs. His expression softened.

"You're provoking, and infuriating and . . . distracting."

"I know."

"I don't have time for this."

"Time for what?"

"Kelahnus . . . Kel. . . . Stop that."

With a sigh, the younger man brought his hands up to rest against Demnor's chest. The sleeve of his robe brushed lightly across the other man's bare skin, causing him an involuntary shudder. The Companion smiled.

"I had business this morning," he explained patiently.

"Business?"

"Companion business."

"And last night?"

"The same. Besides, your itinerary led me to believe that you would be closeted with Alexander DeKathrine on matters of State until nine. I was back before nine." Smoothing the lavender silk of his robe, he returned to his chair, gazing at the Prince in mock exasperation. "Had I known you were planning on quarreling with him, I'd have returned sooner."

"We didn't quarrel. We had a disagreement. I was right. He was wrong."

"Was he upset when you left?"

"I've no idea. Does it matter?"

Kelahnus sighed. "I suppose not. Although it might make your next meeting awkward."

"Nonsense."

The chiming of the porcelain clock on the mantel cut off further comment and Demnor crossed to his arms stand where formal hunting attire and armor had already been laid out. He frowned at the new black surcoat with its stiffly embroidered Royal DeMarian fire-wolf crest. It would be awkward and uncomfortable until it was broken in and by that time it would be ruined by bloodstains.

Jerking the under-tunic over his head, he tried to fasten the collar. After a brief struggle, he left the throat piece dangling. His reflection in the gilt-edged mirror glared back at him, and he turned away and took up his breastplate.

"Do you want help with that?"

"Yes."

Kelahnus rose, and while Demnor held the front, he attached the back.

"That should do it."

Eyeing the effect while the Prince shifted to settle the weight more comfortably, the Companion reached around and fastened the collar, straightening it so it wouldn't bind.

"You should get a valet."

"I don't need a valet."

"Really?"

Running his fingers through the Prince's unruly hair, Kelahnus clicked his tongue and picked up a brush. He stared for a moment at the richly worked tapestry above the bed depicting a DeMarian knight slaying a dragon before he spoke.

"Will you kill a large beast today?" he asked casually, returning to their earlier topic as he worked out the tangles.

"Probably. The scouts reported two or three in the area."

"Then it will be a large Hunt."

"Yes."

"There've been a number of noble visitors to the palace these last few days."

Demnor grunted.

"A number of *DeKathrines* from Exenworth and Essendale."

"I suppose."

"Including the *Earl* of Essendale?"

Demnor twisted around.

"Yes. Why?"

With a shrug the Companion continued to stroke the brush through the Prince's hair, unperturbed.

"Curiosity. She *is* to be your Consort, isn't she?"

"Eventually."

"When will you formally ask her? At the Hunt, or at the banquet?"

"Neither."

"You're going to have to ask her sooner or later."

"Later." Demnor caught the Companion's hand and stilled him. "Kelahnus. Leave it."

With a sigh the younger man dropped the brush. "As you wish." Stretching out on the bed, he clasped his hands beneath his head and closed his eyes in a careful pose of nonchalance.

After gazing at him a moment, Demnor crossed to the dresser below his mirror and opened an old, cherry-wood box. There was very little inside; a child's small signet ring, the DeSandra family crest etched into the face, a smooth lock of white horsehair wrapped in leather, a piece of bone from the first dragon he'd ever killed, and a thin strip of green silk, torn from one of the Companion's shirts years before. This last item he removed. He kissed it and bound it about his right forearm, then clipped the dark blue, enameled vambrace over it.

After fastening the left vambrace and his greaves, he struggled into the surcoat. Sword belt and scabbarded broadsword completed his attire. Drawing the weapon, he saluted his reflection, then touched the hilt to his lips and resheathed it. Stuffing his gauntlets through his belt, he headed for the door.

At the threshold he paused. "You will be here tonight?" he asked without turning.

"If you wish it."

"I do."

"Then I shall be."

With a nod the Heir turned to leave.

"Do you love me?" Kelahnus called after him with a laugh.

Demnor paused once more. *Yes.*

"You're in my blood," he answered and softly closed the door. Behind him, he thought he heard the Companion whisper a reply, but he couldn't be sure.

Now, as he made his way down a wide corridor, he turned the conversation over in his mind again. All right, he admitted, perhaps he had been unreasonable about yesterday. He'd probably been unreasonable with Alexander as well, but the place was crawling with DeKathrines and the mere mention of his upcoming betrothal had been enough to ignite his temper at both of them. Alexander would not fight with him as Kelahnus would, but their responses had been similar.

Demnor sighed. He would make it up to Kelahnus tonight, he resolved. Alexander could just suffer.

Guards, jumping to attention at an interior portcullis, interrupted his thoughts. He nodded as he passed, distracted, until one young sentry caught his attention. He pulled up short, eyes narrowed.

"Gord Rose, isn't it?"

"Highness!" The boy slammed the butt of his pike into the ground.

Demnor nodded slowly. "You took the Squire's Cup last year. But you were marked for the Sword Knights. *I* marked you for the Sword Knights. What are you doing here?"

Rose went red to his hairline, but answered with only a faint quaver in his voice. "Demoted, sir. Drunkenness."

Drunkenness.

"I do not approve of such weakness among my people," the Prince said.

"No, sir." Rose's voice had gotten very quiet.

Searching his memory for the boy's past record, Demnor frowned. "Your father is Sandi Ford of the Watch."

"Yes, My Prince."

The image of the old sergeant came to Demnor's mind, his customary scowl adding life to the memory.

Ford hated excess of any kind and was often called upon to keep the peace in the taverns and inns about the city. His son had been equally serious. Until now.

"I don't expect this sits well with him."

"No, sir."

No, indeed. "On duty?"

"No, sir!"

Suppressing a smile, the Prince signaled for him to explain.

"It was at the last festival, Highness. I got carried away."

"Carried away?"

"Yes, Highness. With the Watch."

"And by them, too, no doubt."

"Yes, sir."

"Hm." While Demnor studied him, Rose stared straight ahead, trying not to shrink into his uniform.

He's a well-disciplined boy, the Prince mused. *Showed a lot of promise last year.* And the Heir could remember scrapes of his own that had involved both the Palace Guard and the Town Watch. Not all that long ago, though sometimes it seemed like a lifetime ago. No doubt Rose's father and the other members of the Senior Watch, proud of their traditions and the two children accepted by a militant order, had torn a strip off the poor lad a mile wide.

"I assume this won't happen again?"

"No, Highness!"

"Good. I'll speak with Captain Fletcher and the Hierarchpriest, but the next time you feel the need to get carried away on Heir's Day, make sure you at least have sober friends with you to carry you home again afterward."

"Yes, Highness. Thank you, sir."

Turning, Demnor nodded to the older guard on watch beside him. "Connie."

"My Prince!"

"Your family is well?"

"Yes, sir, very well, thank you. My father asked to be remembered to you."

"Always. Randolf did good service in his day. Tell him I'll visit in the coming week."

"We'd be honored, My Prince."

Demnor nodded, and his eyes tracked quickly to Rose and back. Connie bowed slightly, the small badge of Gwyneth on her left shoulder flashing with the movement. The badge spoke of desperate service years ago; of honor and dishonor and of the love the Guard held for their Prince; a love that surpassed even their duty to the Crown. A very select few wore the red gryphon of Gwyneth. Many more had died to acquire it. Those who wore it needed no words to catch their Prince's meaning. *He is one of mine as you are. Keep him out of trouble.*

Demnor allowed himself a slight smile before continuing on his way. Connie would look after the boy until he could get him reinstated. Rose, he noted, was standing straighter, his young face less stony above his black tunic. He would recover and be the better for his brief taste of shame.

These few were the backbone of Branion, the Prince mused, happy to change his thoughts to this less complicated line. They were the swords and shields that kept the island Realm strong. An army of them and he could solve the Northern Treaty problem with little difficulty, with or without the Caileins. And he had them, too.

His fingers twitching at the pommel of his sword, he crossed a vaulted gallery and turned down another passageway. The Northern Treaty was the latest in a long series of agreements spelling out the Branion occupation of the Provinces of Heathland; a rough, inhospitable country to the north. Officially Branion for three hundred years, it had been disputed territory for far longer. Not a year went by that didn't see border clashes and violence. This past decade had been no exception.

The Prince grunted. Heathland was like a training yard overrun with weeds. The more you hacked at them, the harder they grew. The last and most decisive

battle had been three years ago. Even with aid from
Gallia, who shared their Essusiate religion and their
hatred of the DeMarians, the Heaths had lost. They'd
been forced to sue for peace and the Northern Treaty
had been the result. Demnor was surprised it had held
for as long as it had. Now rebellion was stirring again
and it would only be a matter of time before the borderlands exploded.

Bending to pass through a low doorway, he absently
took a leftward corridor and then a right. The Heaths
would fight, he knew that as surely as he knew his own
name. It was only a question of when. But Branion was
on the brink of full-scale war with Gallia and the
Aristok would not support one confrontation in the
north with another looming up before them to the east.
An effort must be made to shore up the failing treaty.

Reluctantly the Crown Prince pulled his mind from
the clean solution of the battlefield. The Aristok had
dropped the problem in his lap in Council yesterday
and expected an answer, an answer that did not involve
war. But if battle was out of the question, what
remained? Intelligence of any real value from Heathland was meager. The Branion Constables and War-
dens made their official reports, but the province's true
face was masked behind sullen and grudging obedience. The real Heathland was hidden in barns and taverns and isolated mountain keeps where the spark of
rebellion smoldered. In a land where everyone was
related and alliances were formed along bloodlines and
marriage-ties, strangers were mistrusted and avoided.
How could you manage a diplomatic solution under
those conditions?

Chewing at the scar on his lower lip, he came suddenly face-to-face with a stone wall.

"Where, by the Triarchy's Flame, am I?"

He studied it a moment. The mortar was old and dis-
colored, flaking away where the masons had joined
newer stone to the existing blocks. Idly, the Prince
wondered what was on the other side before turning
and retracing his steps. The palace was full of such

blind alleys. There were at least six different ways to the stables from his suite, and he'd gotten himself lost on more than one occasion.

Returning to a familiar passageway, he made the proper turn and crossing a circular junction, a disused fountain in its center, he ducked under another archway and entered the north tower.

Standing for a minute, he let his eyes adjust before beginning his descent. A set of tiny, blue-glassed windows, their latches long ago rusted shut gave him over to a series of arrow slits choked with pigeon dung, then finally to solid wall as he neared the ground floor level. Sliding his hand along the banister, he moved with the ease of long familiarity, barely slowing his pace. The tower was quiet but for the sound of his own boots ringing on the stone steps; another sign that he was late. Hurrying, he reached the bottom a few minutes later.

The wall torches were lit, marking a wing in use and they sputtered as he passed, adding char to the centuries of blackening on the wall behind. In the distance he could hear the muted sound of the Branbridge bells marking the quarter hour. He *was* late. He lengthened his stride. Another threshold, another sentry stiffening to attention and he stepped into the soft lantern's glow of the Royal Stables.

Built for his mother's grandmother, Kalandra the Great, the building had been designed to house the mounts of half an army and those who served them. Huge beams from the forests of Gwyneth stretched the ceilings thirty feet high, and two rows of wooden pillars cut the central room in thirds. Wide box stalls marched along either side and the back was stacked with bales of hay and bags of grain. The center, forty feet wide and a hundred feet long, was designed so that the Royal Family might arrange itself in procession before showing its members to the populace.

It was an awesome structure, but it had been years since it had impressed Demnor. Now, he was simply caught, as usual, by the comforting fragrance of lamp

oil, hay, and leather and by the soft whickers of the
horses who, alerted to his presence before any other,
craned their graceful necks over their stall doors
to greet him. A quick glance took in the assembled
retainers lounging and talking, the pages and handlers
rushing back and forth, and the knots of activity
which marked the presence of three of his four younger
siblings.

Of course, he reflected as he strode forward, *that
comfort is usually when the family isn't together.*

Silence descended as people turned and bowed.
Giving a curt nod that encompassed them all, the
Prince crossed to the box stall where Titan, his charger,
stood ready.

Before the door, his young squire leaped up from the
bale of hay where he'd been dozing. Straightening his
surcoat, he stood, trying to appear alert and noble, a
serious expression on his fair, Gwynethian features.

Demnor gave him an approving glance. Holding in
the smile that twitched at the corners of his mouth, he
tossed the boy his helm and bent to check his charger's
gear. It lipped at his hair and the Prince stroked its nose
absently as he reached around to slip a hand under the
saddle girth. Around him muted conversation slowly
resumed. He straightened.

"It's loose. Fix it."

Stable hands scrambled to do his bidding while
he continued his inspection. Finally, he grunted in
satisfaction.

A derisive snort to his right made him turn, eyes narrowed, to face his younger sister, the Lord Quindara,
Duke of Yorbourne.

She sat on a stone bench before the stall of her own
mount, sharpening her sword. Her thin face held a
haughty look and the legacy of Flame that pronounced
her DeMarian heritage gave her green eyes a tinge of
red. She returned his glare with one of her own.

"Yorbourne," he said stiffly.

In one fluid motion she rose, graceful despite the
restrictions of armor and padded surcoat, and returned

her sword to its scabbard. Tossing her copper braids
behind her, she eyed him critically.

"Gwyneth," she replied.

In twenty years they had never called each other by
name, only by title. Natural rivals, both for their
mother's affection and for the power she would one
day pass on, they had never been close. Usually they
avoided each other, but today that was impossible. His
temper already short, Demnor made to speak, but
turned at the sound of sentries coming to attention.

The door opened. Two soldiers in the colors of the
Shield Knights, the traditional Royal Guard, entered
and took up position before it. Seconds later Her Most
Regal and Sacred Majesty Melesandra the Third,
Aristok of Branion, Heathland, Kormandeaux and
Aquilliard, Gaspellier, Poitienne, Roland, hereditary
Earl of the Danelind Islands of Columba, Gracious
Sovereign of the Triarchy, Most High Patron of the
Knights of the Sword, and Vessel of the Living Flame,
strode into the stables. Silence reigned.

Tall and uncompromisingly erect, Melesandra
glanced neither to the right nor to the left as she
crossed the floor, four guards keeping pace behind. In
a ripple of bowed heads and bended knees, the assembled knelt before her.

Demnor's thoughts evaporated in a chill rush. A hard
lump of awe caught in his throat, making his breathing
ragged, and as she strode toward him, his heart began a
painful hammering in his chest. Even at a distance, her
presence was a physical blow.

Melesandra DeMarian, fortieth Avatar of the Living
Flame, was accounted the most powerful Vessel since
the founder of her line. Of the thirty-nine to follow
Braniana DeMarian's path, seven had been driven mad
by the Flame's consuming power, five had died in
childhood, their young bodies unable to withstand the
tide, and three had not been strong enough to call it to
their will in times of peril and the Land had suffered.

The Aristok had raised her firstborn son in the
shadow of those fifteen failures. The wielding of the

Living Flame was the most sacred of duties and the awesome self-control necessary was the driving force
behind every lesson. It made the fear of failure rise in
Demnor's throat whenever he faced her. Before him
was his birthright; in her image as unreachable as the
moon. Even with the Flame's tide held firm behind the
battlements of her control, it enveloped her like a
cloak, entwined together with the tradition of her more
secular regalia.

The gray DeMarian Plaide crossed her black surcoat,
pinned at the shoulder by a huge sapphire clasp. At
her hip, in a blue-and-black scabbard, hung Justice,
Kalandra the Great's broadsword, bequeathed to her
former squire and granddaughter on the deathbed of
the legendary warrior. Around her waist her silver warrior's belt carried the Dagger of Divine Right, symbol
of earthly supremacy. Her vambraces were of engraved
metal, as was her breastplate below the surcoat, and her
crowned helm. Beneath it, her lean face was a mask of
unsparing severity. The fiery outline and golden eyes
of the fire-wolf crest flashed in the lantern light as she
approached her eldest son. Eyes narrowing, she held
out her hand, the Seal of the Realm on her finger.

Demnor bent over it stiffly. Brushing the golden seal
with his lips, he fought to keep himself from trembling.
When he straightened, he kept his countenance rigidly
blank.

Stone gray met blazing green, but it was the stone
that fell at last before the fiery gaze.

Demnor dropped his eyes.

The Aristok smiled. "My son," she said.

"Majesty." His voice was ragged, the depth of pain
in it surprising even him. He met her eyes with a
defiant stare, waiting for her comment, but she merely
regarded him a moment longer, then swept past to greet
her daughter.

Once free of her presence a measure of calm
returned, and he kicked his self-control back into place.
He watched his sister bow, a smile on her face. At
twenty she bore a startling resemblance to their

mother. Tall and spare, she had the Aristok's movements and rich, alto voice, as well as her features and
brilliant copper hair. Her eyes held the identical red-
green fire, and when she grew angry, it blazed with the
same molten heat.

Demnor was his father's son. Darker hair and face;
tall, but thick-set, with the DeKathrine features and
burly frame. The Consort Markus had died in a hunting
accident on his southern estates when the Heir had
been eleven, and Demnor's earliest memories of the
man had been of solitary drinking and weakness. Com-
parisons between them were never made in public, but
the Prince could not deny the evidence of his mirror.

The Aristok laughed then. Mother and daughter
sharing some jest, standing at ease together. If he could
have seen her face, he knew what expression he would
see there; the same one he'd seen the day she'd held up
the new Prince for the adulation of the crowd. Pride.
And love. As second child, Quindara lived under no
sword of failure. Its shadow would only pass over her
if he fell. Until then she was free.

Why, his mind asked for the thousandth time, *does
she only love you?*

With one last word, their mother moved on. In the
haze of childish jealousy that suddenly filled him, he
saw Quindara turn and smile. The smile said triumph.
The smile said challenge, and the stables grew very
dark.

All he saw was his rival's face. All he heard was the
echo of her laughter. A throbbing pressure behind his
eyes beat in time with his heart, covering his vision in a
red haze as, roused by the strong emotion, the Living
Flame, diluted by only one degree, began to stir. He
barely felt his hand grip his sword hilt.

Through the tide of crimson a needle of disquiet
began to prick at him. It grew stronger, like an itch, and
spoke one word. *Don't.*

His eyes refocused, past his sister's face to a darkened corner and his brother Atreus. The younger Prince
stood by his twin, Marsellus, one hand on his brother's

arm as if supported, the other at his temple. A faint nimbus of red-gray light surrounded them. Atreus' face was pale with alarm and when he saw that he had his oldest sibling's attention, he shook his head minutely.

Sanity returned in a rush, but the anger remained. Shaking with the effort to control himself, Demnor took a deep breath and snapped the sword down again. Relief showed in Atreus' gray eyes, the spark of fire that announced his DeMarian blood fading as his power retreated. The nimbus of red-gray light dimmed. Hurriedly, he turned away. After a whispered conversation, the twins moved toward their own mounts. Studiously examining the tension of his reins, Atreus refused to meet his eldest brother's eyes.

Demnor returned his attention to Quindara, but the chain of tension between them had been broken, and she, too, was mounted, leaning down to stroke her horse's neck.

Demnor returned his attention to Titan, mounting quickly.

Unfairly, he wished his brother had minded his own business, but underneath he was relieved. The twins were powerful Seers, like many indenticals. Unlike most, the Dukes of Lochsbridge and Kempston had chosen to enter the Knights of the Sword, the militant order the Royal Family traditionally patronized instead of the priestly order of the Flame. Often they'd been the only bulwark between Demnor and Quindara, both senior members of the same order.

The thought made Demnor's teeth clamp shut.

Sensing his rider's mood Titan sidestepped nervously beneath him. Reining him in, the Heir pulled him back to position as his leg scraped against the stall's wooden wall. Forcing himself to breathe slowly, the Prince stroked the stallion's neck, murmuring assurances in a soft voice.

When Titan relaxed beneath him, Demnor urged him forward, walking him to the front of the stables as the company began to form the Processional. The Heir rode in front, as the Defender of the Realm, then

Quindara as the DeMarian Cadet. The Aristok, four
Shield Knights flanking, held the center position with
the twins behind, squires carrying the lances of
their Lords, and a dozen others filling in the places
surrounding.

At the Aristok's signal, pages ran forward with their
shields. Pushing on his gauntlets, Demnor accepted his,
the DeMarian fire-wolf rampant, facing to the sinister,
hovering protectively over a Gwynethian gryphon
couchant. Slipping his right arm through the straps, he
rested it against his knee, then accepted his helm.
Drumming the fingers of his left hand on his saddle
pommel, he stared at the stable doors.

Behind, all was ready and he knew, without having
to see, the Aristok signal Metellus Galvin, the Lord of
the Hounds, to release the dogs. There came the hollow
boom of the kennel bar being dropped and the wild
commotion of barking dogs and neighing horses in the
courtyard outside.

One voice, raised above the din, shouted, "Ho!
'Ware the hounds!"

With a frown, the Crown Prince imagined the chaos
as the nobility of the Realm scrambled to make themselves presentable; each quickly arranging their features and poses; each fighting for the position that
conveyed the most attentive posture to the Aristok.
And to himself. Despite the false smiles and flattery, he
knew what they thought of him. Most considered him
cold and violent. Only the ones who would tell him so
to his face were worth considering, and few had the
courage. Just one family had ever dared to fight for
their convictions against the DeMarians and they had
been wiped out in one terrible night of killing.

Scratching at his arm below the shield strap, he
snorted. He supposed it was for the best. If he was
restrained by position from pitching the bulk of the
court bodily from the top of the main arch, they were
equally restrained by fear.

The two guards marching forward to stand before the
stable doors snapped him out of his reverie and back to

the tension of the moment. He straightened, and at the trumpet's sound, threw back his head to meet the challenge of the day.

With visible strain the guards forced open the massive oak and metal doors. A shaft of sunlight escaping from the heavy pall of storm clouds slid over him, and he narrowed his eyes against the glare as he urged his mount forward.

Slowly and with much dignity the Royal Processional moved out into the north courtyard. In twin waves the Hunt parted before them and from the battlements there came the sounds of cheering. Heartened, Demnor turned to salute the line of servants and children who'd gathered to see them off. The cheering grew louder. He allowed himself a faint smile. As a boy, he'd stood on those very walls, watching in awe and envy as his mother and his grandfather, Quinton the Second, rode out beneath him. Flashing copper hair ringed with silver and swathed in the deepest blue and midnight black. He'd been as impressed as those who'd stood beside him.

Then finally, the day of his first Processional arrived. The memory was with him still. Unfaded by time, he carried it like a jewel in his mind. The dream of his childhood, to ride at its head, had been realized; the dream of his youth, to ride in its center, was yet to be. That had been the Hunt of his blooding also. His second cousin, Alexander DeKathrine, had performed the ceremony. A heady day for one just past his eleventh year. A good day, but one long since gone. He returned his gaze to the courtyard.

The Hunt, resplendent in their formal family colors, bowed low. They looked, he had always thought, like so many brightly garbed puppets, each blend chosen to most effectively clash with the others.

The Gwynethian-born DeLlewellynnes in their quiet white and light green rubbed shoulders with the garish light yellow and lavender of the DePaulas. Mixed into the seemingly endless hordes of somber black-and-forest-green-garbed DeKathrines, the first of the noble families, could be seen the occasional red-and-black checkerboard DeFay, or the vibrant harlequin diamonds of deep purple and red which distinguished the DeLynnes. A dozen cross-bred combinations and the paler shades of several minor houses added to the heraldic nightmare.

The worst, Demnor had always felt, was the DeSharon-DeYvonne brood. Olive green of a particularly vile shade and brown had combined with dark yellow and orange to create the impression that the progenitors of the cross had been violently ill after eating a wedding banquet of molding, poisonous mushrooms. Their descendants lived up to this lack of refinement zealously.

For a moment he caught himself scanning the crowd for the light blue and gray of the DeSandras. Something he hadn't done in years.

The DeSandras are dead. You're the only one who searches for their ghosts, he reminded himself bitterly.

Had he time, though, he might have attempted some jigsaw puzzle heraldry to ascertain who *did* ride to the Hunt this morning—the dozens of complicated designs, some with six or eight different devices on shields, surcoats, and pennants were enough to cause blindness—but at that moment the dogs rushed forward and the Processional was engulfed by the Hunt.

Beside him now as they began to fan out, Quindara bent and swept up a small hound that a DeKathrine youth held out to her. It wriggled madly in her arms, licking her face and nipping at her gauntleted fingers. Laughing, she stroked it and looked down inquiringly.

"For luck, Highness!"

She smiled at his boldness. "Mine or ..." She flipped the dog over and it made a lunge for her wrist, wrestling it like a bone. "His?"

"His, Highness. Your kennels are renowned, and this is his first Hunt."

"And yours?"

He smiled, sweeping ash-blond hair from his eyes

with a quick toss of his head. "My first in Branbridge, Highness, but I mean to do Exenworth proud today."

"Do you now? Good for you." She regarded him with a speculative eye. "Well bred, is he?"

Her intent was obvious and the young man caught it immediately. "Very, My Prince," he replied with a smile.

She grinned back. "Good. Well, then, perhaps I'll breed him with one of my own. If he shows well today, of course."

"Oh, he will, Highness. He will."

"Excellent. We must discuss it. You'll be in Branbridge long?"

Disappointment darkened his features. "No, Highness. Only today and tomorrow."

"No time to waste, then." Holding the squirming dog under one arm, the Duke of Yorbourne began to pick at a strip of blue cloth woven into her tunic sleeve. "What's your name?"

"Troy DeKathrine, My Lord. And he is Runner."

"Well, then, Troy, you will call me Quindara—else we'll never reach the level of informality we both wish to—and see how well we can get to know each other in the time available, hm?"

She pulled the strip of cloth free. Gripping Runner firmly with her elbow, the Duke tied the strip to his tail, then handed him back.

"I'm up to the challenge," she said with a wink. "Think you are?"

"Absolutely High . . . Quindara."

She laughed happily. "Keep my token safe, then, and show it to the guards at the Royal wing. One of them will bring you to my suite."

With a last smile of promise, she turned her mount aside. Troy watched her go, the squirming dog forgotten in his arms. His face held a mingled look of disbelief and anticipation.

Two bloodings in one day, Demnor thought dryly. *Lucky boy.*

He glanced around. The Aristok, surrounded by the

court, was accepting the salutations of the Cailein family of Heathland, allies of Branion since the days of Kassandra the Sixth, over one hundred years ago. The twins had disappeared. Before him, the DeKathrine family awaited his formal greeting, the woman who one day would be his Consort in their midst. Their stance said they expected him to be difficult. Already her brother, the Viscount Alerion glared at him with open hostility in his gray eyes. Although Demnor allowed this third cousin more insolence than most, he was in no mood for it today. There had to be some errand of importance that demanded his attention, at least for a moment or two.

Off to one side, the Lord Julia Fletcher, Earl of Norbrook and Captain of the Palace Guards, stood watching her sentries with a deadly stare. After thirty-five years of DeMarian service, she was still as powerful a fighter and as demanding a Captain as ever. Knighted by Quinton the Second and titled by Melesandra, she remained for the love of the Guard. The Royal Family was the better for it. The scar which ran from beneath her gray hair to the base of one ear, caused by a blow taken for Demnor himself, had earned her the Heir's incredulous respect and devotion.

Riding over, he returned her salute. A good time to make good the morning's promise.

"Captain."

"My Prince."

"It's about Rose. How long were you planning on keeping him?" he asked, coming to the point immediately.

Only the faintest twitch of a smile cracked her precise stance. "I thought another week or so, Highness. Teach him how to hold his drink before he's sent back to that aristocratic rabble in the Knights."

"Good."

She was obviously busy and so was he. This was not the time to sit and talk at their ease. They were both on duty, as it were. He turned his mount, but stopped when she cleared her throat.

"Yes, Captain."

"It's been a long time since I saw you in the practice yard, My Prince."

"Yes, three days."

She said nothing, merely waited.

"Tomorrow."

"Very good, sir. I shall look forward to it."

Demnor laughed suddenly. "So shall I." Feeling absurdly better, he turned his horse and rode toward the gathered DeKathrines.

Nodding a curt greeting to Alerion, he stopped before a tall, blonde woman, the rampant DeKathrine bear holding the yew bow emblem of the Knights of the Bow emblazoned on her surcoat. She gazed at him in speculative invitation.

"My Lord Earl of Essendale," he said, trying without success to keep the stiffness from his voice.

"Your Most Royal Highness," Isolde DeKathrine replied, bowing smoothly.

"You, ah, had a pleasant journey to Branbridge?"

"Yes, thank you, Highness." She smiled, ignoring his obvious discomfort. "I'd recently returned from the fighting in Fenland when my Uncle Alexander invited me to visit with him. I thought it would make a diverting holiday."

"I'm sure." Despite his wish to greet her and run, he found himself drawn into conversation by the mention of the summer's Continental fighting. "Not as exciting as Fenland."

"Your Highness is too kind. We were but a little skirmish in the grand scheme. Your Highness brought the army much glory in Perinout. I should have liked to have been there."

Surprisingly pleased by the observation, Demnor nodded. "We all did our part. Fenland was as important."

With a smile, she accepted the compliment. "Next year shall see the end of it, I think. The Gallians have little fight left in them."

"They had little fight to begin with."

"Too true, Highness, but they show well when pressed.

About to argue the point, Demnor was interrupted by Flairilynne DeFay, Lord of the Hunt. Raising her horn to her lips, she blew a short blast, the signal to make ready.

There was chaos once more as the court brought their horses into position. Keeping war-trained stallions apart in such a confined space was no mean feat, and the animals screamed and lashed out at each other. Hemmed in on all sides, Demnor barely managed to turn his mount to face the gate. Isolde gave him an enthusiastic smile and he returned it, too restless and excited to care that he was surrounded by DeKathrines who courted him for a sibling.

Finally, when he sure he could wait no longer, the gates were thrown open. Flairilynne, her long, black braids streaming down from beneath her helm, stood high in the saddle and blew one clear note into the rising wind. Then she dropped and shot through the gates, the Hunt at her heels.

They fanned out to either side, thundering across the fields, and from the walls, those watching sent up another cheer.

Surrounded now by warriors as intent on death as he, Demnor lost himself in the rhythmic pounding of his horse's hooves against the turf. A light rain began to fall and he raised his face to it, his mind singing.

They fought through the sodden underbrush for two hours, moving in a ragged line about ten feet apart. At the edge of the woods, four of the dogs scared up a hart, and baying, shot off after its flashing tail. The Hunt checked, then continued while Metellus and his apprentices controlled the rest of the pack and the Royal Coursers followed the four into the gloom. With luck there would be fresh venison at the banquet tonight.

It grew darker as they passed into the forest. Though the rare glimmers of light barely penetrated the gath-

ering shadows, Demnor found himself squinting
upward more and more often. The ghostly trees and
the prevailing odor of damp, green life inextricably
mingled with rot was oppressive. They called up darker
thoughts like carrion birds, and he'd had enough of
those already today. He slowed his horse and, slipping
one foot from the stirrup, shook most of the accumulated mud and bracken from his leg. After wiping the
rain from his face with a sopping gauntlet, leaving the
scent of wet leather on his mouth and nose, he peered
up through the dripping leaves. Even the heaviest cloak
would not have kept him dry in this constant drizzle.
His tunic, long since soaked through below surcoat and
breastplate, was cold against his skin. Now, with the
outbreak of heavier rain, water traced a stream down
his helm and collar, carrying bits of bark and leaves
with it.

He laughed quietly to himself. Despite the pitfalls,
the dark, the wet, and the stink, he loved riding to the
Hunt; loved the forest with its hidden prey around perhaps the next turn; loved the final wind-rushing race
across the fields, and loved the kill; loved losing himself in the simple puzzle of life or death. With a sharp
toss of his head, he flicked the plastered hair from his
eyes and urged Titan forward again.

Finally, an hour later, he heard the high call of the
Hunt Lord's horn.

The cry was taken up and around him the Hunt
jerked to a standstill, then sprang toward the sound,
drawn by the baying dogs. Demnor threw his mount
forward, ignoring the branch which sent another water-
fall cascading over his head and leaping a fallen tree
without caring what lay beyond.

His horse crashing through the underbrush toward
the barely visible quarry, the Prince threw back his
head and began the wailing DeMarian war cry. The
Hunt added their voices to his, each family's pitch and
timber different, until they blended into a harmonic
discord of undulating howling.

They surrounded the animal, drove it from the safety

of its cover and forced it toward the open fields. The dragon fled down the avenue of escape they'd left open for it and burst from the protective trees. Then, all it could do was run.

A huge creature, taller than the largest warhorse which pursued, it covered the distance across the field in seconds. But before it could plunge into the belt of forest beyond, the Royal twins were past it and wheeling to force it around.

In the center of the field the Hunt brought it to bay. Panting, its tongue flecking foam across its mottled gray-and-green hide, the beast turned. Sharp, barbed quills stood out from its spine in bristling armor, and snarling, it slapped its tail against the ground in challenge.

The Hunters raced around it while their squires shot darts and small quarrels at its sensitive eyes, driving it to panic.

In their midst, despite the wind whipping tears from his eyes, Demnor watched the creature intently. Like the rest, he had taken up his lance in readiness for battle when they'd brought the beast to bay. Now he circled warily, letting the missiles take their toll, waiting for the creature to tire. The art of first blood was in knowing just when to strike. To attack before the beast was winded was to invite a split belly. To wait too long was to lose the first blow. Impatience battled experience as the need to do violence sang in his ears, urging him to attack. He made one more pass, hooves tearing great strips of sod into the air. Soon. One more. He tightened his circle, just one more.

A black-clad figure broke from the throng and charged.

Yorbourne!

Cursing, he kicked his horse forward. At that moment a DeYvonne lordling, eager for his first blooding and seeing the DeMarian Cadet lead the way, shot for the center. He and the Prince collided with a crash, Titan staggering with the force of it. Screaming in shrill fury, the Royal charger lunged, its teeth clacking

together an inch from the other animal's neck. The
DeYvonne boy sawed desperately at the reins, but his
grip was unsteady and as his mount spun and reared to
face the other stallion, he was flung from the saddle.
The smaller stallion flailed its forehooves, ears flat
against its head and its lips peeling back from its own
teeth. Demnor kicked out at it, cursing. Titan lunged
again, striking like a snake at his adversary's spine.
This time he drew blood. The other horse backed up.
Jerking at the reins, Demnor fought to keep Titan from
following. The great, black head twisted and the Prince
barely pulled his leg back in time to avoid his
warhorse's bite. Slamming his shield into the side of
the charger's skull, he dragged on the reins again,
forcing its head down. Finally Titan relented. The boy
was nowhere in sight, so Demnor turned back to his
sister.

Quindara had set her mount at a slightly diagonal
charge at the creature's head. Used to such sport, the
horse did not shy away, but thundered forward, trum-
peting out its own challenge. The Royal Duke dropped
her lance point and struck.

At the last second, the beast turned and the weapon
hit its back above the shoulder. A large chunk of short
quills and flesh tore free. The creature shrieked and
leaped for her, but she was already away and turning
for her second charge. At the sound of the animal's cry,
the Hunt screamed in answer and swept forward.

They rushed in and out, striking wherever they
could, the dogs, wild with excitement, racing between
them, tearing at the creature's soft underbelly. Soon the
field was churned into a bloody froth as the Hunt
worked off its first reckless fervor.

But the dragon was no helpless prey, and it took its
toll on the dogs and on any hapless knight who came
too close or lost control of his or her mount. With
alarming speed it disemboweled a horse, crushing the
skull of its rider as she fell. Two hounds died instantly
from its kick and another was torn apart when the creature snapped it up in viselike jaws and broke its back

with great wrenches of its head. One of the Cailein
family took a swipe from its tail and fell, screaming,
hands clutching at the dozen quills embedded in his
face and chest. His horse, mad with pain, blundered
into a DeFay. Veteran of many such Hunts, this was his
last. He was thrown from his mount and trampled by
his kin as they passed.

The Hunt continued with cold deliberation now,
urged on by the blood of their own. Following the lead
of the Royal Family, they fell into patterns of alliance
or rivalry.

Attacking in symmetry, Atreus and Marsellus mirrored each other's movements with a grace that was
eerie to behold. Around them, the half a dozen sets of
twins, both identical and not, emulated their fighting
style with elaborate concentration. The Aristok led a
pack of followers, the air surrounding her crackling
with the rising power of the Flame, and through it all
raged Demnor and Quindara. Not a few Hunters fell to
blows taken from rivals, egged on by the sight of the
Royal feud. Most rose to remount with the help of their
squires. One or two did not.

Oblivious, Demnor had been fighting alongside Alerion. Now he pulled back, breathing hard. He had connected with at least a dozen cuts against the beast and
his hair and surcoat were soaked with blood. It stuck to
his flesh beneath his tunic and pulled at his face where
it had begun to harden. His lips tasted of copper. Far
from being sated, however, his very veins sizzled in
frustration.

She has the head was all he could think and the repe-
tition made his own head ache. She had the head and
soon the beast would be down. He could see it in its
staggered gait and weakened defense. She had the
head. There was only one thing to do now.

Ignoring the others who scrambled from his path, he
thundered forward, hurling his lance from him in disgust and drawing his sword.

At that moment Isolde was caught across the chest
by a swipe from the animal's tail. She was thrown,

quills sticking from her surcoat, to land with a crash at
the creature's feet. Too far away, Alerion shouted,
"Zold!" and flinging himself from the saddle, raced
toward her.

The beast rose, madness in its blood-filled eyes. It
made to strike, but suddenly Demnor lunged between
them. Titan screamed and danced sideways, kicking
out at the creature. Scrambling away from the iron-
shod hooves, Isolde collapsed in her brother's arms.

Above them, Demnor returned the beast's howl of
fury and thrust his sword upward. The weapon pierced
the creature's throat, up through its mouth and out.
Something flared in the Prince's mind, a brilliant spear
point of light, that was suddenly quenched as hot blood
splattered into his eyes. It blinded him and the thick,
sickening, copper odor filled his nostrils.

The dragon jerked its head up, tearing the sword
from the Prince's hand. One ragged claw cracked him
across the mouth, sending his helm spinning and then
he was flying from Titan's back. The force of his fall
knocked the air from his lungs as his breastplate drove
into his chest. For a moment he lay stunned, the echo
of the blow ringing in his ears. Warmth filled his
mouth and he bent his head to spill crimson onto the
bloody ground.

I'm injured, was all his mind could grasp as the beast
rose before him. The air around him took on a hazy,
blood-colored hue.

He never saw the streak of fire that slammed into
Isolde's stallion, already mad from a ragged wound
across its flank. The force of the psychic blast flung the
horse toward the dragon just as it lunged to finish him.
The stallion took the death blow meant for him. As he
stupidly watched it die, hands gripped him by the
shoulders and pulled him to safety. Then the world
grew very dark for a time.

One hand on her breast to quiet the awakened Living
Flame, Melesandra DeMarian returned her attention to
the Hunt.

* * *

Safe from the fray, Dimitrius DeLlewellynne, squire to Prince Demnor of Branion, sank down beside his fallen Lord, trying to stop the flow of blood with his hands. He looked about him dazedly as Isolde rushed to his side, crying for the physicians.

Meanwhile the slaughter abated. The Hunt drew back in a semicircle around the wounded creature. With one last, feeble snarl, it fell, to lie twitching, its eyes still glaring at its killers. The nobles watched its death throes in silence, some seated, some dismounted and leaning against their lances. Finally the circle parted. Quindara, a cocked crossbow in her hands, approached it on foot, her squire carrying her sword across his arm.

The creature snapped at her weakly, and she saluted it. Then, raising the weapon, she shot it through the ruins of its right eye. The dragon grew still.

2. Kelahnus

Kelahnus had spent the morning running errands in the city and was damp and hungry by noon. As he made his way back to the palace, he stopped in the West Market for a sausage pastry and a cup of beer. Keeping well under the awning, out of range of the drizzle, he dropped his hood and let his hair spill out over his shoulders. With a sigh, he wiped the moisture from his face. He hated the rain.

The vendor, leaning against the stall's wooden counter, accepted the overpayment the Companion held out to him without comment.

"Afternoon, Kel. A wet day for your gracious self to be out nosing about."

"A miserable day, but it can't be helped," the Companion replied, tasting the pastry with a frown. "A bit burned, isn't it, Jan?"

"Break my heart, why don't you. My cooking is the best in the marketplace and you know it."

"Perhaps. How's your hearing?"

Jan regarded a mole on his forearm with mock concentration. "Open to the Wind's message as it always should be," he answered piously.

"No doubt, and what message has it left you today?" Kelahnus indicated the pocket where the golden crown had disappeared with a questioning eyebrow.

"Nothing you probably haven't already heard," the vendor sniffed. "Rebellion stirring in the north, war in the east, price of flour up ten percent from all that rain this summer, the betrothed of a Prince in town with her kin to insure he doesn't balk on his promises, and speculation on just what that Prince will do since he already loves another."

He turned to serve a member of the Town Watch, who looked at Kelahnus with frank appreciation. The Companion smiled, accepting the compliment of her regard with easy grace. When she left, he returned his attention to the vendor.

"Flour up ten percent, you say? Really?"

"Come on, Kel," Jan leaned forward. "You can tell me. What will His Highness do? The betting in the city is two to one he tells the DeKathrines to bugger off. Others say his love for you will fade once he weds."

Waving an overly curious fly away with one fine-boned hand, Kelahnus kept his features carefully nonchalant. "And what do you think?"

"I think, that if you were my Companion, I'd climb into a box with you and close the lid."

"Don't you think Brand would object?"

"He could come, too."

Balancing the remains of his meal in one hand, Kelahnus flipped up his hood. "Was that everything, Jan?"

The vendor looked disappointed but shrugged. "Word has it the Wind's changed. Unusual for this time of year. Street Seers say it means something big's coming. Maybe a war. Maybe a wedding."

"Maybe a thunderstorm."

"Maybe. Just don't say I didn't warn you."

He swiveled to serve a pair of wine merchants from across the market, waggling his eyebrows at the Companion as he did so.

Kelahnus turned away. Licking the grease from his fingers, he studied the crowds as he went over the day's errands. Apothecary, herbalist, tailor, and the School of Companions visited. Packages to be received tomorrow. Diviner and the half a dozen merchants like Jan on his payroll with only one piece of news of any import to impart: the influx of DeKathrines from

Exenworth and Essendale; come to support the suit of
Isolde, Earl of the Realm and Knight of the Bow.

With a frown, he tucked a stray lock of hair back into
place as he considered the best way to proceed. He
could visit the docks and question the sailors and
handlers who'd brought Branion's most influential
family to Branbridge, but one glance at the rich cut of
his clothes decided against it. Besides, he thought,
glancing up at the gathering storm clouds, it was going
to rain. Again. Better to be somewhere dry. Inside.
With most of their noble guests riding the Hunt, the
palace would be nearly empty until well past dark.
Time to do a little investigating.

Brushing the crumbs from his cloak, he gave the last
of the pastry to a beggar and handed Jan the cup,
another crown in the bottom. Then he continued on
his way.

Some time later, he nodded to the guards at the east
gate and slipped into the training yards. Weaving
between pairs of fighters wrestling or sparring, he
made his way to the east tower.

"Hey, pretty boy!"

The shout was scornful and snapped him instantly
from his peaceful mood. Setting his features into a
mask of disdain, he turned.

The woman in the fighting tunic leaned lithely
muscled arms on the fence that separated the training
circles, her black eyes gleaming under her stained
sweatband.

Kelahnus relaxed. "Florence."

The Aristok's youngest Companion grinned wick-
edly as he walked over to greet her. Three years his
senior, Florence had always merited the title Older
Sister, a ranking by age and experience that the Companions followed. At the School she'd protected him
and taught him; covered up for him at times, held him
at others. At the palace it had been the same.

"How's my favorite cock robin?" she asked.

"Singing a song of bliss, thank you. And your most
gracious self?"

"I manage."

With a smile, Kelahnus leaned against the other side of the fence. "Is there news of the Hunt?"

"Not yet. But as they say, no news is good news."

"Except when your messenger has been waylaid. Mistrust silences," Kelahnus added, finishing the quote from their school days.

Florence chuckled.

"Still, it's early yet. They've barely had time to ruin their clothing." They both laughed.

He smiled at her. She returned it with her usual—*What has my Younger Brother been up to now?*—stare. Usually he brushed it off with one of his—*Sodomy in the hayloft, what do you think?*—looks, but today he was in a peaceful mood, so he merely glanced down at the array of weapons piled at her feet.

"Impressive."

"Care to join me?"

"Flori, it's raining."

"So?" She flipped him a wooden practice knife. Catching it by the handle, he held it at arm's length with finger and thumb.

"Fighting after dinner is barbaric."

"So's fornication before breakfast. Knives or hand to-hand?"

"Such language. Knives, I suppose."

Draping his cloak over the fence, he slipped between the rails and followed her to the center of the practice circle. The palace could wait for an hour or two. He placed the knife on the ground before him.

"So who's fornicating before breakfast?" he asked as he rolled his neck and did a few quick knee bends.

Florence bent and brushed her elbows across the ground before answering. "Well, you did leave the palace awfully late this morning." After a quick somersault, she began a series of kicks.

"Were you spying on me, Older Sister?"

She smiled and made a jab for his head. With a sweep of golden hair, he neatly avoided her.

"Someone has to keep Master Klairius informed of

how you waste your time," she answered. "The Heir's Companion flirting with farm boys!"

After a slow backflip toward the fence, Kelahnus stretched one leg over it, gripped his ankle and touched his forehead to his knee. His contact from Demnor's Ducal lands in Kraburn had arrived early that day with the season's tithe. Although he'd had little to report, he'd had plenty to share. Kelahnus smiled at the memory. "He was a very pretty farm boy," he said, glancing around at her from under his lashes. "He had blue eyes."

"Did he end up with blue balls?"

"My, my, you have had a Kelahnus morning, haven't you? Bored or business?"

"Both. I wanted to see if you would notice you had company. You were otherwise engaged."

"If you'd been anyone else, I would have noticed."

"And he was a very pretty farm boy."

"Indeed."

They shared a long, lazy smile, then Florence laughed. "Well, since you're through on your stomach, care to get knocked on your arse?"

"Flori, I hadn't thought you cared."

She snorted. "You wouldn't know what to do with a real woman if she bit you on the tip."

"I'm a fast learner. If I have a good teacher." Dropping his leg, he gave her a languid look. "Think you're up to it?"

She matched the expression. "Without question, but first, we fight."

"Oh, very well." Sweeping up his knife, he bowed. She reciprocated and crouched.

"Ready . . ."

"Oh, no, you don't. Last time you called it, you cheated. I'll call it."

"And have you return the favor? Don't be absurd, Younger Brother."

Glancing around quickly, she spotted an off duty guard leaning against an outbuilding, munching an apple.

"Mark? Yell ready, set, go!"

Mark looked over and grinned. "Ready, set, go!"

She lunged.

They fought in silence for a time, the only sound an occasional soft whoosh of breath or splash as a booted foot slapped down into one of the growing puddles. Finally, Kelahnus misread a step and Florence grazed him across the chest.

"First blood. Disadvantage."

Eyes narrowed, he acknowledged the point and shifted his knife to the right hand.

"Feel the need to use the comfort hand, do you?" The older Companion's dagger shot forward in a blur. At the last moment, she tossed it to the other fist, then swung under and up for the killing blow. Anticipating the move, Kelahnus twisted aside and caught her wrist with the blunted tip of his own weapon.

"Point. Vein. Disadvantage balanced and exchanged," he intoned.

Florence flushed. Springing forward, she jolted the knife from his hand and knocked him over backward. Following him to the ground, she landed on his chest with a thump. Her hand grabbed his, pinning it and her knife came down. Just before the point touched his throat, he managed to catch her wrist. They strained for an instant, then Florence grimaced in triumph.

"Blood. Slippery. Disadvantage," she panted.

"Blood. Weakness. Disadvantage balanced," he replied with a gasp as the blade dropped a fraction. Florence grinned slyly.

"You lighten your hair!" she said suddenly in mock surprise.

Kelahnus knew this game. "So? You darken yours to hide the gray."

"At least I don't pluck my eyebrows."

"No, but you do shave your breasts."

"Brat!" Her arm loosened as she raised it to strike. With the extra space, Kelahnus twisted and brought his elbow up sharply. It caught her on the chin, knocking her sideways. One foot lashed out as she fell, but

Kelahnus had already rolled free. Diving forward, he came up on top of her. He snapped his stiffened fingers down to just above her throat and grinned.

"Death blow. You lost your temper."

The older Companion gave him a rueful but approving look. "A knife death's too good for you anyway."

He smiled, acknowledging the compliment, and stood, offering her his hand. She waved it aside and rose. Reaching for the bucket at the side of the circle, she drew a ladle of water and drank thirstily. The corners of Kelahnus' mouth twitched.

"Care to go a round of hand-to-hand, since you're so inept at knives?" he asked.

The ladle, still half full, cracked him across the head, soaking his hair. "Little worm!"

Florence shook the ladle under his nose, then tossed it into the bucket. "No, I don't want to go a round of hand-to-hand," she mimicked. Taking his arm, she maneuvered him back to the fence. "I'm comfortably worn out now, thank you. I want to talk to you."

"About what?" His tone was so suspicious that she laughed.

"Not about you, you needn't fear. Not that your insolent behavior doesn't merit it—that or a kick in the arse. No, this is serious."

They reached the fence and Kelahnus disentangled himself. Leaning against it, arms crossed, he blew the water off his nose and assumed a look of bored disinterest.

"Well?" he demanded.

Her expression hardened. "I said it was serious, Kel. Don't feed me this tripe, or you can walk into it blind. It's about your man."

The arrogance flowed off the younger Companion's face with the rivulets of water, leaving him looking anxious and vulnerable. *What now?*

"It involves the Royal Wedding," Florence said when she saw she had his attention. "Or rather the lack of it. The official courting inquiry was accepted over a year ago. It's bad enough that His Highness has done no actual courting since then, without adding his obvious reluctance to go through with the wedding at all. And that is your fault."

Kelahnus opened his mouth to protest, but she waved him to silence.

"You should have pushed him to some outer show of intent: a ball, a ride in the country, something. It didn't have to be a weekend alone playing, 'I'll show you mine if you show me yours,' for the Wind's sake. That's going to be hard enough to accomplish on their wedding night."

Her tone was acerbic and, despite his carefully held control, Kelahnus winced.

"It's not a matter of what he wants," she continued. "It's a matter of how it looks. Everyone knows he has no interest in this marriage, but there's less than no point in rubbing it in the face of the most powerful family in Branion. He's made his statement of independence by not marrying sooner. Now he should act before it becomes a political issue. If he doesn't soon . . ."

"The Aristok will force him to," Kelahnus finished, a lump of fear growing in his stomach. *The last time they fought . . .*

"It's come to that?" he asked lamely, trying to banish the memories and the panic they invoked.

Florence merely stared at him. "What do you think, Kel? The DeKathrines are here in force. Their very presence is a pressure. Not on him, on Her Majesty. And she doesn't like being pressured."

"Neither does he."

"Better he wields the dagger, then. Have it seen as being his idea, not theirs."

And not hers.

The unspoken words hung between them like a sword; a threat of violence to come.

"I'll speak with him," Kelahnus said finally. *Tonight. As soon as he gets back.* The panic rose up again, and he took a deep breath to calm it."

"Soon, Kel."

"I said I will!"

The unexpected burst of temper drew Florence's brows down in a frown.

As surprised as she, Kelahnus passed a shaking hand across his face. "Forgive me, Older Sister," he said stiffly.

Cupping his cheek in her hand, Florence gave him a sad smile. "Nothing to forgive, Little Brother. It's hard to give them up, isn't it?"

With a rueful glance, he gently pulled away. "Don't be silly," he said, regaining his composure. "I'm not giving him up. Consort or no, I'll never lose him."

"Of course not."

He flushed. "Don't patronize me, Flori. I've been through too much for that. We both know how he feels."

"Who doesn't? The youngest stable hand knows you hold his heart, but he's the Heir. He can give you no more."

With a shrug, Kelahnus drew on his cloak, swiping absently at the mud on his breeches. "As you say, I hold his heart. What more do I need?" He ran a hand through his hair. "He'll wed and have children. I know his duty, and as much as he would like to pretend otherwise, so does he. From where I stand, it changes nothing. Really, Flori, I'm content."

She smiled. "You are, too, aren't you? I shouldn't worry. You're always fine."

"No, not always." He squeezed her hand. "Was there anything else?"

"Just that I heard that a certain farm boy had a certain indelicate disease," she teased, trying to lighten their parting and bring a smile to his face.

Recognizing her intent, Kelahnus made himself laugh. "Oh, you wish. Do you think I'd give you the opportunity to say I told you so?"

"No."

They shared a smile, slightly tinged with sadness, then Kelahnus bowed and turned away.

Florence watched him go, her expression slowly

changing back to a worried frown. Then, with a sigh, she returned to the circle.

Weaving his way through the various parlors and conservatories, Kelahnus skirted the guest wings, too agitated and too grumpy to follow his original plan. His clothes were damp from the rain and caked with mud. They clung to his skin, making him feel constrained and uncomfortable. When he reached his own suite, three cream-colored rooms off the Prince's, he stripped quickly and sat naked by the mirror. The breeze from the open window dried him, bringing goose bumps to his flesh and raising the pale hair on his arms. He shivered but didn't bother to put on a robe or close the window. Chin in hand, he stared into the mirror's depths.

Why, he thought, could Florence unsettle him faster than any other? In spite of his love for her and his need for her company and advice, he sometimes wished she would keep it to herself. She made him feel out of control and that bothered him. There was too much he needed to stay in control of.

Sighing, he poked his finger into an open jar of cream. Swirling it around, he took a deep breath to bring his mind back to the problem at hand.

The DeKathrines. He needed to know how many were here and who they were. That meant Gilbraith, the Aristok's secretary. He wrinkled his nose. The man was expensive, and he didn't think he had enough powder. Tomorrow when the Apothecary's packages arrived, but he needed the information today. That left Ariston, the Court Historian. Not as close to the palace goings on as Gilbraith, but infinitely pleasanter. And he kept his own counsel, not running to Martina, the Aristok's First Companion, with every scrap. Also he was cheaper, asking little in return save the exchange of information.

"And that means hoist your lazy rear into those guest rooms."

Wiping the cream on an embroidered hand towel, he

rose and entered his bathroom. The window was open
here also, the sachet of dried herbs before it scenting
the air with a faint touch of lavender. The washbowl
was already filled with warm water. Kelahnus smiled
in appreciation. Someone was thinking. Or spying.
Moving swiftly, he washed the mud from his face and
arms and rinsed his hair, brushing it dry until it shone.
Then he returned to his bedroom.

After a moment's study of his wardrobe he decided
on comfort above discretion. Blue velvet pants and soft
boots, a gold silk shirt to match his hair and a brilliant
blue sash around his waist. Garrote and lockpicks concealed in its folds were within easy reach and his slim
stiletto fit snugly into its wrist sheath. With one last
glance in the mirror, he smoothed an invisible wrinkle
and left.

It took twenty minutes of brisk walking to cross the
west and central wings of the palace. A reticent man,
Demnor had chosen their rooms for isolation, not convenience, and Kelahnus sighed dramatically to himself
as he passed his fifth set of Palace Guards. The rest of
the Royal Family resided in the central wing, in the
midst of the hustle and bustle of palace life. The most
ancient wing in the palace, the Royal apartments were
riddled with spy holes and blocked and unblocked
passageways. The Royal Companions knew every twist
and turn and moved about as they pleased with little
observation. Kelahnus consoled himself with the
knowledge that sooner or later they would have to
move whether Demnor liked it or not. In the meantime
he put up with the inconvenience because it was
equally inconvenient for those who might want to spy
upon them.

Down a short flight of wooden stairs, through an
archway flanked by two stone dragons, and he stood
before the palace residence of the Hierarchpriest of
Cannonshire, Alexander DeKathrine, Duke of Werrick
and Earl of Cambury. His Lord's second cousin. The
door was locked.

A slight pressure and a twist to the left with his

pick and it was unlocked and ajar. A glance told him that no overzealous servants occupied the outer room, and a step took him inside. The door closed softly behind him.

The hush of the windowless antechamber made him move quietly, his ears cocked for any sound that might alert him to another's presence. Nose twitching at the faint odor of incense, he made a quick search of the rooms, then stopped before a heavy mahogany desk.

The rectangular box, Alexander's crest and the device of the Knights of the Sword carved into the lid, was locked. It posed as little difficulty as the door had. He almost laughed out loud.

"Well, My Lord Duke," the young Companion whispered. "What do you have for me today?"

On the top of a pile of parchment sat a small packet of correspondence. A small packet of correspondence from the Duke Isabelle DeKathrine of Exenworth; Isolde's mother.

Unable to make the journey to Branbridge at this time due to the imminent arrival of her eighth child, she had sent more than explicit instructions to her brother. Demnor and Isolde would wed. Period. The waiting was over.

The Companion replaced the ribbon around the letters with a sigh. He'd thought as much.

Digging deeper, he found little else, a petition from a rural prelate requesting support against an ambitious neighbor, a few notes and details about upcoming religious ceremonies and events, a handful of sketches for the renovations at Ludford Castle and a guest list for a reception held last week. The usual. He replaced the letters on the top of the pile and closed the lid.

Born to an older school of Court intrigue, the Hierarchpriest believed in the often proved adage, *What isn't written down can't be read at your trial.*

His secretary, however, was an entirely different sort of man. Kelahnus entered his office with a smile of anticipation. He loved secretaries. They had such orderly and exacting minds. They were a spy's best friends.

An hour later he left, the smile broadening to a smirk of satisfaction. Guilden had a full itinerary of the entire DeKathrine entourage, appointments, petitions, and plans, most centering on one event, the Royal Wedding.

He skirted Alerion's rooms. The Viscount lived like a priest sworn to poverty. Besides, he had little time and the DeKathrine guest suites which now housed Isolde, Earl of Essendale, and her retinue offered a much sweeter temptation.

He was not disappointed. They overflowed with exquisite gowns, perfumes, and jewelry beside armor and hunting gear. A pile of finely crafted weaponry meant for bodices, boots, gloves, and hairnets shared equal importance with cruder pieces, including a carved longbow, backsword and a light, wicked looking ax. At least the Heir's intended would be able to hold up her end of a battle as well as a ball. This was a good thing. Moving a forest green cloak out of his way, he went through the Earl's trunk.

It held much the same, but at the bottom he found an ivory box containing a supply of contraceptive tea and a jade vial filled with sleeping powder. Kelahnus wrapped a sample of each in one of Isolde's many handkerchiefs and went on his way, content.

Weaving through the DeKathrine wing, he passed through the closed courtyard which led to the DeLynne and DeLlewellynne apartments and stopped in the center of a glass-roofed atrium. Beneath his feet a ceramic mosaic circled out to three tiled arrows: lavender for DePaula, hawks soaring above a tall aerie; red for DeFay, the huge tusks of the family's wild boar crest done in two curved tiles of gold; and the DeSharon olive green surrounding a brilliant white stoat with black ears. Here and there the Companion could see one or two gray tiles forgotten in the artist's haste to change DeSandra colors to DeSharon. The stoat adorned the family's new crest, but the ancient eagle could still be found, carved high on a ceiling or woven into an old tapestry. It was easier to wipe out a family's future than a family's past, the Companion mused. Murder some, execute others, hold the most powerful prisoner until the rest paid a ransom that bankrupted those spared and built a castle for the newly born Duke of Yorbourne.

Kelahnus considered the crest. The family hadn't changed much in the years that followed, and if anyone had a plan to exploit the tensions between the DeMarians and the DeKathrines, it would be the DeSharons.

Two hours of gossip and speculation went by quickly and the young Companion left in a thoughtful mood. The DeSharon servants had no qualms about speeding rumor on its way, and the word was the family was waiting to benefit from the DeKathrine fall from favor.

Mulling this over, Kelahnus made his way to the more public areas of the palace. Guilden had made a visit to Gilbraith unnecessary, but he still needed to speak with Ariston. Close to Her Majesty in earlier years, his advice was usually sound in matters concerning her, and the young Companion needed advice. Demnor he could handle, but how the Heir was to handle his mother when he asked her permission— avoided her order—to wed was a bit beyond them both. And it would have to be soon before the DeKathrine pressure erupted into a battle between the two oldest families in Branion.

He subdued the shudder that crept up his spine. Ariston would know what to do.

The halls were quiet and deserted of all but the occasional guard. The unusualness of this did not penetrate his thoughts until a glance out a large, rose-tinted window showed him the darkening sky. It was late. The Hunt must be finished and feasting begun by now. At least one of his people should have already sought him out.

He cast his mind back. Granted, he had been doing his best to avoid being seen earlier, but not for the last two hours. And there'd been precious few servants

about and none of his own people. The comment he'd
so flippantly made to Florence that afternoon returned
to him amidst a chill of unease. He waved down a
passing page.

"Have you seen Eddison or Terrence, lad?"

The child eyed the bright silk of the Companion's
shirt with awe, but pocketed the penny as soon as it
was offered.

"No, Yer Grace."

"Find them for me, will you? Tell them I'll be in the
Octavian Library."

The second penny disappeared and the boy made an
awkward bow and darted off. Kelahnus watched him
go with a frown. Mentally he ticked off where all his
people should be. Two at least should have sought him
out by now.

Likely Eddison was waiting for a report from one of
his own people. Terence was probably at the lodge.
Bright, but inexperienced, it had doubtless not
occurred to him to send a page.

Unconvinced, Kelahnus felt fluttering panic bloom
in his chest. *Silence is as dangerous as chaos,* an
unwanted voice in the back of his mind lectured,
*because silence is blind and therefore more easily mis-
interpreted.* He quickened his pace.

Halfway down an ornately carved staircase he found
he was running. Forcing himself to slow, he fought
down the rising fear.

"There's no reason to panic," he told himself sternly,
unconvinced even as he spoke. "There could be any
number of reasons why you haven't received a report
yet."

Right. Either all my people have turned traitor or
none of them have the courage to face me because he's
dead."

Once voiced, the fear flowed out of him, leaving his
knees weak. He sagged against a miniature stained
glass window and pressed his cheek against its cool
panes. Unwelcome thoughts chased each other through
his mind. He couldn't breathe. With some effort he

forced himself to move, to turn the tiny latch and open
the window.

Outside, rain clouds covered the twilight sky. To the
west, the high, keening cry of a wyvern was answered
by another. Lightning skipped across the clouds, illuminating them in chaotic patches, the thunder chasing
it down even as it flashed.

That's how I feel, he thought. *Overtaken and
scattered.*

A gust of wind rippled through his hair, sending
shivers down his back. Soothed by its intimate touch,
he smiled faintly. The Wind, freest of the Four
Aspects, often called the Messenger, was the patron of
Heralds, merchants, and Companions. Kelahnus sent It
a silent prayer that Its news would not be what he
feared and closed the window.

The tiny panes shuddered with the movement and he
ran his fingertips along them and over the delicate
leaden seams. The scene depicted the birth of Aristok
Dorian the Third who'd brought the Continental religion of Essusiatism to Branion in force. It had
remained the dominant faith for over a hundred years,
upheld by four Essusiate Aristoks, until Atreus the
Bastard had returned the traditional Triarotic beliefs to
their rightful place.

In the finely crafted window, the head of the baby
and those of the DeMarians gathered around were
wreathed in white in the sixth century style. Tracing
the features of the child with one finger, the Companion brought his mind firmly back to the present, the
escape into history having left some measure of calm.
He sighed, and continued down the stairs and along the
paneled corridor that led to the Octavian Library.

Just as he passed the door to the first reading room,
he heard his name called. Turning, he saw a thin boy of
sixteen, sandy hair falling in his eyes, waving frantically at him from the top of the stairs he'd just
descended. When he saw that he had the Companion's
attention, he hurried down, taking the steps two at a
time. His brown, Triarchy robe was bunched up in one

fist so he wouldn't trip but even so he stumbled at the bottom and nearly went flying.

Kelahnus shook his head, amused. Terence was all feet.

Son of a camp follower who'd died in Gallia, he'd been brought to Branbridge by Demnor, who, for reasons known only to himself, had taken a liking to the boy, handing him over to Ariston with the words, "Feed him." The confused Historian had obeyed, taking the hard-eyed five-year-old as his apprentice when no other instructions had been forthcoming. Surprising everyone, Terence had flourished under Ariston's gentle tutelage.

The Companion had no idea what Demnor planned for the boy, but on finding he had other attributes, had taken him into his service as well. Now, Terence was one of his best, albeit these days, clumsiest, lieutenants.

Today however, his smile faded as the boy righted himself and hurried over, his face pale. Taking the Companion by the arm, he pulled him into the reading room.

"Have you heard? Did they tell you?" he panted, leaning against the door and struggling to catch his breath. "I couldn't find you. I checked your rooms. You weren't there. Must have gone the wrong way. Poxed-up son of a sow palace! I've been all over. *Have you heard?*"

Kelahnus took him by the shoulders and spoke quietly. "No. I haven't. Heard what?"

"The Crown Prince Demnor . . ."

A nasty chill worked its way up the Companion's spine, raising the hair on the back of his neck. One image, clear and bloody, came to his mind and would not be banished. Tightening his fingers until the boy winced, he forced himself to take a deep breath.

"What about the Crown Prince Demnor?" His voice, flat and distant, sounded strange to his ears. Terence went white and, stammering incoherently, tried to pull away. Kelahnus held him where he was.

"Tell me." The command was soft, but the tone was so deadly that the boy's eyes widened in fear. He tried to speak, choked, then cried out as the Companion's fists twisted into the fabric of his robe and jerked him forward.

"He took a fall! A blow! A . . . a head wound! Casey said there was blood all over! But he's alive, I swear it! He got up! Please, Kelahnus, don't! I couldn't find you!"

Frantically he finally tore himself free and stumbled backward.

Kelahnus watched him go, his face impassive. Now the quiet of the afternoon made sense. A feeling of numb inevitability crept over him. Deep inside, something within him began a low, keening wail, while something else fought the paralysis in his limbs. Fought to run . . . where? To the lodge. To Demnor's side. But his training and the numbness won out and he waved his hand toward a chair.

"Sit. And report on the Hunt," he said quietly.

Terence obeyed, fumbling for a seat, while never taking his eyes off the Companion's face. Kelahnus sat opposite.

"Now. From the beginning."

The boy wet his lips. "I . . . I went to the stables after twelve to see who had come back and who . . . They took down a dragon in the fields west of the lodge. Five dogs were killed . . ."

Kelahnus cut him off with an abrupt gesture. "I said from the beginning."

Terence went red. "Ah, Your Grace, I . . . I don't have a full report."

"I see. Proceed."

"They lost three, no, four hunters."

"Who?"

"I . . . don't know. One was in the Cailein party."

Knowing the answer before he asked, but asking anyway for teaching's sake, Kelahnus repeated, "Who?"

"I . . ."

"You don't know."

Terence stared at his feet. "No."

The Companion sighed. "Very well. The Crown Prince Demnor."

The boy looked up quickly, then resumed staring at the floor. He wet his lips again and coughed. "The beast knocked him from the saddle," he began, trying to keep his voice level. "Casey, one of Metellus' apprentices . . ."

"I know who he is."

Terence coughed again. "Ah, yes, Your Grace. I . . . I didn't mean . . ."

"Never mind. Go on."

"Ah, I, that is, Casey said he, I mean, the Crown Prince got back on his horse, but that he was covered in blood. She wasn't sure if it was all the Prince's because His Highness often, that is, he . . ."

"Often seems to bathe in it. Yes, I know." Kelahnus leaned forward suddenly, putting his hand down on Terence's and ignoring the boy's cringing reaction. "Terence. Calm down. Take a deep breath and put your thoughts in order. You are becoming unintelligible."

Chewing at his lip, the boy obeyed. "His Highness rode to the lodge. His squire had to help him down, but he walked inside. Casey had to leave then, so I don't . . . I'm sorry, Kelahnus, I wanted to ride out there at once, but I couldn't find you. I didn't know what to do. Casey and the rest were so afraid after seeing him fall. No one ever thought *he* could be hurt."

No one but me.

"It's all over the palace. The rumors of his injuries are getting worse by the minute. No one wanted to be the one to tell you. I couldn't find you. I . . . Forgive me," he whispered.

His expression was miserable. Kelahnus sighed again, studying the young man before him and choosing his words carefully. "Well," he said after a long pause, "I suppose you can be forgiven for forgetting your training in this instance. It is the first emergency you've had to deal with, and as it's about His Highness, well, it's understandable how you might panic. I had thought that your life in the battle camps would have given you a clearer head, but no matter. Sometimes maturity has to come with age."

Terence dropped his head into his hands.

"I take it that I may now rely on you to send a page to the lodge for a proper report?"

"Page?" Looking up, the boy's face grew even more bleak.

"Yes. That is what they're for, you know. I expect a number have been sent already."

"Yes, Your Grace. I'll see to it at once." Terence drew in a shaky breath as tears spilled from his eyes. He dashed them away and made to rise. Kelahnus gently pushed him down again.

"It can wait until you've composed yourself. Everyone makes mistakes, Terence. I know how much you love him. For the next time, send a page to the scene immediately. Send one to find me. And wait. For now, I'll be in my sitting room. Have the others, the ones who didn't want to be the ones to tell me, summoned there. Then come yourself when you have a complete report. And, Terence . . ."

The boy looked up miserably.

"Of course, I forgive you. Thank you for telling me."

Terence nodded. Kelahnus stroked his hair, then squeezed his shoulder and left. As he made his way to the west wing, his mind darted out in panicked fear toward the lodge, trying to pierce the clouds of distance and see what had occurred. But he was no Seer and must rely on others to bring him comfort. He reached his rooms and entered, resigned now to the one thing he hated most. To waiting.

At the lodge the revelry had already begun. The injured were being tended to; the hale were drinking and trading tales of their own prowess. In the Royal apartments, the Court Physician had tended the Crown Prince and returned downstairs to report his condition to the Aristok. Upstairs, the Heir slept fitfully, the pain in his mouth echoing another from years before.

* * *

Demnor was six years old, and her voice was like steel on stone.

"What is strength, boy?"

He blinked, unsure of what she wanted. She said so many things he didn't understand.

"Strength," he repeated, his voice sounding hollow in the great empty hall that was his training room.

"The strength of the Aristok?" Her tone was icy now.

The Aristok. His grandfather was the Aristok. He was strong. As strong as a mountain or a thunderstorm. As strong as the flames that often surrounded him in a nimbus of red fire. Demnor had never stopped to ask why.

"The Aristok is strong because," he began, his voice low and uncertain.

"Not like that." The blow cracked against his ear, the sharp pain sending his vision spinning. But he managed not to fall and not to cry out. The small pride in that stiffened his back.

"Speak like a ruler, not like a peasant."

He felt her power grip him. Raising his eyes to meet hers, he found himself falling into a whirlpool of blazing fire ringed with green ice. He made his own eyes unfocus slightly and the pressure eased.

"The Aristok must have the strength of stone," he intoned.

"And your enemies?"

Again he met her stare. "Everyone is my enemy."

She nodded. "And they will kill you if you show the slightest weakness, the slightest hint of fear. They know nothing of what it means to rule. Their only care is for power. They covet what you are. What you will be. If you relax your vigilance for an instant, they will be on you like a pack of jackals upon a fallen lion, and the country will be torn apart. I will not allow you to bring this into being. That boy, Julian, is your enemy. His family are all traitors, and they used him to use you. Do you like being used?"

Her voice was that of a snake waiting to strike, but

he was a Prince and her words had made him angry, so
he answered, "No!" with a defiant glare. She merely
smiled coldly.

"You must be strong enough to see through false
praise and false love," she continued. "What is behind
them? A dagger. The words and the deeds that shout of
love are a trap, waiting for you to be drawn in for the
kill. When someone strikes you, you must stand and
stare them down until they cower, then crush them
underfoot. Your enemies will see that you cannot be
defeated, and they will slink away like the curs they
are."

Flames burned openly in her eyes now. He could feel
the heat of it on his face. He felt trapped by her voice,
by the passionate rhythm of her words. Not much of
what she said made sense to him, but he strove to
understand so that one day he would be what she was:
strong and powerful. Stone. So the fire would blaze
within him and not turn on him and destroy his mind.
So the new baby that she loved would not steal away
his birthright. Deep inside one lonely voice, the voice
of a gentle man now dead, cried out but he ignored it. It
was weak. Her words washed over him.

"You're a DeMarian. One day you'll be Aristok, if
you're strong enough. For, mark my words, boy, if you
fail, I'll cast you aside without a second glance. The
Aristok must be the Guardian of the Land and Vessel
of the Living Flame. It is a sacred duty. For that reason
you're not free to scatter your trust as a fool scatters his
money. Your Great Uncle Amedeus had that weakness
and he was murdered by a DeSandra he thought was
his friend. The Flame saw his flaw and abandoned him
to death and the duty fell to stronger shoulders: your
grandfather's and mine."

He knew. He remembered. He remembered his shy,
quiet great uncle, who'd lifted him into the trees in
Collin's Park and laughed when the boy had shouted
that he wanted to fly. He had flung himself in the air,
confident that this man would let no harm come to him
and had been caught in his strong arms.

He remembered Marri, his nurse, taking him to his great uncle's garden, and sitting patiently, listening to tales of olden days while the great master, Harold of Daedlesburg painted his portrait for the children's gallery. He remembered games of tag in the halls before the appalled gaze of the Court and the amused smiles of the servants. He remembered his first pony, a gift, and riding proudly by his great uncle's side to inspect the Guard. Amedeus had been so tall and beautiful that day, like the Essusiate god.

He remembered, but he didn't understand. Great Uncle's eyes hadn't burned; the red-gray fire had been warm with love and he'd told him that was what the Flame was. But as the months marched by in their bleak and lonely parade the memories grew faint and distant. Marri was gone and Great Uncle was gone. Only *she* remained; a growing, fearful presence like the Shadow Catcher of Death. Her words burned in his heart, charred all other truths to ash. He no longer felt sorry for his gentle kinsman or for the DeSandra family hunted down and destroyed. He no longer cried for them in the night when no one could hear him. Great Uncle had been weak and they were traitors. All of them. He thought. He couldn't tell what feelings were his and what were hers anymore.

She was pacing now, back and forth, one foot placed firmly before the other, hand on her breast. She always moved that way when she was angry or obsessed with an idea. It reminded him of a dawn last summer in Kormandeaux; of her speech to the army before she'd led them into battle. He'd been excited then and proud. Wrapped in a blanket in the arms of Alexander DeKathrine, in the midst of her generals and Lords, he'd watched her pace back and forth before him, calling on the Triarchy to grant them victory. Her voice had been commanding and harsh, each clipped word shouted at the sky that had glowed red from the force of her desire and the power of her people's will to do battle in her name. She'd raved at her troops to bring her the head of the Gallian king on a spear, to level his cities and crush all resistance. To defeat this Essusiate crusade so utterly that no puppet ruler of an absent pontiff would dare send arms against them. They'd almost managed it. The king had escaped, but her troops had brought her province after province to lay before her father's feet in triumph.

The army worshiped Melesandra. With her at their head, they had carved out an empire greater than any in the history of the DeMarian reign. In their midst, Demnor had felt her power of command reach out and lift him, demanding all his abilities, all his loyalty, and all his love, but she hadn't been speaking to him then.

She wasn't speaking to him now. Lost in her own words, she seemed to have forgotten him altogether. He used this respite to gather his scattered defenses and watch her warily for the signs of a renewed attack.

Her voice had dropped to an introspective murmur. "You must be strong enough to sentence a hundred to death. Yes. And strong enough to send more into battle. You must be strong enough to kill.

"If a man came into your room at night to murder you, could you execute him with your own hands, then rise and seek out his accomplices and put them to the sword?

"Are you strong enough to rule?

"Do you hate me, boy?"

He'd been waiting for a trap. A sudden question meant to startle him into showing some weakness or fault, but he'd learned that lesson. He studied her face. It remained as impassive as a statue's, offering him no clue. The fire in her eyes was dampened, for now. Did he hate her? The answer came easily enough.

"Yes, Mother."

She nodded. "I will send the boy away. You are dismissed."

The dream shifted on a tide of green-and-red fire. Demnor was fifteen, and her voice had not changed, but he had. Two years on the battlefields in the company of soldiers and mercenaries had both hardened and softened him. He had known friendship and loyalty and a duty he could understand. The Aristok and her world of cold scrutiny had been far distant.

His Marshal had been Captain Fletcher. She hadn't called on him to live a life in the shadow of a dead man. She'd trained him and praised him; fought with him and taught him to be a leader. Then she'd almost died for him.

Now there was peace. The Captain was recovering in Aquilliard; he was in Branbridge and so was the Aristok.

The blow snapped his head back, numbing one side of his mouth. Slowly he turned to face her.

He was a soldier, but he was also a DeMarian, Heir to the Throne. Her words were his words now, spoken in his voice, harsh and dangerous. He could not afford to be weak, to trust. Only on the battlefield where loyalties were clear could he relax.

But not here. Especially not here. His eyes met hers, reflecting the royal madness back at her. He was strong, he was stone, and the red-gray fire that glowered in his own eyes burned a darkness through his mind.

But the voice that cried inside was stronger, too, and now it no longer wept, it screamed.

Blood began to run from his lip where the Royal Seal on her finger had split it, but his expression never wavered.

"Are you strong enough to rule?"

"Are you strong enough to stand, Your Highness?"

Demnor glared at the page for a long moment, then abruptly gestured her out. She fled. Sitting groggily on the edge of the bed, he gazed at the overcast sky and wondered how long he'd been asleep. Two or three hours.

Downstairs, the hunting lodge's hall clock chimed four. Three hours, then. No wonder he felt so thick. His throat hurt, and his mouth seemed to be swollen shut. Rubbing his eyes, he tried to pull himself together.

In his mind, the remnants of an unpleasant dream still lingered. Something about his mother and . . . He shook his head to clear it. Pain rippled up the left side of his face and he stifled a gasp as the movement tore at the stitching on his jaw.

Flames.

He glanced down at the ceramic flagon on the table by the bed. Empty now. The physician had come and gone, doing his work and leaving a list of unwelcome advice and a softweed posset to numb the pain. The Prince had ignored the advice and thrown the drink into the garden. He wondered now if perhaps it might have been better to have drunk the vile brew. His face felt as if blunt needles had been driven through it.

Clenching his teeth and holding onto the bedpost for support, he pulled himself up. He hurt everywhere. It hurt to stand. It hurt to breathe. It hurt to think.

With deliberate care, he crossed the room to a small dresser, clutching the edges, white-knuckled, as a wave of dizziness made his stomach do a flip.

Burn it, stand up! he shouted at himself, upset at his shakiness. *There's nothing wrong with your legs!*

Breathing hard, he closed his eyes until the weakness passed.

You don't have any broken bones. Your skull's not cracked. In one hour you've got to face a pack of drunken Lords, so shake this off! You've been wounded before!

And had felt the same humiliating trembling and frailty before. It hadn't stopped him then, though, and it wouldn't stop him now.

Coward! he berated himself. *I said, stand up!*

The gilt-framed mirror above the dresser swam in front of him as he glared accusingly at his own reflection.

His face was bone white, the twin coals of his eyes burning into his image. The ragged, stitch-covered wounds stood out as two angry gashes, the lower starting just below the ear and following the jawline to the chin, the upper smaller but wider, running parallel about an inch above. By the Earth, he was lucky the beast hadn't taken his head off. Below his lip, the

puncture where his teeth had driven through his mouth
still bled. He wiped at it, but the dried blood on his cuff
scraped against the fragile scab and opened it farther.
Dropping his hand with a sigh, he shook his head. He'd
really made a hash of his face this time.

His expression grew bleak. How many wounds and
how many scars had he accumulated over the years?
And for what? Nothing worth all that spilled blood. He
tried to remember the first and couldn't. He tried to
remember a time he'd had none and couldn't.

Hazards of war, he told himself, recognizing the
downward spiral of his thoughts and trying to halt
them. But the mood persisted. Too few had been taken
in war.

He shook his head gingerly. The ride to the lodge
was a blur, but the physician's visit and his own curt
refusal to allow Dimitrius to undress him was an
uneasy memory. He'd been too sick and too drained to
bother with niceties, but that was no excuse to treat his
people that way. The old Healer's blunt words came
back to him then.

You should thank the Triarchy for that DeLlew-
ellynne boy of yours. Was him pulled you from the fray
and saved you from a crushed skull or worse.

Demnor had given a noncommittal grunt. Agrippa
was a nagging old fart, but he was also usually right.
As he was this time, the Prince admitted. He would do
something for Dimitrius later when his head straightened out and stopped ringing like the bells of Bran's
Tower.

His thoughts returned to the present as he stared into
the mirror once more. By the Sword, he was a mess.
His collar was shredded and stiff with dried blood. It
had stuck to his neck and stuck to his hair, and dirt and
gore were encrusted on his face and tunic. A far cry
from his people's view of their Crown Prince, he
thought wryly. With a grimace that was only partially
due to his condition, he began to pull at the clumps of
matted hair.

A soft knock at the door moments later made him

look up as Dimitrius put his head in. "I've come to help you dress for dinner, My Prince. I've brought another posset."

Demnor waved him inside. With just his squire to see him, it would probably be easier to drink it this time.

The clock was chiming five as the Prince and squire left the room. With gritted teeth, Demnor forced himself to take the lodge's stairs at his usual pace, Dimitrius hovering protectively at his elbow. The Heir bit back a snarl of ill-temper. *Boy's only doing his job,* he told himself.

From the dining hall the sounds of music and shouted laughter told him the banquet had yet to begin. They crossed the main gallery, and were ushered into the hall by two liveried servants, who bowed as they passed. Inside, the mingled scents of roasting meats, burning logs, and blood-covered bodies soaked in perfume hit the Prince like a blow. Some had changed, but like himself, hadn't bothered with the fuss of bathing. This wasn't a day for cleanliness. Usually he never noticed, but today his stomach twisted with nausea. He swayed for an instant, but as heads turned his way, he straightened and strode into the room, a menacing scowl on his face.

The gathered bowed as he passed, all watching as he made his way to the head table. Watching to see how the fall had affected him. Watching for weakness. His eyes narrowed.

The Aristok was already seated, speaking to Quindara. Her eyes tracked his face as he bowed, cutting through his stiff stance to the fatigue and illness beneath. She did not speak, merely nodded and returned to her conversation. Taking his place beside her, Demnor sank into the soft velvet of his chair with an inaudible sigh. Around them, now that the Royal presence was complete, the Hunt took their places and servants came forward, huge platters of food in their arms.

*   *   *

The banquet seemed to last forever. Unable to pass anything through lips too swollen to open properly, Demnor didn't eat. He managed half a goblet of cider, spilling the rest down his chin, but soon, even that small stretching split the lower wound. He dabbed at it from time to time and soon his sleeve was soaked with blood.

Dazedly he stared out the hall's great bay widow, watching the sky darken and wishing for night. Lightning skipped across the sky as it began to rain.

To his right, the Lord Isolde attempted a few sympathetic remarks, but on finding him unresponsive, turned to her uncle Alexander. The older man shared a number of pointed looks with Alerion whose eyes shot daggers at the Prince. Demnor noticed once or twice but chose to ignore him. He felt like death. The whole family could have fits on the tables for all he cared.

The banquet continued, the noise and chaos rising. As the clock chimed seven, the first of the guests, full of an afternoon's reveling, began to fall beneath the table.

At one end of the hall two young Lords began a mock duel with the ornamental swords pulled from the walls. It soon degenerated into a fistfight with the rest of the Hunt cheering them on, pounding on the tables and shouting out bets. The Aristok threw a brooch to the winner. She caught it with amazing dexterity before collapsing, to general amusement.

Demnor's head began to pound.

By the time the meal had ended and the Lords who could still stand had retired to parlors and conservatories to digest before the dancing, the Prince was reeling with fatigue. He made his way heavily across the room and out the crystal-paned doors to the gardens beyond.

The trees, with their accompanying statues, blended into a blur of indistinct shadows. Leaning against the damp, ivy-covered wall, he raised his face to the rain. It felt soothing on his skin, the drops almost sizzling as they touched his cheeks. He must be feverish. Perhaps that was why he felt so ill. The shattering beast had poisoned him.

Beside him Dimitrius silently filled a pipe and offered it to his Prince. Demnor accepted it, sucking in the harsh smoke as best he could. The herb stung the outside of his mouth but numbed the inside. Fenweed worked better than a softweed posset, and more easily.

The Lord and squire stood quietly for a time, watching the rain splatter against the flagstones. Before them, vaguely illuminated in the torchlight, a tribute to the first of his name, Demnor I, stood as silent as they. The centuries had worn deep rivulets in the statue's marble face, giving him a tragic look of tormented weeping where once he had held an expression of stern nobility. The effigy had always made the Prince uneasy, but tonight it seemed appropriate. Ruler at nineteen. Dead at twenty-seven. Dead quelling a rebellion in Heathland that sparked up again two years later, and fifty years later and one hundred and . . . futile.

He shook his head. The fenweed was making him maudlin.

Sensing his mood, Dimitrius accepted the empty pipe and filled it again without comment. From within, the strains of a Dachiem waltz drifted out to them, but Demnor made no move to rejoin the company. The garden was quiet and peaceful. The cool breeze lowered his fever and the silence soothed his head. Thinking was not so difficult out here, nor so unwelcome.

The waltz ended and another one began. Imagining the scene inside made him curl his lip in disgust. Laughing faces, flushed with drink, above blood-and-dirt-encrusted finery, torn and food splattered. Fighting and drinking and fornicating in the private rooms. The decadence of it came to him then, and a sudden longing for the battle camps rose up, constricting his chest.

Life was simpler there, more immediate, more real. He remembered the laughter and the singing of the troops around the bonfires; the outbursts of violence when overenthusiastic gaming led to cries of cheat; the tenderness between veterans seeking each other's comfort between battles, or the fumbling nervousness of fledgling fighters seeking release for their excitement; the exotic mercenaries companies, those soldiers for hire who followed the wars from country to country. He remembered the meals snatched between skirmishes; the sleep snatched between Command Councils and fighting and more Councils. He remembered the wounded and the dying; the blood-covered soldiers too numb to feel anything but relief at being alive, at being able to rest, and he remembered the resting; the deep, dreamless sleep after a battle was over.

Behind him, a giggling couple pranced into the garden, but on finding the rain-soaked lawn and the glowering Prince too dark for their comfort, soon scurried back to the safety of the brightly lit hall.

Beside him Dimitrius shivered.

Dimitrius. Demnor's thoughts snapped back to the garden. The boy was cold. And probably soaked through. All because his mad Lord wanted to feel sorry for himself in the rain. They would return to the hall. But first, there were words that needed to be spoken. He touched the boy lightly on the arm.

"What . . . you did . . . today," he said thickly, speaking with difficulty through the stiffness and swelling of his lips, "I shall . . . not . . . forget. When . . . I am able . . . we will . . . speak more . . . of . . . it."

The speech left him almost gasping, the throbbing pain sending his head spinning again. For a moment he was afraid he hadn't made himself clear, but after an initial expression of confusion, Dimitrius' fair complexion reddened. He opened his mouth to speak, closed it, then stammered, "Thank you, My Lord. I . . ."

Demnor smiled inwardly and the pain eased a bit as he watched the young man before him try to find an appropriate response to his Prince thanking him for saving his life. The pride that shone in his eyes spoke it well enough, however, and Demnor nodded his understanding. Distantly he noticed that the music had stopped and the pitch of the murmured voices had changed. Time to leave.

"Horses."

Dimitrius hesitated an instant, then, dropping quickly to one knee, he grasped the Prince's hand and kissed it fervently. "I'm so glad you're not killed, My Prince!" he blurted out. The look of horror which then crossed his face almost had Demnor laughing out loud, but he suppressed it. Blushing furiously, the boy rose and without looking up, hurried off to do his Lord's bidding.

Wiping the rain from his cheeks, the Prince of Gwyneth saluted the timeworn image of his forebear. Then he followed his squire into the dining hall.

The journey back to the palace was cold and uneventful. Satiated with the violence and revelry of the day, the Hunters still able to ride did so quietly. Squires led the mounts of their Lords, or rode beside to support them in the saddle. Those unable to mount had stayed at the lodge. The darkness surrounded them like a blanket and even if they'd wished to break the silence, the somber, dripping trees seemed to forbid it. Lost in their own individual thoughts, the Hunt passed out of the fields and onto the North Road.

Demnor rode wearily, his head pounding with every step. Once in the saddle the dizziness and nausea had returned and he clenched his teeth to keep from losing the cider he'd had for supper. The cold air, no longer refreshing, cut through his clothes like a knife. Huddling more deeply into his cloak, he concentrated on riding, and tried not to think of how far it was to his bed. He looked up.

The moon was a vague form in the sky, surrounded by an eerie ring of cloudy light. Perhaps it was this almost spectral sight, conjuring up images of spirits and death, or the expression of confused questioning on its face, that made him think of the dragon. Did it know why it had died? he wondered. And did it really matter. Its bewilderment and pain matched his own inner face too well; that was why it had died for him.

Sending an inner salute to its spirit, he wished it good speed on its journey to the Earth's Shadow Realm of Death. Then his gaze fell on Dimitrius riding tired but upright at his side, proud that, despite his injuries, *his* Lord could ride unassisted. The boy's face held a new maturity this night, some of the child having washed away in the rain. Somehow, that seemed to make the whole wretched day worthwhile.

I'll knight him. He's ready for it now.

Turning his face toward Branbridge, the Heir's thoughts traveled to the golden-haired man waiting for him to come home.

3. Arren Elliot Armistone

It was raining heavily in the south of Heathland, turning sheep and shepherd alike into miserable huddles of soaking wool. The horseman who splashed over the hills of Liddestane was little better, but he pushed on, now and then shielding his eyes with one thin hand to peer into the storm.

Finally a faint glimmer of light told him that he was nearing his journey's end. He sighed. It was good to be home. He could feel the influence of his years in Branion falling from him like a false skin as he neared the place of his birth. Neared the place where his family had held the dream of centuries in desperate hands. Now their leaders gathered to make that dream a reality and his hands would aid in the molding.

The outline of a towering fortress shimmered through the rain. Herndale Castle. Its history stretched back before the DeMarian conquest and the slaughter of the Royal House of Elliot. Their ancestral home, turned ruins, turned Branion fief, turned ruins once again, was now the headquarters of the latest Heathland uprising.

Gordon Elliot Croser, known as Sergeant Grant Cross of the Palace Guard to his Branion employers, crossed the courtyard haphazardly, avoiding what puddles of mud and cow dung he could see. The torches on either side of the entrance flickered, promising a hot fire and the warmth of a family's welcome to a son returning home from danger. Yes, it was good to be back on the eve of battle with news of the enemy and a plot on the brink of hatching.

When he reached the ancient guardhouse, an armed figure appeared in the rain to challenge him. Gordon smiled.

In the great hall, the fire crackled, sending sparks showering across the stone hearth. Its warmth denied the damp seeping in from outside and threw a somber glow across the tapestried walls. Around the table, the leaders of the Heathland rebellion were gathered. Four of the most powerful families in the country were in attendance: Armistone, Duglas, Greyam, and Croser. Five more stood ready to receive the call to arms.

At the head of the table, Arren Elliot Armistone, acknowledged Heir to the ancient throne of Heathland, sipped at a cup of mulled ale and stared sightlessly into the fire.

He looked older than his thirty-five years. Gray streaked his sandy hair and the years of fighting the DeMarians had hardened his features, adding bitter lines around his mouth and along the thick scar that twisted through his beard. Pale eyes hooded and unreadable, he sat, ignoring the conversations around him, his thoughts deep in the past.

Born at Herndale Castle, the eldest of the Elliot Heirs, he'd been educated in Gallia and trained in the art of war at the Panishian schools of Maderio and San Valdeville. At sixteen he'd returned home to take on the Royal Obligations. Traveling the length and breadth of the DeMarian-held island, he'd studied his enemy closely.

Disguised as a tinker, he'd stood before the north balcony of Bran's Palace and watched the latest DeMarian Demon cast her fiery spells over the people. Knowing he must somehow conquer this metaphysical power if Heathland was to be free, he'd remained in Branbridge, studying the Living Flame, learning Its weaknesses and Its limitations.

At the same time, he'd bolstered the strength of the

Essusiate Churches of Branbridge. An unswervingly devout follower of the Continental faith, Arren had channeled money and supplies from Gallia, kept the Branion Essusiates in touch with the Continental hierarchy and tied them as tightly as possible to the alliance of Heathland. When Essus went to battle against the Living Flame, the Triarctic faith would contain a great Essusiate hole in Its center; a second front of Branions fighting Branions.

To further his goal, Arren had aided the Churches in placing people sympathetic to his cause in the Town Watch. With their help he infiltrated the palace servants and stable hands, and managed to maneuver his own cousin Gordon Elliot Croser into the Palace Guard to spy on the comings and goings of the Royal Family. With so many varied lands under their control, Branion was used to strangers and, arrogant and confident in its invincibility, never assumed those in its pay to be enemies.

Seven years later, Arren's careful plan went awry as four high-level Essusiate clerics were arrested and put to death for protecting their Branion congregations. The religious tensions in the capital exploded. Essusiate and Triarctic mobs rioted through the streets, burning and looting. The Watch was called out and then the Militant Orders. Scores of people were arrested, the bulk being Essusiate Clerics and lay people. Arren himself dared not set foot outside for fear of being taken. Gordon hid him in a remote wing of the palace itself until it was safe to smuggle him out of the country. When the tensions eased, the Heathland leader struck one more blow against the DeMarians, an attack on the Crown Prince, then raced for the border.

Once back at Herndale, he'd stepped up his offensive. Leading a picked band of kin, he'd rampaged across the poorly guarded borderlands, burning farms and villages and driving livestock into the Heathland hills. Twice the DeMarian had sent an army to find him, and twice he'd led it a wild and twisting chase before stripping its supply wagons and disappearing.

Meanwhile the Greyams and Duglases, the two most powerful fighting families in Heathland, had been engaged with the northern Branions in the West Border Wars. Arren had brought his seasoned hill fighters to their aid and quickly gained a reputation as a daring and savage general. When the three families had stood side by side at the ill-fated Battle of Falkeith, Arren himself had brought down the leader of the treasonous Cailein family.

He'd returned to Liddestane, his reputation made, to unite the splintered families. When Heathland rose in rebellion, it would rise under one, all-encompassing banner.

The country grew quiet. Messengers trickled back and forth and feelers were put out for allies from Gallia and the Essusiate Church. Four years later the country was behind him. The influence of the Branion-allied Caileins was waning with their Captain's death at Falkeith. Arren had the blessing of the Pontiff in far-off Florenzian Tiberia and the tentative support of King Henri-Jean of Gallia. Ironing out the last details of this alliance was the final stage. Heathland was on the brink of revolution.

Arren stretched and refilled his cup from the clay jug at his elbow. Those around the table stirred, conversations cut off as they waited for their leader to speak. He took a short sip, laid the cup aside and turned to the aged Gallian Envoy seated with his bodyguard across from him.

"My Lord Marquis de LaRoche, I trust you've had a pleasant meal?"

The Envoy wiped his lips fastidiously with a lace handkerchief. Tucking the delicate cloth into his sleeve, he inclined his head.

Arren nodded. "Fine. We'll now to business. I and my Council have discussed your offer, and I'm afraid it is not acceptable in its present form. Hilary?"

Arren's younger sister passed him a scroll, King Henri-Jean's seal shining in the firelight.

Arren unrolled it and scanned the contents before placing it on the table in front of the Envoy. "I've no need for either Advisers or Commanders, Armand-Pierre. What I do want," he leaned forward slightly, "and this term is nonnegotiable, is a guarantee that Gallia will attack Aquilliard and Kormandeaux as we attack Branion. You will admit that it asks little of your army, since the bulk of the DeMarian forces will be engaged on our borderlands.

"I will not talk trade or future political alliance at this time. I will not give up lands on this island. In exchange for your assistance I offer Gallia, as I've stated before, whatever lands it can wrest from the Branions on the Continent and my assurances that they will have little chance to defend their claims. That is all."

LaRoche pursed his lips unhappily. "Captain Armistone," he began after smoothing his goatee with one hand. "I see your position, of course, and it is understandable, as far as it goes. However, His Majesty requires some assurance that it would be to Gallia's advantage to aid you in this enterprise. After all, your people have attempted this before and failed. To be frank, you need our help. Without it, you will, no doubt, fail again. And if our conditions are not met, I cannot promise my Sovereign's response. The DeMarian Aristok is, after all, distantly related . . ." he trailed off and shrugged indifferently.

There were angry murmurs from the Heaths around the table. Stephan Elliot Croser, Battle Captain of the Armistone related south-land family, dropped a hand to the pommel of his claymore, but one glance from Arren stilled him. The only indication of the Heathland leader's reaction was the barest narrowing of his eyes.

"So, what you're saying, Marquis, is that if we don't bend to your demands and allow you to take control of our enterprise, you'll aid the Triarchs? Have I heard you correctly? You'll ally yourselves with those whom the Pontiff Herself condemned and called for a crusade against not two decades ago? May I remind you that we have Her Eminence's blessing and wish that all those of the true Essusiate faith will give aid to us in this endeavor.

"Surely you haven't fallen victim to the iconoclastic heresy that is even now weakening your country's spiritual health?"

The old, worn Essusiate medallion of Merrone, dragon guardian of the Faithful, around Arren's neck glittered in the firelight, as sharply as his pale eyes which never left his guest's face. The sudden tension in the room made LaRoche cough nervously and his bodyguard scanned the gathered Heaths, ready for an attack.

Hilary smiled. "The price for heresy is death," she said, drawing the blade of her knife across the table's edge.

The Envoy coughed again. "You misunderstand me, Captain Armistone. No one is suggesting that Gallia will ignore its ecclesiastical duties." He laid a hand on his bodyguard's arm, and she subsided. "I was merely pointing out," he continued, "that despite all your valiant efforts Heathland has rarely won a battle against the Branions without aid, and has never completely gained the freedom and independence it has sought for so long."

"And I believe it was remarked when this was brought before Council that we didn't need a history lesson from a man whose ancestral lands in Gaspellier now pass through a DeMarian subline." Eilene Elliot Duglas, Head of the most powerful of the south-land families, delivered her reply with a contemptuous snort.

The Envoy touched his lips with his handkerchief. "If I wished to trade insults with you, Captain Duglas, I might reply that your ancestral *country* is held by the DeMarian *Royal* line and that not once in over five hundred years has it lived under its own free banner, whereas, there has been Gallian occupation in Gaspellier in the recent past. We are merely their enemies. You are their subjects."

Before she could reply, he continued. "However, I do not wish to trade insults with you. That would be a waste of all our most valuable time. We are here to discuss the final details in an alliance that will be truly profitable for us all and add a new page to the history books." He turned back to Arren. "Surely we can put aside our differences to this end, Captain Armistone. And if you look at our offer rationally once again, I'm convinced that you will see that our suggestions are not at all unreasonable."

He sat back, a slightly condescending smile on his face, all earlier traces of nervousness gone.

Arren returned the smile, but when he spoke, his voice held no warmth. "Are they not? Well . . ."

"Sire, rider coming in."

Arren swung his attention to his young cousin, Colleen Elliot Armistone, seated by the window.

"Can you see who it is?"

Colleen stared intently through the break in the curtains, then shook her head. "No, the damned rain's too thick, but Michael's taken his horse and he's coming in. He's not escorted, so they must have passed him at the gate."

Hilary turned to Arren. "Messenger, maybe?"

"Possibly."

They waited until a soft knock at the door broke the silence and the Castle Steward put his gray head into the room.

"Pardon the interruption, Sire, but it's Gordon."

As the tension changed to shock, the tall man stepped into the room, smiling at the identical expressions of surprise on the faces of his kin.

The faint patter of rain against the window announced a second bout of rain and Arren allowed his fingers to drum out its rhythm against the padded arm of his chair. The meeting with LaRoche had ended inconclusively,

with the Castle Steward escorting their Gallian guests
to their rooms in the west wing while he and his people
met to hear what Gordon had come all this way to tell
them.

Across the table, his Croser cousin polished off a
bowl of mutton stew, wiping up the last bit with a hunk
of bread.

Arren leaned forward.

"Finished?" he asked politely, his impatience registering in his tone of voice.

Gordon smiled, savoring the moment.

"Yes, thank you, Sire. It's a cold night and that went
down well."

"I'm sure. Now maybe you can reveal what's so
important that you had to leave your post in Branbridge
without warning."

The reproach was obvious and Gordon dropped his
gaze briefly before looking up sideways at his Royal
cousin.

"Isolde DeKathrine, the Crown Prince's Intended, is
in the capital with a host of kin at her back. Some say
it's to pressure the Heir into making a further statement
of intent. It's caused a lot of tension in the capital. Tension we might do well to capitalize on."

This brought the expected stir of interest from the
gathered Heathland generals. Rubbing the scar in his
beard absently, Arren indicated that he should explain.

Gordon leaned back. "The churches are ready to aid
us come spring and our people in the capital will cause
what strife and confusion they can, but they'll still
have little effect with the militant nobility firmly
behind the Living Flame. Tensions between the
DeKathrines and the DeMarians could be exploited and
no one would think of looking toward Heathland for
the source until it was too late."

"And what sort of exploitation were you contemplating," Hilary asked.

"Whatever the situation calls for; a scuffle or two
between the Palace Guard and the DeKathrine
retainers, seemingly approved by the Crown, rumors

and gossip spread around about Royal reaction to the DeKathrine presence, and more rumors about their plans; whatever it takes to stir the pot. If we had enough momentum, it could even go as far as armed insurrection.

"It's happened before," Eilene observed.

"And not that long ago either."

"But would DeKathrines behave like DeSandras?"

"Why not?" David Elliot Greyam, the southern Battle Captain to the great mid-lands Greyam family snorted. "They're all Branion heretics, not one of them loyal to their ruler or their kindred."

Gordon shook his head impatiently. "You're missing the point, David. The key here is not the DeKathrines; it's the DeMarians."

Arren frowned. "Explain."

"In 875 the DeSandra family brought armed insurrection to Branion. The DeKathrines were squarely on the side of the Crown. There's a lot of history between those two families, and a lot of blood ties holding them together. It would take more than misunderstanding and royal reluctance to turn them.

"But in 886 it was the Crown Prince himself who brought civil war to the country. It split the families, the palace, the people, and most especially the DeKathrines, in two. Dozens fought on both sides of the battlefield. That quarrel's never quite healed and could be opened again with very little effort."

Eilene leaned forward, her dark eyes shining. "A rumor here, a rumor there. Push the DeKathrines to pressure the DeMarian. She pressures the Crown Prince, he reacts against both of them, and the allies start to line up. I like it."

David nodded. "And we can only benefit from the tension. When Heathland rises, Branion could be in the midst of its own civil war.

Stephan laughed. "Brother, you're a genius."

"Branion Triarchs fighting the Flame. A dream come true," Hilary murmured, her mind already busy with plans.

"And an important one," Arren added. "The more off balance the Flame, the more clouded Its prophecy and the weaker It becomes on the battlefield. And that strengthens Essus." The Heathland leader touched the medallion around his neck. "So we will exploit this confusion. Gordon, I want you to return to Branbridge tomorrow, but keep in close touch. I'll send Sister Marie-Claire with you to prepare the Branion Essusiates. As for the rest of our plans, I'll see the Marquis tomorrow and concede . . ." he ran his fingers through his beard, "short-term political alliance and trade. That should keep Henri-Jean happy and ensure the troops we need on the Continent. Eilene, you and David should return to your families to finish preparing for spring. Stephan, I'll need you and your kin to remain here for now if Janet can spare you."

The Croser Battle Captain laughed. "She'll be glad for the peace and quiet, Sire."

"Good. We'll speak again in the morning."

The three leaders filed out. Hilary glanced at her brother, then, after receiving a faint nod, she turned to Colleen.

"Gordon will be tired. Will you see if his rooms have been prepared yet, Cousin?"

Smiling a little at the unsubtle ploy, Colleen nodded and followed the others from the room.

Seating herself on the arm of Gordon's chair, Hilary brushed a finger down her cousin's cheek. "You look so different without the beard."

He smiled up at her. "I'll have one again soon, very soon."

"How's your lady keeping."

"Good, fine, as committed as always."

"And how does she figure in your ideas regarding Branion?" Arren asked.

Gordon turned to his liege. "That actually was the true reason behind my visit, Sire. You see, we had an idea."

With a smile he began to outline the plan he and

Heathland's most dangerous ally had concocted one warm summer evening.

Kelahnus waited in Demnor's apartments, a small book held absently between his hands. Now and then, he ran his fingers along its soft leather cover, but left it closed. He'd given up trying to read an hour ago. Now he simply waited. It seemed to be the only thing he could concentrate on with any degree of success. Eyes slightly unfocused, he stared at the spiraling, cream-colored candles set in the chest-high candelabra at his side. The delicate, leaf-covered branches reminded him of the forest. The smell of damp fields wafting up from the open window reminded him of the Hunt. The empty room reminded him of Demnor, which in turn reminded him of everything he'd been trying to avoid thinking about. Separating a lock of hair, he twisted it nervously around his finger.

Once he'd learned of the Heir's injuries, the rest of the afternoon had fallen into place. He'd had a good scream at his senior lieutenants, the ones who should have known better, and had been somewhat more understanding with the junior. It had calmed him, but he still felt edgy; edgy and insecure. If he couldn't trust his own people . . .

No, he chided himself. *You can trust them. You just can't expect them to bring you bad news about the Prince without some qualms. They love you both and they're afraid.*

Running his hand through his hair, he held it up to the light, watching the flickering candle flames dance behind it. The highlights turned and flashed, as golden as the candelabra. He smiled a little vainly. His people loved him because he was beautiful and because he paid them very well. They loved Demnor because he was the Heir and that vague, intangible coin bought loyalty far beyond anything gold could obtain.

The Companion shook his head. It always surprised him somewhat that so many people loved the Prince, considering his arrogance, his temper, and his morose silences. Kelahnus smiled as he ticked off each point. In fact, sometimes he was surprised that *he* loved the Heir as deeply as he did. A fact that he kept from everyone, including, he thought with a tinge of sadness, from Demnor himself sometimes.

He kept it hidden from his superiors at the Companion's Guild as well. It wouldn't do at all to let them know how much his love blinded, tied, and held his actions to the Prince's service. Companions weren't taught to love. They were taught to serve and to protect the Companion's Guild interests. Their love was reserved for the Guild and their Guild Siblings. To make their Lords love them—oh, yes—but not to reciprocate. Duty demanded a clear head and love . . . love worked best with a clouded one.

He smiled again, remembering one of his teachers, Master Marian, speaking of love. A small woman with boundless enthusiasm, she had espoused her theories of "Love as a Skill" with such energy and good humor that it kept the most cynical of students from becoming jaded, while still teaching a valuable lesson.

Love, she had said, *is like any other emotion. It must be felt. It must be honored. But you can't let it rule you. As a raw feeling it's as blind and heedless as hatred or grief or lust. Mind you, lust is a little better at being blind and heedless. It's also less work. But that's tomorrow's class. I trust you'll all be in attendance?*

Love. He loved Demnor. He loved . . . well, a lot of people who paled considerably when in comparison with the Heir. Pleasant musings, but they served little purpose. He knew why he was dwelling on them, submerging his worry in memories.

Master Adell on daydreaming: *It relieves the nerves. If you can find a safe time to do it, by all means, indulge. However, time is to be utilized, not wasted. One shouldn't dwell on trivial matters, but rather on the more important issues. Very often a knotty problem is the more easily solved by tossing it from hand to hand, rather than by staring at it directly. This,*

*however, does not apply to this lecture, Younger
Brother. . . .*

Kelahnus returned to the present and found himself
staring, chin in hand, at a small oil sketch of Demnor,
hanging by the Heir's wardrobe. He'd been young, four
or five years old. The artist had captured the boy's
intense seriousness before it had been overlaid by the
man's unyielding anger. There was still laughter in
his eyes behind the solemn expression. It reminded
the Companion of Terence. With a sigh, he brought
his mind back to business; going over the youth's
report. He had summed up the Prince's condition
quickly and the news had helped to ease some of
the fluttering panic in the Companion's stomach,
though not all. That would come, he knew, only when
he saw for himself that Demnor was alive and whole.
Then the boy had continued with the less urgent news
of the day.

*The Duke of Yorbourne made a tryst to bed a
DeKathrine tonight. His name is Troyanon. He's sixteen and the Hierarchpriest's third cousin.*

That had been interesting. In a way it was a shame
that Demnor would need him tonight. He'd have loved
to eavesdrop.

*The DeKathrine boy is seeking a position at Court
and is here in the company of two older sisters. The
younger wants a privateering commission from the
Aristok, the eldest, the Earl of Wiltham, is seeking a
husband. Rumor has it she's planning a foray against a
DeYvonne neighbor and needs money for troops. She'd
like to find a knight willing to throw his fortune and his
troops in with hers.*

That hadn't been as interesting, but he'd look into it.
It didn't hurt to be up on territorial feuding.

Terence consulted a sheaf of paper in his hand before
continuing on with the rest of the day's report: the
casualty list.

*Lord Dana DeLlewellynne, only daughter of the Earl
of Stafolk, crushed. Virgil DeSharon, third child of the
Earl of Dorsley, unblooded, trampled. They say he got*

*in His Highness' way, Your Grace, and fell from his
mount.*

*The Count Markus DeFay, also trampled. Lord
Barkarus DePaula, a political rival of Caroline, Earl
of Buckshire, again, trampled. Also stabbed. They've
been fighting for years. There may be an investigation,
but she's high in Her Majesty's favor.*

Sigh. Now he'd *have* to see Gilbraith.

At the next name, Terence had frowned.

*Angus Cailein, brother-in-law to the Cailein Earl of
Dunley of Heathland. Spined by the dragon. No breastplate under his surcoat, just leather.*

That had been an eye-opener. No one went against a
dragon in leather armor. Anyone who tried was either
brave to the point of being suicidally stupid, or stark
raving mad. Kelahnus had met Angus Cailein. He put
his bet on stupid. The man would wager on the wind
and it was likely an enemy had offered the dare. However, his association with the Branion-allied Heathland family's new Earl made an investigation necessary. With an inaudible mutter, he added it to the
growing list.

That had been the last of the fatalities, a heavier toll
than usual. The list of injuries taken was of little
import, save one.

*The Lord Isolde DeKathrine, Earl of Essendale,
daughter of Isabelle DeKathrine, Duke of Exenworth,
thrown from her horse. A bit black and blue apparently, but otherwise unharmed. Her squire says that
His Highness, the Crown Prince, threw himself
between her and the dragon, taking the blow meant
for her.*

Strange. Not like him at all. Well, perhaps something
had happened to thaw the Prince's attitude toward
his Intended. That was good. Terence had watched
him curiously to see how this news would affect the
Companion whom everyone said had hooked the heart
of a Prince. Kelahnus had kept his face professionally expressionless. Florence's words came back to
him then.

. . . now he should act before it becomes a political issue. If he doesn't act soon . . .

He would speak to him tonight if the Heir was up to it. If not, then tomorrow. Waiting was no longer safe.

The Companion sighed, resting his cheek against his palm. This marriage had to take place. It wasn't the age of the Bastard anymore. He accepted it. Why couldn't Demnor?

Because he's stubborn, old-fashioned and stupidly romantic, his mind answered.

Because he loves you and thinks it would hurt you if he bedded or cared for someone else.

As it hurts him when you do it.

There was no answer to that. He was a Companion. Companions lived by different rules. They couldn't change that anymore than they could change the rules by which Demnor lived. It was life.

The candles sputtered in a sudden draft, drawing him out of himself. There was a quiet knock at the door.

"Come in."

One of the older servants put her head in. "His Highness has arrived at the stables, Your Grace."

Instantly the half-submerged fear rose up again to constrict his chest, but he merely nodded and she withdrew.

He sat very still, battling the fear which fought for control of his limbs with surprising strength. Finally, unable to keep still, he stood and stared out the window at the night sky.

It's all right. He's back. He's safe, he told himself firmly, but being this close to discovering the magnitude of his Lord's injuries had him shaking all over. The calm he'd managed through rational reassurances vanished. Terence's report, devoid of hope, kept repeating in his mind accompanied by a parade of images, each one more frightening than the last.

Facial wound, facial wound, wound, wound, scar, disfigurement, mutilation, infection, death, death, DEATH . . .

"No!"

He slammed his fist on the windowsill, then stared at it in shocked amazement. Slowly, his years of discipline reasserted themselves.

You've been around him too long, he chided himself, sucking at his little finger. *Reacting violently! Be still. Face whatever is to come with dignity.*

Quieter now, but no more reassured, the young Companion rested his head against the cool glass of the window. He swallowed, his throat suddenly aching with unshed tears.

"Oh, please," he whispered to the Wind. "Don't let him be ugly."

He lost track of how long he stood there, staring sightlessly down at the rain-slicked courtyard, before he heard the Heir's footfall in the anteroom. Straightening, he turned.

Demnor rested his weight against the door to his bedroom for a moment. Not long enough to alert Dimitrius, who followed, arms laden with gear, but long enough to prepare himself for Kelahnus' frantic nursing.

The day was over. That was all that really mattered. He'd made it past the shy and fearful glances of the stable hands, past the formal greetings of those of the Court who'd just happened to meet him in the halls, past the worried eyes of the Palace Guard. His step deliberately firm, he'd retraced this morning's walk, showing no sign of weakness or fatigue. Now it was over. Time for peace and oblivion. He pushed the door open.

The room was dark save for the candelabrum by the window. Beside it stood Kelahnus. The Companion's face shifted from strained fear to guarded relief, and he came forward quickly as Demnor dropped into a chair.

Too weary to even wave a greeting, the Prince simply leaned his head back and closed his eyes. Now that the need to maintain a strong stance was over, his injuries rushed in at him on a wave of pain. Behind him he could hear Dimitrius leave his armor by its stand

and speak briefly with Kelahnus. Something about food and a bath. He almost groaned aloud. Food he was sure he couldn't handle. Already his mouth seemed swollen shut. As for the bath, he feared that if he allowed himself to relax, he would surely drown. He felt terrible and so scorching tired. His chest ached with every breath and his jaw throbbed pain up through his skull. When he closed his eyes, his head spun in sickening circles in time with the heaving of his stomach. In all, he decided, it had been a cow dung of a day.

Around him, servants crept in and out on whispered instructions from Kelahnus. There was a whoosh and crackle as the fire was built up and splashing from the bathroom as water poured from the cistern and boiler above. The sounds were peacefully familiar, blunting the day's experience and he gave himself up to fatigue and dozed.

Much too soon a light touch on his hand woke him. Opening his eyes, the room lurched sideways before righting itself, more or less. Kelahnus knelt beside him.

"Your bath is ready," he said quietly.

Demnor shook his head. The pain in his mouth had dulled and all he wanted was to take advantage of it and sleep. The thought of moving was unacceptable.

His refusal drew a frown from the Companion. "You're covered in blood. It's unhealthy. Besides, if you sleep now, you'll wake up in knots. Your muscles need a chance to relax. The bath will help, then I'll give you a massage."

Working the words around his swollen lips, Demnor managed a thick, "Go 'way."

Kelahnus eased back on his heels and stared up at him, his expression reminding the Prince of his old nurse. Demnor sighed. It simply wasn't worth it. Dragging himself to his feet, he allowed the Companion to undress him, wincing as the movements wrenched at bruised muscles and blood-caked hair. After one loud hiss of breath, Kelahnus looked up sharply.

"Are you in a lot of pain?" he asked with a worried frown.

"No!" Demnor snapped, instantly regretting the word. The pain in his mouth mirrored the pain in the younger man's eyes, but when the Heir's vision cleared, Kelahnus stood watching him with sad understanding. Demnor cursed himself. Allowing the Companion to lead him into the next room, he hoped his cooperation might make up for his unthinking snub.

Once inside, the green-tinted water steamed invitingly, smelling of lime leaves. He sank into the tub with a long, drawn-out sigh.

As Kelahnus washed him clean of blood and dirt, the Prince could feel the day's tensions slowly melt away. The light caress of the Companion's hands soothed his jangled nerves, and he drifted off again. With a faint touch to the uninjured side of his face, Kelahnus lilted the Heir's head forward and began to wash his hair. He held up one, dark auburn lock.

"It's getting long," he murmured, the light note in his voice masking the worried undertone. "Soon you'll be able to braid it."

Mother and daughter standing at ease, sharing some jest, long copper braids hanging down behind them.

Slumber bleached some of the anger from the memory, but left Demnor irritable and quarrelsome. "Gon . . . t' hev' . . . it . . . cut," he muttered peevishly.

Clucking his tongue in exasperation, Kelahnus reached for a towel.

Later, wrapped in a black velvet robe, Demnor tried to call back the sense of groggy peace he'd felt in the bath while the Companion worked the knots from his feet and legs. Supper had been a clumsy mess. All he'd been able to manage had been broth—he hated broth—and half of that had spilled down his chin. He'd refused Kelahnus' aid, swallowing about five spoonfuls before giving up in disgust. He wasn't hungry anyway. Ignoring the growling in his stomach, he'd glared at the Companion, daring him to comment. Kelahnus had simply reached for the jar of oil warming by the fire and begun to massage his calves.

Now with the fire spreading warmth through him, his irritation eased, replaced slowly by sleepy complacency. His hand dropped to caress the younger man's mane of golden hair, shining all the more metallic in the dancing firelight. Kelahnus gazed up at him with a lazy smile. "Bed," he whispered.

Demnor nodded. Rising gingerly, he staggered the few feet and sank into woolen blankets and soft, down-filled pillows. Once there he let his breath out in a long sigh. The cursed day was finally, truly over.

Kneeling on the bed, Kelahnus kissed the Heir softly on the neck and poured a thin line of oil down his spine. While working it into the tense muscles of his back and shoulders, he mentally ran over his arguments for Demnor's betrothal. It had to be brought up before the Prince could sleep—but subtly, or he would refuse to discuss it.

The Companion's hands moved instinctively while he thought, running smoothly over flesh and the broad scar on Demnor's right side. Years ago he'd asked the Prince about it. Demnor's answer had been short. An Essusiate fanatic had stabbed him when he was sixteen. The Companion had managed to piece the rest together from other, related remarks.

Melesandra had executed several Continental leaders after they'd been accused of stirring up Branion's Essusiate minority. There'd been riots and a number of their supporters had gained entrance to the palace. Returning from the Ecclesiastical Courts, Demnor'd been approached by a Heathland man, and had stopped to listen to his pleas. The man had attacked him. Driving him off, the young Prince had then made the long walk to his suite without alerting the Guard to his injuries. Once there he'd dismissed his valet and crudely bandaged the wound himself. He'd told no one of it and it had healed poorly. Kelahnus always wondered if the scar pained him, but was unwilling to ask. If it did, the Heir gave no sign. He never did.

The Companion moved down to rub Demnor's lower back. "I take it that the Hunt was successful?" he asked, keeping his voice lowered to a tone of mild curiosity.

The muscles in Demnor's back jumped, but he made no answer.

Kelahnus continued the massage, seemingly unconcerned, but alert for every nuance of the Prince's reactions.

"No one important fall, I trust?"

There was the barest shake of the Heir's head.

Oh? No one? Just a host of the country's nobility either dead or wounded. Why must you be so blind to their power, my love?

Considering it, Kelahnus was sure that Demnor had no idea who'd fallen, nor cared. After all, no DeMarians were counted among the dead. But it still rankled the Companion's professional sense. Demnor *should* know.

He remembered a terse comment of the Prince's years ago when the Companion had been young and inexperienced with the callousness with which Demnor's class treated its members.

It keeps the clumsy and the stupid from begetting children.

Kelahnus was no longer shocked by such remarks. In fact, he had often thought later that it wasn't particularly effective. But Demnor's words always carried a bitterness that belied his indifference.

"And the Lord Isolde?" the Companion asked.

Demnor turned his head to stare searchingly up at him.

Kelahnus chose to ignore his expression. "She is well?"

". . . Was there. Re . . . turned."

The Prince dropped his head again, signaling the end of the conversation. With a hiss of pain, he jerked it up, then laid the right cheek gingerly against the pillow.

His face was pale and drawn, the ragged wounds along his jaw still leaching blood. Each time Kelahnus looked at them, he wanted to cry, or rail, or gather Demnor up to protect him. Lightly, he wiped away the red smears with a corner of his handkerchief. The Heir was so worn out. He would let him sleep. What was one day?

What was a command by the Aristok? What was a fresh outbreak of anger and steel wills clashing against each other? What was Demnor's life? No. It had to be tonight. One day could be one day too late.

He decided on the blunt method. Subtlety went straight over the Prince's head, and it was too late for a conversation full of prolonged manipulations.

"Did you discuss marriage plans?"

"No!" Demnor half rose, a scowl on his face. Calmly, Kelahnus pushed him back down and continued to massage along his ribs.

"But you will soon."

There was a long silence. Finally Demnor said softly, "If . . . you insist."

The sadness in his voice made the young Companion want to take him in his arms, but he merely began to massage the Prince's buttocks and said, "Good," in a voice carefully neutral.

"I suggest you speak with Her Majesty tomorrow. The formal request can be delivered to the Lord Isolde before the banquet, and the betrothal can be announced then. With that out of the way, the bulk of the DeKathrines can return home until, say, the Oimelc Festival, when the marriage can be celebrated. That should give all parties equal time to prepare." *And get the DeKathrine host out of the capital.*

Demnor lay, feigning disinterest, but the tense set of his shoulders told the Companion how much he disliked the conversation.

"How's your jaw?" Moving from a sensitive subject to a sensible one with practiced ease, Kelahnus was glad to see the Prince relax slightly.

"Aches."

"I'll get you something for it."

He slid off the bed and padded to his own rooms. Unlocking a trunk by his dresser, he rummaged through neat piles of jars, vials, and cloth bags until he found what he wanted, a small, ceramic urn with a cork sealed in wax. He broke the seal and sniffed delicately. One tiny drop on his tongue satisfied him and he closed the trunk, carefully locking it once again.

Back at Demnor's side, he ran a hand over his rear.

"Roll over."

The Prince complied with a grimace.

"Now tip your head up."

As Demnor opened his mouth to protest, Kelahnus put a finger to the Prince's lips.

"It's imported. All the way from Ekeptland and very expensive. Too expensive to dull the pain in the sheets. Now, tip your head up."

With exaggerated deliberation, Demnor obeyed.

Uncorking the tiny urn once more, Kelahnus poured the thick, silvery liquid carefully, drop by drop onto the Prince's tongue. Now and then he ordered him to swallow, watching the pale line of his throat as he did. Then, satisfied with the amount, he recorked it. A moment, and it was back in its place amongst his medicinals.

When he returned, the Prince had sunk under the covers. Kelahnus twitched them aside and continued with the massage. Demnor glared fuzzily at him, but made no comment, save a blurred, "Pushy." Kelahnus just smiled.

Running his fingers lightly around the dark purple bruise that stretched across the other's chest, he finished with his upper body. Then, stretching out beside him, he traced a pattern down between the Prince's legs.

"You're tired," the Companion whispered. "Sleep."

Demnor muttered something incoherent. His hand reached out and clasped the fingers of the younger man. A moment later his breathing deepened and he slept.

Kelahnus' face lost its gentle, teasing smile, hardening as he stared down at the twin wounds on Demnor's jaw.

"Burn her," he said quietly.

4. Marsellus

Night. Careful not to wake his sleeping Lord, Kelahnus slipped from the bed and moved quietly to the window. Taking up the delicate, golden candle snuffer, he went from one climbing spiral to another, slowly dipping the room into darkness. Then, firmly dispelling the day's troubles from his mind, he returned to bed and slid beneath the sheets. Instinctively, the Prince reached over and wrapped his arms around the younger man without waking. Pushing the unruly hair from his lover's face, Kelahnus brushed Demnor's lips lightly with his own.

In the fire's fading glow Demnor's expression had smoothed. The fine, red hairs, scattered over his forearm, seemed like wisps of flame, and the Companion brushed a hand along them, absently turning a small ring on the Prince's finger. It was a simple piece, a thin silver band with a ruby oval set flush in the center, the first and only gift he'd given the Heir, other than his love.

Kelahnus smiled, remembering. The ring had taken all his savings to purchase and he'd been in a fever of nervousness over it. He'd presented it shyly, all his training forgotten, a week after they'd first met. Demnor had been surprised, and for a second Kelahnus had feared he'd overstepped himself. He almost snatched it back, but something in the Heir's face had held his hand. Chewing at a scar on his lower lip, Demnor had gazed at it with an expression of uncer-

tainty, then he'd looked up with a tentative smile.
Kelahnus' heart had skipped a beat. The Heir had put it
on, and his brows had drawn down in consternation. It
was too big.

The student's panicked offer to replace it brought an
embarrassed smile to his face even now, but Demnor
had covered it quickly with his other hand, then slipped
it on his middle finger. Quieting the youth with a long
kiss that grew more confident as it was returned, he'd
whispered that it was perfect, a little big, but perfect all
the same.

They'd laughed together and made love in the sunshine amidst the remains of their lunch. A special afternoon, one to cherish. Demnor had seldom laughed in
those days, although when he did, it seemed to lighten
his whole countenance. It had made the young student faint with desire. It still had that effect on him
today, though the Heir laughed even less now than he
had then.

Kelahnus shook his head sadly. He knew the laughter was still there, buried deep like the love. It was just
harder and harder to find.

"Torch her," he murmured fuzzily, sleep leaching the spark from the words. His mind spiraled down
as the night strengthened its grip on him. His thoughts
left the present troubles, touched on older, happier
times, until he, too, fell asleep, remembering.

The School of Companions was in turmoil, students
and servants rushing to make ready while the Masters
snapped at them to move at an even more frenzied
pace. The most promising of the graduates were
dressed, perfumed, and ready to exhibit their skills, but
the mirrors were still crowded as they checked and
rechecked their individual effects. The younger raced
through the halls on last minute errands, shrieking and
giggling with excitement.

Today was graduation day for the Senior Session of
886 and the first audience was to be in a few minutes.
All day the nobility of the Realm would come to buy

the contracts of the new Companions, the first guest
being the Aristok herself, Melesandra the Third.

Master Klairius, the Guild Leader and Head Master
of the Branbridge School, applied his own makeup and
took a swift pull from a small, silver flask. Quelling the
shocked expression of the young student assisting him
with a piercing stare from beneath his white eyebrows,
he returned the flask to the pocket in his multicolored
robe and smoothed away its bulk.

Moments later after one final glance in the mirror,
he swept regally from his suite and down the stairs.
The halls were suddenly empty. He smiled. Servants
scuttled past, trying to appear perfectly efficient, and
when he seated himself on a low divan in the School's
Audience Hall, a tray of wine appeared at his elbow as
if by magic. He nodded. All was in order.

Messana, the School's Steward entered the hall,
formal and impeccable as always. He bent to whisper
in Master Klairius' ear.

"The Aristok and party approach, Your Grace."

Klairius inclined his head. "Show them in as soon as
they arrive," he said serenely.

"Yes, Your Grace."

Several minutes later, the hall's huge, double doors
were thrown open and Messana bowed in the Royal
Party.

"Her Most Regal Majesty, the Aristok Melesandra
the Third, His Royal Highness, the Crown Prince
Demnor, and His Lordship, Alexander DeKathrine,
Earl of Cambury," he announced, then disappeared,
closing the doors softly behind him.

Klairius stood and bowed deeply.

Hidden in a mass of plants behind a pillar, Kelahnus, fifteen, watched their arrival with awe. It was his
first glimpse of the Aristok and he shivered at her air of
fiery command.

This was the woman who'd led the "Charge of Carnage," winning Aquilliard for Branion and the worship
of the army for herself. She'd been just fourteen. This
was the woman who'd sentenced over one hundred

Heathland rebels to hang for insurrection in 877, and had stood calmly discussing tactics with her Guard Captain while the sentence was carried out. It was said she gave no quarter, either on the battlefield or in the courts; that to contest her will was to die. She ruled Branion with a fanaticism as molten as red-hot steel, but it was also said that times had never been so prosperous, nor the Realm so vast.

Granddaughter of Kalandra the Great, the most brilliant military leader in centuries, and daughter of Quinton the Second who'd crushed the DeSandra family in one bloody night of killing, she was a true DeMarian Avatar.

Kelahnus frowned, remembering his studies. It seemed impossible to see her as kin to the wise and magnanimous Atreus the Second, who'd given his name to a century of enlightenment; or Kathrine the First, commissioner of the great Branbridge College of Art. He couldn't see them sharing her blazing stare or her fanatical possession of the Realm.

Then again, she was also descended from Octavius the Mad and Marsellus the Black, the only two Aristoks to be assassinated for their bloody excesses. He could see their legacy plainly. It came off her like smoke. It was said she could outstare a demon and cow a dragon with her presence. Kelahnus believed it. Watching Master Klairius bow before her, he felt sure that if that fierce gaze ever fell upon him, he would be struck dead on the spot. Instinctively he shrank back into his leafy cover.

Master Klairius spoke briefly with the Aristok, then turned to bow before the Heir. Kelahnus turned his attention that way also and fell instantly in lust.

The Crown Prince was a young man, not much older than the student himself, but already wearing the warrior's silver belt proudly. He was tall and muscular with a thick mass of unruly, auburn hair that flashed in the sunlight when he moved his head. Flecks of red fire touched his cheeks and chin and burned in his smoldering gray eyes. He held himself stiffly, giving a sharp nod in reply to Klairius' greeting, his formal expression masking a barely concealed hint of impatient boredom.

Demnor, Prince of Gwyneth, Kelahnus breathed, recalling the tales of the Heir that were already passing into legend; tales of his violence and intractability, of his prowess on the battlefield and at the Hunt. He'd seen two years' fighting on the Continent, following conflicts as they occurred, learning the skills of a Warrior Lord, and now he was once again home in Branbridge.

Kelahnus and his year-mates had studied the Prince's progress in their Military History class. He was said to be a model if impatient Commander. A man for whom experience would soon polish the rough edge of youth. He was popular with the troops and deferred to those who earned his respect. It was believed that the Flame would burn brightly for the Realm when he ascended the throne.

But at home he was a different man. Reckless, moody, liable to take offense at the slightest remark. Only the Aristok could control his outbursts. If he kept a lover, none knew of it.

Kelahnus sniffed. There wasn't a secret in Branion the Companion's Guild didn't know. Perhaps he'd had affairs in the army. Perhaps his love had been tragically slain in battle, and he had sworn never to love again. The student studied the other man intently. The Prince was sixteen. He *had* to have had an encounter of *some* kind by now. He didn't look impotent, diseased, shy, or deformed. In fact, he looked quite . . . virile. Kelahnus swallowed.

The preliminaries over, the Royal Party seated themselves and Master Klairius clapped his hands. Instantly Messana appeared with a tray of cakes. As the quiet strains of a flute threaded down from the balcony, the doors at the end of the hall opened and a line of graduates moved into the center of the room to bow before the Aristok. They turned gracefully in their silken gowns, sleek and sensuous.

Kelahnus felt a sudden stab of jealousy. He would be as poised, he thought to soothe his ego. On his graduation day, he would be as tall and graceful and would dance before the Heir in a robe of blue and gold.

Idly, he compared himself with each of the new Companions. Darian was taller than he, although his hair was not so soft, nor his features so fine. Yarius had the most beautiful blue eyes, and his skin was like smooth honey. By comparison his own was almost transparent in its paleness, the veins tracing blue lines along his hands. But he sang better. The others were all beautiful and elegant. Kelahnus was sure he could be as composed as any of them. Except Florence. He sighed, eyeing the red-robed woman as she swept past his hiding place. Florence was good at everything. She could sing, compose, dance, ride. She knew five different fighting styles and was fluent in six languages. Assassin, spy, physician, adviser, lover, Florence could play each part equally well. She was the top of her class, the very best the School had to offer. It wasn't fair.

He glanced back at the Heir, and their eyes locked.

In horror he realized he'd somehow moved from his protective flora. Panic seized him. He would be ruined! Expelled! Disgraced before the Prince who wouldn't want him and wouldn't look at him like that again and . . . Firmly he brought himself under control. A quick glance showed him the truth of the matter. The others couldn't see him, situated as he was. Only Demnor who stared at him with open interest. Then his expression softened, and he smiled almost shyly. Kelahnus felt his heart leap.

Out of the corner of his eye he saw Master Klairius and the Aristok rise. Ducking behind the plants, he burrowed as far back as he could. Thanking the Wind that he had chosen green today, he prayed that he was completely concealed.

They passed him by without incident. Two of the graduates followed, and he saw Florence glance down at his hiding place and smile. The others returned upstairs to wait for the next audience.

After a few moments, when he felt it was safe, he peered out over the leaves. The hall was empty, almost. The Prince had remained, staring at a piece of stone sculpture with stiff absorption. When Messana entered to clean up the tray, he called him over. They held a whispered conversation, then Demnor walked briskly out a set of glass doors to the gardened courtyard beyond. Messana came directly toward Kelahnus' hiding place.

The student pushed back again, his heart pounding.

"You might as well come out with some dignity as I know you're in there."

Kelahnus considered it. Then, putting on his best look of extreme innocence, he emerged.

"Hello, Messana," he said lightly.

The older man glared at him. "Don't you hello me," he snapped. "This sort of behavior will get you into a great deal of trouble some day, maybe sooner than you think. His Highness, Prince Demnor saw you in there and now he wants to speak with you in the garden."

"With me?" Kelahnus squeaked, unable to keep the excitement from his voice.

"Yes. And if you'll take my advice, you'll say you're indisposed, or that it's not allowed. Which it certainly wouldn't be if Master Klairius knew about it."

"Oh, ah, I couldn't say that," Kelahnus answered quickly. "It, ah, it would be rude."

Messana gave him a skeptical look. "Rude. I see."

"Ah, when does he want to see me?"

"Now."

"Now? I can't go now! I have to change and . . ."

"If you'll take my advice," Messana repeated. "You won't bother with any of that. You obviously caught his eye with your face all red and leaves in your hair. Disgraceful." He reached over and brushed one away. "And if he didn't mind that, you should have no worry about being seen in a practice tunic."

Kelahnus squirmed. Messana ignored it.

"If you're determined to go," he continued. "And at this point I can't honestly see how you can avoid it, I'd go now. Her Majesty won't be long, and if Master Klairius discovers what you're up to . . ."

He didn't need to finish, for Kelahnus was already heading for the gardens. As the student pushed open the doors, he thought he heard Messana chuckle.

Once in the garden, he ran a hand through his hair as he scanned the paths and rookeries. To one side he heard a group of young students playing a game of skip rope. The ancient rhyme wafted over to him through the trees, causing a tremor to run through him.

> *"Who will buy my contract?*
> *Who will pay the price?*
> *Hope it's someone pretty,*
> *And I hope it's someone nice.*
> *DeMarian, DeKathrine, DeLynne and*
> *   DeLlewellynne,*
> *DePaula or DeYvonne or a DeFay or a*
> *   DeSharon."*

It broke off abruptly and he smiled. No, the Prince wouldn't be that way. There was a small fountain with a marble bench farther inside that guests often waited by. It afforded greater privacy and quiet. He hurried toward it.

The Prince was seated where he'd expected, staring up the path. When Kelahnus appeared, he rose with a smile.

Resisting the urge to wipe suddenly damp palms on his pants, Kelahnus advanced with an air of languid dignity that would have made his teachers proud. He bowed.

The Prince inclined his head. "You are?"

"Kelahnus, Your Highness," he answered, praying his voice wouldn't crack.

"Kelahnus." The Prince seemed to savor the word and the student felt a rush of heat on his face. The greeting over, they now stood in awkward silence, each

at a loss over how to continue. The silence stretched.
The Prince shifted slightly, opened his mouth, then
closed it again, chewing at a scar on his lower lip.
Wanting to chew on it too, Kelahnus racked his brain
for something innocuously polite to say and kicked at
his self-confidence. What would Master Klairius say?

"Will you sit, Highness?"

His voice, calm and warm, surprised him, but a
relieved expression crossed the Heir's face and he
dropped back onto the beach. Kelahnus joined him.
The silence grew again.

Acutely aware of the other's presence, Kelahnus
tried not to squirm. The Prince smelled wonderful; like
new mown hay and herbs. It brought to mind images of
clothes carefully laid away in trunks. Demnor seemed
uncomfortable in his finery. Kelahnus wondered what
he would prefer to be doing. Hunting or riding or . . .
The thought of the two of them rolling through a field
of green grass and flowers suddenly came to mind with
a rush of heat that made his breathing labored. Firmly
he pushed the thought from his mind.

The image would not be entirely banished; somehow
the outdoors seemed to suit the Prince far more than
the ornate Audience Hall inside. He seemed more
relaxed amid the plants and trees, less intimidating,
more desirable. His hair was wind ruffled and unruly,
and Kelahnus kept his hands clasped tightly between
his knees to stifle the urge to reach up and smooth it.
The pressure of his thighs helped a little, too.

Out of the corner of his eye he saw the Prince shift
away and tug at his breeches. It brought a flood of
relief in its wake. Good. That at least answered one
question.

"We don't do this very well, do we?" Demnor suddenly commented.

Kelahnus shook his head. "No, Your Highness."

"No. Look, couldn't we just make it Demnor and
Kelahnus? It would make things a lot easier, I think.
Your Highnesses always get in the way."

Kelahnus nodded. "Certainly, Your . . . I mean, ah, Demnor."

"Good."

They sat in silence once again, and then they both laughed.

"All right. Let's try this again." Demnor said. "How about we try and talk like we're old friends. You pretend that I'm just another student . . ."

Internally, Kelahnus snorted. If Demnor had been, "just another student," they would *not* be talking.

"And not the Heir," Demnor continued. "And I'll pretend that you're a noble's son and not, not so . . ." He stopped abruptly.

"Not so what?" Kelahnus asked, unsure of whether this would have been a compliment or not.

Demnor shifted uncomfortably. "Well, not so, well . . ." He gestured vaguely at the student and then took a deep breath.

"Look," he said in a sudden rush of words. "I saw you and I wanted to talk to you because I think you're really beautiful and I wanted to get to know you, but there isn't time and there probably won't be another opportunity that we don't make ourselves, so could you just talk to me and tell me about yourself, because I'm not very good at drawing people out and I'd feel a lot better if I could just listen because everyone is always asking me about myself and I'm sick of making things up and there isn't anything to say anyway."

Kelahnus just stared at him.

Demnor blushed, going the color of his hair. "Ah, I mean, tell me about yourself," he stammered, turning away and chewing at his lower lip again.

"Well," Kelahnus began after a deep breath. "I'm a student here." *He knows that, stupid!* "And, ah, I live here." *Cringe.* "It's nice. Ah, we eat well." *Peasant! Talk about something he's interested in!* "I'm learning to ride."

"Could you get away? I mean, without anyone seeing you?"

About to add an anecdote about his Riding Master,

Kelahnus was caught off guard by the sudden question. He opened and closed his mouth a few times, confused. "Yes," he answered finally.

"Good. Ah, go on."

"Go on. Right. Where was I? Um . . ." He stopped and looked at the Prince. "Why?"

It was Demnor's turn to be taken aback, although he answered quickly with just a hint of bravado. "Because I want to see you again."

"Really?"

"Yes."

"When?"

"Well, tomorrow night. At midnight. At the base of Dorian's Tower. Do you know where that is?"

Kelahnus nodded, then gave the Prince a skeptical look. "Can *you* get away without anyone seeing you?"

"Of course. I do it all the time. I'll just climb out my window," Demnor bragged.

"What if you should fall?"

"Fall? Then, I'd just swim the moat."

Kelahnus laughed. "There isn't a moat around Bran's Palace."

"I know," Demnor replied with a grin. "Just this big rosebush under my window. They planted it there when I was seven, to keep me in, I think. I've only fallen in it once."

"Did you get hurt?"

"Not really." The Heir dismissed the accident with a wave of his hand. "But I've got all these scratches on my arm. See?"

He pushed up his sleeve to show the student a number of thin, white scars on his forearm. Kelahnus bent to examine them.

"I've got a bigger one," he said finally. "From when I fell off the table in the alchemist's laboratory. Master Louisa almost had a heart attack for fear it would disfigure me."

"Where?"

"On my leg." Kelahnus' nonchalance matched Demnor's from moments before.

"Can I see it?"

"Oh sure. It's . . ." He stopped and began to stammer. "No, I mean, well, um, it's too high up. I'd have to, that is . . ."

Suddenly realizing how close they'd come, they quickly drew apart again. Demnor glanced around the gardens.

"So will you come tomorrow night?" he asked without looking at the student.

"If you want me to."

"I do."

"Then I will."

They looked at each other in silence again, this time at ease, content to simply drink in what they could of each other's presence. After a time, Messana rounded the corner.

Kelahnus leaped up with a start and Demnor's hand dropped to the pommel of his sword. If the Steward noticed, he gave no sign, merely advanced and bowed to the Prince.

"Yes?" Demnor asked tightly.

"Please forgive the intrusion, Your Highness, but Her Regal Majesty and His Lordship are taking their leave of the Head Master."

Demnor drew himself up. "Thank you. I shall return presently."

"As you will, Your Highness." Messana bowed again and withdrew with a parting frown at Kelahnus. The student glared back at him. Demnor turned.

"I have to go."

"I know."

"I'll be waiting."

"I'll be there."

With a smile, Demnor bent, kissed him lightly on the lips, then strode off down the path without looking back.

Kelahnus watched him go, his heart thumping in his chest and an erection straining painfully at his breeches. How, by the Earth, was he to get away in the middle of the night with no one finding out?

On a breath of wind, the strains of the skipping rhyme's last verse came to him from over the trees.

> *"Will I teach when I retire,*
> *In schools as I was taught?*
> *Or will my first love be My Lord,*
> *As minstrels say they ought?"*

He sighed. And because there was nothing else to do, he shrugged off any worry of the consequences and concentrated on their meeting the next night.

I'll wear my blue and gold shirt. No, the lavender and gold shirt. Oh, it's going to be such a wonderful night!

The Companion stirred in bed, curling closer to his sleeping Lord. A smile played across his lips, but he did not awaken. Around him, the palace settled down to sleep.

It was hot, stiflingly hot. He tried to rise, but some unseen weight held his limbs immobile. He tried to speak, but his throat was swollen shut. It was difficult to breathe. A thread of disquiet wormed through him, some half-felt hint of danger. Something was wrong.

He was too hot! Sweating, he tried to rise again, couldn't, struggled, fought against the paralysis and fell back. Something was very wrong.

Then the first cramp hit. It corkscrewed inside him, tearing at him, clawing at him, then slackened off. Another hit and then another. He couldn't breathe, couldn't talk, couldn't see. A roaring filled his ears, and on the edge of his hearing someone whispered, "Die." Everything grew suddenly clear.

Die? Someone wanted him to die? Someone was trying to kill him!

Fury rose up to fill him with the flaming strength of hatred. Die! He lunged at the unknown voice, hurling every ounce of will and strength and spite against it. For an instant, he seemed to be winning. He managed to rise, to turn and vomit whatever poison held him in its grip out onto the ornate rug. Die! Never! Never, never . . .

The paralysis struck again and he fell back. On the edge of vision growing gray, he saw the Shadow Catcher beckon. "NO!" Lashing his head from side to side, he willed the nightmare figure away from him, but it only drew nearer. He fought to spew again, knowing that if he didn't, he was finished. Panic threatened to snatch his last chance away and he struggled against that too. His throat closed.

Crowned in a purple haze, the Shadow Catcher approached his bedside and bent over it. He felt himself lifted, cradled in its frozen arms. Unable to breathe, unable to scream, he looked full into its empty face and knew the final terror and the final comfort. It kissed him on the brow and then there was nothing. The fire in his eyes grew faint and then was snuffed out like a candle flame in the wind as he screamed his final denial.

Marsellus jerked awake, the last, agonizing cry echoing in his mind. He stared wildly about him, then drew in a shuddering breath as he recognized his own bedroom. Beside him, arms thrown back, Atreus slept on, undisturbed. The quieter of the Royal twins pulled his legs up and sat shivering as he tried to disentangle himself from the threads of his nightmare. The images flowed through his mind leaving a sense of dread in their wake. Someone was going to die.

Passing a shaking hand over his face, he was surprised when it came away wet. Tears? Probably. He'd wept in his sleep before. Even awakened, sobbing, to find his brother holding him, soothing him from a nightmare he didn't remember. But that had been years ago. He was no longer spared the waking sight of what the future held. He always remembered his prescient dreams now. Someone was going to die. Someone close.

Dreading what he might see, Marsellus slowly looked down at his brother's sleeping form. Atreus' face was smooth and slightly luminescent in the moon-light. No pall of death hung over it. He sighed in relief.

Suddenly the heavy blankets were too restrictive and he slipped out of bed and padded quietly to the fire-place. The coals glowed sullenly in the grate. He crouched and poked at them with a taper, watching as they flared and died and flared and died. Concentrating on the rhythm, he sank down into his mind and reached out with his senses, the flames in his eyes reflecting the fire's glow.

The bond that tied him to his brother was still strong. he could feel it stretched between them, linking their hearts and minds and gifts. Absently his hand brushed the smooth scar on his hip, the tearing made by the birth that had separated the twins in flesh, though not in spirit. No, his sense of it had been correct. The doom did not lie over them.

Who, then? His mind moved on, reached out. It touched the flickering of something cold and fell back.

He sighed. It was no use. He was too fully awake now and his gift slumbered once again. Tossing the taper into the coals, he watched as it was consumed, then returned to bed.

Disturbed by his brother's movement, Atreus stirred and wrapped one arm about him. Careful not to wake him, Marsellus squirmed under the covers. He would tell Atreus about his dream in the morning. Together they would pierce the fog that held the future and pre-vent it if they could. They'd fought his dreams before. Sometimes they'd won. Sometimes they'd lost. The images returned, and he shuddered. They had to win this time.

Running his fingers nervously through his brother's copper hair, he thought of each friend and family member, one by one, wondering which the Shadow Catcher had chosen him to lose.

In the west wing, Demnor muttered fitfully in his sleep, then sank deeper into a dream of candlelight and anticipation.

Tomorrow night, tomorrow night, tonight, tonight, tonight . . .

Demnor had been in a fit of agitation ever since his meeting with the student Kelahnus. The time had crawled along, and it had been all he could manage not to scream at people to get away from him and leave him be. Actually, he admitted, he hadn't managed that at all well.

He stood before his wardrobe, trying to decide what cloak to wear and grimaced. Why hadn't he said to meet last night. Then he wouldn't have had to wait. *Because last night was the performance by that Eireon Minstrel and you couldn't get away until four in the morning,* his mind supplied.

Scorch off, he answered himself and chose the unadorned black cloak over the dark blue one. He could've missed the singing. He hadn't really needed to be there, and it would have made today easier to bear. The memory made him frown.

He'd been in a panic all day that someone would discover he'd arranged a secret tryst and even more panicked that his frenzied behavior would evoke some suspicion. Ironically it had taken a fight with his twelve-year-old brat of a sister to put the worry to sleep. Quindara's parting scream of, "You're always such a prick!" before throwing a three-hundred-year-old plate at him, had shown him how foolish the worry had been. If he was always such a prick, then today's behavior should go unremarked.

He threw the cloak onto the bed and began to pace back and forth. Soon he'd be with Kelahnus.

The dizzying memory of the student; his hair, his eyes, his body, had been a constant distraction all day. No matter what the Prince had been doing, riding, hunting, training, the golden-haired boy kept stealing into his thoughts. His Arms Trainer had twice hammered through his guard because of it.

Demnor probed at the purple bruise across his ribs and sighed. He couldn't get Kelahnus out of his mind. His face, his smile, the way he spoke and walked and . . . *You've got it bad,* his mind remarked. He ignored it.

Feverishly, he went over his plan for the hundredth time. Five minutes to make ready, five to climb down the wall. Thirty minutes around the palace grounds to the northwest wings, avoiding guards and dogs and servants. Ten minutes to get onto the roof of the Marsellus Chapel, then another twenty over the roofs to Dorian's wing. Finally, fifteen minutes to negotiate that spooky, old nest of ghosts and rats to the main courtyard and the crumbling tower in its center. One hour and twenty-five minutes in total. So he should leave by ten thirty, or around there. He stared at his clock by the door. It was just past ten now. Twenty minutes to go.

He continued to pace. He had to be at training at six, so if he left when Bran's Bell tolled four, he would have four hours with Kelahnus and a half an hour to sleep. That should be enough to keep him from dropping off during training. He could sleep in the afternoon, rather than go to dancing lessons; a better use of his time anyway.

Dropping into a chair, he stared broodingly at the fire. Fifteen minutes left.

Dorian's Tower was a good choice, he thought. Subsequent construction had moved the center of government and the Royal Residences farther and farther east and decay caused by storms, scavenging builders, and an ancient tale of murder had kept it empty ever since. Empty of all, that is, save the Heir to the Throne.

Demnor liked its isolated location and its air of abandoned sadness. Scoffing at superstition, he reasoned that no descendant of Marsellus the Black need worry about ghosts. So far none had appeared to challenge that belief.

He'd discovered it one day while running away from lessons at age four and had returned often. Mostly he'd gone alone, now and then he'd brought another. He'd taken Julian DeSharon there when they'd both been young and unaware of politics and treason and a family's name changed to pay a blood debt to an

Aristok for the death of his brother. They'd played as children do. But children are watched more closely than adults and although his mother had not discovered the playground, she had discovered the playmate. He'd never seen Julian again.

He'd taken Alerion DeKathrine there three times. They'd played as older children do with the first tentative attempts at love and sex. Then he'd gone to war. On returning, fearing the same reprisal from the Aristok, for no other reason than that they cared for each other, he had broken off that friendship himself. But he was a man now, and he would take Kelahnus there. They would play as adults do and his mother could go hang herself.

The clock chimed the half hour and he rose. In one series of fluid movements, he swept up the cloak, threw it around his shoulders and disappeared over the windowsill. Minutes later he was running through the south gardens.

The journey had taken longer than he expected and the echo of the Branbridge bells had long since faded before he hurried into Dorian's Tower. Breathing hard, he made a quick search of the straw-and-leaf-covered lower rooms. They were empty. He chewed anxiously at the scar on his lower lip. Maybe Kelahnus had been delayed as he had. He paced across the front room. Maybe he'd fallen asleep or had forgotten or been discovered or injured on the way.

Reaching the far wall, he turned and leaned his back against it. Maybe, maybe. *If maybes were must bes, we'd all be Street Seers,* he told himself, quoting his old nurse. Where was he? A thin patter of rain began, and he stared gloomily out the window.

The moon was waning. Partially covered by cloud, it cast a ghostly luminescence over the empty courtyard, conjuring up images of demons and phantoms. Demnor's hand dropped to his sword. Drumming his fingers nervously on the pommel, he tried, unsuccessfully, to banish the thought of headless horsemen and armies of the walking dead led by the Shadow Catcher, shuffling silently toward him.

Ahead, between two crumbling walls, was the tournament field where it was believed two DeMarian brothers had battled to the death for the right to woo a cousin. She'd loved the vanquished and on one cold, rainy night, much like tonight, she'd murdered the victor and thrown herself from the top of the tower. It was said, on stormy nights she stood atop its peaked roof, wailing and bemoaning her fate, while below, her cousins fought once more across the rain-slicked grass.

Movement to one side snapped the Prince's head around. Everything was quiet and still. Peering through the broken shutters, he stared out across the tower's yard, at the rusty, iron fence, its gate hanging dejectedly by one hinge, at the dead tree next to it, and the hollow stump that crouched in its shadow. The stump scuttled sideways.

With a gasp, he jerked back into the darkness, cursing himself for a fool. Enemies all too real lurked outside the protection of his guards; assassins and dissatisfied nobles, crazed fanatics and madmen, any one of whom would rejoice to see the Crown Prince alone and undefended. The barely healed wound across his right side, caused by just such a one not two months before, throbbed dully.

He pressed his back against the far wall, clutching at his sword with one hand, while digging through his cloak for his dagger with the other. Ears straining against the splatter of rain, he heard running feet, a muffled curse, and Kelahnus was framed in the doorway.

His hair was windblown and beaded with a fine mist that wreathed his face in a glittering halo. Pushing it from his eyes with one slender hand, he peered into the gloom of the main room.

Relief drove the fear away, leaving a heat both heady and painful in its wake. Demnor sheathed his sword and took a step forward. Before he realized it, he had crossed the room and taken Kelahnus' face in his hands. The nearness of the student's beauty stopped the breath in the Heir's throat and he drew in a shuddering gasp as he ran his hands through the other's hair and along the fine line of his jaw. His skin was like satin under his fingers, smooth and soft and cool. The rough calluses of the Prince's sword hand caught at the delicate wisps of pale hair on his cheeks.

Kelahnus shivered and looked up into his eyes.

They kissed.

Somehow, they ended up on the stone floor, the student's thick cloak spread out beneath them. Somehow, but Demnor would never be able to recall how. All the world was taken up by the golden-haired vision in his arms. He propped himself up on one elbow and fumbled at the student's belt. With a happy smile, Kelahnus reached up to untie the laces of the Prince's tunic. In the distance the bells of Branbridge tolled the quarter hour and the rain began to beat harder against the tower.

He was warm and cold, comfortable and cramped. Something sharp dug into his back and his right arm was numb. He felt wonderful. For a second, he stared up at a cobweb-covered beam, disoriented, then his memory cleared. Kelahnus. Last night. Turning his head, he gazed at the sleeping youth curled up, spoon-fashion, beside him. Yes.

He savored the memory, eyes closed. They'd made love for what seemed like hours, frantically at first, then more gently as the initial burst of lust had cooled. Other nights and other lovers had passed from Demnor's memory like ghosts, leaving him a nervous virgin once again. He'd done all right, though. He thought. If Kelahnus' reactions had been any indication, he'd done just fine.

Shivering in the early morning cold, he pulled his cloak up closer about his neck with his free hand. Where had his tunic gotten to? The line of scratches along his ribs protested the movement, leaving him with a stupid grin on his face. At some point last night he was sure Kelahnus had drawn blood.

The student stirred beside him and Demnor smoothed the hair away from his face. Winds and clouds, he was beautiful.

The bells tolled six.

Six?

Demnor threw himself up, yanking his arm out from under Kelahnus. The youth was on his feet in an instant, locked in a defensive, fighting position and staring blearily about him.

"Wha . . . ? What's wrong?"

"Blast and burn it to ashes!" Demnor cursed as he hunted desperately for his clothes. "I'm late for training!"

"Oh." Kelahnus fetched his boots, while the Prince pulled on his pants and struggled into his tunic. "But you're the Crown Prince. Can't you do what you want, when you want?"

"I wish! Thanks." Demnor snatched the boots from him and jammed them on. He didn't have time to explain Royal obligations. "I've got responsibilities," he answered simply. "That go beyond doing what you want. See you later." Grabbing the student by the shoulders, he kissed him firmly, then darted for the door.

"When?"

The forlorn tone of Kelahnus' voice stopped Demnor with one foot over the threshold. He turned back with a sigh. He was late anyway and sometimes responsibilities conflicted with each other. Returning more slowly, he took the student in his arms.

"I'll send word tomorrow," he whispered as Kelahnus leaned into his embrace. "With Sarah, my page. She's discreet. I can't see you tonight. There's a banquet. And tomorrow I'm doing the High Sabat Mass at the Holy Triarchy Cathedral. I think I can get away the night after that. Can you?"

Kelahnus gazed up at him. "I can be free any night you want me to be."

"Good." Bending his head, the Prince kissed him

again, this time more tenderly. Then he sighed. "Now, I really have to go."

With a nod, Kelahnus disentangled them and silently offered Demnor his cloak. The Prince took it and did up the sapphire clasp without taking his eyes from the other's face.

"Till then."

"Till then."

After one last smile, Demnor turned and left the tower. In four steps he was at the fence and over it. In six he was through a hole in the dilapidated wall and leaping over seven centuries of rubble, feeling freer than he had since he'd returned from the Continent.

The crash of thunder snapped Demnor's eyes open and he lay, staring into the darkness while the dream slowly melted away. That old dream. He shook his head, wincing as the movement pulled at his mouth. Blood, seeping in from the tear in his chin, had encrusted over his lips, sealing them together. With an inward groan, he leaned over and groped for a goblet of water. Beside him, Kelahnus stirred, but did not wake. Good. He didn't need to be fussed over at this time of night.

Pouring a little water on a handkerchief, he scraped at his mouth. That old memory.

It resurfaced now and then. It was always the same and he always mistrusted its timing. He didn't need to be reminded of his youth. Those days were gone. Often, he wished he could control his dreams like the Seers could. He would will the whole experience, dreams and all, out of his memory. A vision of Kelahnus, fifteen, sleepy-eyed and smiling from within the folds of his cloak came to him then. Well, he softened, if only he could banish the latter half of the experience, he would be satisfied.

The latter half. The half after the first meeting and the second and the third when he'd had to face the one thing he feared. He'd faced his mother with the most vulnerable part of himself, his heart, laid bare and with something he cherished carried openly in his arms. He couldn't hide it. He couldn't protect it, so he'd risked it and . . .

No. With deliberate control, he set the goblet carefully down on the side table. The middle of the night was no time for such memories. He scrubbed at his face. No time was time for them. The past was dead and best left buried and forgotten. He'd won. The cost had been almost too great, but he'd won. He would *not* remember.

Mindful of the sleeping man beside him, he lay back and closed his eyes. Silently thanking the storm for waking him before the rest of the dream played out, he willed himself to sleep. After some time his rebellious mind obeyed.

In the central, Royal wing, the open windows of Quindara's suite blew wafts of fresh night air into her bedroom, sweeping it clean of the mingled odors of sex and wine and incense. In the center of the bed, the Duke of Yorbourne slumbered peacefully, one arm draped over Nadia, her Companion, the other across the chest of the young man she'd met that day. At her feet a black-and-white cat washed its face with long, even strokes, pausing now and then to swat at the dog asleep beside it.

Quindara slept, dreaming of the day's Hunt and the night's sport, untroubled by visions of the past or of the future.

In the Aristok's apartments all was quiet. If Melesandra dreamed, none knew of it. Three of her four Companions slept in their own rooms, the fourth lay awake beside the Aristok, thinking her own thoughts.

The next morning, the junior knights on duty at the entrance to the Sword Tower saluted the Royal Dukes of Lochsbridge and Kempston as they made their way inside. As one, the twins sketched the sign of the Triarchy, then walked quietly down the right aisle of the main chapel, greeting those who'd already gathered with silent nods.

Today was Di Sathairn, the day of prayer for those of the Triarctic faith, and as usual, the twins had chosen to worship with their fellow Knights of the Sword at the Branbridge chapterhouse rather than in their private chapel at the palace. Ordinarily, the presence of so many sworn to the same tradition wrapped a comforting balm about their Sight, but today Marsellus was too edgy to take it in. Feeling his brother's disquiet through the joint bond of their birth and their Gift, Atreus was also tense and uneasy. After bowing before the symbols of their Order, the twins took their seats.

As members of the Royal Family, they shared one of the ornately carved box stalls running along both sides of the chapel. They'd chosen the second on the right, next to their sister Quindara's. Across from hers, to the left of the Aristok's throne, was their brother Demnor's. Both stalls were empty today.

Marsellus gave an inaudible sigh of relief.

Ever since last night he'd been afraid to look anyone in the face, afraid to see if the pall of death from his vision hovered over one of them. The fear of it had gnawed at him all night, robbing him of sleep.

He'd told Atreus as soon as his twin had awakened this morning. His brother had listened gravely, then suggested they go to the Archpriest of the Flame for help. They'd sent a page immediately.

Gwynne DeLlewelynne would see them later that afternoon. Marsellus had wanted to wait in their suite, hesitant to go out, afraid of what he might see, but Atreus had prevailed upon his more reticent twin. It was essential that they follow their normal schedule so as not to cloud the prophecy with sudden change. They'd planned to attend Mass at the Sword Tower and that was exactly what they were going to do. Recognizing the wisdom of his brother's words, Marsellus had reluctantly agreed.

Now, sliding to their knees and raising their eyes in the Triarctic tradition, both twins prayed for the inner peace and clarity they were going to need if they were to discover the meaning of this vision.

Slowly, the years of sanctity that pervaded the Sword Chapel settled over them. As one, they breathed deeply, tasting the faint acrid flavor of incense on the back of their throats, then sat back.

Atreus tilted his head, passing the time before the service, as he'd done every Mass since they were children, staring up at the tall windows and the ceiling above them. His gaze passed languidly over each painted crest set above each elaborately carved box stall, over each vaulted beam and inner buttress that ran between them, and over every brilliant stained glass window that together depicted the history of their Order.

Usually Marsellus studied the people filing into their places as his brother studied the architecture, but today he kept his eyes averted. Only when their older sister, Quindara, entered the chapel, flanked by two junior knights, did he glance up in trepidation. The Duke of Yorbourne strode past them with a faint nod and Marsellus let out a breath he hadn't remembered holding. Her face was clear of the pall he'd Seen last night. The doom did not lie upon her. Atreus gripped his arm comfortingly for a moment before returning his gaze to the ceiling.

Marsellus found himself relaxing. Quindara frequented the Sword Chapel often, and her presence this morning suggested that Demnor was unlikely to attend as well. The two oldest royal siblings did not seek each other's company and rarely appeared at public functions together unless absolutely necessary. Kassandra, their other sister, was too young to enter any Order as yet, and the Aristok herself only appeared on days holy to the Sword as she had many other commitments.

Marsellus leaned into the plush, dark blue velvet of his chair with a sigh. That was all the family accounted for, then; he could breathe easily for a while.

Around them, the chapel slowly filled with Sword Knights and their squires. Junior knights lit the heavy

silver incense urns while Alexander DeKathrine bowed
before the altar. As Hierarchpriest of the Sword, it was
his right to sing the Mass unless the Aristok or
Demnor, as Defender of the Realm, was in attendance.
Often, he passed that duty to others, prefering to worship as a simple knight. Today, it seemed, he would be
exercising his right. With a half smile, Marsellus
settled in for a short service.

But, as the Duke of Cambury knelt to begin his own
silent prayers, a stir at the entrance made him pause.

Flanked by four junior knights, Demnor, Prince of
Gwyneth, and Archpriest of the Sword, strode into the
chapel. Those seated rose at once.

Barely pausing to accnowledge the greeting of his
fellow knights, the Prince made a swift sign of the Triarchy, then strode down the left aisle of the chapel, his
boots ringing against the flagstoned floor. The Hierarchpriest bowed and made to move aside, but Demnor
waved at him to continue and turned to enter his own
stall.

As his brother knelt and raised his face to the great
flame-covered sword that hung above them, Marsellus
cast a swift glance over his features.

The Heir's face was pale, the wounds across his jaw
standing out in angry relief. Dark shadows surrounded
his eyes and hollowed out his cheeks, but if his injuries
had weakened him, he showed no sign of it. Marsellus
was not surprised.

The twins had spent most of their early years on their
father's ducal estates of Lanborough. They'd seldom
come in contact with their elder brother, but on the few
occasions they were brought together, he'd been both
stiffly polite and somewhat distant. Now, in the capital,
he listened with neutral attention to them in Council,
and endured their company on the Hunt and in the
training yard with neither pleasure nor hostility. Quindara was much the same.

For their part, Atreus and Marsellus accepted their
siblings' reserve with easy grace. It was better than the

alternative. Now, both Demnor and Quindara were studiously ignoring them and each other.

The tower bells rang once.

At the sound, the main doors were closed. Alexander DeKathrine stood before the altar, facing the gathered knights, and held up his arms in benediction. The chapter raised their heads to receive his blessing. Only then, with the invocation of the Flame to protect him, did Marsellus DeMarian look fully into the face of his brother Demnor, his Sight open to whatever he might see.

For a moment it was as if someone had passed a veil of red silk over his eyes. His vision grew hazy, his brother's face indistinct. It was only after he willed himself to stillness and looked again, that he saw the misty aura that hovered over the Heir's features. He closed his eyes.

The Archpriest of the Flame agreed to see the Royal Dukes immediately. The initiate sent to escort them to Her Grace's private rooms gave no sign of the curiosity she felt, merely bowed and directed them to follow her. Although no strangers to the Flame Temple, the Royal Seers were not priests and as such had always respected the temple tradition that demanded secular visitors make appointments and be escorted by a temple acolyte at the very least, especially on Di Sathairn. The Dukes' shared Gift could, officially, avail them of more immediate attention, but until now they had never demanded it. The Initiate cast a surreptitious glance in their direction. The Duke of Kempston looked nervous, the Duke of Lochsbridge, determined.

Gwynne DeLlewellynne was seated before a small fire in her outer chamber. She remained seated as Atreus and Marsellus were ushered into the room.

An old woman when the Elder Conclave had named her Archpriest of the Most Holy and Powerful Order of the Flame, she'd held that post for over twenty years. Second in ecclesiastical circles only to the Heirarchpriest of Cannonshire, and even then only by ancient tradition, she stood by the side of the Aristok in all matters regarding the Triarchy. She was counted the most powerful Seer in a hundred years and, at the age of eighty-three, still partook of the Potion of Truth at her Avatar's demand. She had trained the two young DeMarian Seers who now stood before her.

She gestured for them to be seated.

They obeyed, placing themselves unconsciously to either side of their old teacher as they had when they were children. She noted this without comment, merely waited, her hands held loosely in her lap while Marsellus spilled out the reason for their unorthodox visit, recounting his vision of the night before and his observations of that morning.

When he was finished, she pursed her lips and gave him a keen stare.

"You believe this vision to be a direct prediction of the future and not the symbolic portrayal of some perilous change."

It was not a question, but he nodded anyway.

"You are the most qualified to interpret your own Sight, of course," she agreed. "Do you believe the aura you saw about your brother to be the manifestation of your vision of death?"

Marsellus opened his mouth to answer, then closed it again. Did he? He'd been asking himself that same question since he'd first been aware of it in the Sword Chapel. Usually he was confident of his interpretations. This time . . . this time he wasn't sure.

"No, Your Grace," he said finally.

"But your sense of it was what?"

"That it was not benevolent."

"Was it a strong aura?"

"No. I had to concentrate to see it at all. It seemed to waver, but it *was* there."

"Did you perceive this as well?" She turned suddenly to Atreus.

He shook his head.

"The prophecy has predicted violent and dire

happenings for the future," she said. "If your vision of last night was so strong and the ensuing pall so weak, then it's best surmised that the event you've foreseen is in the far future, whoever it may involve. Do you concur?" She turned her bright black eyes full on Marsellus.

He slowly nodded.

"Do you know of any event of such magnitude revealed in the future that might fit this profile?"

Both twins thought for a moment.

"The fighting in Gallia is escalating," Atreus finally offered. "By spring the entire family will likely be taking the field on the Continent."

"And does this vision feel like a vision of war?"

Marsellus shook his head, his confidence returning in the wake of her familiar approach. "A battle death would feel much cleaner," he answered. "This feels more . . . political."

"The Essendale DeKathrines are in town," Atreus said. "That could mean our brother's betrothal will soon be made public."

"And is that cause for dire predictions of death?"

Atreus snorted and even Marsellus cracked a smile.

"You could say that," the more demonstrative twin answered wryly. "He has about as much enthusiasm for marriage as a merchant has for bankruptcy."

The Archpriest leaned back in her chair. "I sense these two events to be connected," she said, "but how is still hidden from my Sight.

"Are you willing to partake of the Potion of Truth to attempt to glean the answers to your vision," she asked suddenly.

Marsellus grew very silent.

Atreus glanced at him.

"Mars?"

The quieter twin frowned, staring into the fire as he considered what she asked. He'd always steered clear of the potion with which the Seer Priests entered the Prophetic Realm and called forth the future for the Aristok. It sharpened his already sensitive Gift to the point of pain and overwhelmed the bond he shared with his twin. He needed that bond to feel secured to the world. Without it, he'd always been afraid that he'd be cut adrift, unable to return. It had frightened him enough as a child to drive them both away from the Flame Temple where their Sight should have taken them. But now . . . now if he didn't risk it, he risked losing a brother.

He turned back to the Archpriest, his expression firm. "Yes, I am," he answered. "We have to know what this means."

Pleased by his answer, she clapped her hands and an initiate appeared at the door as if summoned there by magic.

"Have Mandius prepare three doses of the Potion of Truth and have him meet us in the Seeing Room with three scribes and three assistants."

The boy bowed and disappeared.

The Archpriest returned her attention to the Royal Seers. "Now then, my lads, if you will help an old woman to her feet, we'll see what we can do about finding an answer to your questions."

As one, Marsellus and Atreus rose, offering their arms to their old teacher, certain that, with her help, they'd not only See the future, but prevent it as well.

5. Melesandra III

Dawn. Kelahnus stretched sleepily in bed, watching Demnor dress for training. It had been four days since the Hunt; three since the Heir's request for an audience with the Aristok to discuss his marriage plans. Raventarian, the Royal Herald, had brought her reply. She would see her firstborn son in three days.

Three days. The Companion tugged at a fine silver thread in the bed-curtains as he pondered this decision. The Aristok would not be rushed, not by the DeKathrines and not by the Crown Prince. Secure in her strength, she could ignore the warning rumblings of political unrest in the city. The Palace Guard and the Town Watch did not like the invasion of armed DeKathrine retainers and already there'd been minor clashes between them. The sooner the Betrothal announcement was made the better, but the Aristok would not be rushed, and she would see her son in three days.

Today.

Demnor had shown nothing but polite interest in Raventarian's message, but Kelahnus knew his Lord; knew that the last three days of frenzied training and audiences were more than just devotion to duty; and it had taken its toll. Demnor was gaunt and gray, swaying slightly as he hoisted the heavy mail shirt over his head. The underpadding of soft leather and cloth protected his bruised ribs somewhat, but he still winced as the weight settled against his chest.

Chewing on a lock of hair, Kelahnus wished, not for the first time, that he could say something, do something, but there was nothing he could do. Comfort was out of the question, counsel was out of the question. The Prince would reject each offer, making it obvious that he saw such acceptance as a weakness. He would handle it his way. Carry it, suffer it, ignore it.

Kelahnus sighed. There was nothing he could do. He'd learned that years ago. He still tried.

"It looks miserable out," he said, raising himself up to peer out the open window at the dark, cloudy sky.

"Raining," the Heir answered distantly.

"It's too wet to train," Kelahnus observed, a bright smile masking the underlying concern. "Why don't you come back to bed? We could exercise here." He gave an exaggerated leer.

Demnor returned as much of a smile as his swollen jaw allowed, and shook his head. "Can't. I'm expected."

"Nonsense. You could send a message. Declare today a holy day of contemplation or worship of the Earth or something."

"Weren't you satisfied with Calan Mai?"

"That was months ago! Come back to bed." The Companion pushed the covers aside and stretched out seductively.

With a sigh, Demnor crossed the room to stand beside him. Bending down, he brushed the younger man's lips with his own, then straightened again with a faint groan. "I can't. I'm expected."

He made to move away and Kelahnus caught his tunic front and pulled him down for another kiss. He held him that way for a long time, then slowly let him up.

Demnor's expression was slightly unfocused.

"You'll ruin me," he chided gently.

"I'll be the making of you."

"Kelahnus . . ."

"You look terrible. You're about to fall over. Why

can't you rest, just for once, and give your body a chance to heal and regain its strength?"

"I can't coddle it. I'm fine."

"Oh, yes, that's why . . ." The rest of the Companion's retort was lost as the door banged open and a furious, young girl stormed into the center of the room, to stand, fists on hips, glaring at Demnor.

After an initial start, the Heir gazed impassively down at his youngest sister, the Prince Kassandra, Duke of Clarfield. Her tunic was disheveled and her thick, auburn hair, so like his own, stuck out from the leather plaitings of her braids.

"Good morning, Your Grace," he said formally, with just a hint of a smile.

"Don't you good morning me, you traitor!" she stormed. "Why wasn't I woke for the Hunt?"

"You weren't? How remiss of us."

"Don't make fun of me! Hi, Kelahnus." Kassandra turned and waved at the Companion, then whirled to confront her brother once more. "Well!"

"Maybe your nurse felt you needed more sleep."

"Tit warts! She said Atreus told her not to wake me!"

"Then you should talk to him."

"I tried, but he was off somewhere hiding that night, probably so he wouldn't have to face me, and then Ariston made me go on that manure pile of a tour to Albangate, and I've just got back. Besides, you could have countermanded his order if you'd really wanted to."

"I didn't."

"You're a poop head. Will you next time?"

"No."

"But, Dem, it's not fair!"

"It's tradition."

"But you were blooded before your seed!"

"That's different. I'm the Heir."

"And Quindara?"

"She went in disguise."

"And by the time anyone found out it was her, it was too late, right? Maybe . . ."

Demnor's face grew stern. "You will not attempt it."

"But, Dem . . ."

"Promise me."

"But . . ."

"Kass . . ."

"Oh, all right." Her freckled face fell. "It was just a thought anyway."

"A dangerous thought. Without proper training you could be seriously hurt, even killed."

"Yes, I heard. Are you all right?" she asked with a sudden look of concern on her elfin face.

"Yes."

"Good." Chewing at her lip in unconscious imitation of her oldest brother's habit, she squinted professionally up at his wounds. The angry red swelling around them had faded to be replaced by a spread of black bruises. "Were they deep?"

"Yes."

"Then they'll scar prettily."

"There is always that." Demnor's tone was sarcastic. Kassandra ignored it.

"Why can't I go on the Hunt? I *have* trained," she demanded, jumping to the attack once more.

Demnor raised his eyes heavenward. "Because you're too young!"

"I am not! I'm practically an adult!"

"If you will excuse me, My Lord, Your Grace," Kelahnus interrupted, his face contorted with the effort to maintain a serious expression. He left, closing the door to his own suite. From behind it, they could hear the sounds of muffled laughter. Demnor turned back to his sister.

"How old are you?" he demanded.

"Almost twelve!"

"Just past eleven, you mean."

"Two months past! That makes almost!"

Forgetting his injuries, Demnor burst out laughing, then gasped as the room tilted and his vision grew hazy. After a time the pain subsided, though the urge to laugh did not. He glared down at her in mock ire, then, throwing up his hands in resignation, lowered himself carefully into a chair.

"You're impossible," he said finally.

"I know," she answered with a toss of her braids and a smug look. "You taught me how to be. Also arrogant, egocentric and self-centered. That's what Ariston says."

"Does he?"

"Yes. But he'd do anything for me, so I don't mind."

"I see. Are you tormenting him?" He gave her a measured look, which she countered.

"No! And anyway, I *have* trained," she repeated, returning to the attack. "I'm *much* better than I was. I took down a yearling hippogriff all by myself this spring, And Flairilynne says I'm the best rider she's ever trained. I beat Kassius DeKathrine last week and he's two years older than me, but then *you* wouldn't know that since it's been *forever* since we've done *anything* together."

Her words were teasing, but Demnor heard the loneliness behind them and his expression sobered as he searched her face, so like his own. Bursting with energy one minute, serious and sad the next, she reminded him so much of himself at her age that sometimes it was painful to be with her. And she was right, it had been weeks since they'd done anything together, just the two of them. He realized with surprise that he'd missed that as much as she had. But then, Kassandra had always been special.

At her birth, she'd been just another unwelcome sibling; one more guarantee of the continuation of the line; one more reminder that he could be removed with little effort if he failed. But as she'd grown, that had changed. She hadn't been content to live her life as a solitary affair. She'd demanded love from all those around her, especially from her eldest brother.

Demnor had complied. He refused to explain it, to himself or to anyone else. He enjoyed her company. He left it at that. As the years went by, he found himself seeking her out, talking to her, teaching her, and watching over her as she grew. Taking her from the arms of tutors and trainers, he'd brought her into his world, the world of horses and armor, of quiet religious duty filled with peaceful silences and of long rides in the company of the wind and the rain, much as a quiet man had done for him years before. She'd grown up open and vibrant, willing to view the world as an adventure and a game. He guarded her jealously, from the machinations at Court and from the hardness of their mother. He told himself that he did it out of duty, and yet the more he fought to safeguard her life from the shadows that veiled his own, the fainter those shadows grew when they were together. He loved her as he did few others and allowed her more familiarity than anyone else. She knew this. He also, usually, gave in to her demands and she knew this, too.

Setting his features into a mask of severity, he gave her a level stare.

"So you've trained, have you?"

"Yes!"

"Every day?"

"Yes! Mostly."

"Mostly? Mostly isn't good enough. The Hunt is a very serious affair. Only the best . . ."

"But, Dem . . ."

He held up his hand for silence. "Quiet. I'm lecturing. Only the best . . ."

"You mean the richest."

"Warriors in the land . . ."

"In Branbridge."

"May ride to the Hunt. You're too young, you're not sufficiently trained, and your Arms Trainer concentrates on battle techniques, not on hunting skills."

"Then you train me!"

"Fine. We start today."

"What?" Caught off guard, Kassandra's flame-flecked gray eyes widened.

Demnor smiled, having anticipated her reaction. He had not, however, anticipated an assault as Kassandra, crying out, "Oh, you're wonderful!" threw herself into his arms.

He paled, biting back a grunt of pain as she squeezed his bruised ribs, but the sharp intake of breath was enough to cause her to release him, looking contrite.

"Oh, I'm sorry, Dem. It's just so wonderful! This morning?"

"Yes. Go and fetch your leathers and meet me in the west circle."

"I'll be down there in a flash of lightning! Betcha I beatcha down there!"

With a bound, she was up and out, the door slamming dust from the tapestries behind her.

"No bet." Smiling, despite the pain in his chest and face, he rose and took up his practice tunic. At least now Captain Fletcher would have someone else to harass.

The mantel clock was just chiming twelve when, for the third time that day, the door to Demnor's bedroom slammed, this time with enough force to knock a painting from the wall. Kelahnus, doing stretches by the window, nearly dislocated a shoulder with the speed at which he turned, but relaxed when he saw the Prince.

Seething, Demnor jerked the heavy, black, woolen Triarchy robe over his head, ignoring the protestations of bruises and wounds and threw it savagely into the corner. By all the spirits of the Shadow Realm, he hated heresy trials. Naked, he threw himself into a chair.

Kelahnus, wisely, said nothing, and merely waited.

Leaning his head back, Demnor closed his eyes. Although the day had started in fun, he'd found his mood darkening as soon as he'd returned from the training yards. His Secretary had wordlessly handed him the day's itinerary, then slipped quickly from the room. He'd wondered about that until he'd glanced down. Heresy trials.

Technically the Hierarchpriest of Cannonshire sat as

High Judge in such cases, but Demnor's position as the Defender of the Realm placed him above his second cousin. He could have passed it on, claiming other responsibilities; many had before him, but he would not. It was his duty and his right.

He knew the Hierarchpriest thought he should pass it on. The head of the Knights of the Sword wanted a cooler head; one well versed in the laws of the Triarchy and Its degrees of penance, with a more orthodox approach. Too often, Demnor judged on instinct or on personal bias, ignoring the advice of his deputy judges. Alexander DeKathrine did not approve of such methods.

But the Hierarchpriest was wrong if he thought the Prince unversed in the penitential rites of their faith; Demnor knew them only too well. It was simply that he chose to judge in the ecclesiastical courts in the same way he did in the secular, or in any other matter: as he saw fit. And he hated heresy trials. They were not why he had sworn his oaths to the most ancient of the Triarchy's Militant Orders. To the Crown Prince, heresy was a sickness, not a crime, caused by a lack of guidance and a lack of compassion. If there was any chance of redemption, Demnor gambled on it. It was his way of honoring a quiet and compassionate man whom even he would not speak of in public.

He thought back to the last man to come before him that morning. Boy, really. The lad couldn't have been more than seventeen and scared out of his wits, though trying hard not to show it. Daniel Fellows, minor nobility, a third child to seek admittance to a Militant Order and bring prosperity to his house. The Knights of the Bow had tested him and found him wanting. Their answer had been no and, too proud to return home in failure, he'd taken to drink. Bitter and angry, he'd found sympathy in the city's taverns. One thing had led to another and now he was on trial for his life.

The prosecutor's words were brief. He had preached rebellion against the Triarchy. He had spoken against the Militant Orders and their hierarchy and therefore against Demnor himself. The prosecutor wanted him condemned.

The Prince, who viewed the prosecutor as an officious little prick who couldn't break wind without the Hierarchpriest's permission, did not. He pronounced his judgment.

"Penitent crusade. Go to the Continent. Grow up. Make a name for yourself. Come back when I'm Aristok."

Recognizing Demnor's intent, the Hierarchpriest had been quietly furious. The Prince had ignored him. Ordinarily they managed a negotiated peace in matters where their individual powers crossed. In fact, Demnor did respect and rely on the older man's experience. But today he was unable to look at him without seeing the host of kin gathered at his back to force the Heir into an unwanted marriage. Viewing this show of might as one step below armed treason, Demnor was barely able to keep from reaching for Alexander's throat.

The DeKathrines were more powerful than any one family had a right to be. They were about to become more so and there wasn't a thing he could do about it. He closed his eyes as his jaw began to throb. *Burn him and her and the whole world to ashes.* Opening his eyes, he looked into Kelahnus' worried face. *Well, everyone but you,* he amended.

The younger man leaned against the chair, one hand resting lightly on the Heir's arm. Demnor sighed and covered the Companion's hand with his own.

Later, his ire dampened by the other man's quiet understanding, he stood before the ornate clothes spread out across the bed. The Companion had anticipated his needs, laying out the Heir's formal garb; what he wore as the Defender of the Realm, and not his elaborately ugly High Court attire. This was an occasion brought about by duty. That was the statement he would make.

Demnor glared down at the stiff finery. Submission was submission, no matter how well you dressed it. With a grimace, he began to dress.

Black woolen breeches and undertunic went on easily enough, but he grunted in pain as he struggled into the heavy, silver-embroidered, dark blue tunic. Kelahnus helped him into the breastplate and the richly woven surcoat; the Crown Prince's personal device with the Defender's sword and helm emblazoned on the front. Ceremonial vambraces and greaves over polished black boots went on next; then a heavy, dark blue cloak, trimmed in black fur and bordered by a line of sapphires.

"Thank the Wind it's cold out today," Demnor muttered, "Or I'd never make it."

Kelahnus chuckled.

A wide leather belt, tooled in silver, completed the attire. Its bejeweled scabbard housed a silvered broadsword, the pommel encrusted with precious and semiprecious stones, including the third largest sapphire in the world; a sword that was only unsheathed during the rituals of Royalty. Demnor's fingers brushed reverently at the pommel.

Defender. The earthly symbol of his faith, his love of the Realm and his duty to the Crown. It had only been blooded three times since its forging: once at its consecration two centuries past when it had nicked the palm of the first Defender of the Realm; once when it had been plunged into the heart of a traitor to avenge a brother's death nineteen years ago, and once, in a quiet, private ceremony in 886 when a young Prince had drawn his own blood across its edge to cleanse a debt of honor he could not have withdrawn from. Defender. With it at his side he could brave any trial.

Behind him, Kelahnus brushed his Lord's hair until it swarmed about his shoulders like dark fire, then placed a silver circlet on his head. The Prince turned to the mirror. His own reflection stared morosely back at him.

His face, swollen and purple with its four days' worth of stubble, made him look like some half human, half demon from the Triarchy text. His eyes, burning like hot coals in the dark hollows around them confirmed it. How had he become so grim and cheerless in so few years? The answer gave him no more peace than he expected, so he thrust it aside. Feeling the Companion's eyes on him, he turned and met his gaze a little sadly. Kelahnus smiled, his own eyes dark, and reaching up, he touched the uninjured side of Demnor's face. They stood that way for some time, each caught up in the same memories until the clock chimed the half hour, pulling them back to the present. With a grimace, Demnor turned and strode from the room.

Unmoving, the Companion stared at the door and spoke the words he had been unable to utter in the Prince's presence.

"Come back to me soon. I love you."

He turned back to the empty room, the love spoken, the fear remaining unuttered. There was little point. The Aristok, no doubt, had this interview planned. She wanted this marriage. That was to their advantage. The meeting would be brief and Demnor would return to him. That was all that mattered.

The hall was long, tiled in a marble blue-and-black diamond pattern. Elaborate tapestries, hung between the floor-to-ceiling stained glass windows, marked the deeds of past rulers, and at every third window, twin alcoves housed two formally armored Palace Guards, facing each other with mirrored blank expressions. Demnor paused for a moment, looking down to the far end of the hall and the thick, oaken door at its end. The door to the Aristok's private office and audience chambers. How often had he made this journey with his heart in his throat and fear drying his mouth and knotting the muscles of his stomach? Too often. And had he ever made it without them? Yes. Only once and look how that had turned out. He shook himself and, gritting his teeth, started down the long hall. His expression was grim, and the guards who slammed to attention glanced at each other in mutual apprehension. The whole palace knew what happened when the Heir and the Aristok met. Demnor ignored them, concentrating on the hated audience to come and remembering.

He was sixteen and he was in love. Coming in from training, Demnor felt as if he'd sprouted wings. Everything was enjoyable, training, Council, even Court duties. Sometimes he feared he would begin whirling in circles and never stop; at other times he thought he'd taken ill. His attention had a habit of wandering and he'd begun bumping into things again. In the midst of daydreaming about Kelahnus he would start guiltily and glance about him in fear someone had noticed, or stare blankly at the courtier who'd been talking to him for ten minutes without a response. But overall, he found it hard to continue to worry. No one seemed to have noticed, so he assumed he wasn't acting as strangely as he was feeling.

In fact, the whole palace had noticed and come to the right conclusion. The Prince had found a beau. The younger servants blushed when he passed, the older hid approving smiles. The Guard, always allowed more liberty with their Prince, grinned openly. Demnor never even noticed. He was in love and the feelings were so new and wonderful that he threw caution to the wind and simply enjoyed them. He was to remember this time as three of the happiest weeks of his life.

The Court had also noticed, and they, too, had made an accurate diagnosis of his condition. The Prince had taken a secret lover. There were jealous whisperings in the ballrooms and dark glances from across the audience halls. Where did the Heir go when he was alone and when did they meet? Three spies were chased away by the Prince's bodyguards, once when Demnor was bathing, twice when he was in meditation. The Palace Guard didn't know when he held his secret meetings either, but they'd be drowned in horse manure if they allowed some poxed-up courtier's worm to discover it. One man barely returned to his master in one piece after Randolf's less than gentle

handling. The Guard had made their intent plain and
the Court drew back, momentarily thwarted.

Laura, the Aristok's Second Companion, was not.
Top of her class in espionage and clandestine concerns
and Head of Melesandra's private security force, she
neatly sidestepped the Guard and the Court and set a
watch on the Prince's window. She found the place,
she found the boy.

Unaware, Demnor continued to meet Kelahnus two
or three times a week, whenever they could both get
free. They made love on cloaks laid out on the cold
stones and afterward they lay, wrapped around each
other, spent and sleepy. They shared cider and cakes
and talked of their dreams, their fears, and their lives.
On that final night, lying listening to the rain's gentle
sweep across the tower, they'd talked of their future.

"What will happen after—to us, I mean—after
you're Aristok?" Kelahnus snuggled deeper into the
crook of Demnor's arm, looking up at him through a
halo of tousled hair. The Prince felt his heart do a backflip as he met the student's eyes.

"You'll be my Companion. You'll live with me and
I'll fill your life with music and jewels and fine
clothes," he declared.

"Hm. That would be nice. I'd rather it be filled with
you, though."

Another look and Demnor felt his tongue swell to
the roof of his mouth and his ears go red. Scorch it,
the youth had that affect on him so often. He tried
to speak, blushed furiously, then gave up and simply
held him.

The student sighed. "It'll be a long time until you're
Aristok, won't it?"

"I expect so."

"What if it's too long? What if it takes years? Sup-
posing Master Klairius wants me to sell my contract
before that? To someone else?" His voice rose with a
tinge of fear.

Demnor took his hand firmly, using the pressure to
reassure him. "He won't. I won't let him."

The certainty in the Prince's voice calmed him, although when Kelahnus spoke, his voice was still edged with worry.

"But what if . . ."

"Sh. No more what ifs. There won't be any. *I'm* going to buy your contract. Me. Now. Today."

"What?" Kelahnus stared at him in shock, while a smile spread across the Prince's face.

"Today?" the student asked weakly.

"Today. Well, later this morning. No one's up this early except us."

Kelahnus suddenly took him in a fierce hug. "Oh, I do love you! I've been so afraid that this was just a dream. Everything's so perfect, it just couldn't be real, but when I'm with you, I know it's true. It seemed so unbelievable that it could be so much better. That I could be your Companion and wake up in your arms in the morning and be with you all the time. But if you say it can happen, I believe you."

Demnor laughed, a carefree sound that echoed through the old ruins. "Of course it can happen." He would go to the School that afternoon. He smiled as he imagined servants scurrying to pack Kelahnus' things while he and Master Klairius discussed the terms of the contract: price—whatever it took, length—forever, naturally.

Of course, he had to get his mother's permission first. But there had been no friction between them in weeks. In fact, the last time they'd even been together was five days ago at a banquet to honor his second cousin Alexander DeKathrine's victories in Gallia. The older man had spoken at one point of the Heir's valor and promise and the Aristok had actually turned to him and nodded. She wouldn't say no. All the high nobility had Companions, even the ones in the Militant Orders. Some even went to war. Not that Kelahnus would, but he'd be there when Demnor came home.

He kissed the student gently. "Of course it can happen," he repeated. "And it will. I give you my word."

*   *   *

Demnor practically flew down the hall, startling each pair of Guards to a hasty attention. The marble floors, usually treacherously slippery, helped his progress today. Scattered patterns of light flowed over his face as he passed the tall, stained glass windows. Usually they and the elaborate tapestries filled him with awe. Today he didn't even notice them. His whole attention was fixed on Kelahnus and what he must say to his mother and to Master Klairius.

His stomach fluttered nervously, but he told himself not to be a coward. This was a formality only. Hadn't she agreed to his military postings, his titles and ranks. This was merely an extension of those. The only stumbling block might be that she wouldn't see him without a formal audience. And then it would just be a matter of waiting. But it should be all right. He'd delayed until midday when she wasn't usually too busy.

The door loomed up before him. The two Guards came to attention, and the one on the left pushed it open. With a deep breath he entered.

The wide anteroom had no windows. It was lit instead by delicate lanterns encased in tiny stained glass panels and a small fire in the hearth. Paintings covered the walls, rugs from the East covered the floor. At the far end, two Royal Guards, Shield Knights, stood to attention before the Aristok's private audience room and office. Facing the outer door was a small desk, from which Klaudius, the Aristok's Chief Clerk, was rising, an alarmed expression on his face. He bowed nervously as Demnor strode up to him.

"Klaudius, I need to see the Aristok. I don't have a formal audience, but it's important. Ask her." Demnor looked the aging man firmly in the eye.

Klaudius stammered and glanced at the inner door. "Your Royal Highness, I, that is . . ." He stopped and wiped a handkerchief over his face and the thin wisps of hair on his head. "Ah, yes, Your Highness, at once." He withdrew through an inner door.

Demnor perched on the edge of his desk and glanced

down at the huge audience ledger. Amber DePaula, probably a land request. Megan DeFay and Barius DeYvonne, a reconciliation. The neighboring Viscounts' hatred for each other was well known, and only the Aristok could douse their rivalry for any length of time. The Marquis Jean-Pierre de LaRoche, Ambassador of Gallia. Demnor frowned. Trade maybe. That had been at ten. The Prince doubted he still lingered.

Klaudius returned and bowed once more. "The Aristok bids you enter, Your Royal Highness. She's in her office." He still acted as nervous as a hare facing a wolf, and at the back of Demnor's mind an alarm bell began to toll. He ignored it. The man had served three generations of DeMarian Aristoks. Who wouldn't be skittish? The Prince nodded his thanks and entered the waiting room.

The guards at the inner doors were ushering Katrina, the Aristok's Secretary, and her young apprentice—what was his name?—Gilbraith, out when Demnor entered. They bowed low. The woman's face was a mask. The boy looked frightened. Demnor nodded and pushed past them. His hand on the door, violent misgivings suddenly made his stomach twist in nausea. He hesitated. Maybe this was the wrong time? Maybe he should request a formal audience or send his Herald? He shook himself. It was too late. She was expecting him. Schooling his features to an expression of respect, he entered.

The Aristok was seated at her desk, the top laden with documents and scrolls. She'd put aside her formal cloak and circlet and was dressed for work, her long copper braids wrapped about her head and her tunic sleeves rolled up.

At the sight of her, Demnor's heart began to pound painfully in his chest. Emotions he didn't have time for chased themselves around inside him. Even with her regalia put aside, the aura of power that surrounded her was as strong as ever and all his misgivings returned to labor his breathing. She did not look up as he advanced and bowed.

He waited, the silence stretching out, his nervousness increasing. Finally he saw her shoulders tense.

"What, by the Flame, do you want?" she snapped, and all his carefully planned words left in a rush.

He chewed at his lip uncertainly, then blurted out. "I want a Companion."

That got her attention. The blazing green eyes rose from her paperwork to fix on him. "Tired of the kitchen maids, are we?"

A rush of chill air went through him. She was in a vile temper. So that was why everyone danced on ice today. He should have seen it. He should withdraw. But he'd given Kelahnus his word, so he pushed past the lump of fear and tried reason.

"I'm sixteen, Majesty. Many of the nobility my age have Companions."

"So get a dog." Her voice was dangerously low. "I'm busy, boy, and your wanting a bedmate is hardly important. Get out."

She didn't understand. It wasn't that petty. Did she really think him so shallow? The words stung his pride and his sense of honor and that brought up the old ache of unworthiness. He had to make her see that she was wrong. To leave now would be to admit to her beliefs about him. This was an honorable request. She had to be made to understand this.

"But, Majesty," he began.

"I said get out!" Her hand slammed down on the desk. "We may be at war, and I have no interest in your wish to fill your bed with some painted, overpriced whore. Do you hear me, boy? You'll get a Companion or not when I decide, not before." Her eyes narrowed. "Why this sudden desire?" she asked suspiciously. "I was given to understand you cared only for the sword."

Unprepared, the soft question caught him off guard. He stammered, "I've met someone."

As soon as he spoke, he knew it was the wrong answer. The weeks of lovely haziness burned away like the dawn mist, leaving him shaken and cold. Had he really marched in here believing she would allow him someone's friendship merely because he asked for it? He was a fool.

The Aristok regarded him with a reptilian stare.

"Where?"

It was over. There was nothing for it but to answer and hope that this victory would satisfy her, hope that she wouldn't ask who? "At the School of Companions, Your Majesty," he answered hoarsely, fighting to keep his tone even.

"Oh? And when were you there?"

"With yourself, Majesty, and the Earl of Cambury some weeks ago."

"Some weeks ago? You take some weeks to make up your mind, then interrupt my work with no audience to demand that I give you this person. Who is it?"

The flames in her eyes burned into his, and he felt his self-control waver.

"A student there, Majesty," he answered, teeth clenched.

"A student there, Majesty." She gave a harsh laugh, mocking his feeble attempt to keep the youth's name from her. They both knew he was one question away from revealing it. Triumphant in victory, the Aristok leaned back with a humorless smile. "No."

No.

"But, Majesty,"

"I said no. The subject is closed. The only answer that has any bearing on the discussion now is, 'Yes, Majesty.' "

The years of training nearly voiced the words for him, but he caught them on the edge of utterance. He was a DeMarian, and he had given his word. He must have her consent. Desperate now, he used the only argument that offered him any hope. It might enrage her, but at least she might listen before she had him thrown out.

"Most Holy Majesty, Vessel of the Living Flame," he began formally. "I, a Knight of the Sword and your sworn liege man, do beg the boon of an audience on a matter of honor."

She could refuse him. It was her right. But she was the Leader of the Faith, and his request took the interview into the bounds of religion and called upon her oaths of holy patronage.

Melesandra eyed him with malice, but she nodded. "Well, then, My Lord Duke of Briery, my knights kneel before their Aristok."

The room went ominously quiet. The contest of wills had begun. He knew this game. He had lost it often enough, but this time she would not emerge victorious. Slowly, he went down on one knee, forcing his eyes to the floor.

"Your boon of an audience is granted, my Lord of Briery. Speak." The words were disdainful, daring him to challenge her, the Flame damped and unnecessary.

Ignoring the tone, Demnor cast urgently about for the words that would reflect her anger and make his need plain. A blurted comment would lose everything, but committed now, he found to his horror, that his mind was a complete blank. Panic threatened to overwhelm him. He fought it down and took his fluttering senses firmly in hand. "I did not intend my words as a demand, Most Holy. If they seemed so, then I beg your forgiveness."

The words made him feel ill, the portion of Flame within his own breast restless behind his self-control, but he forced himself to continue. "I have given him my word, Most Holy. I see now it was rash and premature, but . . . please, aid me in this."

My word, Mother. Please, don't you see? My word, my honor is tied up in this. Please respect that.

The Aristok did not speak for some time. Demnor did not look up. The die was cast. He had done the unimaginable. He had asked for her help. Now all he could do was wait.

When she spoke, her voice was like ash. "Well, that was stupid of you, wasn't it?"

The words snapped his head up, and he met her eyes. All he saw there was contempt.

Melesandra leaned forward. "Yes, stupid!" she

repeated and the red-green fire blazed. "What have all these years of training been for, the years of work, of time I've given you? What have they been for? For you to give your word of honor to some painted whore? You're no better than your Uncle Amedeus! Weak! Stupid and weak!"

He had never seen her this angry before, her face dark with hatred. Rising, she stood over him, fists raised and he flinched before the madness in her eyes.

"Well, I'll tell you this, boy," she hissed, flecking spittle across his face. "Your ill-judgment got you into this mess and you can burning well wallow in it! And the next time you think to give your word so rashly, maybe you'll consider the consequences of breaking it!"

He stared at her in horror. She couldn't force him to do that. This went far beyond Kelahnus, far beyond their love. Everything he was was tied up in this, everything. Any authority he held, and rank, was useless, was false, if she denied him now. This wasn't a matter of pride, of will between them. This was a matter of honor. And she was going to smash that asunder just to prove to him that she could.

No. The dam broke as a flood of red-gray fire rushed over him. She had beaten him, she had humiliated him and terrified him. She had forced him to become as hard and empty as a statue. She had made him drive away his friends and stand alone against the world, to revel in killing and run from healing. But this he would not accept. This would destroy him.

Above him, the Aristok continued to rave. "You will not have this whore! Not ever! You will learn this lesson and be the stronger for it!"

No. If his word was broken, he was nothing. Then he was truly unworthy of the crown. The red tide of anger began to beat at his defenses, forced upward by the pressure of her attack.

"The Aristok must stand alone in heart and in soul and may not be weakened by sentiment and desire. Only then are you strong enough to rule!"

Her power crackled across the room, covering everything in a red and greenish haze. Slowly the air around
her son grew hot as his own heritage rose up to meet it.

*No. You have four Companions, five children, count-
less advisers. Are you alone?* The Flame built, formed,
drove one heated shaft of power past his control, then
froze, absorbed into a defensive wall as strong as stone.
He stood.

"No."

The quiet word shocked her into silence. She stared
at him, the rage frozen in her eyes, and only then did
Demnor realize that he stood above her. Melesandra
was tall. A tall woman, strengthened by war, who rode
armored into battle. Demnor, her son, was also tall. At
sixteen, he topped six feet by three inches and Captain
Fletcher believed he would be taller still. The knowledge added strength to his defenses and he felt himself
calm. *No.*

"I will not break my word."

The fury rose again to the Aristok's face, but when
she spoke, her words were as ominously calm as her
son's. "And I order you to do so. Everything you are,
you are under my suffrage. I made you. I can break
you. There are others more suitable than you to take
the throne."

There it was, her final threat. If he did not submit to
her demands, she would cast him aside, execute him,
for that was the only way the Flame would pass, and
take Quindara as her heir.

His pride, his desire for the throne, honed by sixteen
years of preparation, screamed in the trap she had
sprung, but his heart remained untouched, the Flame
undisturbed. What was the throne without honor?
Shadow. "No." He faced her proudly now, the fear
defeated by the conviction of his decision.

The Aristok smiled faintly. "You will break it, one
way or another. I give you a Royal command, My
Prince of Gwyneth. To disobey me in this is treason.
You will be forsworn in every oath you've ever held,
because they are all sworn to me. What will it be, My

Lord of Briery, Knight of my Faith, Duke of my Realm, will you break your word to this childish whore, or to your Sovereign?"

The tendrils of her words drove their way through his resolve, and inside he began to shake uncontrollably. She would do it. He knew she would. She never bluffed. But neither did he. He stared into her face, unable to believe· that she could hate him that much. Where had it come from—this implacable enmity? What had he ever done to deserve it?

The Aristok smiled again. "You are silent. So you realize the seriousness of your crime. And yet you begged a boon of me as one of my Elite, and for that I will give you this. You will tell me this boy's name. I will send to Master Klairius demanding his dismissal. You will reswear your private oaths to me and we will consider this matter closed."

Demnor was unable to control the fit of shaking now. His head reeled with her demands. Dismiss Kelahnus? He couldn't let that happen. But—treason. The word made him physically ill. Dishonor, the throne in Quindara's hands. But Kelahnus. Aghast, he looked up and saw triumph in his mother's eyes. The Flame lapped against his mind, wild still, but waiting now in obedience to his will. *No*. He met her gaze.

"That I cannot do, Majesty. He is under my protection." He would not let her blacken Kelahnus' life, too. "If I have erred, it is my error, not his. He should not be made to suffer for it."

"He should not be made to suffer for it," she mimicked. "If I say he shall, he shall. Do you dare thwart me? Name him!"

"I cannot!"

"By the Faith, you can!" Her voice was rising again. "And you'd better! Disobey my wishes and you'll regret it, I promise you! Now I want your obedience this instant, or I'll declare you outlaw and every hand in the Realm will be turned against you! Choose!"

Demnor felt the cool touch of pure rage fill him. Threaten him, bully him, babble nonsense at him. It stopped here. He let the anger rise up and cover him in an armor of righteous fury.

"If I break my word, I am not worthy to rule!"

"You are not worthy now! Disobey me, and you break your oath of fealty!"

"You're forcing me to it! All I asked was that you back my word of honor! But you will say no out of spite. Out of hate! You dishonor me!"

"ENOUGH!"

They were standing within inches of each other, faces and limbs contorted with madness. Demnor checked at the harshly spat word, and Melesandra's eyes glittered with malevolence.

"You will not take that tone of voice with me," she said, her words threateningly low. She was once more the ruler, and his years of discipline kept him silent while the rage dissolved before its control. "I am your Sovereign. You will remain civil or I'll have you taught how to be." She turned and strode back to her desk and sat down. "You will submit to me, one way or another. Guards!"

The two Royal Guards, hovering outside the door, obviously uncertain of whether they should have broken in by now, thundered into the room. They crashed to attention two paces behind the Prince. Uncertainly flickered across the face of the younger.

The Aristok leaned back. "You are to escort His Royal Highness to his chambers. He is not to leave until I send for him."

"Majesty!"

Her gaze returned to her son, all traces of anger smoothed away. "You will remain there until you have recovered your senses. I will have this boy's name, either from you or from other sources. This will be your only opportunity for absolution. Don't waste it. If you do, I'll have you disowned and you know what that means."

The Guards' shock was palpable, and Demnor's hatred for her blazed because he knew it would be all over the palace in an hour. He glared at her, pride

refusing to allow him to submit to this final indignity
in silence. Let the palace have another morsel to chew
on. "If you harm him," he grated, "I'll save you the
trouble. I'll abdicate." It would mean his death, but one
self-chosen and not inflicted.

They locked eyes with a measured stare, the Flame
sheathed and unnecessary. They were committed. Both
knew now where the battle lines were drawn and what
was at stake. Then the Aristok nodded to her Guard and
Demnor was escorted from her presence.

The crash of spear butts against marble brought him
forcibly back to the present. He stood before the two
Palace Guards who held the door to the Royal wing.
Silently they moved out of his way, features woodenly
expressionless. Demnor made his own face match
theirs. He had ridden to war a dozen times, faced death
and dismemberment and not faltered. He had never
shown fear in the face of an enemy before and he
would not do so now in the face of the Aristok. Whatever they thought, the Palace Guard would not think
him a coward. But then, they never had, not even in
that summer of 886.

He thrust the memories aside. This time it was different. This time he asked for something she wanted
and he didn't. Her only victory was that he had to ask,
and that was an old bone. The Guards held the door
open, and he stepped over the threshold and into the
Aristok's anteroom.

It was much the same with one exception. Klaudius
had died in the interim, leaving his post to his son,
Peerik. Demnor thought no more of the new clerk than
he had of the old.

The man was waiting inside, looking pale and
nervous. He bowed deeply as Demnor entered, then
scuttled past the Royal Guard and through the door to
the Aristok's private audience hall. The Prince was left
on his own to wait.

His gaze swept the room. A gold leaf table held a
decanter and one goblet, both of elegantly cut crystal.

Rainbows danced across their surfaces as Demnor
lifted the decanter and sniffed. Cider. Knowing his
aversion for alcohol, someone had replaced the wine
usually served to waiting guests. He couldn't imagine
who that might have been, a servant, probably. He
poured himself a goblet and continued his inspection of
the room.

To his left was a dark blue divan, the wood stained a
deep, reddish brown. It faced a huge portrait on the far
wall of the Aristok at her coronation. Painted by
Harold of Daedlesburg at the height of his skill, it was
not a portrait he wished to face. Melesandra had been
twenty-five, one year older than the Crown Prince, but
the artist had captured the fanatical will she'd possessed even then. The red-green fire burned in her
eyes, reaching out to pierce his thoughts. Demnor
turned away.

To one side of the entrance sat a large urn enameled
in bright yellow and white. Tiny, multihued fish swam
between waving plants that had been carefully placed
in the sand at the bottom. Demnor stared down at it for
a time, watching their movements cut tiny ripples
across his reflection. It mirrored back at him the naked
fear in his eyes and he turned away with a scowl. The
Guards at the door stood as still as statues, staring
straight ahead. Peerik chose that moment to return.

He bowed apprehensively.

Demnor glared at him. "Well?"

"The Aristok bids you enter, Your Royal Highness,"
the man announced hesitantly, holding the door open.

His face set, the Prince moved past him.

Melesandra sat on a small carved throne, set on a
two-step dais. The platform widened at the base for
advisers and courtiers to hover near at hand when she
gave audiences. Demnor himself had stood there on
occasions that merited a show of Royal solidarity. He'd
felt no more comfortable than he did now. No one
stood there this day, no Chamberlain, no Generals, no
Companions. This was a private audience between
Ruler and Prince.

The Aristok's face was stone as the Crown Prince marched to within nine paces and bowed.

She regarded him silently. Attempting to control his breathing, suddenly ragged, Demnor stared past her shoulder to the brilliant flag of Branion.

The silence stretched. Finally, he dropped his gaze and met her eyes. The Aristok regarded him regally, the faintest smile touched her lips. She knew the war he fought. She'd forged the weapons each side carried. Suddenly he felt very tired, but he kept his face expressionless. He could wait.

"My Lord Defender." Her tone was flat, a statement, not a greeting.

"Your Majesty." He matched it.

"You requested an audience?" Her tone was bored, although her eyes watched his face with a predatory gleam.

"Yes, Majesty. It is my duty to request your permission to marry." There it was done. It was said. The hammering of his heart subsided a little. Deep down a voice dared her, *Say no, go on, say no.*

The Aristok merely raised one copper eyebrow. "To whom?"

A milkmaid, a servant, a Gallian He hated this game. She knew flaming well to whom, but he kept his face blank as he answered. "The Earl of Essendale, Lord Isolde DeKathrine, Majesty." *Mother.*

"I see. Is that all?" Her tone was disinterested.

"Yes, Majesty."

She inclined her head. "Our permission is granted."

He bowed once more, dismissed. That was all there ever would be. He left.

The polished wooden door was warm to his touch and he pushed it open gently. Avoiding the loose stone beyond the threshold, he stepped into his tiny, private chapel and closed the door. Comforting darkness enfolded him.

Taking a moment for his eyes to adjust, he crossed the room and genuflected before the altar. The single candle, placed in the center of the white silk altar cloth, flickered in the draft caused by his movement. He stared into its light for a moment, letting its warmth reach out and touch its twin, mirrored in his gaze, then rose and walked quietly to the back and sat. Resting his arms on the pew before him, he laid his head on his hands and closed his eyes.

By the Faith, he was tired. His jaw ached like an old wound in the rain. But at least it was over. Now he could rest.

The faint traces of the morning's incense were a balm on his jangled nerves as he half dozed. He should get back. Kelahnus would be waiting, would be worried. But he couldn't face him yet. Shoving one arm under his head, he laid his undamaged cheek on the cool metal of his vambrace.

The walk back to the west wing had been made in a barely remembered fog. Guards and servants had bowed, come to attention, or scurried away. He didn't need to see their faces to know what they were thinking. The whole palace knew of the struggle between the Aristok and the Heir, had known of it since the beginning; the day when he was sixteen and he'd first risen up to challenge her power over him.

The memories had been nagging at him all week, poking sharp little needles into him whenever he'd tried to relax. They wouldn't be satisfied until they forced him to relive them again and again, for as long as he lived. Some memories were like that. They ruled your life whether you willed it or not, and the only way to banish them was to let them have their head until they tired. At least, that was what his uncle had told him so many years ago. And today he was far too tired to fight. He closed his eyes once more and remembered.

The decision had been made within seconds of entering his suite. Kelahnus was in danger. He had to go to him. Except he would be seen in daylight. He would have to wait until dark. Seething, he paced the room, barely hearing his Guards exchanged with ill grace for those of the Aristok.

He crossed to the other side of the room. Kelahnus was in danger. He should send someone, send a message, but how? He could summon a servant to fetch wine or food and then take a message, but that would mean requesting it of the Guards outside. His pride would not allow him to do that. He chewed anxiously at his lower lip. Was pride more important than Kelahnus? Burn it, he had to do something.

An hour passed, his impatience driving him to his feet every time he sat down. Now he stood, staring morosely out over the gardens, his mind blank. To leave would stir up coals already about to burst into flames, but the longer he waited, the greater the chance that the student would be discovered. He considered and discarded a dozen ways of warning him. They all depended on him breaking his imprisonment and that truly would be disobeying a Royal decree. The thought of the consequences made him shudder.

Slamming his fist on the metal balcony he derided himself for a coward. Kelahnus was in danger! He had to *do* something and if that meant breaking his confinement, then so be it.

There was a knock at the door. He whirled.

"Come."

A grubby six-year-old, sandy hair falling in his eyes, advanced into the room after carefully closing the door. He gave an awkward bow.

"What, Terence?"

" 'Cuse me, Yer Highness. I was sent ta see if you wants anything from th' kitchen, or anything else Yer Lordship kin think of." He checked a motion to wipe his nose on the sleeve of his ill-fitting gray tunic.

Demnor studied him. He'd given Terence to Ariston, not the kitchens, and scholar apprentices wore brown robes, not gray tunics. The boy gave him a sly look, and the Prince nodded.

"Come here."

Terence grinned and ambled over to receive his message and the coin Demnor pressed into his hand.

The scrape of a foot against stone snapped Demnor's head up, but it was only a young acolyte, come to trim the candlewick. The girl knelt reverently before the altar, unaware of the Prince seated in the darkness.

Slowly the memories let go their death grip on him in the wake of the familiar ritual. Even Demnor himself had performed that function when he was young. He shook himself. It was getting late. Kelahnus would be worried.

Waiting for the girl to leave, he firmly pushed away the past. It served no purpose to relive old pain. He had work to do. Making the sign of the Triarchy, he rose and left the comfort of the chapel.

Kelahnus was waiting in his study, flanked by his Secretary, his squire, and his Herald. The Companion held a wide piece of parchment, the marriage proposal, in one hand, a stick of sealing wax in the other. They had anticipated him and readied this task for him. All he had to do was seal it. Demnor met his Companion's eyes, and they both smiled a little sadly.

6. Isolde

The Lord Isolde DeKathrine, Earl of Essendale, sat on a stone bench in one of the south wing conservatories. The cloudy sky cast a strange, translucent glow through the glass, tinted green from the surrounding flora. Idly, Isolde traced the leaf pattern on the edge of the bench. If she closed her eyes she could almost imagine herself at home amidst the quiet, growing things of her own conservatory; sitting, watching a storm coming in, and thinking.

At home, she would then have taken her horse and ridden for hours alone with the sky and the rain. She might go out later, but for now she was content to sit and watch the darkening sky fill the conservatory with shadows. At her feet, Tania, her young Companion, played a quiet tune on the mandolin, every now and then resting her head against Isolde's knee. It was an almost perfect afternoon. Almost, except for her brother.

Alerion had broken into her solitude some moments ago, growling curses about the Prince Demnor and stomping about like an angry bear. Isolde had listened for a while and then ignored him. It was nothing she hadn't heard a dozen times before.

Running her fingers through the other woman's dark curls, she mulled over a different problem. Whether it would be better to wear Quinton the Second's Consort, Evelynne DeKathrine's wedding regalia, or have her own commissioned. It was a decision she'd put off until after she and her tailor'd had a chance to study it. Preferring a simpler style, if she could get the design she wanted clear in her mind she could speak to Carrie today, but Ler *would* go on distracting her. With a sigh, the Earl of Essendale brought her attention back to her brother.

Alerion was pacing in front of her, his broad face twisted in annoyance. "Burn him," he grated. "How long does he expect us to swallow this insult." He turned, saw that she was finally listening, and stopped. "Why are you taking this so calmly?" he demanded. "Aren't you aware of what people are saying?"

Unconcerned, Isolde glanced down at her Companion. "Tania, play 'The Whisper in the Wood.'" Humming along with the first few bars, she smiled and then turned back to Alerion. "I'm not the least bit interested in what people are saying."

Her brother opened and closed his mouth a few times, his face going red. Finally he sputtered, "Don't you care how this affects the family's reputation? The official inquiry was answered over a year ago!"

Isolde laughed. "Our reputation will survive. The Heir is a boor, but his Companion is not. I expect to receive the final proposal quite soon now. I wonder if I shall accept it." Playing idly with the green tassels on her sleeve, she looked up at him from beneath her lashes.

Alerion began a protest, but on seeing that she was teasing him, cut it off abruptly, feeling the fool. Breathing heavily, he threw himself down on the bench beside her.

Isolde patted his hand, unable to resist teasing him again. "Don't worry, Ler, you'll find some way to punish him for his horrid behavior and then everything will be well between you again."

He jumped up angrily. "There's no need to be insulting. I can handle my own friendships, thank you. I'm simply concerned for the family!"

"Then have no fear. The family has never been

stronger. Now come, sit beside me again and stop worrying."

She smiled up at him and he felt the anger melt before the warmth of her gaze. With a sour smile, he returned to his seat.

"He doesn't deserve you."

"Thank you. But we shall get along fine, he and I, you'll see."

"I'm sure. I almost feel sorry for him."

"Do you? Poor Ler." She rested her hand on his arm. "You're so much alike, you two. You need a war, both of you, so you can ride off, feeling brave and useful, and pound out this estrangement between you. No, I mean it." With a touch to his lips, she silenced his newest protest.

"Men like you are never quite comfortable unless your problems and their solutions are clear and simple. There are your enemies, and there are their armies. If you can but defeat them, your problems are solved."

"You've fought in your share of battles," he reminded her stiffly.

"Yes. The difference is that I can find something to do with myself in peacetime."

"Someone has to protect the Realm."

"Of course, dear, but someone has to run it, too. Leave that part for me to play. You'll only muddle about and get your sword caught in the curtains."

With an elaborate sigh, Alerion rubbed at his temples before asking querulously, "Why is it that your comfort so often ends in an insult?"

Isolde laughed. "To keep you on your toes, dear brother, and teach you not to take me for granted. Now, if you don't mind . . ."

Her gaze shifted past him, and he turned.

A young woman in the livery of a DeMarian Herald advanced through the conservatory, weaving gracefully between the plants and flowers. She bore Demnor's personal device on her sleeve and carried a thick scroll under one arm. Approaching the two

DeKathrines, she bowed and, dropping fluidly to one knee, held out the document.

Isolde smiled. "Yes?"

"My Most Noble Lord, it is my duty to bring you this proposal of marriage from His Highness, the Lord Demnor, Prince of Gwyneth. It is his request and hope that you will accept this union in keeping with the customs of the Royal line. He offers it sealed with his own crest and witnessed by one of the College of Heralds as proof of his intent, this twelfth day of Mean Fhomhair, eight hundred and ninety-three."

With an air of supreme dignity, Isolde accepted the scroll from the kneeling Herald. "I thank you, ah . . . ?"

"Robinarden, My Lord Earl."

"Robinarden. Your arrival has caught me somewhat off guard and at a loss for words. If you would do me the kindness of retiring for a time to allow me to gather my scattered wits, I shall oblige you with an answer to His Highness."

"Of course, My Lord."

"Tania?"

The Companion looked up at her name, laying the mandolin down beside her.

"Perhaps you might escort our most honored Herald to a place where she may wait more comfortably and partake of some refreshment."

"As you wish, My Lord." The woman rose languidly and bowed. Together, she and the Herald left the conservatory. As they passed through the doorway, the Companion whispered something in the other woman's ear and Robinarden chuckled.

With a sigh of contentment, Isolde cradled the document loosely in one arm and glanced up at her brother through her lashes. He returned her smug look with one of grudging admiration.

"Well, Most Fair, now that you've won our argument, and proved you can magic what you wish out of thin air, will you grant a humble petitioner the friend you think he wants and the advice you think he needs?"

Isolde chose to ignore his mocking tones. "Of

course, my dear brother," she murmured. "All in good time."

The marriage proposal was accepted, sealed, and returned within the hour and the official announcement made the next morning on the north balcony. As was customary, Demnor and his new Consort-to-be threw silver to the crowd, who cheered the more vehemently for it. Street Seers predicted wealth and prosperity to come and pickpockets realized it as the crowd jostled to get a look at their future ruler and his betrothed. And if the Heir's countenance was bleak, few remarked on it. It was, after all, the Heir's usual appearance. The Court Artist made the rapid sketches that would form the basis for his painting of the event and the Heralds sent messengers out across the land with the news. The people cheered and shouted for speeches and were only driven back to their homes and businesses by the drops of rain that quickly grew to a major downpour.

Demnor and Isolde returned through the balcony's crystal doors, and parted with few words. The Earl swept off to meet with her tailor and the Prince escaped to the quiet of his study. He wanted a few minutes to compose himself before facing anyone in his new capacity.

Kelahnus was waiting for him. Settling into one of the study's comfortable, stuffed chairs, he steepled his fingers.

After dropping into another chair before the fireplace, Demnor closed his eyes. They sat in silence for a time until finally the Prince looked at his Companion.

"What?"

"I beg your pardon?"

"You've got your innocent face on, the one you wear when you're about to bring up a subject I don't want to talk about."

"I'm sure I don't know what you mean, but if you're asking for my thoughts, I was wondering when you're going to begin your Progress?"

"What Progress?"

"Your Betrothal Progress. The one you and the Lord Isolde are now going to take across the country to show yourselves to the populace."

"Why?"

Kelahnus gave an exaggerated sigh. "It's tradition. It helps bind the country together. It gives Royalty the excuse to exercise a bit of muscle, the nobility the excuse to show how loyal they are, and the rest of us the excuse for a party. Besides, a jaunt in the country will do you good. You're looking pale."

Demnor rubbed his eyes irritably. Kelahnus always did this to him; dropped concern into the middle of a discussion, and it never failed to catch him off guard. Biting back the retort he might have made, he gestured resignedly for the Companion to continue.

Kelahnus accepted the acquiescence with an easy smile. "I thought north. It's not too cold yet. Leiston, Linconford, Yorbourne, then up through maybe Castldown or Carisley, with the smaller towns on route, then back. It would take some weeks, but you should be home by Calan Gaeaf. It would be the first excursion you've taken since your tour of Gwyneth."

"What's wrong *with* Gwyneth, then?"

"You've been there. You haven't been north."

"I was north four years ago."

"With an army. It doesn't count."

"Why not Kraburn?"

"Kraburn is south. And you've been there, too. You're just being difficult."

Demnor sighed. "Fine," he said tightly. "North. But not Yorbourne."

Rubbing one finger along the bridge of his nose, Kelahnus considered it. "It might not seem appropriate."

"It will be expected and save both Quindara and myself from an awkward visit," the Heir retorted.

"As you wish. Not Yorbourne. Grimscombe, then."

"Braxborough."

"Braxborough! That's in Heathland!"

"What of it?"

"It's not safe, for one thing!"

"Nonsense. It's a fortified city."

"Exactly, fortified against its own citizens."

"All four Militant Orders have chapterhouses in Braxborough. It's as safe as Branbridge. Besides, it's the northern capital. If I don't go, it will look like I'm afraid."

The Companion shook his head. His first reaction was to caustically suggest the Heir visit the Gallian border provinces, then, but in this mood Demnor just might agree. Far better to simply accept his decision and hope that someone else, like the Hierarchpriest, would throw a fit and the Aristok would forbid it.

"If you insist. Grimscombe, then Braxborough?"

"Fine."

That settled, the Companion rose, and coming around behind the Prince, began to work the stiffness from his shoulders. "Hungry?"

"No." Despite himself, Demnor felt his muscles relax and he closed his eyes. "Playing Princeling always dulls my appetite. But I am restless."

"Well, why don't we go riding, then? Shake some of the ill-temper out."

The Prince's eyes snapped open in surprise. "It's raining, Kelahnus. I thought you hated the rain."

"I do, but you need to get out. And I suppose I won't melt away, or drown ..." He shuddered. "... too much. Call it a peace offering."

The Heir was silent for a moment. The Companion's cologne twitched at his nostrils and strands of his hair tickled at his neck. The urge to touch him was strong and he gave in to it, resting his hands on the younger man's.

As usual, he marveled at their softness. Kelahnus had fine, slender hands, but Demnor had seen him crack a walnut shell with two fingers. He was an enigma. As sensual and indolent as any courtesan and yet as deadly as an assassin. From the safety of an upper window, the Prince had watched him train with Florence one afternoon. The contortions they'd gone through had made his own muscles creak in protest. They were far more than they seemed and yet, in private, in bed, Kelahnus was once again the beautiful, young student who'd captured his heart.

Demnor closed his eyes again. By the Faith, he loved this man so much it made his chest ache, but the words stuck in his throat every time he tried to say them.

"You're not the one who should be making peace offerings," he said softly. "No riding. Why don't we walk the galleries? The north ones should be empty."

Kelahnus smiled, accepting the gift at face value, pleased that he wouldn't have to catch his death in the name of love. "Is this an urge for art or for history?"

"For advice. I want to consult an ancestor."

The Companion nodded. The greatest of the north galleries held the collection of pieces depicting the life of Atreus the Third, Aristok two centuries previous.

"The Bastard?" he asked. "His statue stands in Collin's Park."

"I'd rather see him face-to-face. Canvas is warmer than stone."

"It is that." Kelahnus relaxed slightly. That Demnor would be reasonable about his betrothal had been more than he'd hoped for.

He laughed suddenly, relieved that the storm had been avoided and pleased at Demnor's remark about warmth. It was a good sign. He decided to see how far it went.

"You can't get out of it, you know," he teased. "Marriage has been legal for over a century. He won't be able to offer you any strategy."

"No, but it will give some comfort. As will . . . your company."

The Heir was not looking at the younger man as he spoke. If he had, he would have seen Kelahnus' face soften and take on an expression of sad longing. But the Companion quickly pulled himself together and rose.

"Then let us go."

Demnor nodded, and with no further words they left his study.

His Guards were posted at the gallery doors with orders to bar the entrance, and for a time they walked together, playing at the peace neither of them had.

That afternoon Demnor's personal Herald was sent to the Aristok requesting permission for the Crown Prince to leave the capital on Progress with his Consort-to-be.

Melesandra's reply was brief. She would consult with the Archpriest of the Flame before giving her answer. Demnor accepted this response with a disinterested shrug.

Word of the Progress soon filtered through the palace. When Atreus and Marsellus heard the news they immediately sought out their elder brother to urge him to rethink his travel plans. They found him in the aerie with Captain Fletcher and, after some argument, convinced him to retire to his study to hear them out.

His response was curt.

"I don't run from prophecies," he said bluntly, eyeing his younger brothers with displeasure.

Marsellus looked away, but Atreus met Demnor's frown with one of his own. "We're not asking you to run," he said. "We're asking you to reconsider a possibly dangerous and unnecessary course of action."

"It's the same thing."

"No, it's not. It's using foreknowledge to anticipate the future and then changing it."

"And if the future cannot be changed, it's simply delaying Fate. Better to meet the future face-to-face, than have it sneak up on you when you're not expecting it."

It was an old, theological argument. Some maintained that if enough forces were arrayed in the same direction, the future could not be changed. Others believed that the future was malleable, every uncharted action causing a new future to be instantly created. The Royal Seers were of the latter belief. Demnor was of the former—at least during this argument.

Atreus threw up his hands and Marsellus took over.

"We have drunk from the Potion of Truth," he said, ignoring Demnor's surprised expression. "The future is filled with danger, for you and for the Realm. We have Seen it. Why won't you listen?" His voice was strained with worry and with the effects of the prophetic drug. Demnor knew what his younger brother had risked in taking the Sight-enhancing infusion and, with a sigh, he took a seat.

"All right, Mars," he said. "I'm listening."

The quieter of the twins took a deep breath. "I saw fire covering the world. You were at the center of that fire. You weren't here, and you need to be here. I *know* it, I have *Seen* it. *Don't go.*"

His eyes were wild and Demnor raised one hand to forestall another outburst. After a moment, Marsellus dropped his gaze, his mouth set in a tight line.

"My itinerary is already before the Aristok," the Heir said evenly. "If she approves it, I'm going, Mars. I *have* to go."

"Why?"

Demnor rubbed irritably at the barely healed wounds on his jaw. They were starting to ache, a sure sign that he was grinding his teeth. "Because this Progress is necessary to cement the goodwill of the DeKathrines—" Seated to one side, Kelahnus' brows rose, and even Demnor's expression suggested he didn't think much of that reason. "—and to bring the country together on the eve of war. But more importantly, because I won't run from the future. It's cowardly. And that's the last word I'll entertain on the subject," he added as Marsellus made to speak.

The twins exchanged a look, but did not pursue the argument.

"Will you at least take care while you're there and not do anything reckless?" Atreus asked finally.

With gritted teeth, Demnor nodded. "Yes," he answered stiffly.

"That's all we ask."

Marsellus opened his mouth to protest but Atreus placed a restraining hand on his arm. "That's all we *can* ask, Mars. And maybe the Aristok will veto Braxborough, anyway," he added under his breath.

"Don't count on it," Demnor said.

Later, after the twins had reluctantly departed, Kelahnus glanced over at his Lord, an amused and exasperated expression on his face.

Demnor returned the look with a frown. "What?"

"I was just wondering," the Companion mused, "if someone told you not to jump off Bran's Bridge, would you jump?"

Biting back his initial response, Demnor smiled, recognizing the humor in his sudden switch from refusing the progress to defending it. "I suppose that would depend on who said it," he answered.

Kelahnus just shook his head.

Later that evening as the palace readied itself for sleep, an old woman was ushered into the private chapel of the Living Flame. The Shield Knight who helped her over the sill accepted the blessing of the Realm's most powerful Seer, then closed the door softly behind her. Gwynne DeLlewellynne, Archpriest of the Flame, advanced on the fiery throne before the hearth. Kneeling, she kissed the outstretched ring, then seated herself with a groan on the stool indicated.

The Aristok regarded her with glittering eyes.

"Our most honored Archpriest."

"Most Holy."

"We have summoned you here to gain insight on our son's visit to our northern provinces. The Flame flickers," she placed one thin hand upon her breast, "and we would have an explanation for Its concern."

The Archpriest cracked one swollen knuckle as she nodded. "The Flame has been very active of late, Most Holy. Things are brewing in the future, huge and terrible things."

"Such as?"

Sinking to the floor, the old woman stared past the throne to the yew fire crackling in the hearth.

"I have drunk from the Potion of Truth, and the prophecy will do your bidding. Ask."

Melesandra leaned forward, speaking the ritual words. "Tell me, Seer, what do you see?"

"Fire," the old woman whispered, her eyes widening as the vision took hold of her mind. "Fire everywhere. The Flame covers the future. I can't . . . can't . . ."

Reaching out, the Aristok gripped the Archpriest's shoulder. The contact with her Avatar snapped the old woman's head back, the veins in her neck standing out in sharp relief. She choked, then spat out, "The Living Flame stands in the center of the maelstrom, waving a fiery sword. The dragon and the thistle battle it together, and as they fight, first one then the other grows stronger. I see the past raising a fortress in a vale of green meadows and the future hovering over another on a towering mountain. Their battlements point toward a field of fire." Her voice grew faint. "I see a many faceted gem, the color of blood, a flame burning deep within its core, balancing on the fulcrum of the future." Her eyes grew dark. "The Flame covers the future. I . . . I can see no more."

She sagged, and Melesandra knelt to catch her in her arms. After a moment the Archpriest raised her head.

"All the signs point to war, Most Holy, the Flame of Branion battling the combined strength of Essusiatism."

"And my son?"

"He is the gem that stands upon the fulcrum of the future."

The Aristok stared over the woman's gray head, her own eyes hooded. "This gem has appeared in the prophecy before as a flawed vessel."

"Yes, Most Holy."

"If this gem is my son, as I have suspected before, then my son is flawed."

"The flaw is the fulcrum, My Avatar, which will determine the future. The field upon which it rests is Heathland."

After a moment Melesandra nodded slowly. "We do

not run from prophecies, we face them, as does our son. He shall go to Braxborough and there meet the future as befits a Vessel of the Flame. If he fails, we may yet wrest victory from defeat with other Vessels trained to take the field. If the Flame covers the future, the Flame controls the future, and I am the Flame. We shall win."

The Aristok allowed her priest to lay her head against her breast. "You may rest here in Our Presence until you have recovered your strength, then return to Our Most Holy Order and tell them to prepare for war."

"Yes, My Avatar."

A week later the Royal Progress of the Prince of Gwyneth and his Consort-to-be clattered its way toward Timber Gate, Branbridge's most northwestern trade gate. Isolde threw roses to the cheering crowds along the route. Demnor threw money. It caused a minor riot, but eventually they escaped the city limits and turned onto the Linconford road.

Throughout the chaos of the preceding week Demnor had remained unusually calm. Having won his point about Braxborough, he was content to let others see to the particulars of the journey, and to his surprise, he found he was anxious for them to be on their way. They would be visiting Terion DePaula, the Earl of Linconford. Demnor hadn't seen his old friend since the fighting in Gallia two years ago. They would talk and relive old campaigns. Then he'd go to Heathland. A beautiful place of wild country and violent weather, this time he might actually get a chance to see it. He wasn't afraid of Marsellus' prediction of danger, rather he was looking forward to confronting it. And Kelahnus was right. Getting away from Branbridge would do him good, whatever the circumstances.

He accepted the Hierarchpriest's gift of ten Junior Knights of the Sword as escort with such good grace that he did much to soothe the still ruffled feathers of the DeKathrine family. The new Guard fit into the ranks of the Shield Knights, the traditional escort, with little maneuvering. The Earl of Essendale added three servants and four Fenish guards, and the Companions managed a mountain of luggage between them. All agreed it would be a most enjoyable journey.

Then the Prince caused a minor panic when he refused to go by carriage, thus committing the entire entourage to horseback. Several advisers, including his Secretary and Kelahnus, predicted dire consequences—namely brigands, demons, and torrential downpours. But the Heir was adamant. They would ride. The escorts were more philosophical. They would ride regardless. When the whole company finally formed in the north courtyard, they made a fine show of martial splendor before the Aristok, then made their way through the crowded streets and finally out into the autumn countryside.

The days passed pleasantly. The weather obliged with little rain and cool, clear skies and the small towns and hamlets they passed bedecked themselves in festive attire to honor their Crown Prince. Demnor heard cases and passed judgments; hanged a bandit in Barnlow, and pardoned another in Austindown. He spoke with the village elders, hearing their needs and concerns and watched the farmhands and youths show off their prowess with the bow or the quarterstaff. He took one fellow into his service immediately with barely a word to the boy's parents. Robin Miller found himself pushed into the ranks of His Highness' escort until he could be handed over to Captain Fletcher.

Slowly, the stiff set of the Prince's features eased.

Kelahnus, riding quietly behind, watched his Lord respond to his people's welcoming with a satisfied smile. The progress was accomplishing exactly what he'd hoped. Once free of the tensions of Court, Demnor had calmed and the charismatic charm he usually repressed slowly reasserted itself. Content to watch it unfold, the Companion eased himself into the background, spending his traveling time with Tania

and studying the Prince's growing friendship with the
Earl of Essendale.

Isolde, too, had relaxed once the formality of Branbridge had been left behind. Riding beside Demnor,
she stepped easily into the position of Consort, providing a smooth bridge between the Prince and his
more reticent subjects. She was as attentive to the
stumbled compliments of a farmer's daughter as she
was to the attempted flattery of a young nobleman
barely come into his title, and was gracious to all who
gathered to see them. Between them, Kelahnus and
Tania agreed that the Prince and the Earl would do.

Three weeks after they left Branbridge, they arrived
in the free city of Leiston. The south gate had been
thrown open and people lined the streets to the center
square. Many had been waiting since early morning
and the general state of inebriation added enthusiasm
to their greeting. A delegation of city elders met the
Royal Party on the steps of Leiston's town hall and, as
they rode up, the Mayor, a portly woman, came
bustling from the Green Boar Inn next door. She
bowed unsteadily. From her and the other elders' condition, Demnor assumed they'd spent most of the
morning inside. The Heir acknowledged her with a nod
and a short word of greeting. Beaming, the Mayor
threw her arms wide as if to embrace the Prince's
entire entourage.

"Welcome to Leiston, Your Most Royal Highness
and My Lord! We remain always your most devoted
servants! All the city lies at your command! You have
but to voice your desires, and we shall endeavor with all
the powers at our disposal to see that your visit, however long or short as Your Highness deems fitting, shall
be as pleasant as humanly possible and one that, we
pray, shall remember us kindly in Your Highness'
memory as your most humble . . ."

The was a great deal more of this, with each of the
City Council waxing poetic in their loyalty. Demnor
blotted it out after the first. Years ago, he'd learned the

art of seeming to be sternly attentive while sleeping.
The afternoon wore on.

Finally the Mayor made a grand gesture, and a
young page dressed in the livery of the city of Leiston,
stepped forward. She held two large brass keys on a red
satin cushion and, stretching to full height, she presented them to the Prince. Demnor received them
solemnly, tucked them into his belt, and left her the
customary silver piece in their place. With a bow, she
stood aside, her young face aglow, while the Mayor
made another speech.

Eventually, it was over. Mounted on a snowy white
gelding, the Mayor led the Royal Party up Highgate
Street to her own manor house and they were able to
escape the crowds for a time.

Meanwhile, the town celebrated as if a major victory
had just been won. Jugglers, tumblers, and musicians
competed at every corner with Street Seers, wine
sellers and prostitutes. The poor bedecked themselves
in whatever bright clothes they could find or steal and
the wealthy strutted through the streets in their gaudi-
est festival finery. Anyone who could claim even the
most remote connection to a high noble family wore
the appropriate colors. Several duels and brawls broke
out over this, the crowds either moving around the
combatants, joining in, or cheerfully harassing the
Town Watch on their way to the scene.

Outside the manor gate, a number of entertainers had
gathered, hoping to catch a Royal eye. One young minstrel, after slipping into the gardens, roamed confi-
dently down the flagstoned paths until he caught sight
of the Earl of Essendale taking the air on the balcony to
her suite. Unslinging his harp, he began a long, sweet
ballad to her beauty.

Having soaked the dust away in a hot bath, Isolde
was feeling invigorated and she listened, amused, to
the young man's words. The tune was an old one,
although the lyrics were new. She could only assume
he was making them up as he went along. She
applauded his abilities, and threw him a purse just

before she called the Guard. He was firmly escorted to the gate, where he bowed low, much to the amusement of his fellow musicians.

Isolde returned to the balcony, and a few minutes later Tania joined her there. The two women stood in silence for a time, then the Companion leaned over and plucked a tiny white flower growing amidst the ivy. Weaving it through her hair, she smiled.

"A pretty young man."

"Hm."

"I wonder if he dances as well as he sings."

The sounds of the town's merriment filtered up to them and Isolde raised one eyebrow at her Companion, curious as to which form of dancing she referred to.

"Is that all you ever think about?"

Tania laughed. "Not at all, My Gracious Lord, but beauty is such a fleeting thing, it should be appreciated when it presents itself." She turned. "Shall I brush your hair?"

"Please."

The Companion withdrew, returning a moment later with a brush and a bottle of perfume. Isolde seated herself on an iron bench while Tania scented the brush, then began to work it into the mass of golden curls. The Earl's gaze moved slowly about the garden, taking note of the strategic positions of the walls and topiary.

"What have you heard about the night's festivities, Tania?"

"Well, there's to be a banquet, of course," the Companion began as she parted her Lord's hair into two great plaits. "It should include the Mayor; there's no gossip about her, she's just as she seems, foolish and prone to drink; her husband, equally foolish; her two daughters, Gwendolynne and Terlynne; the one is a fair hand with a bow and the other serves as the Mayor's messenger; and her son, who has a tendency to throw food, so he'll likely be seated well out of range."

The two women laughed.

"How old is he?"

"Just over a year, and his parents adore him."

"Sweet. Who else will be there?"

"The City Chamberlain. A woman named Lasalle Gilies. She runs the city in fact though the Mayor holds title. She was a weaver by trade before this appointment and her name still heads the Guild List. She has no particular connections outside Leiston, though it is believed she'll rise in power, either in the city itself or within the Weavers' hierarchy. She's shrewd and very fast on her feet. It might do well to cultivate her, My Lord."

Tania laid the brush aside and ran her fingers absently through Isolde's hair.

"The rest of the Town Council will be in attendance, of course. The usual types, pompous old men and women, enamored of their own power."

"And just the sort to annoy His Highness into an impolitic remark."

"Quite."

"Quite." Tapping her fingers against her cheek, Isolde's thoughts turned to the Heir and the family she was marrying into. Distant, bitter folk, so unlike her own demonstrative kindred. It was odd. Their respective families had wed for years, long before Kathrine the Second had granted the noble title to the first of their name eight centuries ago.

They shared common ancestors, common features, and often common powers in the ecclesiastical and even secular worlds, but there was something about the Flame that marked the spirits of the Royal Family as well as their eyes. A hardness was born into them, a coldness that belied the traditional warmth of fire.

Isolde shook her head. The Living Flame was like a fiery tree, branches of power spreading out from the trunk that was the Aristok. The farther from the central core, the fainter the fiery touch, until it faded altogether. Melesandra's eyes blazed in the darkness and Demnor's smoldered like angry coals. One day, his would blaze forth and Isolde would look down into the burning gaze of her own children. Would she see strangers that day? Babies with her face and Alerion's burnished, shining hair and the DeMarian madness swimming in their innocent eyes?

She shivered, and Tania checked the slow, rhythmic stroking of the brush.

"Are you cold, My Lord? Should I fetch your cloak?"

Hugging her arms to her chest, Isolde shook her head. "No, I was just thinking."

"They must be dark thoughts to chase away the sun on such a beautiful day." The younger woman came around and knelt before her Lord. "Share them with me?"

The Earl smiled, trying to shake off the sense of foreboding the image had invoked.

"I was just thinking about the future."

"And that makes you shiver? Why, My Most Gracious Lord, the future couldn't be warmer. You're soon to be one of the most powerful people in the Land, wed to a man who's at least passing fair in looks, and Kelahnus tells me he's softer than he seems."

"It's not the man I fear, Tania, it's his nature, his family's nature coming out in my children. The Flame is harsh and it makes harsh people."

Cocking her head to one side, Tania considered her Lord's words before rising. Companions were taught a more secular faith; belief in the Guild. They acknowledged the esoteric abilities of the Triarchy, while only recognizing its power in holding sway over the nobility as a useful lever. The Flame was a metaphysical phenomenon; the recipients of Its powers were men and women, and their needs were no different than anyone else's. Thus their actions were predictable within the framework of power and desire. Tania, concealing a practical, even cynical philosophy behind the Companion's Guild's silken facade, believed in her own powers of observation and persuasion.

"Well, as to that, I couldn't say," she remarked as she picked up the brush again. "It would seem more likely that a harsh and heartless upbringing is what makes a harsh and heartless man, no matter what his eyes speak of. Her Majesty's uncle Amedeus was a just and kind man, from what I'm told. His brother, however, now there was a cracked vessel if ever there was one."

"Tania!"

"I'm not speaking treason, nor ill of the dead, My Lord, merely simple truth. Quinton DeMarian was an unstable man, and his mother's and brother's untimely deaths and the passing of the Flame was too much for him. It broke his mind."

"How can you say that? He was a great ruler and a great Aristok."

"Certainly, My Lord, but what kind of father was he? And what kind of mother did he make of his daughter?"

Isolde grew thoughtful, her mind dwelling on the summons Melesandra had issued her shortly after she'd returned the marriage proposal to the Crown Prince. The summons had been brought by the Aristok's Second Companion and had been blunt and to the point.

You are ordered to accompany me, My Lord, to the presence of Her Most Regal Majesty. At once.

Isolde had been at the training yard with her Uncle Alexander's Arms Master. As a result she'd been hot, sweaty, and not at all presentable when she'd bowed before the Aristok ten minutes later.

Melesandra had not deigned to notice. Her green, fire-washed eyes had burned into Isolde's own. When she spoke, the Aristok's voice was clipped and flat.

"My Lord Earl of Essendale."

"Your Most Regal Majesty." Afraid her own voice would emerge as a frightened squeak, Isolde was surprised at the even tone. It gave her the courage to meet her Sovereign's gaze and for a moment she thought she saw a faint smile on the other woman's lips.

"You are to wed my son, produce children for the Realm, and rule by his side. Are you prepared for such responsibility?"

Numerous answers came and went in the split second before Isolde answered with only a slight hint

of bravado. "Yes, Majesty. My mother has schooled
me in all my duties."

The Aristok gave a short, mirthless bark of laughter.
"Of that I'm sure. My Lord of Exenworth is an astute
and expedient woman. I'm sure she has taught you
well. You may tell her when you next correspond that
the position we discussed for your sister Alexandra is
confirmed and I shall expect her by Calan Gaeaf."

Inwardly Isolde shuddered. Poor Sandi, squired to
such a frightening Lord. It would make her fortune,
although Isolde wasn't at all sure it would be worth it.
She showed none of this on her face, merely murmured,
"Thank you, Your Majesty," wondering if Sandi had
been a private payment between the two older women.
And wondering also who was paying whom.

The Aristok nodded. "You will accompany my son
on Progress within the week. Take care how you travel,
My Lord of Essendale. The future travels with you,
remember that. That is all."

Isolde'd found herself back in her room and pouring
a drink before she'd collected her wits. The Aristok
had rattled her, the more so because she was still
unsure why the interview had taken place. To show her
it was still Melesandra who ruled? No. None dared
challenge the granddaughter of Kalandra the Great in
any matter. To catch Isolde off guard, then, and
glimpse the woman behind the courtier's mask that
everyone wore here as a matter of survival, to find
some exploitable weakness in her new wed-daughter
that might taint her grandchildren. That was most
likely the answer. Melesandra was a hard woman who
had raised her son to be a hard man. She would have
her own ideas on how his heirs should be brought up.

A sharp pain brought her back to the present, and she
was surprised to see she'd clenched her fist until her
nails had dug into her palm. Tania paused and made an
inquiring noise. Slowly, the Earl relaxed her fingers,
foreboding hardening into resolve. The Aristok would
find a different sort of foe in Isolde, Earl of Essendale,

one not nearly so predictable as Demnor, Prince of Gwyneth.

"What were we speaking of?"

"The late Aristok, Quinton the Second, My Lord."

"Oh, yes. Well, he may have been as you say, Tania. It makes little difference. His Highness' children will also be mine, and they will have no harsh and heartless upbringing. They'll have a proper DeKathrine family life whether they're DeMarians or not, and we'll see what Flame and Throne can do against that."

"Very little I would think, My Lord," Tania murmured approvingly into her hair. She set the brush aside. "Will you come and change for the banquet now, or we might dance a little, if My Lord remembers the minstrel's song."

Her dark mood lifted as the Earl looked into the fresh, beautiful face of her Companion. How Tania was able to insinuate her way into the gloomiest thoughts and toss them out with a well placed shove, was beyond her. Isolde was grateful for the ability nonetheless. With a sudden laugh, she rose. Tania was right. It was a beautiful afternoon, too beautiful to be marred with fears of the future. Linking their arms, the two women returned indoors.

The Royal Party dined that night with the Town Council. Fortunately for all, before Demnor was called upon to return the Mayor's effusive compliments, a speech he was sure would have ended in civil war, the woman, having been celebrating all afternoon, slipped beneath the table. The Crown Prince spent the evening talking tactics with the Captain of Leiston's Guard while the Earl discussed city improvements with the Chamberlain. They both retired in good humor.

Kelahnus and Tania had spent a quiet evening together, and when Demnor returned to his room, the Companion was curled up by the fire with a sleepy, sated look on his face. They conversed quietly about their respective evenings, then retired.

Long after Demnor's breathing had grown deep,

Kelahnus lay, watching the fire make shadows on the walls. He smiled sleepily as he reviewed the night's events. He and Tania were developing a good working relationship and he was confident they could navigate any storms the new Royal couple might encounter. Slowly, he, too, fell asleep to peaceful dreams.

The next morning the entourage was through the north gate and back on the road by noon. The weather continued fair, and slowly they made their way toward Linconford.

They were less than a day's ride from Terion's Earldom when Demnor felt the last of the tension ease. They'd picnicked beside a stone bridge that afternoon, and the Prince had found himself laughing with Isolde over jests he later couldn't remember having been that funny. It was quite beyond him to understand why.

Yawning, he stretched in the saddle. He'd been riding half asleep for a mile or two, enjoying the taste of the fall wind on his face. Behind him, Isolde's Companion sang a comic tune, the music adding a soothing thread to the rhythm of his horse's stride.

At that moment, one of the Sword Knights who'd been sent ahead reined up beside the Heir, breaking into his thoughts.

"Yes?"

"The city of Linconford lies ahead, My Prince. I've sent Gord Rose with word of your arrival."

"Thank you, Deverne." Demnor smiled to himself. Rose had been reinstated in the Knights the day the Progress had set off and had begged the Prince to be allowed to serve in his escort. Demnor had been happy to grant his wish.

He turned to Isolde.

"We're approaching the Earl of Linconford's lands, My Lord of Essendale. He . . . we fought together in Gallia. You'll like him, I think," he added, trying to make conversation, although he wasn't sure why he felt the need. "He lays a fair table and has the largest menagerie in the Realm."

Isolde turned the warmth of her smile on him, and he almost believed the brilliance of it.

"I've never seen a menagerie before, Your Highness," she said. "Perhaps you and the Earl would be so kind as to grant me a tour of it."

"Ah, yes, I don't see why not."

"If you gain a fondness for them, My Lord, there's quite a passable one at Bran's Palace," Kelahnus called out from behind them.

"Really? No one told me that. Perhaps you might escort me through it on our return, Highness?"

"I, yes, of course. If you wish." Five animals tended by a blind, old woman could hardly be called a menagerie, and Demnor said as much in the glare he shot his Companion. Kelahnus only smiled.

"If I like it, I might even add to it, if that's possible. I hear there are quite a few exotic animals in the East."

"Oh?"

"Yes. The Captain of my ship, the *Phoenix,* mentioned it on her return last autumn."

Demnor thought a moment. "The *Phoenix?* Wasn't that the ship that brought those Tersian mercenaries five years ago?"

"Yes, Highness."

"Good soldiers. Wish they'd stayed."

"So does Alerion. I prefer the Fenish."

Demnor nodded. "I remember you speaking of them before. The Fenish are good infantry, but you need more than that to fight the Gallians."

"With Fenish infantry and Gwynethian archers, what more could you desire, Highness?"

The Heir smiled. "DeKathrine cavalry."

"Why, thank you, My Prince."

Behind them, the Companions shared some whispered secret and their mutual laughter made Demnor frown nervously. Isolde merely smiled.

Dropping her hood for a few moments of sunshine, the Earl shook her hair free. The mass of golden curls swept down and Kelahnus murmured in appreciation. She turned her head to acknowledge the compliment, and he bowed gracefully in the saddle. *Oh, yes, he was a piece indeed,* she thought. *Extremely ornamental but, like all Companions, much more than he seemed.*

Turning her attention forward again, she caught Demnor watching her out of the corner of his eye. Well, that answered that question. He wasn't stone blind after all. At least he'd *noticed.* She supposed that was all she could expect at this stage of the game, but it pricked her vanity despite what the minstrels sang about Kelahnus. If Demnor were even half a man, she'd have bedded him by now. In fact, she'd have married him by now.

And had at least one child, her mind added sardonically. The dark thoughts of the day before hovered in the wings, but the day was much too fine and she waved them aside. Her mother had birthed seven children. Dropped them regularly with no hint of trouble. And had probably had number eight by now. Maybe even eight and nine. The last two had been twins, after all. Isolde had no doubts about where the Duke of Exenworth would be when the time came for her first grandchild.

No, pregnancy was to be expected with marriage and as long as there was someone around to help when they screamed, there was nothing wrong with having half a dozen or so. A keen grasp of politics and a good supply of contraceptive tea kept them to when you wanted them; not during the warring season and spaced decently apart so that one wasn't hanging off the tit while another was growing in the womb.

She glanced at Demnor from behind her hair. He was a handsome man when he smiled, even with the new scars along his jaw. Actually she was rather grateful for them. They were the only things that, at a quick glance, told him apart from her brother, Alerion. They were that alike, as cousins will be sometimes. Ler was slighter and more disposed to laughter, so he looked more dashing and less brooding. They had similar mannerisms, though, and Isolde kept having to catch herself from treating the Prince with the same cavalier teasing with which she had always handled Alerion. But he was a handsome man. They would make pretty babies together.

"Look, Your Highness, I can see a turret in the distance. Is that Castle Linconford?"

"What?" Demnor pulled himself from his own thoughts and squinted in the direction she pointed. "Can't see a thing. Is it?" He turned to Deverne.

The knight stood in his saddle, one hand shading his eyes from the afternoon sun. "I can barely make it out, My Prince, but, yes, that should be it."

"Then we should reach it before dark." The Heir turned back to Isolde. "You have good eyes, My Lord Earl."

"Thank you."

Behind them, Kelahnus breathed an inaudible sigh of relief. Maybe this marriage wasn't going to be like forcing a hawk and a hound to share the same bowl.

Shifting uncomfortably, he sighed again. Riding in the open paled fast and he was relieved their journey's end was drawing near. He was stiff and saddle sore. Hooded like Isolde, not so much to keep wind-tossed hair from his face, as to keep the sun from his pale skin, his hair felt heavy and limp. He could brave the sun a little, but he must look a fright, and he had no intention of presenting that face to the world. He would be glad of a little peace to reorganize himself.

Beside him, Tania hummed contentedly, watching the others behind the folds of her hood. Things were moving along smoothly, just as she'd known they would.

An hour later they entered the southernmost end of the city of Linconford.

A large and prosperous town since the earliest Essusiate Wars, Linconford housed numerous guildhalls, merchant warehouses and religious chapterhouses. To their right, just before the new southern gates, the Royal Party passed the short, sturdy tower of the Order

of the Earth across the road from the ancient Essusiate church of Marta le Wessleuvre. For centuries the
two religions had lived comfortably together in Linconford, even paying a mutual tax for their joint flocks
of sheep. As one, monks and scholars from both orders
emerged to gape at the heavily guarded entourage clat-
tering past them.

Crossing the ancient stone bridge over the Wiltham
River the Royal Party passed through the original south
gate and entered the center of town. Word of the Heir's
arrival had spread, and the streets were choked with
people. From the gate's Guard Tower, members of the
Watch leaned out to catch a glimpse of their Prince,
then hurried down to join the growing throngs. As
Demnor and his party turned onto Low Street, the
crowds began to cheer.

Slowly, with much difficulty, the entourage inched
its way through the city. The crowd threw autumn
flowers in its wake and petals over the Royal Couple,
shouting out good wishes and good fortune.

Everyone wanted a glimpse of the Heir and his new
Consort. The city elders, less nimble than their fellow
citizens, found it impossible to push through them to
reach their Royal guests. The Mayor had his cap
knocked off by an enthusiastic potter, and when he
objected, was jostled so violently, he gave up and
simply added his voice to the din. The city's High
Priest of the Flame had wisely stayed home, knowing
eventually Demnor would come to her. The other
elders craned their necks and gawked with the rest of
Linconford's citizenry.

As the Royal Party began the climb up High Street,
the people started chanting Demnor's name.

The late afternoon sun blazed across the castle's
outer bailey as Demnor and his entourage reached
Castle Hill. They rode past the huge cathedral, dedi-
cated to Terion's and the Prince's parent Order, the
Knights of the Sword, and up to the main gates of
Castle Linconford.

Rising in his saddle, Demnor saluted the crowd.

The responding cheer was almost deafening. As the Royal Party rode through the castle's wide tunnel vault, and the guards closed the massive doors behind them, the crowd shouted, "Long live the Prince of Gwyneth!"

7. Linconford

The vault was quiet after the city's tumultuous welcome. The wide tunnel curved under the castle's outer walls, dripping moisture from the stone's mossy mortaring, and Demnor breathed in the cool air with a sigh of relief. Using the darkness as a shield, he rubbed at the scars along his jaw and told himself sternly to sit up. The day's ride was almost at an end, but there were hours left before he could sleep.

Passing under the vault's arched ceiling, the Royal Party emerged onto the inner common. Before them loomed Linconford's ancient keep, lights beckoning in the windows, and people already emerging from its various entrances.

The Lord Terion DePaula himself, eighth Earl of Linconford, met them at the main doors. Running a hand hastily through his unruly, graying hair, he bowed and grinned.

"Terion," Demnor said with a smile.

"Welcome to Linconford, My Prince." The Earl's eyes tracked across the Heir's face, taking in the new scar tissue and the tight, tired smile. His own smile faltered for just an instant before he was all cheer and enthusiasm once again. "My apologies for the state of confusion you find us in, but we're birthing a calf and I barely had the chance to wash after your messenger arrived."

Demnor laughed. "Some things never change."

Dismounting, he embraced the older man. "What do you think a Cattle Master's for, Teri?"

"Oh, I have one, of course, My Lord," Terion ran his hand through his hair again, "only she's laid up with a sore tooth, and her lad's just a bit of a fellow, and, well . . . Still, I suppose . . ."

A discreet cough behind the Prince interrupted the Earl's explanation. Demnor turned.

"I'm remiss. My Lord of Essendale, Terion DePaula, the Earl of Linconford. My Lord of Linconford, the Earl of Essendale, Isolde DeKathrine." He turned to Isolde. "As I told you, Terion and I fought together in Gallia. Terion, the Earl of Essendale is, uh, my betrothed."

Terion bowed and Isolde inclined her head.

"His Highness has spoken of you with much fondness and admiration, My Lord," she said. "I'm pleased to finally make your acquaintance."

"And I yours, My Lord. When we heard the news, the city celebrated for a week. But then, we are prone to merriment here," he replied, his eyes dancing.

Demnor snorted. "We noticed."

"Oh? Oh, yes, of course." Terion cocked an ear at the city where they could still hear the shouting and laughter of the crowds before the gate. He turned back to the Prince. "Actually, I was afraid you might need rescuing."

"We almost did."

They laughed together, then Terion pulled himself together.

"You'll be tired and want to rest before supper, My Prince. Please, forgive me for keeping you standing in my yard. Denis!"

A small boy of nine or so came running.

"Denis! Oh, there you are. How many times do I have to remind you to be here as soon as guests arrive? Hm? Well, never mind, you'll remember next time, aye? Take the Lord's horses to the stables now. If you need help, call your sister. And send for Marian. She's my Stable Master, Highness. She'll tend to your mounts and find lodgings for the horses of your Guard."

The Royal Party dismounted. Denis looked up at Demnor's gelding, Challenger, with alarm, then putting two grubby fingers in his mouth, he gave a piercing whistle. When no answer was forthcoming, he stamped his foot impatiently and gave another. Moments later a small girl appeared, trailing a toy horse by the tail. She stared at the assembled with openmouthed awe.

"Sarah, you got's ta help me take the Lord's Horses ta the stables. Come on now."

" 'Kay, Deni." She made an awkward bow and accepted the reins held out to her.

Demnor's squire appeared at his elbow.

"Yes, Dimitrius?"

"Perhaps Flewellynn and I should take Your Highness and Her Lordship's mounts, Sir. Challenger is a bit of a handful for a child."

Demnor nodded, and between them, the two DeLlewellynne squires and the children led the horses away.

Terion beamed after them. "They're my Steward's," he explained as he led them toward the door. "Bright as buttons, they are."

"No doubt," Demnor answered. "And how is Dorin?"

"Stuffy and irritable and deaf when he wants to be. But I couldn't be without him and that's the truth. Not and raise three children on my own, anyway."

"And how are they?"

"Oh, fine, fine, My Prince. The eldest; you remember Willona, Highness; is married and expecting. I'm to be a grandfather. Strange, isn't it? She and her husband are traveling on the Continent." He held the door open for them, much to the silent disapproval of the Steward hovering in the hall.

Demnor and Isolde entered the keep while Kelahnus indicated that the Earl of Linconford should precede them.

"Your other children?" Demnor prompted as they made their way through the vaulted entrance hall.

"Oh, yes. Well, Harold's on the Continent, too. Training to be an artist in Florenz, of all places, and Katrina, well," Terion sighed. "Katrina's at home."

"You say that with the weight of the world on your shoulders, old friend."

"Oh, no, Highness, not really. It's just that she's sixteen. She's *very* sixteen and so is her latest beau."

"Beau?" Demnor's tone was amused.

Terion shook his head. "Beau. He's a nice lad in his way. He's just very . . . well, very. You may know him, actually, My Lord." He turned to Isolde. "He's one of your kin, Phillip DeKathrine."

Isolde thought for a moment and then shook her head. "Sixteen? No, I don't think so. Mother may know of him, of course. She keeps an eye on most of the family."

"Well, *his* mother tried, but eventually I offered to squire him here. He was always here anyway. And besides, she has so many. One less was probably a relief."

"Yes, probably." Isolde smiled.

They paused before the keep's main staircase, and Terion bowed.

"I'll leave you to rest and bathe the dust away, then, Highness, My Lord. There are baths drawn, I believe, aren't there, Dorin, in the guest rooms?" He turned to the Steward.

"Yes, My Lord."

"Good, good. Well, come down whenever you're ready. I'll be, oh, somewhere. Supper at seven, Highness?"

Demnor smiled. "Seven would be fine, old friend." He looked to the others. "I'll be up presently."

They bowed and followed the Steward up the stairs, Kelahnus shooting his Lord a curious look.

When they'd passed out of sight, Demnor turned back to the Earl.

"Who else will be at the table tonight, Teri?"

"Just Phillip, My Prince. I thought I wouldn't invite the city elders just yet. I did take the liberty of sending word that you'd see them tomorrow, however. Duties are like taxes," he added with a grin. "You can avoid them for only so long before you have to pay up."

"With interest. Thank you."

"It's nothing, My Prince. However, I did want to ask you about later tonight. There's a troupe of players staying in the castle fields. I thought I might have them in to entertain us after supper. They're passable actors, though the soloist is a bit flat. If you don't mind, sir."

"Not at all." Demnor looked the older man over. "It's good to see you, Teri."

"You also, My Prince. It's been a long time."

"Too long."

They stood in silence for a moment, then Terion shook himself.

"Too long indeed. Betrothed, is it? Well, well. You'll be a father next."

A shadow passed across Demnor's face, but he quickly schooled his expression. "Yes, likely."

"Likely, but you'll want to change."

"I'll be down later."

Terion's face brightened. "We could play strategy. We haven't matched wits since Gallia. Do you remember Highness, the night before the Battle of Troysailles?"

"I remember. You kept using the poor light as an excuse to cheat."

"Did I? Oh, well. It didn't help, did it?"

"No."

"No. Thought not. Well, no one here knows how to play properly; except Katrina, that is, and I'm tired of her gloating over the carnage." He sighed.

"I'll look forward to it." Demnor smiled down at his old friend, feeling the last shred of tension work itself free in the Earl's easy company. It reminded him of happier times and easier problems. Perhaps they'd stay a month.

* * *

Kelahnus was curled up in a large, stuffed chair, one toe poking from under his robe toward the fire. When Demnor entered, he rose.

"I thought you'd never come. Did you want to bathe?" he asked, trying to mask his enthusiasm. "There's hot water."

"Later. You go ahead."

The Companion let the robe fall softly to the ground, then stepped out of it. Giving the Heir an inviting smile, he turned and entered the bathing room. Demnor watched him go with a faint smile, then followed him in.

"Is there room for two?"

Allowing the soft golden locks to cascade over his shoulders, Kelahnus inclined his head. "Of course."

Some time later, feeling sated and a little sleepy, and dressed in clean, comfortable clothes, Demnor made his way back downstairs. The main hall was deserted. Glancing about, he chose an archway at random and stepped through it. A large gallery stretched out before him. Music came from somewhere beyond and he followed it, past a dozen portraits of Terion's family and two stuffed dragons' heads, to a tiny solar.

The alcove was draped with faded tapestries and the stone benches were padded with lavender cushions. Beyond the barred window, the final strokes of the sun touched the faces of the young couple within. The woman, black hair tied in a loose braid, sat playing a flute. At her feet, the man, stylishly dressed in the DeKathrine green and black, sang the lyrics to an ancient love song. His dark hair was long and curled about his ears in thick disarray, and he gazed up at her with coltish admiration as he sang.

When Demnor approached, the two fell silent, then leaped to their feet as the shadows parted to reveal the Royal intruder. The young woman was the first to recover, making a deep bow. The young man followed a second later. Demnor nodded.

"You are?" he inquired with what he hoped was not growled menace.

The youth opened his mouth, then darted a quick look at the woman.

"Katrina DePaula, Your Highness," she answered with only a faint quaver in her voice. "And this is Phillip DeKathrine, my companion, I mean, um, my friend." She blushed.

"Yes." Demnor nodded, purposely ignoring her mistake. "Your father spoke of him. Where is Terion?"

"I believe he's in his outer chamber, Your Highness," she answered, quickly regaining her composure. She was, after all, the woman of the manor. Demnor could almost see her firmly telling herself that. "If you wish it, I can conduct you to him."

"That will be fine. Lead on."

Katrina bowed once more and swept from the solar with as much dignity as she could muster. Demnor followed.

Leading the Prince back through the gallery, up a winding flight of stairs and down a corridor, she stopped at a small door and knocked.

"If you would abide here a moment, Your Highness."

She slipped inside. From without, Demnor could hear her side of the muffled conversation.

"Father? Father! His Highness, Prince Demnor is here. Please put your tunic on and try to look presentable."

The door opened once more and Katrina, her young face annoyed, stepped aside. Her father rose from a desk, as Demnor entered.

Terion's outer chamber was a comfortable room with thick rugs thrown before the fire, heavy tapestries on the walls, and drapes over the windows to keep out the chill. A small table held a beautiful strategy set—the wooden pieces carved as Branion and Gallian soldiers—beside a crystal carafe of cider, pressed from Terion's own apples, and two chased goblets. The fire crackled invitingly and Demnor settled himself in the chair on the side of the board where pieces painted

Branion crimson awaited. The Earl, in his shirtsleeves, joined him, pipe in hand.

Demnor poured them both a drink. "To old times."

"And to future times, My Prince. May they become memories as pleasant."

They drank.

"Your Highness found his way through this crumbling pile of rock, then? Or did Katrina meet you at your rooms?"

"I found the western gallery. After that she guided me to you." The Heir pushed a foot soldier forward for his opening move, then lit his own pipe.

"Good, good. Katie's convenient that way." Terion countered with a mirroring move. "Did you meet her paramour?"

"Yes. He seems harmless."

"Oh, quite. A nice boy, but stuffy." The Earl covered another move by the Heir's advancing line of infantry. "That's the trouble with children these days. No sense of humor. Oh, blasted knight, didn't see that. Anyway, children. They think they can save the world, if only the world would stop going about its business and let them." He stared morosely at the white-painted foot soldier now standing beside the board.

"Were you any different, old friend?"

Terion's eyes sparkled. "Perhaps not quite as stuffy. But for all that, I quite like having them around. They're so marvelous to tease." He touched his priest experimentally, then with a shrug, moved its twin.

Demnor brought up his other knight before answering. "I wouldn't know."

With a quick glance, the Earl gauged his mood, before taking it and commenting, "No. I suppose Your Highness is still as serious as ever, yes?"

"Worse."

"Oh, my." Terion's pipe had gone out and after sucking ineffectually at it for a time, he reached over and lit a taper from the fire.

Demnor made a move. "Flanked and overridden."

"What!"

The Prince smiled. "Perhaps not quite as serious."

After staring at the board, confused, Terion began to laugh.

Three games later, Dorin put his head in the door to announce supper. The Earl sighed and leaned back. "Just as well, I'm getting a terrible crick in my neck."

"And you were losing."

Running a hand through his hair, Terion looked down at the few Gallian pieces remaining in a sea of Branion. "Yes, well, I'd have rallied."

They left the room, the older man pausing to slip into the light purple tunic the Steward wordlessly held out for him.

The others had already gathered in the long, candlelit dining hall. Isolde stood by a wine service, sipping at an aperitif and speaking with Kelahnus. She had changed into a dark green gown, low necked, and trimmed with black brocade. Emeralds gleamed from her ears and throat, and she wore one emerald ring next to her family seal. She smiled as Demnor entered the room. He found himself smiling back without thinking. Kelahnus raised a sardonic eyebrow.

The Companion had also changed. He now wore a soft blue tunic with slashed, trailing sleeves and tight maroon hose. His hair swirled about his face like living gold and Demnor's breathing became labored. Swiftly, he swung his attention elsewhere.

Isolde's Companion was dressed in a silken gown of green, a shade lighter than the Earl's. Its simple cut and deep neckline, set off the swell of her breasts and the graceful line of her throat. Demnor was reminded of the swans at Bran's Palace.

He caught Kelahnus' eye. The younger man's lips twitched upward in the faintest of amused smiles, and Demnor found himself irrationally annoyed. He turned toward the younger guests.

Phillip was attired in the latest court fashion, a thickly embroidered, dark green tunic, with slashed, trailing sleeves and gold ribbons woven into the fabric. Stiff lace at the wrists and throat accented his pale features and dark hair, as did the gleaming emerald stones in his ears. His hose were tight, the codpiece black while the hose were green.

Of all of them, even Terion, Demnor was the most simply dressed in a plain, dark blue tunic and black breeches. The Prince hated hose, preferring the more loosely comfortable breeches and hadn't worn a codpiece since letting his valet go when he was sixteen. Nodding a greeting as Phillip bowed, he turned his attention to Katrina.

The young DePaula wore an ornamental surcoat of pale yellow silk, trimmed with cream-colored lace. Her family's hawk and aerie crest endowed the front, embroidered in stiff gold and lavender brocade. Beneath, her sleeves were slashed, tied with ribbons, showing the violet undercloth. Lavender breeches and soft ankle boots completed the attire. She and Tania had been deep in discussion, but now they bowed and moved apart as the Heir and the Earl entered.

With a cheerful greeting, Terion gestured them in to supper. He sat Demnor at the head of the table with himself at his left hand and Isolde at his right. Katrina sat beside her father and Phillip was placed, with some show of misery, between Isolde and her Companion.

Tania smiled with toleration at his lack of enthusiasm and at his obvious attempts to touch Katrina's foot under the table. Kelahnus, on the other side of the Earl of Essendale, amused himself throughout the meal by substituting his own foot, and then looking suitably surprised.

Dimitrius and Flewellynn DeLlewellynne completed the table.

Supper passed without incident. The food was excellent as were the wine, ale, and cider. Terion kept his guests entertained with accounts of the life of a North Country Lord and soldier, alternately telling stories and listening with rapt attention to return tales of Isolde's campaigns in Fenland and Burguntoise. He even managed to pull a story or two from

Demnor, and the animation with which the Prince spoke of soldiering did much to put the young people at ease.

Katrina managed to extract a promise from Isolde to view her skill in the days to come. The Earl assured her that if she were as good as her father believed, she would personally induct the younger woman into the Knights of the Bow, Isolde's own Order. Blushing with pleasure, Katrina agreed.

Phillip, after some prodding from Terion, put forth his ideas on siege craft and Demnor found himself listening attentively to the young man's ideas. The Prince and his Companion shared a look. Here was the makings of a good sapper, though the boy wanted to be a Triarchy Knight, like Katrina. Demnor made a mental note to speak with Geoffrey Harper, the Captain of the Royal Engineers.

The conversation wound on through each dish, moving from battles to history to current politics and back. Over dessert the talk dwelled on Heathland, the mood around the table growing serious as Demnor and Terion relived the fighting of four years ago.

"A bad business," the Earl observed, making his perpetual gesture through his hair. "Heathland's a terrible country to fight in."

Demnor gestured and a servant refilled his goblet with cider. "I disagree. The Heaths are the only worthy adversaries left. When you can bring them to battle, that is."

"Well, that's just my point, Highness. The buggers are forever springing down from the hills and then running off before you've had a chance to saddle up."

The Prince laughed. "The Heaths are hill fighters," he explained to the youngsters around the table. "It's madness to try and play by their rules. Do you remember 883, Teri?"

"I had hoped Your Highness would let me forget," the Earl groaned.

Phillip and Katrina looked interested, so with a smile, the Prince related the story.

"It was during the fighting ten years ago. As we've said, the Heaths fight on the run. Small groups dashing in for short attacks, then breaking off and disappearing into the hills again. A difficult tactic for an army laden with supply carts and foot soldiers to counter. They carry their food, porridge for the most part, in bags on their saddles. It makes them very mobile.

"So Terion decided to fight fire with fire, or porridge with bread if you like." He winked at the Earl who gave him a long suffering look back. The Prince continued. "The only problem was that bread and horse sweat do not mix to an appetizing meal, and the experiment was discreetly forgotten by all."

"All but yourself, My Prince," Terion replied reproachfully as the others laughed.

"True. But the only way to fight the Heaths is and will always be to make them come to you, fight on your terms, and to beat them with numbers."

"Like Falkeith?"

"Like Falkeith."

"But Heathland's been peaceful for some time, hasn't it, Your Highness?" Katrina asked.

"Yes. We won't see another battle like that for years. But it will rise again. It always does. Fortunately." He helped himself to a wafer. "For now, though, a Royal Progress is completely safe. And as dull."

Terion chewed on a nail, his face suddenly drawn. "So Your Highness is bound for Heathland, then?"

Demnor nodded. "To Braxborough at least. After that, we'll see."

"Yes." The Earl nodded distractedly. "Braxborough, on the banks of the Braxen River . . ." He strained as if to catch sight of something in the distance.

The others exchanged glances across the table. Katrina went very still.

Demnor turned to the older man. "You sound worried, old friend. Do you know something I don't?"

"Know . . . something . . . ?" Terion repeated, rubbing at his eyes, his expression vague. "I . . ." His voice faded.

"Has there been trouble in Heathland?" Kelahnus asked with a worried frown. When the Earl didn't answer, he turned to his daughter. Katrina shook her head.

"Everything's been quiet. Here at least, but then we're rather south. Father has these spells sometimes. He's all right." Her young face held a protectiveness that drew a nod from the Prince.

"My brothers act much the same way at times. And they're usually accurate. So is your father."

She glanced up at him with a questioning frown.

"He saw a surprise attack one night many years ago. We were able to defeat it. At that time, a Priest of the Flame tested him. He said your father had the Sight, though only dimly. It might increase or decrease as time went on."

"Yes, Highness. Father?" She touched the Earl lightly on the arm. "Father, do you feel that His Royal Highness will be in danger in Heathland?"

"Danger ... perhaps ... I ... I'm not sure ... I can't see ..."

Terion's eyes cleared as he glanced about, somewhat confused. Then he sighed. "It's gone. It's like something you see out of the corner of your eye. If you turn your head, it vanishes."

"You said you saw danger. What kind of danger?" Demnor probed.

Terion closed his eyes, then shook his head. "I can't grasp it. I'm sorry, My Prince. It wasn't a strong enough feeling. I couldn't really say if it portended an enemy or a thunderstorm." He ran his hand through his hair and sighed.

Demnor and his Companion exchanged a look.

"Do you believe we should abandon our northern journey through Heathland, My Lord?" Kelahnus asked.

"I don't know. No." He straightened. "No, not for this. I'm sorry I can't be more specific, My Prince."

"Don't fret, Teri. We'll simply proceed as scheduled, but remain on guard."

"Yes I'm sure that will do." The Earl shook himself. "Foolish. I used to be able to grasp the meanings of these visions. Now . . . I'm getting old."

"Nonsense."

"Maybe." The Earl pushed a hand through his hair again. "I get twinges in my legs when it rains and my hands stiffen up something terrible on these chill mornings. Soon they'll be no good for anything save lifting grandchildren into the saddle." He winked at Phillip with a trace of his earlier humor. The youth blushed furiously.

"You're just tired, Father," Katrina said in a firm voice.

"Perhaps. Well, we seem to be finished. Shall we adjourn to the great hall, Highness? The players I told you of should be ready."

Demnor frowned. "You're sure you're all right, Teri?"

"I'm fine, My Prince. Truly. Ask Katrina. The spells only affect me for a moment, and then they're gone." He made a gesture in the air. "Like a puff of smoke."

When the Heir turned to her, Katrina nodded, though her brow was furrowed. Regarding his old friend with a long, even stare, Demnor finally nodded. "Very well, I'll believe you." He stood and the others quickly followed. "Lead on, My Lord of Linconford."

The Rose and Gryphon Traveling Players were indeed ready when they arrived. The room had been divided roughly in half, the front curtained off by two large squares of patched cloth, the back set up with chairs. When the Earl and his guests seated themselves, a small boy blew out all but the two candelabra flanking the makeshift stage, and the room dropped into darkness.

"Welcome, Highness, and gentle company all!" a voice spoke from the shadows. There was a swirl of curtain and a tall, ginger-haired man stood before them. He was dressed as a fifth century Herald, and as he bowed, he swept his hat to the floor.

"Tonight our players would present, with your indulgence, a story of both great magnificence and of humble piety; of fearsome battles, bravely fought and mighty countries won and lost; of love and lust; of treachery and trouble. And so, with no more speeches, no more words, let the scene be set in Branbridge amid the pageantry of that most regal court of 438! We do present to you, *Demnor the Third, Part Four!*"

The curtains opened.

The troupe was a large one, consisting of some twenty people ranging in age between five and fifty. Most bore similar features, and the Prince assumed, like many such groups, they were family based. In the open, most would have, no doubt, served as tumblers, ushers, and thieves. Indoors, however, their parts became more limited. Demnor was amused. He should have so many servants.

The play got off to a shaky start, the actors unused to Royal audiences, but eventually the familiar lines and scenes took hold and the darkened room disappeared to be replaced by the subtle intrigues of the late Aristok's court and the wide fields of Gallia.

Part Four was the finale, mostly battle and love scenes. Scene three ended with great fanfare as Demnor the Third, played by the ginger-haired actor, was slain by a dozen Gallian adversaries. The man expired most dramatically after a long soliloquy. He was carried to a couch to be wept over by his Consort Elisha, a heavyset, black-haired woman, and by his fourteen-year-old daughter, the future Kassandra the First, played by a strikingly beautiful, well-endowed woman of at least thirty.

The love interest, Kassandra's future husband, Desmond DeKathrine, stood by her side comforting her. They made a tearful couple, setting Katrina to sniffing and Phillip to comforting her. Out of the corner of his eye, Demnor caught Isolde's amused smile. He assumed it was at the young lovers beside them and not on stage, for by all accounts the Royal

Couple had loved each other deeply, and Kassandra's untimely death at thirty-one from childbed fever had almost destroyed the Consort.

Her older brother, Demnor the Fourth, the next Aristok after their father, stood at his parent's deathbed with sword in hand and delivered a thrilling speech of revenge and retaliation. It was reasonably performed, although interrupted by fits of coughing by the emaciated youth who played the part. The boy looked ready to expire at any moment, but managed to carry on and slay the villain of the piece, a Gallian Marquis, played most convincingly by a curly-haired man of about twenty.

Demnor watched intently, drawn into the battle scenes, despite their inaccuracies. Somehow, the ginger-haired actor managed to hit the exact feeling just before a major battle. The Prince was carried back to the times he had stood, listening to predawn speeches and feeling his blood rush to the excitement and the fear of the coming battle.

Earlier, in scene two, when the Aristok had stooped amid the carnage to weep over his fallen brother, Demnor had actually felt a lump in his throat. Glancing over, he'd seen that Isolde had been as deeply moved, her eyes moist and her jaw clenched with the effort not to cry.

It was a good play, despite the literary license the playwright had taken with his ancestor's reign. The war, far from being decisive, had been a disaster and the young Demnor the Fourth had committed suicide four years after assuming the throne. The troupe had, however, chosen the play obviously to honor him and Demnor found himself absurdly flattered. The end was met with genuine applause.

As was the custom, when the actors had taken their final bows, the Prince and his company threw coins onto the stage. Most were snatched from midair, the troupe forgetting its newly found dignity in its haste to possess the thick, silver sovereigns.

Next there was somewhat subdued tumbling and juggling, and finally the black-haired woman came out and sang. Her voice was a little flat and droning, but her enthusiasm gave it force and Demnor found himself wishing he was ten or twenty feet back. It was a martial song, one of the many written to celebrate Kalandra the Great's victories. As she rolled into the fourth verse, he tried not to wince.

Some years before he had heard the great Eleanor of Lanborough sing the same song in the Atreus Hall in Branbridge. He'd been strongly affected by her voice and had found her charming company at the banquet afterward. Luckily this woman either chose not to sing or didn't know the other five verses. She ended to polite applause and more money.

While Dorin handed wine and cakes to the actors as they bundled up their props, Terion presented the leader of the troupe, Arthur Dickey, to the Prince. The actor who had played Demnor the Third bowed low with only a hint of nervousness.

"Have you ever been to war?" the Heir asked.

Dickey smiled. "No, Your Highness, but I've listened well to those who have. To be honest, sir, the very thought of battle makes me weak-kneed."

"A pity. You'd make a good general."

"I'm honored that Your Highness finds me so convincing."

"I do. Bring your troupe to Branbridge. You'll find others there who will also."

The actor's eyes lit up, and he gave a gracious smile that held only a hint of avarice. "Might we have the honor to present ourselves before Your Highness once again?"

Demnor smiled, knowing full well what success he granted these people if he agreed. But his mood was light and he decided to push ahead.

"Yes. Paint my crest above your troupe name if you like. Then I'll remember you when you arrive. You could perform in the Great Hall at Bran's Palace."

The man's expression was almost comical and Demnor found himself smiling with pleasure. With a stammered thanks, Dickey accepted the sizable purse the Prince held out. He bowed, and Demnor moved on, feeling absurdly happy.

After a word with Terion, the Royal Party retired for the night and the Rose and Gryphon Traveling Players returned to their field, far richer than when they'd left it.

Demnor sat on the edge of the bed, tugging at his boots and whistling the evening's song quietly between his teeth. Kelahnus, already disrobed, reclined on the bed and yawned

"That was quite a performance," the Companion noted.

"Yes."

"You certainly seemed to enjoy it."

"I did. It reminded me of Gallia and the battle camps. They were good memories."

"The Lord Isolde seemed equally taken."

Demnor grunted and tossed one boot aside.

"You have a lot in common, you know."

"Oh?"

"Yes. The love of mud and sweat."

"Very funny. We've more in common than that. She appreciates a good fight. And the reasons behind one."

"Oh?" The smile Kelahnus showed to the Heir's back belied the offhand, curious tone.

"Yes." Demnor yanked the other boot off, dropping it beside the first.

"I'm pleased, then, that you're getting along so well. I'd thought you were. It's refreshing, actually, after sitting beside young love all night to observe an older, more dignified couple."

"You could have always watched the play."

"Why? I live with a hero. I don't need to watch a bad performance of one."

Flattered despite himself, Demnor smiled. "I thought he managed quite well."

"You manage better." The Companion leaned over

and looked up at the Prince through a cloud of tousled hair.

Shaking his head, Demnor stroked the golden mane. "Not always. I might if life were a play. Then at least I'd know my lines."

"Yes, but most plays end tragically."

"So does life."

"Only if you let it. A life well-lived and well-loved is never a tragedy."

The Companion reached up and wrapped one arm about the Heir's neck, drawing him down in a deep kiss. They lingered over it, lips brushing lips for a long moment. Demnor's hands roamed down the other's hips while Kelahnus tugged at his Prince's buckle. Slipping him out of his clothes, the younger man began kissing him lightly on the chest, moving slowly down while his hands traced patterns of warmth along his back. Demnor took him in his arms, one hand buried in the silken softness of the Companion's hair, the other reaching down to stroke goose bumps along his sides.

The fire had burned low in the hearth when they finished. Stretched across the rumpled sheets, Kelahnus lay with his head on Demnor's chest, the Heir's arms warm around him. He listened for a time to the Prince's heart beat, then said sleepily, "The Lord Isolde's Companion is very beautiful, isn't she?"

"What?"

"Tania, the Lord Isolde's Companion."

"I know who she is." Demnor shifted uncomfortably, smoothing the sheet under his back. Kelahnus gave an indignant wiggle and the Heir returned his arm to its original position. "Why bring her up now?"

"I was just thinking." Kelahnus twirled his finger in the fine, red hairs on Demnor's chest. "She is beautiful though, isn't she?"

Demnor sighed and closed his eyes. He was sure there was a point to this, but he was too content to try and avoid it. "Yes, I suppose," he relented after a moment's reflection. "She's very fetching."

"Fetching? What a lukewarm compliment."

"I wasn't aware I was supposed to compliment her."

"She has nice breasts, don't you think?"

"I'm sure. Look, what are you after?" Demnor sat up, shifting the Companion off him. "If you want to sleep with her, sleep with her."

"It's not that at all," Kelahnus sighed. "I just noticed you looking at her and admiring her—endowments."

"Oh." Mollified, but wondering if he was now supposed to feel guilty, Demnor shrugged. "Well, they were displayed. I noticed yours, too."

"I know you did," the younger man answered softly. "And I was pleased. Come and lie down again."

"I want to get into bed properly. I'm cold."

Once they were underneath the covers, Kelahnus draped himself over the Heir's chest again. "Katrina's quite pretty. Fetching."

"She's a child."

"And Phillip?"

"He's a child, too."

"I suppose. None of them match the Lord Isolde, do they? The more mature stance and confidence always adds an extra touch of beauty. And her gown was gorgeous."

"I suppose. I liked her better in breeches."

"You would. I despair of your taste. A woman spends an hour doing her hair and dressing herself to take the breath away, and all you can do is remember how much better she looked soaked with rain and covered in mud."

"She wasn't covered in mud."

"We were all covered in mud. She has beautiful hair. I'd kill for such hair."

Demnor shook his head. "You have such hair, you foolish, vain peacock. Now go to sleep. Unless you want to dissect Terion's features next?"

"No. He's nice, and his looks reflect that."

"I'm glad you approve of him."

"I do." He paused. "You never told me he had the Sight."

"Didn't I?"

"No, you didn't. Do you suppose his *feeling* over supper is something we should worry about?"

The Companion's voice was light, but Demnor could hear the worry underneath it. He matched the other man's tone.

"Didn't he say it meant a thunderstorm?"

He grunted as the Companion's elbow dug into his ribs.

"You know very well what he said; that it could mean either danger *or* a thunderstorm."

"Oh. So we should what . . . pack an oilcloth?"

Kelahnus looked down at him, saw the half closed eyes and sleepy expression and decided the Prince was not trying to be funny.

"You're not at all concerned?"

"No."

"Even after your brothers foretold danger on the road to Heathland, and now the Lord Terion has an unsettled feeling about Braxborough?"

The Heir sighed. Rising, he put his arms around the other man and drew him close. "Kelahnus, danger doesn't mean death. And besides, I've a whole pack of Sword Knights and Shield Knights just itching to prove their prowess."

"But what if . . . ?"

"There's no what if. It's autumn. Heathland would never start something in the middle of Mean Damhar; they need their troops for the harvest and they could never maintain an army on winter stores."

"They wouldn't need an army," the Companion argued stubbornly, "just one assassin is all it would take."

"The Heaths don't work that way."

"How do you know?"

"Because I do."

"You've Seen it?" Kelahnus' tone was borderline sarcastic, but Demnor ignored it.

"Yes."

"So you're not worried at all?"

"Only about not getting any sleep."

Kelahnus poked him.

"I'll send out double the advance guard once we reach Heathland," Demnor assured him. "And we'll be extra vigilant on the road. That's all I can promise, all right?"

"I suppose."

"Good. Now may we please go to sleep?"

With a grimace, Kelahnus made a show of getting comfortable, pulling the covers up around his chin and settling in against the Prince's chest with a thump. Demnor sighed but, after only a few moments, began to snore. Kelahnus lay staring up at the canopy above them, going over the Prince's security, until finally he, too, fell asleep.

As the coals glowered into darkness, the only sound in the room was of deep breathing.

As the Linconford bells rang twelve, Phillip DeKathrine wrapped his cloak more tightly about his shoulders as he slipped from the keep's kitchen door and into the chill air. He swayed slightly, unsteady on his feet, but righted himself and stared into the starlit sky, watching his breath puff out.

He'd had trouble with sleeplessness since he was a child and usually found relief in a long walk before bed. He'd have preferred to wander the halls, maybe fetch a book from the Earl's library, but with the Prince of Gwyneth here, he didn't dare loiter about in case he should be taken for an assassin or a thief. There were guards all over the place. So, he would brave the cold and walk down to the players' camp and visit with Drew. In the last week, since the troupe had been playing in Linconford, he'd found the actor an enjoyable drinking comrade, always willing to sit up well into the night playing cards and arguing philosophy and politics.

The curly-haired man was pleased to see him, ushering the young nobleman into his wagon with a gesture of pleasure. "Wine, cards?" he offered.

"Yes." Phillip settled himself into the wagon's one chair. After pouring them each some wine, Drew sat down on a trunk by a small table. "Couldn't sleep again tonight?" he asked.

Phillip drank from his goblet. "No. Thought the wine over supper would help. It didn't."

"Your inconvenience is my company, then." The actor pulled out a worn pack of cards and began to deal them out.

They played a few hands, Phillip ruefully handing Drew a small handful of copper at the end.

"So," the player said casually as he shuffled. "Did His Highness like the play?"

"Seemed to." Phillip tipped back his goblet, frowning on finding it empty.

Drew refilled it.

"He's a reticent man," the actor observed.

"Scary man."

"Perhaps. I've been told that the stories about him are exaggerated."

"Well, I wouldn't know about that. But they wouldn't need to be exaggerated too much. You should have heard him over supper when the conversation turned to Heathland. All he could talk about was how he loved fighting the Heaths and how he wished they would rise up again so he could."

"Oh, did he now?" Drew asked softly.

After a gulp of wine, Phillip nodded. "He didn't give any thought to the issues or the people. He thinks there'll be another uprising soon. He's positively gleeful about it."

Only a narrowing of the eyes betrayed Drew's interest, but when he spoke, his voice was carefully indifferent. "What gives him that idea?"

"I don't know. Just because there's been so many, I suppose. But he actually smiled when he said it, like he couldn't wait to start the killing. I nearly choked on my drink."

"Hm. It's a bad idea to drink around an enemy."

Phillip looked shocked. "He's not an enemy. He's, well, he's the Prince of Gwyneth. He's just . . ."

"Easy, Phil." The actor touched the younger man lightly on the shoulder. "I didn't say that the Prince of Gwyneth was your enemy. It's just a phrase. It means you should always keep your wits about you." He poured him some more wine.

"I suppose."

"You've seen his shield device, Branion wolf hovering over a Gwynethian gryphon?"

"Yes, of course."

"Well, that's Branion policy isn't it, conquer and control, so if he's not an enemy, you must at least admit he's an ideological adversary? After all, we've agreed that Branion doesn't belong in Heathland any more than they belong in Gallia. You said so yourself last night. And it's our job as responsible citizens to make that clear in peaceful, and if necessary, forceful ways. Your glass is empty."

"I jus' don't like the word enemy," the young nobleman explained after draining half the goblet's contents in one quick swallow. "It makes it soun' like I'm, well . . . It makes it soun' like treason," he whispered.

"Treason!" Drew's tone was one of dramatic horror. Phillip winced.

"Don't be absurd! Is it treason to expect justice to be done by our most high?"

"Well, no."

"Is it treason to take an interest in the destiny of one's country?"

"No, but . . ."

"There are no buts about it." Drew poured him another drink. "Stop imagining things and undermining your own confidence. You simply see more clearly than most people about freedom and the right for a culturally separate people to live under their own rule. Of course, it's a pity that you can't convince His Highness. But then, it's hard to convince a man about justice who only thinks in terms of power and force. He's

like all the nobility, present company excluded, of
course. You know better. After all, how can you teach
a man about a country he's never been to without an
army at his back?"

"Well, he's goin' there now without one." Phillip's
voice was starting to slur, and he gazed blearily at
Drew, who seemed a bit fuzzy. He didn't notice the
returned spark of interest in the other man's face.

"Oh," the player asked, his voice neutral. "When is
that?"

With a shrug, Phillip reached for his goblet and
missed. "Dunno when. End of his tour. Goin' to
Braxborough. Both of them."

"Really? I hadn't heard that end to his itinerary.
Well, I'm sure he'll see reason when he gets there."

"Do you really think so? I mean, if it were up to me,
Drew, I'd give it back, honest. I don't think it's right
for . . . for . . . what was I saying?"

"That it was time you went to bed."

"Oh. Yes. G'night, Drew."

"Good night, Your Grace. Here, let me get a boy to
help you home. Oh, by the way, you still owe me for
that last hand."

"Do I? Sorry, uh, here." He handed the other man his
purse. "Is that enough?"

Drew put it on the table without opening it. "Just
exactly enough," he said soothingly. "Now come on,
up you get."

The player helped the very drunk young nobleman
outside and onto the shoulder of one of the older boys.

"Make sure he gets home safely, Peter."

The boy nodded.

After watching until they were out of sight, Drew
then went to Dickey's wagon to collect his share of the
night's revenue. On the way out he mentioned that it
might be best if the troupe didn't linger in this part of
the world.

Dickey, being no fool, and already thankful for the
bounty of the Prince of Gwyneth's patronage, took the
hint of his most talented but mysterious associate. By

the time dawn spread its light across the fields, the Rose and Gryphon Traveling Players, the paint on the crest that would make their fortune still dripping, were packed and gone and Andrew Elliot Armistone-Post was well on his way to Liddestane.

8. The Companions

Halfway down the main staircase of Castle Lincolnford, Demnor paused to glance out a window. Glowering storm clouds hung in the sky, spitting rain against the glass in intermittent bursts. Faintly, he could hear the sound of thunder. He smiled grimly. It was exactly the weather he was in the mood for. Continuing down the stairs, he passed under an archway and along a gallery to a small door. Beyond was the castle yard and Terion's stables. He would ride, bathe, and sleep. And if Kelahnus had shaken himself from the contrary mood he'd been in all morning, maybe ride, bathe, make love, and sleep.

They'd guested at the Earl's for three weeks now, indulging in Terion's hospitality, his cellars, and his deer. The official meetings and ceremonies over in the first few days, the remaining time had been filled with riding and quiet conversations. Earlier in the week Demnor had accompanied the Earl on a tour of his lands, meeting his tenants and viewing his crops. It had been a pleasant and peaceful day. The evening had been . . . eventful.

Isolde—the Earl of Essendale, he reminded himself sternly; he'd begun to think of her far too casually of late—had spent much of her time with Katrina and Phillip in the training yard, practicing and handing out advice. Her style was clean, graceful, and economical. Watching her, unobserved from Terion's library window, Demnor itched to join in and test her skill, but found himself strangely hesitant. He'd arranged, instead, for his guard to take exercise, inviting her to join them in this small battle.

In the midst of the fray, Demnor had paused, one hand upraised to halt the rush of his attacker. He'd watched, unable to take his eyes off her as she'd advanced over the rough ground, eyes dark with concentration, face an unreadable mask. She'd paused then, aware of his gaze and had turned. When their eyes met, he'd found himself suddenly uncertain and had abruptly left the training yard.

That had been earlier in the week. Two evenings ago, Demnor and Terion had returned from the older man's northern lands to find her and the two youngsters indulging in a large keg of beer in the dining hall. They were still in training clothes, damp with sweat and dust and happily drunk. Katrina was just beginning the fifth verse of a bawdy Gwynethian ballad when the Heir and the Earl of Linconford entered.

She broke off immediately, but the flush of drink and the presence of Isolde, booted feet on the table and tankard in hand, gave her courage. She smiled and greeted them while her father stared at her in blank surprise, and the Prince stared at his betrothed. This was too much for Phillip. With an explosion of laughter, he slid off his chair and sat giggling on the floor. Isolde gave him a look of mild disapproval.

"Children. They just can't hold their beer like they used to," she admonished, peering down at him. "Well, My Prince, and future father of my children, and you, My Lord of Linconford, don't just stand there gaping in the doorway. Come, sit down and cool your throats. There's still plenty of drink. Isn't there?" She frowned at the keg and then at Katrina.

"If there isn't more in the keg, there's more in the cellar. I'll get some tankards." The younger woman rose, and somewhat unsteadily left the hall, heading in the direction of the kitchens.

Terion looked at Demnor. The Prince himself was

standing very still, staring at the Lord Isolde. She gave him a sloppy smile and gestured for him to sit. He did.

The three older Lords remained drinking, laughing, and exchanging tales long after the youngsters surrendered to drunken slumber. Finally, Terion admitted defeat and allowed himself to be helped up to bed by a sleepy-eyed footman. Demnor and Isolde were left to finish off the keg.

Unused to indulging in alcohol of any kind, the Prince had only a few, vague, drink-muddied images of those later hours. There'd been talking and . . . singing? Visions of Isolde's face flushed with drink, her tousled hair falling down in scattered disarray over her shoulders, swam through the memories. They'd had a heated argument about tactics around two in the morning and, later, about who had the greater number of battle scars. It was during this conversation, that Demnor somehow managed to misplace his tunic.

Standing together in the huge bay window of the castle's empty great hall, they watched the first pale fingers of sunrise touch the sky, then made their way up stairs which seemed much higher and steeper than they had the morning before.

Roused from solitary slumber an hour later, Demnor found himself lying on an unfamiliar bed, the coverlet bunched up and uncomfortable below him. Groggily, he looked around. The room was cold and dusty, the open window allowing in a fine mist of rain.

He stood unsteadily, and as he groped for his breeches, the room suddenly tilted and he sat down hard. After a moment's deep breathing to steady the room, he tried again, and once righted, staggered out into the hall.

With a grimace, he wondered just what he thought he'd been doing last night. Memories of his father's weakness and his mother's cold contempt for him, combined with a fear of losing control, had always kept the Heir away from drink.

You're getting stupider with every passing year. A grin forced itself across his face, despite himself. It'd been kind of fun. *Idiot. You probably made a burning fool of yourself. You don't remember what you said or what you did. What would Kelahnus say?*

Kelahnus. As the evening's revelry had continued and the Heir had not come upstairs, the Companion had probably gone to bed. He hoped.

A sense of uneasiness made his chest feel tight. He was forgetting something. Leaning against a tapestry-covered wall, Demnor scrubbed at his face and tried to call the night's details into memory. Nothing. He shook his head impatiently. He'd probably just staggered upstairs, taken a wrong turn, and collapsed on the first bed he'd tripped over, and he was feeling guilty because he'd gotten drunk like some idiot youth and had left Kelahnus alone all night. That was it. That was all. Rubbing arms covered in gooseflesh, he pushed himself upright and headed for their room.

All this had occurred two days ago and Kelahnus had been in the strangest mood ever since. Rubbing at the scars on his jaw, Demnor frowned as he continued down the stairs. He couldn't remember how this morning's latest argument had begun, or even what it'd been about. The Companion had been distant, staring out the window at the courtyard below. Finally he'd suggested the Heir go riding. Demnor, annoyed at the conversation's confusing, circular path, had agreed.

Now as he crossed the muddy common, he put the argument behind him. Terion's stables were large and clean, smelling of horses, straw, and feed; they cleared his mind and put him in a better mood almost immediately. As he entered the wide doorway, his thoughts elsewhere, he almost collided with Isolde, leading her own mount out. He pulled up short.

"My Lord of Essendale. I didn't see you there." Her smile made him uneasy for a moment, and then the moment passed.

"It was entirely my fault, Highness," she answered. "Are you all right? I hope Rogue didn't step on you."

She patted the large roan's neck as it lipped her hair.
"Are you riding this morning, Your Highness?"

"Uh, yes."

"So am I." She looked up into the sky, brushing rain
damp hair from her face. "I love this kind of weather.
Wild and free, the rain swirling over the hills and the
cold bite of the air in my lungs. I feel more truly alive
than anywhere else. But then, I think we've had this
conversation before." She looked up at him, a lazy
smile on her lips and he felt that nervous flutter in his
stomach again as if there was something important he
was forgetting.

"We did," he answered too hastily. "I agreed
with you. The only place I feel more at home is on the
battlefield."

"Yes, My Prince, I remember you mentioned that."

Rogue pawed at the ground and Isolde absently
swatted him. "You'll want to get your own mount,
Highness. I'll wait for you here."

Demnor nodded and moved past the gelding and into
the stables. It wasn't until he was halfway to Challenger's stall that he realized they had somehow agreed
to go riding together. *Did I decide that?*

Challenger, sensing his presence before the Prince
saw him, gave a loud whicker of greeting. By the time
Demnor had entered the wide box stall, the bay's iron
shod hoof had driven a six-inch trench in the dirt floor.
Stroking his neck affectionately, the Prince waved the
stable hands away.

It took several minutes to get the overexcited animal
haltered and out of his stall. Challenger kept pawing
and tossing his head in his eagerness. Now and then the
Heir would smack him lightly on the flank with a short,
"Stop that," and he would be still for a minute or two
before beginning again. When Demnor muscled the
heavy saddle into place, the bay reached his powerful
neck around and tugged at his hair so hard it was
almost pulled out by the roots. Demnor jerked his head
out of harm's way. Challenger then nuzzled his hip,

looking for the bit of fruit the Heir always brought him, and Demnor staggered back from the force of it.

"Later, you wretch," he snapped as he tightened the girth. Challenger tossed his head and gave a little jump. Straightening, Demnor laughed. "Don't you think you're a bit big to bounce? Here." He fed him the piece of apple.

A few minutes later, he joined Isolde in the stable yard. The Earl of Essendale had already mounted, and as he swung himself into the saddle, Demnor felt absurdly excited. Beneath him, Challenger jumped again and snapped at Rogue who took one step back, ears flat. Demnor chuckled. "The brute still thinks he has balls."

Together the two Lords trotted around the castle keep and through the west gate.

From his vantage point, high above in Isolde's window, Kelahnus watched them go, a smile on his face. Turning back into the room, he joined Tania at breakfast. Tapping at a boiled egg, the other Companion glanced up at him through her lashes.

"So, are they away?"

Kelahnus quartered an apple before answering. "Off and running," he replied, licking the juice from his fingers.

"Then good luck to them. You wouldn't catch me out in weather like that, not for all the Princes in the Realm."

"Not when there're so many more amusing things to do within." Kelahnus' smile made the invitation obvious and Tania nodded her acceptance.

"After breakfast, of course."

"Of course. Have some grapes."

"Why, thank you. Oh, by the way," she sipped at a cup of catmint tea. "Did I tell you that My Lord of Essendale has refrained from partaking of her daily teas?"

In the act of buttering a slice of bread, Kelahnus took a moment to understand her words. The two Companions had compared notes yesterday morning, both surprised by the evening's outcome. But this. This had not been a part of the conversation. Kelahnus placed his knife carefully on the plate and stared at the younger Companion.

"I beg your pardon?"

She laughed then, the sound like the chiming of bells. "I've surprised you! How wonderful! It's true."

"But why?"

Tania shrugged. "With the betrothal announced, she felt there was no longer a need. After all, babies have been known to slip by the herb before, so monogamy was the best response, or in this case, celibacy. Who would have thought?" She left the unfinished sentence hang.

Kelahnus shook his head. "Yes, who would have thought?" He finished his own tea in one swallow, then sat, turning the cup between his fingers.

"So there's a chance there might be a child?"

"A small one, yes, she may have been in her fertile time. I could check back if you like."

"Please do. A child. Oh, my." Despite the seriousness of the situation, he couldn't help but smile. "He'll be surprised." Now there was an understatement. If he knew Demnor, the Heir would be appalled.

Tania nodded. "So will she. Although less so, I think. Has he said nothing at all about that night?"

"Not a word. I don't think he remembers." At least not completely. The memory was there, however, submerged just below the surface. He could see it in the other man's eyes, in his unease and his inability to meet and hold his Companion's gaze, which wasn't like him at all.

"Should we inform the Guild?" Tania asked.

Kelahnus tapped a finger against his cup a moment before setting it carefully aside.

"No, I don't think so. It's a bit premature yet. If she hasn't caught, there's no rush. There'll be plenty of time to discuss the situation with Master Klairius when we return to Branbridge. In the meantime, we must stay vigilant for any sign that the night's dancing has changed their relationship. But if he doesn't remember it . . ."

"She does."

"So you said." He shook off a thrill of disquiet. "But that's all for the best. It will make things easier between them later."

Tania helped herself to more grapes. "What if they fall in love? Aren't you worried?"

Kelahnus smiled. "No, Younger Sister. I have an extended contract and a large retirement clause. Besides, they have too much in common, though few would believe it. They'll become friends and that's good. If they grow to love one another, that will be all to the better. Love can be an added benefit in a marriage."

"Whereas it muddles up a contract."

He laughed. "That depends on which side of the contract it occurs."

"True. And they say the Prince of Gwyneth is in love with you."

"*They* are very observant."

"And do you feel for him?"

Inwardly Kelahnus smiled. He had cut his teeth on questions such as these. "Of course I do," he replied in the voice of an older, wiser person humoring a child. "You can't live with someone, share his life and sleep in his bed without growing to care for him. Even to love him. But then, you'll discover that when you've been with your Lord longer. It's perfectly normal."

The younger Companion mulled over his words, distracted by his reference to her Lord. "Yes," she answered finally. "I do care for her. She's kind and passionate and charming, but in some ways . . ." She shook her head.

"In some ways?"

"In some ways she's arrogant and selfish and hopelessly out of touch."

With a laugh, Kelahnus poured them both some

more tea. "They're all like that. Without us, the country would fall apart through neglect."

"So here's to us, then."

"To us."

Their cups touched, and their eyes met. Tania drew her tongue across her lips and Kelahnus rose, hand outstretched. She took it and they moved toward the bed. The Royal Companion smiled. They had most of the afternoon, and there was no better way to keep a young Companion from sleeping dragons best left undisturbed than with sex.

Some hours later, Kelahnus returned to his seat by the window and stared out. *Are you worried? Was* he worried? He had to admit, if only to himself, that after the keep had grown quiet that night and Demnor had still not returned, he had felt a vague, nervous stirring in his stomach. And after he'd heard the two Lords coming up the stairs—it was hard not to, they sounded like a pair of warhorses—and the Heir still didn't come to bed, he'd felt, not worried, but surprisingly jealous.

He sighed and, for the twentieth time, told himself he had nothing to be jealous about. He'd seen within the well of Demnor's soul. He knew the Heir loved him. And he knew how he felt about the Heir.

The young Companion turned his face from the window with a contemplative expression. It had begun so long ago.

The wind caressed his face, pulling him back to another time and another view.

Kelahnus, fifteen, sat in the west study's window seat, gazing out across the School grounds to the turret tips of Bran's Palace. Somewhere in that maze of beautifully furnished rooms and corridors Demnor moved about his day, eating, drinking, maybe thinking about him. The thought made him itch. The Prince had sworn to make him his Companion and Kelahnus had no doubt that he would, he was only a little worried about when. Companions graduated at eighteen and not before. Never before. He still had three years of regular training to go, plus the years of graduate studies that those contracted to the Royal Family and the higher nobility had to attend. Florence had been contracted almost a month now, and still returned to the School for lessons twice a week, and sat on the Council as a junior member. Three years. He wasn't sure if Demnor would be able to wait. For that matter, he wasn't sure if he could.

He leaned his chin on his arms and sucked reflectively at a lock of hair. That was a matter safely left in the hands of Master Klairius. How the Guild Head would manage to stall the Crown Prince without having a Royal fit land on his head, Kelahnus had no idea, but again, he had no doubt that he would. Problem one solved. Problem two, suitability was no problem at all. He knew he was destined for the highest nobility.

At eleven, those who were deemed possible as Companions were split from those whose earlier potential had bloomed in other ways. The latter served the School as Auxiliaries. At sixteen, those remaining were placed in sections that most suited their abilities. The most beautiful, the most talented, the most intelligent, and the most loyal were placed in a special class to be trained to contract to the Lords and Scholars who ruled Branion.

Kelahnus had half a year to serve to Junior Session Three and was top of his class, Junior Session Head, and believed to be the brightest and best to come out of the Branbridge School in years.

He pulled the lock of hair from his mouth in mid chew. He *had* been Junior Session Head. Master Klairius had taken the title from him after the day he'd first met Demnor in the garden. The Master had commended his behavior toward the Prince, while condemning the actions that had brought the meeting into being. Kelahnus' ears burned at the memory of that conversation.

"Careless! Childish! And most unbecoming to one of your status among your classmates. If you've not

learned to control yourself any better by now, you're certainly not ready for the responsibilities of Junior Session Head. You are dismissed. Send Gabriel to me."

Gabriel, his second until then. Promoted to the position his desire had cost him. Kelahnus tossed the lock of hair behind him. It was all right. Nothing had changed between the two students. Gabriel may have been Junior Session Head, but he still deferred to his more gregarious classmate, as he always had. Besides, Kelahnus soothed his injured pride, it was good training as the power behind the throne. And the gamble had been worth the risk. It had won him Demnor. Now, however, he must keep him.

His classmates knew he visited the Prince at night. And if they knew, the Masters knew. There was no such thing as keeping secrets in the School of Companions. Until now. So far, Master Klairius had not seen fit to summon him. He was waiting. Waiting to see what would develop, watching Demnor, getting reports from the Palace Companions on his actions and his words. Kelahnus knew what those reports would say. In the three short weeks he had known the Prince, he had come to realize that the older youth was totally without guile. What he said, he felt, and what he felt he showed, indiscriminately, without thought of the consequences.

Coming from a world where every glance and every movement was schooled to convey a desired effect, this both drew and frightened the student. There was one thing he was sure about, though; if ever a man was in need of a Companion, the Heir was.

The Royal Companions would report that the Prince of Gwyneth was in love.

Leaning out the window, he picked at a sprig of ivy. They would be watching him, too. He had assumed that from the very beginning and had acted accordingly.

He was unable to contain his pride at being noticed by the Crown Prince. Obviously he was the most beautiful and accomplished of them all. He could not hide his triumph from Gabriel; he told him everything. And Gabriel could not keep from spreading this delicious tale about. The others were jealous, rightfully so, and he lorded his new conquest over them, while desperately trying to hide it from them all, especially from the Masters.

His fingers shredded the delicate ivy leaf. The walls had ears and eyes and those walls would report that the Junior Session Second was overwhelmed with the attentions being paid to him by the Heir. After all, who wouldn't be? Bringing his fingers up to his lips, he breathed in the sharp perfume of the crushed plant. Who wouldn't be?

Some years ago Kelahnus had discovered that the west study door creaked. He'd made it his special place ever since, the place where he did his most serious thinking, the place where he could relax and drop his guard, allowing his features to mirror his thoughts and his feelings. By the time Master Klairius' page had navigated the bookcases and chairs, he was curled up in the window seat, looking up curiously from a book at the sound of the soft footfall.

The page was a Second Class. Probably Second Class Head, twelve years old and puffed up with the importance of her mission. Having served in the same capacity three years and a century earlier, Kelahnus hid a smile and heard her message.

"Master Klairius wants to see you."

The Head of the Companion's Guild sat at an elaborately carved desk imported from the East, sipping at a glass of chilled chocolate. When Besalia arrived to tell him that Kelahnus awaited without, he indicated that the student should be shown in. Kelahnus entered and bowed. Klairius waved him to a seat.

He studied the boy intently, letting him know he did so. Kelahnus sat waiting, his features and his stance held in a carefully crafted pose of respectful curiosity. They both knew it was false. Klairius had every faith that Kelahnus knew exactly why he had been summoned, had been expecting it, and had rehearsed their conversation. The Master smiled inwardly. The boy had potential, although it would be some years before it was realized. His task today was to show the student this and to guide him away from the serious pitfalls his pride was leading him toward. The old man fingered the stiff piece of parchment on the desk before him, and Kelahnus' gaze flickered to it. Good, he was curious then. This letter was not something he had anticipated and he had no strategy for it. Time to remind him who was the student and who the Master.

He cleared his throat and Kelahnus looked up expectantly.

"I have here a message from Her Most Regal Majesty, the Aristok. Do you know what it contains?"

Kelahnus inclined his head with a polite expression that both affirmed and invited the Master to enlighten him anyway.

Confident little bugger, the old man thought.

"It states that the Prince of Gwyneth has been carrying on a clandestine affair with one of my students."

Kelahnus nodded.

"It intimates that Her Majesty is not yet aware of who this student is." The actual words had been, *We are not interested in this person's identity* . . . but the Guild Head had no intention of making it easy for the boy.

There was a faint look of relief in Kelahnus' eyes.

Yes, be relieved, you young goat, what I would have done if she had demanded your head, I'll never know.

"It suggests, however, that I contrive to discover it."

Slight amusement pulled at the student's lips.

"It also suggests, since such activities are against the rules of this School, that when I discover it, I discipline the guilty party."

The boy had a measuring look, guarded but thoughtful, wondering how far his Master agreed with the Aristok.

"As she has disciplined the Crown Prince."

The old man had been watching Kelahnus closely,

waiting for the reaction to this last piece of news. The boy's eyes showed alarm for an instant, then went blank, but the Master could see that his breathing had quickened and his pale skin had dropped a shade whiter. Klairius kept his own face expressionless, though his eyes narrowed almost imperceptibly.

"She has also forbidden him to see you again."

Disappointment, but the student's eyes were hooded, masking what?

"And considers this matter closed."

No reaction, and he had expected none. The boy wore his thoughtful expression again, and Klairius allowed him a moment to mull over the message and to collect himself. Sooner than he had expected, Kelahnus looked up, waiting.

"You have been seeing the Crown Prince for some weeks."

It was not a question, although the boy nodded, wariness in his eyes.

"It is said that he has fallen in love with you."

Faint pleasure colored Kelahnus' cheeks.

"Or at least in temporary infatuation."

The young eyes showed indignation, and Klairius kept the smile from his face.

"It is also said in these halls that you are encouraging his attentions."

The student's chin raised slightly, the defensiveness in the position apparent, though he did not reply.

Klairius gave a sigh and schooled his expression to one of sternness with a touch of understanding.

"Kelahnus, I know that he is the Heir to the Throne, and as such wields a power to be reckoned with. If he has demanded your company, it was wise not to provoke him. I am sure, also, that it is flattering to hold the attention of one such as the Prince."

He was half expecting Kelahnus to seize on this excuse, but the boy merely watched his superior, his face smooth of expression. Klairius applauded his abilities while mildly cursing them at the same time.

"However, flattery and wisdom aside, why did you

not come to me when you learned of his designs to continue your acquaintance?"

His voice was gentle, reproachful, his expression that of a father grieved to find fault in his favorite son, although his thoughts were anything but calm. Kelahnus *was* one of his favorite sons; a boy he had watched grow and helped train. It wasn't like him, this flagrant disregard of the rules. True, each success had raised his confidence in his own abilities. Few graduates had such poise and a certain arrogance was necessary and encouraged. But. Klairius stilled fingers wanting to drum on the desk. But He was hiding something. What?

The student was quiet for a moment, several answers obviously chosen and disregarded, then, with a measured look, he answered, "I assumed you knew about my activities, Master, and that if you disapproved of them, you would send for me."

Flagrant disregard indeed. A flash of anger came and went, swiftly smoothed over at this insolent reply. The boy had spoken respectfully, but was gambling that Master Klairius wanted this eventual contract. And he had not answered the question. Klairius continued the attack.

"Fraternization with possible clients outside of these walls without chaperoning is strictly against the rules of this School." The Master's voice was stone with no warmth or understanding evident. "I had thought you knew that."

His words had the required effect. The boy's cheeks grew warm, and his jaw worked with the effort to retain an expressionless mask. He dropped his eyes. After a moment, he spoke without looking up. "Forgive me, Master. I . . . I wanted to come to you, but I thought . . ."

"You thought?"

"I . . ." He raised his head, contrition and pride battling in his eyes. "I wanted to win him without counsel or advice. I thought . . ."

"You thought I would not trust your abilities, trust

that you could make a Prince of the Realm fall in love
with you."

Kelahnus looked away. "I wanted to do it all
myself."

"To prove you were a Companion already?" The
Master's voice was harsh. "To show up your classmates and those farther along in their training? Or did
you think you knew better about such matters than I?
That advice or counsel from your Master would be so
dense and constrictive that it would fail to win you this
young man?"

Biting at his lip, Kelahnus remained silent.

Klairius leaned forward. "Shall I tell you, Junior
Session Second," the words were deliberately biting
and the student winced, "what you have proved instead
and what the consequences of your rash, unthinking
actions are likely to be? You have proved yourself a
vain, foolish child with no thought to your duties, to
your teachers, or to your Guild!"

Kelahnus' head snapped up. With effort, he brought
himself under control, though his eyes flashed with
anger. Klairius went on.

"You have flaunted your abilities in the most
shameful way, proving that you have learned nothing
about the subtleties a Companion *must* possess! No
graduate of this School would be so obtuse! You may
say that you have done this for the Guild, that bringing
this young man under your control will be good for us.
I tell you that you are wrong, you are blind, and that
you are doing this merely for the sake of your own
vanity!"

Half rising from his seat, Kelahnus opened his
mouth to protest, but with a look from his Master, he
subsided, shaking.

Klairius continued, his tone that of lecturing a
Second Class. "The Prince of Gwyneth is a highly
strung, unstable youth. He must be handled with the
strictest control and the most delicate of maneuvering.
Appealing to his ego, as you have so obviously done,
will last only as long as he assumes that *you* are infatu-

ated with him. Should he ever suspect that it is false
flattery, he will turn on you with all the force he has
shown to others in the past. You may believe you are
skilled enough to handle this. I tell you that you are
not. At one time, I might have believed that with
training you would become so. Now . . . what you have
exhibited here is the most juvenile form of thinking."

The student's face was dark, his eyes burning into
those of his Master with an expression that reminded
Klairius suddenly of the Crown Prince and gave him a
tremor of disquiet. That Prince Demnor should have
such a flawing effect on one of his best students was
more than alarming. That effect would cease as of this
moment. But this was getting out of hand. Willing himself to calm, the Master studied the student once more.

There was no maliciousness in Kelahnus, no willful-
ness or recklessness. In fact, some of his teachers worried privately about his abilities to actuate certain
aspects of his training. Master Terri, who taught techniques in assassination, firmly believed this though her
superior Master Elias, Head of Guild Security, did not.
Neither did Master Klairius. All it took was training
and necessity.

There was no maliciousness, although there was
overconfidence and presumption. The Head of the
Guild cursed himself for not noticing the signs of this
sooner.

I must be getting old.

The Heir must eventually have a Companion, he
mused to himself. When he took the Throne, likely
more than one. Master Klairius had made up a list of
alumnae some years ago who would be appropriate as
Initial Companions; however, the Aristok had refused
the first inquiry, so he'd put it aside. Now, of course,
the youth was too old. The Master sighed.

*The contrary, young savage would choose a course
of action like this; guaranteed to cause the greatest
degree of inconvenience.*

Like Kelahnus, the Master knew that once the Prince
had the bit in his teeth, he would not be deterred. The

Aristok had halted his desire for the moment, but that would not be the end of it. And also, like the student, he knew Kelahnus was ideally suited. It was an opportunity well worth the risks, even more so now that the boy had indeed managed to hook the Heir's emotions. It was well done, if rash. And that brought his thoughts back around to Kelahnus and his reasoning.

In his pride, the boy did truly believe he was bringing control of the Prince to the Guild. His *loyalty,* at least, could not be questioned, though Klairius was disappointed that good sense had shown itself to be one of his weaker suits. That could be learned. Egotism and Royal high-handedness, traits obviously picked up from the Prince of Gwyneth, were not, however, to be tolerated. With several years of careful training and limited access to the Heir, Kelahnus would be ready to serve as Companion to such a man. But he must be pulled away from the Prince's influence. The Master picked up the Aristok's letter.

"What Her Majesty has done with His Highness, I have yet to discover, although you may be certain it has done nothing to alleviate the tensions between them. As for any punishment you may have brought upon yourself, I have yet to decide upon it. Be assured, however, it will fall. It is very possible that I shall hold up your graduation to Senior Session, as it's clear you're not ready."

Kelahnus paled, growing suddenly very still. Klairius could see him turning over the humiliation this would cause and marshaling his arguments. Before he had a chance to speak, Klairius pressed on.

"Further, the Aristok has demanded that the two of you never meet again, and I think I concur."

That brought the reaction he was expecting. Kelahnus started, his eyes wide and disbelieving. Klairius merely gazed at him. He knew what raced through the student's mind. He had gambled it all, his standing, his reputation, the whole game on the idea that the capture of the Royal Knight was worth it. Now the Head of his Guild was telling him not only that it was not, but that the former were lost as well. Kelahnus' mouth worked, his eyes suddenly filling with tears. He bowed his head, defeated. Klairius nodded.

"It was a good try, child." The Master spoke softly now, gentle in victory. "And I can't say that I wouldn't have tried the same in your place. It's very hard being the best at a very young age. Hard to remain patient and learn the polish you must have to carry out such an ambitious idea."

Kelahnus dropped his head into his hands, totally undone, his shoulders shaking. Klairius let him cry.

"I'm sorry, Master," the boy finally gulped out. "I didn't mean it to seem that way, I swear. I wanted to do it for the School, you must believe me."

"I do, lad, I do. Now stop crying. It's undignified."

He handed him a handkerchief, and Kelahnus swiped at his eyes, his expression embarrassed.

"I'm sorry."

"I know. Now bring yourself under control, please. I wish to discuss this with you seriously, and I want you to answer as honestly as possible."

The boy looked up, hope mingling with despair.

"Is the Prince of Gwyneth in love with you?"

Taking a deep breath, Kelahnus looked him in the eye. "I believe so, Master."

"Do you believe it will stand the test of time?"

Kelahnus took longer to answer this question. "I don't know," he said finally. "If we're not allowed to see each other, it may fade or he may turn his attentions elsewhere."

He was loath to say the words, and Klairius almost forgot himself and smiled.

"But," the student went on, "his possessiveness may outlast his affection."

Klairius nodded.

"And, Master . . ." the student hesitated, uncertain if he should speak.

Klairius indicated that he should continue.

"He may not wait."

Interesting.

"Explain."

"He may move before his affection fades, but also before he holds the power to do so."

Klairius snorted. "Nonsense. I told you, the Aristok has forbidden him to see you again. To move, as you put it, would be to directly disobey a Royal command. Speak sense, boy."

Kelahnus dropped his gaze.

Klairius sighed, suddenly remembering just how young this brilliant pupil of his really was.

"Kelahnus, I know his no doubt fierce desire for you is heady, like a potent wine. But you mustn't allow yourself to become drunk on it and ignore the very obvious traits of your Prince. He is unswervingly devoted to the Realm and slavishly obedient to the Aristok's demands. No. If you are to become Prince Demnor's Companion, it must be by our hands, not by his."

A look of joy flashed across the boy's face, then was quickly smothered. "You mean, I, that is, you . . . ?"

This time Klairius allowed himself a chuckle. "Yes, child, it's an opportunity we shouldn't waste. But," he held up his hand to forestall another outburst, "in this you will, you must, be guided by me, for now we must not only outmaneuver your Prince, we must out-maneuver the Aristok. And that will not be easy."

Kelahnus nodded, the thoughtful expression returned.

There was a knock at the door. At Klairius' reply, Jeaniel, his secretary, put his head in. "Excuse me, Master, a child from the palace has gained entrance to the grounds. He says he bears a message for Kelahnus."

Once back in his rooms, the student collapsed onto the bed he'd shared with Gabriel for two and a half years and gave himself over to a fit of shaking. He was sweating and his teeth chattered together with the release of the nervous energy that had kept him going through his interview with Master Klairius, his meeting with Terence, and back to the Master's office again.

"I don't ever want to go through that again," he whispered.

After a time, the shaking subsided and he lay, hands behind his head, staring up at the ceiling. The late afternoon sun sent strips of light across the beams and he counted dust motes circling above his head. Slowly, a smile spread across his face. He'd done it. Given everything he had in the performance of his life. A hysterical giggle forced its way between his lips, and he clamped his hand over his mouth in case any more emerged. He'd done it. He had fooled the Head of the Companion's Guild.

He sobered quickly. He'd done it for the moment, he reminded himself sternly. This was just the beginning. He went over the interview. He hadn't believed he was going to be that nervous. Sitting there, fighting to keep a blank expression while Master Klairius racked him with his eyes. He'd felt naked and foolish, sure the Master could see through his plans. But the Guild Head had believed the performance Kelahnus had orchestrated before his classmates. Believed he had over-reached himself, that pride and arrogance had prompted his actions.

He frowned. The Master had believed, believed him shallow and boasting and reckless and—what was the word he had used—juvenile. That hurt. Tears burned at the back of his eyes, and he hastily ran his sleeve across them.

Foolish, he chided himself. *That was what you wanted him to believe, wasn't it?*

The hurt remained, a lump of disappointment in his throat. For over a decade the School had been his home, been mother and father and world to him and Master Klairius had been his teacher and his friend. Now a wall had grown up between them. A wall built by Kelahnus' emerging talents that were greater than even that astute, old man suspected. And for what? For a man who made his arms ache to hold him and his body tingle with the memory of his touch. For a man who frightened him with the intensity of his need and the force of his desire. For a man who cried out in a self-imposed exile, bleeding from wounds he would not allow to heal. For a man he loved.

With a sigh, the student turned on his side, resting his head on his arm. At the beginning, he'd believed his feelings were much as they should have been. He *had* been overwhelmed and flattered by the Heir's attentions. Master Klairius was right in a way. It'd been a heady brew, one he had been completely intoxicated by. And one that had led to his first break from his complete submission to the dictates of the School. He had met the Prince secretly, knowing that he would be safe from discovery this one time because Gabriel slept soundly despite all Master Terri's training and because no one would suspect him of such a thing.

Kelahnus closed his eyes, the memory of that first night, both frantic and tentative, bringing a flush of pleasure to his face. The budding feelings were new and totally irresistible. But the Prince had duties and in the week between that night and their next meeting, reality had imposed on his pleasure like a bucket of ice water. He couldn't count on not being discovered the next time or the next and why was he sure there would be a next time and why did he need there to be. His first suspicion felt the most accurate, and until he understood his feelings better, he planned for the worst. He was in love. It turned out to be the truth.

Remembering his panic brought a smile to his lips. He'd had no idea what to do or how to proceed. All he knew with absolute certainty was that neither Master Klairius nor anyone else must ever suspect his feelings for the Prince. For Demnor to fall for him was one thing, and all for the good. Love was easy to control and manipulate. But for him to fall for the Prince? No. He would be suspect in his loyalty to the Guild. Love blinded you, made you vulnerable. The vows he had taken at thirteen and would reaffirm at his graduation were quite clear. Love and loyalty was reserved for the

Guild. As for the nobility, the clients outside the safety of these walls whose beds they would fill, they were the means to the power of the Guild and the Guild Council. Nothing more.

He sighed, chewing on a lock of hair. Nothing more, until now. What, by the Four Winds, had he gotten himself into? Master Klairius was right about one thing; the Prince *was* high-strung and violent. But the Master was wrong if he thought him—what had he said—slavishly devoted to the Aristok's demands. This afternoon's message had proved that. The student mulled over Terence's words.

The grubby child had stared up at him, unimpressed by the beauty of the garden and the people around him. He had delivered his message, carefully memorized, then turned and darted away without waiting for a reply.

"There's been some trouble. Hide. Tell no one about us. Be ready to run."

Be ready to run! Kelahnus had felt a thread of fear trickle down his spine. Just what kind of trouble had he gotten them into?

The presence of Florence in Master Klairius' office when he returned had confirmed that it was of the worst kind. The Aristok had named the Prince forsworn and placed him under arrest.

Master Klairius was not happy, and his words were brief. "I must think. Return to your studies."

Kelahnus had bowed and retired, catching a sympathetic glance from Florence. That'd helped a little. *Please don't let him do anything stupid,* he'd thought to whatever powers might feel inclined to listen, although he feared it was already too late. Somehow he had made it to his room and after several deep breaths, had managed to calm himself. Then the day had finally caught up with him.

Now he sat up and tucked his feet underneath him. Enough wallowing in emotion. Time to rationally review the past and orchestrate the future.

First, he had to know more about what had

transpired between Demnor and the Aristok. Then he must get a message to him. He wished he could speak with him alone, but that was impossible now. Now he must play by Master Klairius' rules. For the first, he would ask Florence. She would tell him without drawing any suspicious conclusions from his asking if he worded it right. And she might have some advice on contacting the Prince if he convinced her it was to persuade him to mend the rift between himself and the Aristok. He thought he could influence him that far. Kelahnus was sure he would listen to reason if someone listened to him. That, the student felt, was the Heir's greatest problem. Nobody cared.

Tears welled in his eyes, and he allowed them to drip onto his sleeve for a little while. He cared, and he would make Demnor know it, and together they would defeat anyone who stood in the way of their happiness.

A splash of rain on his arm brought the Companion back to the present. Brushing futilely at the wet fabric, he smiled at the memory of his younger, more melodramatic self, before folding it up and tucking it safely away.

He squinted up at the swollen clouds before closing the window. Demnor and the Earl of Essendale would be far out in the fields by now, enjoying the biting wind, the rain, and the muck. *May they have joy of it together.* He shivered, sudden misgivings chilling his skin and raising goosebumps between the fine hairs on his arms. He hoped he was doing the right thing.

Trotting easily along the north bank of the Wiltham River, Demnor and Isolde had been content to ride silently for several miles, both busy with their own thoughts. Much of the land surrounding Linconford was cultivated, and they'd had to travel some distance before the neat furrows of farmland and pasture gave way to rocky ground, patched with pockets of woods and scrub. Finally this, too, surrendered to the tangled borders of Bricklin Forest. The river continued to flow through the trees with barely a ripple to mark its new surroundings, but the banks were high and steep, and no path wide enough to admit them could be seen.

At the edge of the trees, Demnor reined in and wiped the mist from his face.

Pulling up beside him, Isolde removed her gauntlets and leaned forward in the saddle to peer into the gloom.

"Are we carrying on, Highness?"

Demnor considered it a moment, then shook his head. "The Bricklin's a labyrinth of pitfalls and brambles. We'd do better to turn north from here and follow the trees until we make the Bardcaster Road."

"A shame. I've heard so many tales of its beauty that I'd hoped we might journey through it a short while."

Rubbing at the scars along his jaw, the Heir squinted at the sky, trying to gauge the time through the heavy storm clouds. "The Bardcaster runs through a portion of the forest. If we make good time, we might have an hour or so to spend in the Bricklin before dark."

"Then shall we make good time, My Prince?" Isolde's smile was inviting and Demnor found himself responding to it with a smile of his own. Turning her mount to the north, the Earl urged it forward and took off across the fields.

With an indignant neigh, Challenger gave chase. The Heir let him have his head, and before long the two animals were racing neck and neck across the fields.

Two hours later they crested a small hill overlooking the road.

The Bardcaster was one of the ancient highways linking Linconford and the west with the port cities of the east. It cut straight as an arrow through the most northerly tip of the Bricklin Forest to emerge some thirty miles later at Bardcasterfort, the coastal defense town for which it had been named. The two Lords turned onto it and passed quickly into the trees.

Within, it was dark and muted; the trees, like towering sentinels, leaning out over the road to listen to the dull clop, clop of their horses' hooves. Most had begun to lose their leaves although here and there a tall oak still reached dusty, yellow-covered fingers up through the tangled branches to the sky.

They'd gone about a mile when a long, ragged howl broke the silence. Demnor froze, the hair on the back of his neck rising with the ululating cry. When he turned to Isolde, the Duke had gone pale.

"Dragon," the Heir whispered, his voice tight.

She nodded. " A challenge cry, I think."

"Too far off to be directed at us. Still . . ."

Dragon's territories were not vast, but they defended them with wild ferocity. Every winter the tales were told of some unlucky knight or traveler who'd stumbled into a dragon's realm only to be set upon by the beast driven savage by the cold.

The call sounded again, then, from the distance, came an answer. The returning cry was rougher, deeper, and almost immediately the first creature howled again, the rage in its voice unmistakable.

Demnor grinned. "There'll be a burning battle."

Isolde nodded, her eyes bright. "It would be an impressive sight to see."

Turning, the Heir met her gaze, the same thought in both their minds. "With their full attention on each other . . ."

"And the musk and blood-scent so heavy in the air . . ."

"A cautious approach could get quite close . . ."

"And back again in one piece with a story that would make the minstrels jealous."

"Stupid, though."

"Indeed, Highness, both stupid and dangerous."

"Leave the horses. They're far enough away they won't spook."

Past the road, the tangles grew more pronounced, but with unusual patience the two Lords made their way toward the sounds of battle. The crashing of brush and the creatures' high-pitched shrieking grew steadily louder until the trees parted to reveal a wide, burn-scarred clearing.

The forest's open floor was scored and ragged, chunks of sod ripped up and flung against the surrounding trees. Old scars on brush and bark showed the signs of past battles and the ground cover was thin and patchy.

In the center two male dragons paced back and forth. Tearing at the loose soil with their back claws, the quills on their necks standing out in stiff fighting posture, they screamed their challenges, eyes intent on each other's movements.

One was small, the short, deadly spines on its body still showing the faint pattern of adolescence, the spurs on its legs grown to only one barb. As it circled, it kept its head low, weaving to the right and left, seeking its adversary's throat or forelegs. Slapping its tail against the ground, it screamed in rage. Demnor recognized the timber of the first cry that had alerted them. Here was the challenger.

The other was older, the scars of previous fighting showing plain beneath its coarser spines. It was bigger, bulkier, and when it lunged, it threw itself forward, trying to make use of its heavier weight to overbear the smaller creature. But it was favoring its right foreleg, and the younger dragon's eyes kept tracking back to this obvious weakness.

"Clever beast," Demnor observed in a whisper.

Isolde nodded.

The dragons continued to circle, their challenging screams rising in pitch until, almost as one, they lunged. Rolling, they tore at each other, ripping away patches of quills and flesh. Then they leaped back to circle once again.

The scent of blood, mixed with the heavy musk of fighting males filled the clearing and Demnor felt his groin tighten and his lips peel back from his teeth. The ferocity before them was intoxicating, the threat of death adding a sharp taste of fear. Beside him, the Earl was breathing hard, absorbed in the battle, her expression glazed and intense.

With a high-pitched shriek, the younger dragon lunged, the older rising to meet it. They came together, feet clawing, teeth snapping. Drawn by the unbridled ruthlessness of their attack, Demnor found himself unable to look away. No civilization held them back, no armor clothed their vulnerability in iron shielding. This was a desperate, savage fight to the death, and he longed to join the fray, gouging and tearing at his foe with his bare hands.

The younger one cried out then, a hoarse squall of agony, and Demnor shuddered. Caught up in the creature's desperate struggle to hold its ground, his head began to throb as he willed the beast to stand and fight. His eyes grew hot, his vision dancing with blood-red motes as his senses reached out. The animal's rage filled his mind, his own strength wrapping it in bands of flame. As the elder dragon made to lunge, Demnor and his brother creature rose to meet it.

Something held him back from the final attack. The pressure built behind his eyes like a dam and then snapped backward and the dragon lunged alone. Slowly, his vision cleared and he found himself standing, straining toward the clearing, Isolde's hand holding his arm like a vise. The rage retreated, and when she saw that reason had returned, she released him and quickly looked away. The memory of a warm and soft embrace surfaced for an instant and then it was gone. Demnor turned back to the clearing.

The fight was over. The older dragon lay still, the younger standing slumped and bleeding beside it. Staggering back a pace, it gave one ragged cry of victory, then it, too, fell, to lie still upon the bloody ground.

The Prince and the Earl cautiously entered the clearing.

The going was slippery and uneven, pools of blood collecting in the deep trenches. Slowly Demnor approached the dead combatants and stared at them for a long time, his features distorted.

Isolde stood silently beside him. Finally she sighed. "So little gain at the end of it all."

When the Heir didn't answer, she knelt and laid her hand on the still warm flank of the younger creature. "So much strength, so much desire, wasted."

She looked up at the Prince, and, as if he were shaking off a dream, Demnor turned and regarded her.

"What?"

"Well, did it achieve anything in the end, My Prince? This glorious battle, this terrible thirst for victory? It all ended in death."

The Heir shrugged, his eyes straying back to the younger beast. "It gained the pride of the fighting. That's enough. Everything ends in death."

The Earl said nothing.

Kneeling, Demnor removed a few of the barbed quills from the creature's tail and tucked them in his belt. Then he rose. "We should leave this place, My Lord of Essendale, the scavengers of the forest won't be long to the feast.

"As you wish, Highness."

The horses were where they'd left them and they mounted in silence, an uneasiness grown up between them. A cold breeze had begun to blow, and it fanned the fever on Demnor's face as he rode, soothing the throbbing pain in his skull and numbing the memory of the dragon's rage and desperation.

Cantering quickly along the east road, they soon saw the welcoming lights of the city shining in the distance, but for the Heir they held no more warmth. The peace that had settled over him in Terion's easy company had evaporated in the forest, leaving a chill purpose behind. It was time to leave Linconford and carry on with his responsibilities.

9. Braxborough

The fields of Liddestane were awash with sunlight, steam rising from the recently sodden ground. Arren pushed his sturdy Heathland pony into a gallop, its hooves sending sprays of water into the air. At the crest of a low hill, he reined in and stopped, allowing it to drop its head to the grass. Balancing an elbow on the pommel, he rested his chin on his fist and stared out at the misty hills.

Before him a hawk soared across the sky, searching the fields for prey. Arren watched it a long time, his mind running over his plans with the same meticulous care. Finally, his thoughts came around to the latest in a series of Essus-sent opportunities.

"He's coming here, the bloody Prince of Gwyneth," Andrew Elliot Armistone Post had staggered into the hall, dirty and exhausted, to drop this bit of news at Arren's feet. *"To Braxborough Castle with just over a score of Guard. He thinks Heathland is quiet, tamed. A small band could . . ."*

Could. Would. Opportunities like this didn't happen often and had to be taken advantage of. His War Council had seen that immediately and the room had erupted with ideas and volunteers to lead the attack. But Arren had stilled this premature call to arms with one curt word. When the Council had quieted, he'd told Hilary to carry on with the business of the day and had left the room. Saddling Mohair, he'd departed the castle grounds at a gallop.

Now, out on the moor, he could think clearly and incorporate this new piece into the larger plan.

An attack would be made on Braxborough, that much was certain, with the Crown Prince taken or slain. And that would bring the wrath of Branion down upon their heads like a swarm of black wasps. So they must be ready to meet this swarm and that meant moving first. The war must be initiated now, this autumn, despite the harvest, and the key cities with their stores of food secured before winter. A messenger must be sent to Gordon to coordinate the Branbridge operation with the Braxborough attack, and the Churches would have to be informed that they must rise five months early.

He shook his head. So much depended on timing. A nagging doubt tickled the back of his mind and he stilled it firmly. They'd prepared for this all their lives. They were ready. Rubbing his medallion between finger and thumb, he emptied his mind of worry and put his faith in Essus. Together they would triumph.

When he opened his eyes again, a movement on the plains below him caught his attention. A single rider: Hilary, from the way she rode. Nudging his pony into a walk, Arren met her at the bottom of the hill

"Have you concluded the day's business?"

His sister turned her mount before answering, and the two ponies fell into step together.

"As much as could be done. They're like children in there, fidgeting and eager for Market Day."

Arren frowned. "It's too premature for that sort of nonsense," he snapped.

"They'll calm down. With you and I absent, Eilene will lead the conversation to feats of fame and glory until they've spent themselves."

They splashed through a swampy puddle. Scratching at a scar on her wrist, Hilary glanced sideways at her elder brother, trying to gauge his mood.

"This changes things somewhat."

"Somewhat."

The sarcasm in the tone made her smile.

"It could well be the best way to begin."

"With a victory."

"With a hostage."

"Or a death."

"A hostage might make the DeMarian overcautious, a death, overzealous. Either way, we win."

"Whatever way, we win."

"As you say, Brother."

They rode in silence for some time.

"It's not a bad time for it either," Hilary continued. "We're as ready as we'll ever be. All it needs is the word and we could be in Braxborough by Essus' Harvest."

"And Tottenham and Bothsyde, Threkirk, Tantaven and Caerockeith?"

"Why not. They'll not be expecting it, not this close to winter. And Braxborough's the place to start. There's none so caught in the middle as the garrison there. Half of them at least have Heathland families by now."

This was Hilary's strength as a lieutenant and Arren allowed himself to be drawn into conversation. "We'll need one or two on the inside for success. And they *must* be reliable. The garrison is Branion, no matter how sympathetic, and if even one returns to the fold, we're lost." He thought a moment. "Doesn't Mary Ramsen have a man at Braxborough?"

Hilary nodded. "Dion Hill; he's a Guard Sergeant from Vervickshire. They've two children and he doesn't think much of his Triarctic Lords. He's half an Essusiate already.

"And it's said Mary visits him up a secret path," she added.

Arren snorted. "Not so secret if *it's said.*"

"Well, secret enough that the Warden's done nothing to secure it. If one can take a path, then so can fifty."

"Maybe. If the path existed. Find out."

Hilary smiled. "Yes, Sire."

Skirting a wide patch of nettles, they turned east of Herndale. When they reached the next hill, Arren halted Mohair and sat, staring down at their ancient stronghold. Hilary reined up beside him.

"So who's to make up my attack force?" she asked.

Arren squinted down at the tiny figures in the court-yard before answering. "The Ramsens for sure. And David with his lot. And Stephan. It'll do him good and get him out of my hair. He can take his children along. The rest you can pick up on the way and in the city"

"The Lindies have experience at Braxborough. There's a few of them here."

"Take them."

Satisfied, Hilary was about to urge her mount for-ward, but her brother placed a restraining hand on her arm, and she turned questioningly. Arren's expression was distant, but when he spoke, his voice was clear and to the point.

"Take the castle, secure the town, leave someone competent in charge and come north. I'll move on Tot-tenham. Join me there. The rest we'll discuss with the Council this evening."

"And the DeMarian Prince?"

Arren's pale eyes were cold. "Bring me his head or his body enchained, but be careful. The DeMarians are sorcerers who can call up demons when they're pressed. It's said their very touch will blight the soul."

"The Church says, you mean. Clerics and Abbots." Hilary laughed. "Useful enough when you need to be shriven, but a nuisance the rest of the time."

"They know more of the world than you do, Hilary Elliot Armistone," Arren admonished. "So you'd do well to listen. I'm sending Sister Marie-Claire with you . . . no argument!" He held up his hand to cut off his sister's protest. "Her prayers should be enough to battle whatever fire-spawned sorcery he might call up. The DeMarian controls the power, but her son's come close to realizing it in the past. And with the chaos we'll hopefully be spinning in Branbridge, you never know how it will respond. Besides, whatever his other worldly powers may be, he's a fair hand with the

broadsword, so you just make sure he doesn't get his
hands on either weapon, then come north"

"You'll hardly know I've gone."

"Good. Now the Council will be waiting, and I've to
send word to Gordon and the Branbridge Churches."

They came to a small stream and Arren dismounted.
Crouching, he brought a handful of the chill water to
his lips and drank. Hilary stayed seated, though she
allowed her pony to lower its nose to the water.

Remaining motionless for several moments, Arren
stared at his reflection. The time was almost here, and
suddenly he felt frozen, wishing to hold onto this one
last quiet moment before they went hurling down into
the maelstrom of war. The wind blew up from the
north, from Tottenham and Braxborough, bringing an
icy taste to the air. Arren let it trace through his hair,
whispering in Essus' voice of battles and victories. He
would send Hilary to Braxborough and Eilene to Tantaven. The Branions would gnash their teeth and shake
their fists and raise a mighty army for the spring, but
by that time they would be more than ready to meet
them. Essus had blessed him with a sign of victory and
nothing now would stand in his way.

He rose and remounted. With one last, deep breath of
air, he turned his pony and urged it into a gallop.
Hilary kept pace beside him. It was begun. Let the
maelstrom take them and fling them where it would.
Soon battle would be joined, and they would carve
themselves a piece of history.

The sun was a fiery ball of late afternoon glory when
the small pilot ship guided the frigate *Marmoset* into
Braxborough Harbor. Most of Demnor's party had
retired below, but Isolde stood on the sterncastle where
she could watch the ship's progress. She'd been a little
surprised when the Prince had announced a change in
their itinerary at Grimscombe three days ago, choosing
to take their large mounted party by ship instead of
overland. As far as she could see, they hadn't saved a
scrap of time, and Kelahnus had practically had the

vapors, swearing he would drown. Even his Guard Commander had been dubious. But the Prince had barely heard them. Staring hungrily at the huge three-master, his eyes glowing with an almost feverish light, he'd simply repeated his decision.

Having no preference one way or the other, Isolde had agreed, exclaiming that it would be a delightful way to travel. Surprisingly, she'd been rewarded with a genuine smile from His Highness before his expression had grown distant once more. He'd been almost reasonable company ever since. Perhaps they should journey to the Columba Islands after they were wed if this is what the sea did for his temperament.

At the moment, having spent most of the last three days on deck, the Prince was now taking his ease in the Captain's cabin while Kelahnus, no doubt, was going through the woman's papers.

Tasting the faint residue of salt on her lips, the Earl suddenly wished for a cup of something, but that would mean going belowdecks to that stiflingly cramped cabin away from the sea smells and the wind whipping her hair in all directions. Everyone on deck was busy doing something exciting and the low hills that rose up before her were her first sight of Heathland's greatest city, so she licked her lips and gazed out at the land moving slowly by.

They'd been hugging Heathland's coast since morning, running steadily northward. The Heir had joined her briefly at the rail just after dawn to tell her they now looked upon the ancient and war torn south-lands, his voice hushed with the possessive reverence so many veterans of the Heathland conflict carried. A seasoned soldier of the Continental Wars, Isolde understood the sentiment, but the Northern Provinces held no such romanticism for her. It was the thorn in Branion's side and too much DeKathrine blood had been spilled on its rocky, unprofitable ground.

High overhead a gull screeched out its indignation at the ship's intrusion and the Earl of Essendale chuckled. Even the Heathland birds were unwelcoming. She watched it wheel for a time then returned her gaze to the shore, seeking her first glimpse of Braxborough Castle. Docks and warehouses dotted the shore, but the great fortress was still hidden behind the hills.

With a sigh, she turned away. The sea air was drying her mouth out something terrible. She *had* to have a drink.

She'd taken two steps when Tania appeared from below with a flagon. The Earl smiled in appreciation as the Companion moved gracefully across the swaying deck toward her.

The younger woman delivered the cup, then leaned negligently on the rail to watch a small fleet of fishing vessels below. After a time, she turned, a lazy smile playing across her lips.

"There's a lovely young man aboard one of those small boats, My Lord."

"Oh?"

"Mm. Quite lovely. He has such ripply muscles and his skin is like polished bronze."

"Is it now? How can you tell?"

"Because he's taken his shirt off, of course."

"Before or after he noticed you leering down at him?"

"Oh, after."

The winds dropped off, and they could hear quite clearly the strains of an old, explicit, Gallian love song. Tania hummed along, the tune obviously familiar.

"His legs are very muscular, too."

"What? Has he taken his breeches off as well?"

After a dramatic pause, the Companion laughed. "No. Sadly, I'm speculating, although I'm sure he would if I requested it. But I'll wager he does. They really leave very little to the imagination."

Unable to ignore the other woman's tempting any longer, Isolde joined her at the rail, her eyes following the direction of the Companion's gaze.

"He's too skinny," she announced after a moment's scrutiny. "I like my men heavier."

"A good thing."

Isolde snorted and changed the subject, nodding at the shore. "What do you suppose those round copper dishes are?"

"They're for salt."

Demnor's unexpected comment made the Earl of Essendale turn around so fast she almost gave herself a broken neck. Having seen him approach, Tania merely smiled.

Struggling to regain her composure, Isolde tried a relaxed smile. "Your Highness, I didn't see you there." He was very close. Too close. She could smell the leather of his clothes and the faint scent of sweat. It made her feel warm and a little intoxicated, and that wouldn't do at all. "You startled me."

"Oh. Uh, my apologies." He moved back a pace, looking embarrassed. "I just came on deck. The copper pans, they're for boiling seawater to get salt. They're actually about six feet across. They keep fires going at all hours and pour in buckets of seawater. When it boils down, they scrape the salt out and package it for export. You see that big frigate?" He pointed toward the docks.

Isolde stood quite close beside him and squinted. "The one flying the Danelind flag?"

"Is it? Yes, probably." The Prince moved to one side. "The biggest one. It's likely here for that reason. Salt is Braxborough's greatest export."

"Really? How fascinating."

Although Tania had assured her the Heir remembered nothing of their night together, Isolde wasn't convinced. His reluctance to stand beside her and his almost desperate attempts to find a neutral topic of conversation had to be more than embarrassment caused by their strange visit to Bricklin Forest. That he chose neither to admit to it, nor even to suggest that they repeat the evening was an insult.

Not that she really wanted to bed the man again before their wedding night, she amended, her eyes narrowing. His lovemaking was only fair. Well, perhaps a little better than fair. She could wait. Although she didn't see why they should. The *next* time they went to bed together, she vowed, she was going to make burning well sure he did it sober so he couldn't deny it the next morning, the rude, arrogant . . .

This circular argument had been running through her mind with dogged frequency the last few days. Usually it so annoyed her that she either paced the ship cursing to herself or drowned it in Tania's soft embrace, but as she was unable to do either at the moment, she decided to play his game for now and cast about for something innocent to discuss.

"I see there's a great deal of forest. Is there much hunting, Highness?"

Unaware of her displeasure, Demnor nodded. "Yes. Deer mostly, unicorns, no . . . dragons. They've been overhunted. There hasn't been a dragon sighting around Braxborough in a hundred years. The Essusiates consider them holy. That's one of the tensions between our two Faiths here."

"But doesn't the Cailein family hunt dragons, Highness?" Tania ventured. "Surely they're Essusiates like the rest of Heathland."

Demnor snorted. "The Caileins' only religion is money. If Essus paid as well as we do, they'd be as pious as the Armistones. Their defection to Atreus the Third's camp in 674 cost Heathland their greatest stronghold." He stared out across the water, past the harbor and the walled city that drew ever closer. "Braxborough Castle," he murmured. Drawn by the reverent tone in his voice, the Earl and her Companion followed his gaze to the huge stone structure that now dominated their view.

"There's been a fortification on that hill for a millennium and then some," the Prince said almost to himself. "While the Heaths held it, they held the country. But we hold it now, and without it the Heaths can't hope to win. They know that as well as we do."

Tania frowned. "But wasn't there a major uprising a few years later that nearly recaptured the castle, Your Highness?"

Demnor gave a short, barking laugh. "There were many. There'll likely be more. The Heaths don't give up. Neither do we. But you mean the Elliot Uprising of 735, I think."

She nodded.

"I've read of it," Isolde mused. "A bloody time."

"For everyone. Marsellus the Black seldom differentiated between friend and foe."

"But what finally happened?" Tania asked. "Other than that the Branions eventually won, of course."

Rubbing at the scars on his chin, Demnor tried to recall the particulars. It'd been years since he'd studied the family's history, but slowly Ariston's gentle voice came back to him. "A claimant to the Heathland throne surfaced, an Elliot on the distaff side. She raised the country. There'd been bad harvests, corruption under Marsellus' unstable rule, unrests, the usual. The northlands rose, sweeping much of the south-lands with them. Tottenham Castle fell almost immediately. Braxborough held out for three months before my mad ancestor deigned to respond. He brought an army through Heathland like a scythe through a hayfield Relieved Braxborough, retook Tottenham, scattered the Heathland forces. And when the fire was out, he decided to jump on the ashes. He led a massacre of the Elliots. The Heathland minstrels still sing of it."

"The Elliots were the Royal line of Heathland. Not the most politic of moves," Isolde commented. "The massacre caused an upsurge of patriotism that's lasted to this day."

"Yes," Demnor agreed. "But then, he was insane. Who can say what his motives were. The scholars of his time write that he was incredibly quick-witted and shrewd. Perhaps he was trying to keep attention on Heathland and away from the fact that he was losing his mind. Didn't stop his assassination two years later."

Tania frowned. "You sound almost as if you approve, Your Highness."

Demnor turned to the Companion, his eyes smoldering like dark coals though his expression remained

stone. "He was a bad ruler. He deserved to die."
Swinging his attention back to the castle, he refused to
speak further. Isolde shot the other woman an exasperated look. Tania merely shrugged.

The *Marmoset* docked without incident half an hour
later. Demnor stood at the bow, watching the Guard
struggle with the horses, restless and feisty after three
days cramped in the hold without exercise. Turning, he
looked wistfully up at the ship's proud masts before
returning his attention to the dock.

He'd taken the *Marmoset* more on a whim than from
any real necessity. They could have made the overland
trip as fast, with as little risk. The Bjerre Sea was not
calm, nor warm in late autumn, a fact Kelahnus had
pointed out, among others. But when he'd seen the
huge oceangoing vessel riding proudly at her berth,
such a longing to be out on the cold, rough waves came
over him that he'd acted immediately.

A fat purse handed to the Captain overcame her initial resentment to the Royal command of a quick sortie
northwards, and a promise to finance the *Marmoset* for
a journey to the East had so softened her disposition
toward her guests that they'd had an enjoyable trip.

Now they were docked in Braxborough, the greatest
conquered city of the Realm. Despite the festive attire
of the officials awaiting his arrival on the pier, the
atmosphere crackled with tension like the air before a
storm. Demnor breathed it in with perverse pleasure.
This was the kind of tension he understood. Heathland
was Branion only in name, and year after year violence
broke out afresh between two wills equally determined
to win. The Prince swept his gaze across the ancient,
walled city with its sixty thousand citizens and smiled
possessively. "You're mine," he breathed, "and I shall
keep you."

Let Braxborough be trouble, he thought. He hadn't
matched strength with Heathland in far too long.

Below, an outraged shriek forced his attention to the
dock. Under his feet the bow shuddered as iron-shod

hooves crashed against the ship's side. Sailors scattered and Demnor heard Dimitrius curse audibly as he dragged Challenger out onto the dock. The bay was in a furious mood, rearing up on his hind legs and slashing at the air with his forehooves. Diving out of harm's reach, Dimitrius gave his Lord an imploring look before leaping up again to try and calm the animal before it hurled itself into the water. Demnor sighed and left the *Marmoset* to go rescue the boy.

Some time later, the chaos calmed, the Prince and his entourage began the climb to the castle.

With his guard surrounding and the Braxborough officials—Branions every one—behind, they clattered their way up the steep, hard-packed road to Cairn Gate, the easternmost point of the walled city. Already Braxborough was bursting its seams, with shops and homes challenging the dominance of warehouses and dry docks outside the ancient walls, but here, at least, the air was still fresh with the sea breeze and the buildings were evenly spaced apart with room to move between them.

Once past the wall, however, the streets became unevenly paved and choked with grime. The ancient buildings—some as high as fifteen stories—which towered malevolently above them were black with smoke, and the rank odor of sewage was almost unbearable. Tania quickly raised a perfumed handkerchief to her nose.

Around them people lined the street on both sides and hung from windows and over roofs. Although some cheered, most had come simply to see this foreign Prince, for such he was despite the glut of Branion officials, priests, and merchants in the city.

Slowly they made their way up the cobbled ridge. Demnor sensed his Guard were nervous, but they made a good show of regal arrogance regardless.

They needed it. Braxborough, the Royal city of Heathland, had perched on the seven hills overlooking the River Braxen for centuries. It had been the cultural center of the Islands long before Atreus the Second had

wrested away the title for Branbridge in the year 500.
Even today, with its glory diminished, it was still an
awe-inspiring city. Here, the artisans and merchants
vied with the nobility and both Faiths to create the
most beautiful housings for their wares. Copper roofs
and carved balconies topped richly decorated walls and
colorful signs. Every Guild imaginable was represented, from the Scholar's Orders, and the monasteries
of the Essusiate Clerics, to the Wool and other Merchant's Guilds, down through the Artisan's Orders
which included the Sculptors, Stonemasons, Painters,
and Glaziers of the Stained Glass Association, to the
Cooper's Union and the Tanner's Lodge, and others of
the Allied Trade Guilds; each with their own heraldry
and traditions, many occupying whole streets. The spirals of a dozen churches pointed toward the sky next to
the marching crenellations of the mock towers of the
great Branion Militant Orders. The effect was a
dizzying display of wealth and power which gave the
lie to the pockets of tightly packed slums that existed
in between. Even Demnor, citizen of the greatest city
in the world and Heir to a dynasty nine hundred years
old, rode soberly, impressed into silence.

Suddenly the buildings fell away and the most commanding sight of all, Braxborough Castle, rose up
before them. Perched on the tip of the ridge leading up
to it, the ancient fortress made a forbidding sight with
its great tower and huge battlements. Built on a high
hill of jagged, black rock, it crouched, daring the sap-
pers to do their worst. On the north it was guarded by
Mairi's Lake which lapped right up against its rocky
feet. On the west, Gideon's Tower reached toward the
clouds, built on great chunks of rock that bulged out
over the town to make it unscalable. The south was the
same. To the east it was reached only by a narrow dirt
path which wound up to the first of its six gates on the
north side. Through this gate, a stout pair of oaken
doors that opened outward, the Branions now passed.

Demnor looked with approval at the high walls
which enclosed them, crenellations along the top giv-

ing the defenders ample room to fire down from cover. Rock rising up to meet the forewall battery on the right and enclosed battlements on the left almost forced the visitor toward the gate with the need to relieve the oppressive sense of being dangerously enclosed. But once the gate was reached, this feeling was intensified rather than lessened. The centuries-old carving of Merrone, Essus' dragon guardian, etched on the wall above was a chilling reminder that this stronghold represented Essusiatism's northern heart no matter who held its bones.

The horses clattered three abreast through the second gate. Above them the third portcullis gate awaited. In times of siege it could be dropped so that any attempts to force the doors would simply thrust them against its great iron bars. Beneath them, the fourth gate was a wooden bridge capable of being weighted so that anything bigger than a cat would send it, and those on it, crashing down into the dry moat below.

Demnor had an instant's thrill of unease as they crossed, but the fourth gate held and after passing another set of wooden portals, the walls finally widened to open space.

To their right the battlements stretched on until, far to the west, they enclosed wide fields of sheep and cows. To their left higher walls, built on the castle rock, circled away southward and up. Before them a dirt track followed the left battlements. This path they took.

It wound around and up until they were facing north and here they came to the last gate; a narrow archway with a heavy wooden door that stood open. The garrison guard moved aside and the Royal Entourage entered single file.

Now they arrived within the castle yard proper. To their right stood two large wooden buildings, meant to house stock and supplies and stables. Hands ran forward to take the reins, and Demnor and the rest of his party dismounted and allowed the Warden, Kevin Davies, a retired Knight of the Lance, to lead them up the steep path toward a tiny building perched on the bare castle rock.

"Mairi's Church," the older man explained to Isolde's query. "She was the Consort of Gideon the First of Heathland some six hundred years ago. She was an Essusiate. One of the first on the Island. He built it for her that she might hold services. We've left it as such. There are a few Essusiates among the garrison, though most attend service at the Aspect's Chapel beyond." He gestured at the great stone building to their right.

"We had hoped Your Highness might officiate at the Sabat Mass, if our request is not too bold?" he asked as they continued. Demnor nodded.

"I should be honored."

"Thank you, Your Highness."

They turned right past the tiny Church and toward Gideon's Tower along the high battlements. One of the Knights of the Sword fell behind to look down and whistled appreciatively. Meanwhile the Royal Party passed under a diagonal archway connecting the tower with the Aspect's Chapel and entered a stone courtyard where the garrison stood at parade.

"The central living area of the castle," Demnor said to Isolde. "And a comfort, My Lord Warden, that it be so well defended," he added after inspecting the guard.

Davies accepted the compliment with a low bow. "If I may, Your Highness," he said, gesturing before them. "The barracks; the great hall to your left where, if it please Your Highness, we may feast tonight, and of course, the Royal Residence within Gideon's Tower where I shall now conduct you that you and your party might rest and refresh yourselves."

He led them inside and, after showing the Prince to the Royal Apartments on the ground floor, left to guide Isolde upstairs to the secondary rooms.

As the door closed, the distant roll of thunder could be heard. Demnor shot Kelahnus a look, but said nothing.

After a cursory inspection of the hall, sitting room,

and bedroom, Demnor scowled. The rooms were far more ornate than he liked, the bedroom housing besides an expansively carved wardrobe and desk, a wide bed with heavily embroidered bed-curtains and coverlet and pillows tasseled with silver. It looked far too soft for comfort. Rich tapestries covered the walls and thick rugs from the East, the floors. There were no windows. Kelahnus immediately sank onto the bed with a sigh, while Dimitrius eyed the small pallet at the foot of the bed with glum resignation.

"Don't be a fool," Demnor snapped, sympathetic to his look, but the elaborate room making him curt. "I don't want you in here either."

His squire straightened, attempting to hide the effect of his Lord's words. "I, I could sleep in the sitting room, Your Highness," he suggested haltingly.

Demnor pulled himself up short, the boy's expression closing his teeth on an unthinking reply. No matter how uncomfortable or inconvenient the situation might be, it was Dimitrius' right to be here. In Branion he had simply been housed one room over. But in this potentially hostile land, duty demanded that he sleep by his Prince. To refuse would hurt his pride and his love. He should have knighted the boy before they left Branbridge, then this problem never would have come up, but now it would have to wait until their return. In the meantime he must find him a place that would satisfy them both.

"No, lad," he said, "You're supposed to be here guarding my sleep. But I don't want you on the floor. There must be a better place."

He crossed to the far side and opened a small door, peering inside. "You can sleep in here."

His squire followed him and gazed into the tiny room.

It was paneled in dark wood and had a little, leaded paned window looking out across Mairi's Lake. It housed a small, single, curtained bed and that was all.

In the midst of undressing, Kelahnus paused to peer around the corner. "Isn't that where you're supposed to sleep?"

"And where will you be? In the big bed with him?"

"Maybe." The Companion smiled at the young squire who blushed and turned aside.

"Why is it here, Highness?" he asked. "Surely the other bed is meant for Royalty."

Demnor made a dismissive gesture. "It's for privacy and warmth, but what I want is space. Besides, it's too burning hot in here as it is."

Dimitrius and Kelahnus shared a puzzled look before the squire bowed. "Yes, My Lord."

That settled, the Prince turned back into the main room and rubbed at the stubble on his chin. "Have a servant bring water for shaving," he instructed the boy over his shoulder. "And find out when the banquet is. And get yourself something to eat."

"Yes, sir."

Dimitrius bowed and made for the door. Returning to the bed, Kelahnus removed his tunic and stretched. "Have a servant draw a bath, too," he called after him. "I'm covered in salt. Come to think of it, so are you. We could have one together, if His Highness won't let us share the bed."

"Ah, yes, Your Grace, I mean, ah, no, thank you, Your Grace, I don't think so, I mean . . . ah, no," Dimitrius stammered and beat a hasty retreat.

Unable to keep a neutral expression, Demnor allowed the corners of his mouth to quirk up. "That was cruel," he admonished.

"Do you really think so," Kelahnus asked curiously. "I thought I was being quite restrained." He rose and began to unpack their trunks, shaking the clothes out before laying them across the bed. Finding his robe, he slipped out of his breeches and wrapped himself in its silken folds. "Now will you be wanting the blue tunic or the black, Milord Prince. What sort of effect shall we be trying for? Melancholic or deathly."

"How about naked? Then they can see how seriously I take all this pageantry."

"But you do take it seriously, you take everything

seriously. You treat even the smallest detail that doesn't suit your desire as a personal insult."

"Nonsense."

"Well, it had better be the black, then. The blue makes you look too attractive."

"And we mustn't have that."

"No. We mustn't. At least not in public."

The Companion leaned with studied negligence against the bedpost, watching appreciatively as Demnor stripped off his salt-encrusted clothes, then smiled as the Prince moved toward him.

The banquet was long and hot. With his back to the main fireplace at the north end of the enormous Great Hall, Demnor felt the full effect of the tree trunk that burned and crackled in the grate. He wondered idly what it might be like to sit far below the salt at the end of the huge table. Much cooler, no doubt. He cast his gaze down, past his own party, the Warden and his family, the local nobility and those of the Heathland families that owed their wealth and position to the occupying Branions, past his Guard Commander and the Captain of the Garrison, the Royal Guard, the Knights of the Shield, some of whom he had known since he was a child, to the young Knights of the Sword. Nobility for the most part, many would occupy high positions when they'd finished the two years' service required after their squiring; a service he himself had not served due to his position.

Around them, squires vied with servants for the rights to serve their Lords, one indignant young man taking a tankard right out of the hands of a fuming older server, to place it to the right of Commander Hough. Demnor laughed when he recognized Robin, the boy he'd pulled from the fields of Loughborough. That was good, Hough would keep him out of trouble and be a patient teacher until they returned to Branbridge. The Prince himself had learned the battle ax from the old veteran. It was a weapon he liked but seldom got to use. Davies, he noted, was served by a

young woman who resembled him quite strongly.
When asked, the Warden explained that this was his
youngest, Saralynne, serving her time as squire to her
father as her three older siblings had done. Demnor
nodded. It was common these days to squire at home
rather than being sent to another's keep to learn the
trade of war as had been popular a century before. It
was a new tradition Demnor planned to continue with
his own Heir, though, as the Crown Prince, he himself
had never served a true squiring. That was a custom he
planned to change.

The banquet wore on. Dish after dish was presented
to the Prince for his approval before being carried to a
side table to be carved. Roasts of mutton and beef,
whole pigs, venison, and veal were followed by duck-
lings, chicken, capons, rabbits, a boar's head which
Davies proudly told the Prince had been slain by his
oldest son, and a huge stuffed swan in plumage. The
wine flowed like water, supplemented by beer and
cider, and the table was piled high with bread and
wafers. Spiced and mulled wines were served with fruit
at the end, when finally, some hours later, the assembled leaned back to enjoy the entertainment.

Jugglers and acrobats tumbled and danced in
between the songs and ballads by the numerous minstrels; two of the garrison made a demonstration of the
claymore; and a small play was put on of the tale of
the Herald Taniserian and the Faerie Queen. Afterward
the tables were pushed to the side and the dancing
began. Demnor released the guard and most withdrew
to the barracks. From time to time the sounds of dicing
and cock fighting could be heard over the music and
the sound of rain which began to pour down around
midnight.

The Royal Party retired well into the wee hours of
the morning, long after the barracks had grown quiet
and dark.

Dawn was not far off when Kelahnus, unable to
sleep, passed the two Knights of the Shield on guard

before the door. Demnor had been restless in the hour
or so they had been in bed, muttering and thrashing
about feverishly, and finally the Companion had given
up and risen. Dressing quietly, he'd slipped outside for
a short walk.

The air was cold after the storm, and he clutched his
cloak more tightly about him as he crossed below the
arched entrance to the courtyard. Two more Royal
Guards stood watch there, one challenging him before
recognizing his face in the faint dawn light. The Companion crossed the grassy lawn behind the Aspect's
Chapel to the path that ran up to Mairi's Church. Here
at the highest point of the castle, he leaned against the
upper battlements and stared into space.

Somehow, here in the quiet dawn, all the problems
and anxieties of the last seven years seemed trivial.
Demnor and the Earl were becoming friends and for
tonight, at least, he no longer felt threatened by it. He
and Tania had reached an understanding that was also
beginning to warm into the pleasant glow of comrade-
ship. Together, he felt, they would be able to take care
of their Lords with very little difficulty. Soon there
would be children and they would have Companions of
their own for him to train. When Melosandra died, and
with luck and the Wind's grace she'd die soon, he
would stand at Demnor's side in the Privy Council and
in the Aristok's Court and rule his household. The two
of them would grow old together in peace until one day
he would fall asleep and awaken in the Shadow Realm.
In the meantime he had the Companion's Council on
which he'd sat as a Junior Member for five years now.
He could rise there as high as he wished to go and,
should Demnor die before him, even as high as Head of
the Guild. Or there was always the School to retire to
and teach, overseeing future generations of Companions. He might even have children of his own with
Tania maybe or some other highly placed Companion
and live his final days quietly watching over Demnor's
and his own grandchildren. In all, his future stretched
out as rosy as the eastern sky.

Behind him, the top of Gideon's Tower glowed red with the rising of the sun, but before him all was still dark and peaceful across the pastures of Braxborough Castle. Gradually, as he stared into the night, he became aware of furtive movements along the northern battlements.

Quickly he pulled back into the shadow of the Church door and peered over the wall. Dim shapes glided stealthily across the field, indistinct shadows that became a company of cloaked figures. More followed until several dozen stood gathered upon the path. Faintly the wind brought to his straining ears the muffled clink of chain mail and the heavy footfalls of iron-shod boots. Then, by the light of the faint dawn, he saw the glint of steel. Heaths. It could be none other. Marsellus had been right.

He wasted no more time. How enemies had gained entrance to the castle, he had no idea. All he knew was that they were about to be attacked and he had to get back to Demnor.

Throwing himself from the wall, the Companion leaped down the small rocky hill. The dawn had yet to touch this tiny outcrop and, stumbling on the slippery rocks, he fell and went sliding to the bottom. For a second, he lay, the wind knocked out of him, then wincing, he got to his knees. A sharp pain made him gasp as the right one buckled, but somehow, he managed to stand. Behind him now, he could clearly hear the sound of running feet, and ignoring the stabbing pain in his knee, he ran. Fear gave him wings as he sprinted across the lawn behind the Aspect's Chapel and opened his mouth to shout the alarm.

A black figure materialized from the darkness. Rushing toward him, face contorted into a grimace, sword in hand, was one of the garrison guards. Astonished, Kelahnus was almost too late to meet the attack, but at the last second he flung himself aside. Rolling, he came up in a crouch, his knife in his hand.

The man swung and missed. With a curse, he lunged forward again. Diving under the clumsy swing, Kelahnus came up inside and with a quick movement, carved a gash across his assailant's throat. With a choked-off scream, the man staggered forward. Even as he turned to avoid his flailing arms, a gout of blood caught the young Companion full in the face. Blinded, he stumbled back. His knees gave out and twisting sideways, the two fell with a crash.

The seconds stretched to hours as Kelahnus fought to thrust the dying man away. Finally he managed to free himself and scrabble aside, scraping the gore from his eyes. Then, knowing he shouldn't, he looked down.

The man lay on his back. Arms flung out, his body jerked and contorted in a parody of movement. His mouth worked, but only garbled noises emerged through the red froth covering his lips. From the great wound bubbles of blood grew and burst. Kelahnus rose, staring, unable to tear himself away. His stomach heaved. His years of training fled and all he could do was watch the man die. Then slowly his eyes widened as he recognized the Garrison Guard Sergeant.

The meaning of this broke the paralysis of his limbs and as he turned to run he saw the attacking force boil through the gateway, its guards at their head. Just at that moment he heard the alarm sound behind him.

"AWAKE! AWAKE! ATTACK! ATTACK!" One of the knights from the archway came running toward him, his sword drawn. For a second Kelahnus feared that this, too, was a betrayal, but even as he raised one blood-soaked arm to fend him off, the man was past him. Kelahnus stayed just long enough to see the knight cut down by the first line of attackers. Then he ran.

His pursuers hot on his heels, the Companion skidded into the courtyard and dove aside as mail clad figures poured through the archway. They met the first of Demnor's guard with a clash of steel. Those who'd been on duty fought them armed and armored but, surprised from sleep, most piled in disarray from the barracks with whatever weapon they could snatch up. There was chaos in the yard. Somewhere a bell began to sound the alarm, but for most it was too late. They were surprised. For a moment safe behind the statue of a great wolf on the steps of the Aspect's Chapel, Kelahnus crouched, watching.

Very quickly the attackers' objective became clear. Although spreading out to attack the guards, most roared toward the Royal Residence. The two Shield Knights on guard before the door were hit by a wave of howling dervishes. Somehow, using the lintel on either side as a partial shield, they held, but it was clear that overwhelming numbers would soon bring them down. Battle raged before the door and fanned out across the courtyard.

Then a Heath fell, an arrow protruding from his throat and another staggered back, her sword arm useless. Looking up to a small window in the residence, Kelahnus saw the Earl of Essendale fit another arrow to her short bow and let fly, eyes narrowed to find her target in the bright dawn sun. In the next window her squire fired his own weapon and together they rained a hail of arrows down upon the attacking force.

The Heaths checked.

With a screaming war cry, Captain Hough threw his Shield Knights against them. The attackers fell back. Behind his statue, Kelahnus shouted encouragement, cheered by the sudden rush of the Royal Guard. They made the door, relieving their beleaguered comrades. For a moment it looked as if they would push the Heaths back through the archway, but then Captain Hough was down and the attackers surged forward again.

A tall Heathland woman with a wild shock of sandy hair howled like a banshee as she twirled a claymore above her head. She cut down two knights, then turned and pointed at Isolde, shouting orders. The Heaths began to scale the rough wall toward the windows.

Slowly the attackers pushed the knights backward, forcing them away from the Royal Residence. The Branions fought with frantic urgency, but few had spilled from the barracks fully prepared. Casualties

were heavy, especially among the younger, less ex-
perienced Sword Knights. In desperation, many of
them almost threw themselves on their enemies'
swords to clear a space around the door. Kelahnus
watched in horror as one Sword Knight, armed only
with a dagger, fought on long after she was cut to
ribbons. Finally she fell and her body was crushed
underfoot.

The Heaths had almost reached the windows. One
fell screaming, an arrow pinning his arm to his side,
but the others came on. Flewellyn's shot went wide,
and then he was shouting a warning to his Lord. Isolde
put an arrow in the eye of one last assailant and the two
of them disappeared inside. Seconds later the Heaths
gained the upper floors.

They had almost gained the door as well. Savagely
they hacked at the Royal Guard, three and four swords
to one. The sandy-haired leader dispatched one man
with a vicious slash across the face, then turned on
another. Her blow was checked on the sword of Captain Hough.

Miraculously alive, the Captain was a grisly sight.
Minus helmet, with blood-covered features wearing a
savage grimace, he hurled back the Heathland leader,
Screaming in rage he attacked.

But he and his people were too few and flanking
them, the attackers gained the door. His voice raw with
shouting, Kelahnus watched, horror-struck, as they
began to smash at the tough wood. The door split, then
gave under their assault. There was a joyous shout that
changed to a cry of dismay as the first through the door
staggered back, his head split open, blood pouring
down his face. A great figure leaped into the courtyard,
metal singing a deadly song before him. The howling
DeMarian war cry filled the courtyard and was taken
up by his knights as the Prince of Gwyneth joined the
fray, a veil of red-gray Fire surrounding him, vying
with the sunlight in its brilliance.

At four inches past six feet, the Royal Knight was
used to the advantage of height and weight, and he

used it now. Swinging his great broadsword, flames
licking up the blade, he sliced through an enemy in one
stroke. Howling with wild laughter, the Crown Prince
threw himself at another. Terrified, the man gave way
before him.

Their Lord in their midst, the Royal Guard rallied
and charged the enemy. Forming a protective circle
around him and those who'd left the building behind
him, they held their ground. With Hough leading the
defense, they fought their way across the yard. Then a
Shield Knight fell, breaking the ring of protective
swords and the red veil guttered and went out. The
circle faltered. Kelahnus saw a black-robed woman by
the archway, her arms raised to the sky, saw Dimitrius
swept away, and the Earl's bright hair stained with
blood, saw Demnor stumble and then right himself as a
wild, black-bearded Heathland man, tricked by the
feint, lunged forward. The Prince's slash took him
across the gut.

The man gasped. With an astonished expression he
clutched at himself, sword ringing on the bloodied
flagstones. He looked down in disbelief, watched his
entrails push their way through his clutching fingers.
A scream began to form on his lips, and then he
pitched forward on his face. Kelahnus turned away and
was sick.

Kneeling behind his granite shield, the Companion
fought against the cramping heaves. When he finally
gained control of himself and looked past the statue's
great stone muzzle, battle was joined on the steps
of the Aspect's Chapel, and his position was no
longer safe.

The Heir's armed group had made the top of the
stairs. Kelahnus followed cautiously, his back to the
wall. At the door, the Prince turned and saw him. His
arm thrust out, grabbed his blood-splattered Companion by the collar, and half threw him past the chapel
doors. The rest rushed in behind him.

The Heathland leader made one last desperate bid to
stop them, trading thrusts with Gord Rose. The two

clutched at each other in a parody of friendship before their compatriots pulled them apart. For a moment Captain Hough was outlined in the doorway, a demonic, bloodied guardian, then the doors slammed shut, as he and the rest of Demnor's Guard took up position before it. Two Shield Knights inside drove pieces of broken sword into the hinges and the door was secured.

"That should hold, My Prince."

Outside, the battle raged, the fighting greatest near the chapel as the attackers fought to penetrate the wall of swords that Hough had built to protect his Lord. Inside, the thick stone walls muffled all sound but the labored breathing of the few who'd made it to temporary safety. Demnor wiped his sword on a corner of his cloak and returned it to its sheath.

"How many are we?"

His Lieutenant, Paterion Grey glanced quickly around in the dim torchlight. "Ten, My Prince, counting yourself, Her Lordship, and His Grace."

"Ten." Her Lordship, that meant Isolde. His gaze found her leaning against a pillar. Breathing hard, unarmored but unscathed. He released a breath he hadn't remembered holding. And Kelahnus. He shook his head. The Companion had appeared as if by magic in the thick of the fray. He didn't know how he'd gotten there, he only thanked the Earth and Wind that he had. His eyes sought the other man's, then widened. Seeing his expression Kelahnus shook his head, blood-matted hair pulling against the movement.

"None of it's mine."

Almost weak-kneed with relief, Demnor turned to his force. The boy Robin was there, a nasty looking cut across his cheek, but he seemed all right for the moment, a pike held resolutely in his hands. Grey, Benger, and Glicksohn, Shield Knights all, looking grim and ready, but pitifully below strength. All had taken some injury, even Benger, the only one fully armored. Flames. They'd really been caught napping this time. Two Sword Knights, Deverne Jones and

Gord Rose. Deverne was unscathed, but Rose weaved uncertainly in Benger's grip, clutching his abdomen, his face white. One young garrison guard, shaking, his eyes wide with shock and blood dripping from a graze along his temple. Not the greatest fighting force, but it would have to do.

"How many do you think they are, Grey?"

The old veteran rubbed at his chin before answering. "Half a hundred it seemed, My Prince. Maybe more."

"Heaths."

"Aye. The Captain will be hard pressed."

"Yes." Demnor could hear the unspoken words. Grey wanted to be out there fighting alongside his Captain. And he knew without having to see their faces that the other Royal Guards felt the same. That was their job, their duty, to raise their swords in defense of the Royal Family. He understood. His own heart raged at this confinement, believing, as they did, that his one sword could strike the telling blow that would turn the tide of battle to their favor; his heart that berated him as a coward for staying holed up here in safety. But he also believed the lesson that Randolph and Captain Fletcher had beaten into his head year after year; that you let people do their duty, do what they were trained to do, and as much as he hated it, he was the Crown Prince. It was their duty to keep him alive and it was his duty to let them. In this case it meant that they, and he, must await the end. If their enemies won, they would be his last bid for life and freedom. He turned to Grey.

"We wait."

The Lieutenant nodded and turned to the others. "Glicksohn, guard the door. The rest of you see to your wounds."

As if he had been waiting for the order, Rose slowly sank to the floor. His arms dropped to reveal his midsection, blood-soaked and dripping crimson down his legs. Benger lowered him carefully, cradling his head in her lap.

"I think he's hurt bad, My Prince."

"Open his tunic."

The Lieutenant knelt beside them and sucked his breath through his teeth as Benger gently cut away the bloodstained cloth. He looked up at Demnor and shook his head.

Nine. "Will the door hold?"

"Yes, sir."

"Good." He knelt beside the dying man and Benger slowly slid out from under him, as the Prince took her place. Brushing the boy's fair hair from his face with one hand as he took his bloodstained fingers in the other. Rose winced in pain and tried to rise. Demnor pressed him gently down.

"Easy, lad. You've done your share. The fighting's over. You can rest now."

Rose gave a rasping cough, then looked up into the face of his Prince. "Did . . . we win?" he whispered.

"Of course we did. Did you ever doubt it?"

". . . No."

Demnor smiled gently, stroking the lines of pain from the boy's face. "You did well. I'm very proud of you. Now sleep, My Brother Knight. There's still some mopping up to do. Then we'll get you to a physician. Can you wait a little?"

". . . Yes . . . My Prince."

"Good. I'll stay with you. Now sleep."

Rose's eyes flickered, then closed. Slowly his breathing grew more shallow until it finally ceased. Demnor held his hand tightly a moment longer, tears obscuring his vision. Then he signaled and Grey helped him rise while Benger supported the boy's body. Glicksohn left the door and Robin took his place as the three Shield Knights carried their dead brother-in-arms to the altar. Removing his cloak, Demnor draped it over the cold stone and they laid the body on it, placing Gord's sword at his side. Then, one by one, they knelt before the altar, offering silent prayers for Gord Rose's journey to the Earth's Palace in the Shadow Realm. Each of the others followed, Deverne tracing the sword pattern on his brother knight's

chest. Isolde knelt last of all, then moved aside as the
Prince performed the Rites of the Dead. The young
face below him was peaceful and free from pain.
Demnor found himself remembering the boy's pride
at being sponsored into the Knights by the Crown
Prince, his shame at being discovered in his demo-
tion, and the happy eagerness with which he'd discharged his duty as a member of Demnor's escort. Neither one of them had suspected his last breath would be
so soon. Wearily the Prince rubbed at his eyes. One
more spirit too young to wear the red gryphon of
Gwyneth in the Shadow Catcher's army. He turned
away.

Grey offered him his own cloak and with a smile of
thanks, Demnor accepted it. The older man sighed. "A
poor age to die. But no better place to do it in."

"When the time comes for my last journey, he'll
have an honored place among my Shadow Guard," the
Heir answered, his voice thick.

Grey nodded, tears running unabashedly down his
cheeks. "You made his last moments peaceful ones,
My Prince. A comfort to have the Four so close."

The others nodded. His throat constricting, Demnor
bowed his head in acknowledgment of the honor his
people had just bestowed upon him. Only three of the
four Aspects were represented in any chapel, though
torches lined the walls; Earth, Sea, and Wind. The
fourth, Flame, was believed to be personified in the
living Ruler. And the Flame had manifested. When
he'd hurled himself at the enemy and the power of the
Living Flame had burst forth to surround him, none
had been more surprised than the Crown Prince. But
he'd accepted it and used it until it had been, just as
inexplicably, snuffed out. He'd never doubted the
power of the Aristok before and wouldn't now.
Somehow she'd sent the force of her will to aid them,
and he was too tired to wonder how or why. He would
find out when he returned home.

Moving away, he rested his hand briefly on Grey's

shoulder before glancing about the darkened room for
Kelahnus.

The Companion was slumped in a side alcove,
leaning heavily against an altar. After crossing the
chapel, Demnor put his arms around him, the younger
man leaning into his embrace with a sigh.

"Are you all right?" the Prince whispered. "You look
terrible. Maybe you should sit."

"No. I'm fine. Really. I'm fine now." The Companion scrubbed futilely at the dried blood on his face
and shuddered. "Do you think they'll get in?"

"No. Hough and his people are the best in Branion.
They'll win through, and everything will be all right."

"Promise?"

The Companion sounded so much like Kassandra
that Demnor had to hide a smile. Stroking his hair, he
kissed the younger man and said reassuringly. "I
promise."

"Don't leave."

"I won't. Come and sit." He drew Kelahnus up onto
the small altar top. Standing beside him, he put his
arms about him again. Kelahnus rested his head against
the Heir's chest and closed his eyes. Soon he was
breathing deeply. Shifting his weight to a more comfortable foot, Demnor stroked his Companion's hair
and listened to the quiet talk of his guard by the main
altar.

"I saw John Rose fall, too," Benger said softly.

"That's both sons," Deverne added. "Their mother
will be devastated."

"But he died well. He took two of them Essu-arse
heretics with him."

"Aye. He'll have good company on the road."

"And Bollin was wounded. You remember her, don't
you, sir?" Glicksohn turned to the Lieutenant. Grey
nodded. Glicksohn rubbed absently at the stubble on
his chin and glanced toward the doors. Beyond them,
they could still hear screams and the clashing of
swords. "So many outside. And we don't even know
who's dead or alive."

"Well, I, for one, am going to consider them all alive, until I see them dead," Grey said gruffly. "And you'd do well to think the same."

"Yes, sir."

Demnor smiled, then looked up as a figure approached. Isolde was dressed in breeches and a loose shirt, the cloth sticky with blood, a cloud of loose hair falling over her shoulders. She looked tired and worried, but smoothed her expression as Demnor nodded a greeting.

"May I join you, Highness?"

"Yes, of course. Stupid of me not to offer. Here, you're cold. If you can get it off without disturbing His Grace, you can have the Lieutenant's cloak."

"Thank you, no, My Prince. I'm fine. I'm just worried about Flewellynn."

"Ah."

"He's just a boy. Barely fourteen. And Tania, and the servants."

"I'm sure they're fine, My Lord Earl."

"I told her to take them and hide while I led the invaders away. Flewellynn wasn't happy about it." She smiled at the memory. "He wanted to stay and fight. Tania said she'd take him down the back way. I didn't even know there was a back way."

Demnor gave a quiet bark of laughter. "How long have you had a Companion, My Lord?"

Isolde raised an inquiring eyebrow, but answered. "I had an Initial Companion when I was fifteen, Highness. But I've been busy since and haven't had the time. Tania's been with me three months now. The family felt that due to my imminent rise in rank, I needed one."

"Then take my word on it. Never be surprised by what they know. It saves time. Tania'll look after him. I can't imagine she followed us into battle. She probably held the boy back, too."

"And *your* squire, Highness?"

Demnor looked grim. "Dimitrius has been well trained. And he's armed. He'll make it." His tone refused argument, so Isolde merely leaned against the altar and wearily closed her eyes.

Time passed as the nine waited. Outside, the battle raged unabated.

10. Briery

Dimitrius DeLlewellynne drove off his attacker for the fourth time, turning the man's lunge on the blade of his sword. The weapon was heavy as he raised it shakily above his head, his wounded sword arm shrieking in protest. The Heathland man's blade darted forward and, almost without thinking, the young squire hacked it aside and swung his own weapon in a tight arc. Caught across the chest, his attacker fell back and suddenly the space around him was clear. Dropping the point to the ground, Dimitrius leaned on the pommel. The knight pressed into the doorway of the Great Hall beside him slumped, breathing hard. For the moment they were ignored.

Before them the battle continued. Dimitrius could see Captain Hough and his Shield Knights fighting like demons on the steps of the chapel. So far they'd held the door, though as he watched, one knight went down, clutching his face. It looked like the enemy would breach their defenses. He shivered.

It had been less than an hour since dawn when he'd awakened with the Crown Prince roughly shaking him. His Highness had practically dragged him out of bed and thrust his tunic at him. Explanations were unnecessary. Already the sounds of battle could be heard outside as Dimitrius followed his Prince into the next room. The inner Guard was at the door, fidgeting nervously, her sword in her hand as the two quickly armed themselves. They had just enough time to struggle into

mail shirts before they heard a crash upstairs. The
Prince bullied his frightened squire into his breastplate,
then headed for the door, catching up his shield as he
ran. In the chaos, Dimitrius forgot his, though it had
stood right beside the Heir's. He would wish for it
often later.

They met the Earl of Essendale at the door. She was
unarmored and alone, but her bow was in her hand and
her blade at her belt. Turning, she shot the first of those
who pounded down the stairs after her. The others
pulled back, but it was clear they would soon attack.
Out of arrows, the Earl tossed her bow aside and drew
her sword. She smiled tightly at the Prince as he
gripped her arm in greeting. Together, they faced the
stairs.

Heavy blows began to rain against the door. It shuddered, held, then splintered and slammed open as the
first of their enemies swarmed inside. The squire fell
back in alarm, but his Lord spun around, taking the
man across the face with a vicious swing of his blade.
Dimitrius had barely enough time to register the death
before a burst of flames suddenly enveloped the Prince.
Momentarily blinded, by the time the boy's streaming
eyes had cleared, the Heir, aiming a savage kick at the
corpse, had cleared the doorway and leaped outside.
The others followed.

Once out in the courtyard, battle was joined in
earnest. Quickly surrounded by enemies before and
behind, Dimitrius' stomach did a flip as a screaming
Heathland man charged toward him. The sword his
parents had given him on his sixteenth birthday the
month before came up almost of its own accord to meet
his strike. The jar of the two weapons connecting
slammed at his wrist and numbed his arm. He strained
to force the other's sword aside, then dropped his point
and swung under. His assailant leaped backward.

The heady sense of power his brothers had boasted
about came over him then, and he laughed with its
feeling of invincibility. Beating at his attacker's sword,

he screamed out his family's battle cry, the ringing
Gwynethian calling on the man to come to him and die.

The man came. Cutting sideways, he drew a line of
crimson along the youth's arm. Dimitrius knew a
second of fear, then his attacker checked and, mouth
spewing blood, fell. Fighting down a bitter disappointment, the squire watched a Shield Knight wrench his
sword from the man's back. But the enemy were many
and even as the Royal Guard rallied and ringed their
Lord and his party in a protective circle of steel,
another faced Dimitrius and the boy's blade came away
dripping.

Slowly they fought their way across the square. His
Highness moved resolutely forward, his foe unable to
penetrate the shield of Holy Fire around him. Beside
him, the Earl of Essendale dispatched one Heath with a
double slash to the gut, then casually gestured for
another to replace him. She killed her as easily. They
were almost to the Aspect's Chapel. The Prince's foot
was on the steps and the Heaths were falling back.
Then the Heir stumbled and the Living Flame guttered
and went out. A sword point took the knight beside
Dimitrius in the gut. Hanging on the blade, her fingers
reaching past it to scrabble at the hilt, she slowly
folded and collapsed.

Screaming figures filled the space and Dimitrius
found himself swept away from his Prince and the protective ring of Royal Guard. Fear dried his mouth, but
on its heels rushed the battle lust again. He gave himself up to it. Swinging his sword in a wide circle, he
charged. Two of the foe gave way before him, then a
wild-eyed Heathland woman took his strike on the
edge of her own sword and flung him aside. His back
hit the wall of the great hall and chips of stone show-
ered above his head. He ducked, struck out with his
own weapons, and missed.

He saw her swing, watched the blade whistle toward
him and knew even as he twisted desperately away that
he was too slow. The blow took him in the left side, the
shriek of metal hitting metal loud in his ears. The force

of it spun him around and the rough scrape of stone against his face was like a shock of cold water. He fell. Stunned, he could only watch his death rise above him. The gleaming blade streaked down and at the last moment he threw his own sword up to meet it. It was a weak blow, his injured arm trembling with the effort to hold it aloft, but it was enough. Deflected, her point cracked the flagstones an inch from his ear. Dimly he saw a Sword Knight turn and race toward him and knew that the Heath would have at least one more strike before she reached him. Using the wall as a brace, he pushed himself up and kicked out.

It was not a move his enemy had expected. His foot caught her in the shin and she stumbled, her stroke going wide. It was just enough time for the knight to arrive. While she held the Heathland woman off, Dimitrius scrambled to his feet. Together, they brought her down.

The fight continued. How many more they beat off before the battle moved away from their tiny pocket of resistance and massed at the chapel doors, he couldn't remember, but finally, he dropped the point of his sword to the flagstones and leaned against the pommel. The knight beside him slumped, breathing hard.

Around him the wounded screamed, their anguish lost in the hoarse battle cries of both sides. Dimitrius blinked sweat from his eyes and coughed, happy to be on his feet and not among them. One more breath, he told himself. One more breath and he would rejoin the fighting. The knight beside him seemed to be having the same conversation with herself.

Faintly in the distance a noise fought to gain the squire's attention over the sounds of battle; a series of notes repeated over and over. Fighters on both sides paused to catch the meaning of it. A trumpet. In the distance. For a second Dimitrius despaired, believing it to be a Heathland call for reinforcements from the city and then the knight was jumping up and down, screaming, "It's cavalry! They're Branion cavalry calls!"

The Heaths before them paused, then leaped to the attack once more. Now they fought with a panicked desperation, and slowly the Royal Guard began to gain the upper hand.

In the doorway Dimitrius laughed hoarsely. "We . . . we made it," he gasped.

The knight grinned at him.

The trumpet calls grew louder.

"We . . . should reenter the . . . melee."

"A moment. Just let me . . . catch . . . my breath."

One of their attackers lay facedown on the cobblestones before them. While he stilled his breathing, Dimitrius stared sightlessly at him for a time before the man's uniform caught his flagging attention. Uniform. Castle garrison uniform. His eyes widened as that sank in and he turned to his comrade.

"The castle garrison are . . ." he started.

She nodded grimly. "I know. One tried to split my . . . head open as I left the barracks." Pushing a clump of bloodied hair from her eyes, she shifted the weight of her shield, the only piece of armor she'd managed to salvage.

Dimitrius opened his mouth twice before the words he was trying to say emerged. "But if the garrison's turned, what's happened at the gate?"

She paled. "Oh, shit! If the gates are secured . . . oh, shit in a saddlebag!"

The two stared at each other for a breath, then bolted from their protective doorway. The race around the battle's flank took only a few seconds. Fortunately they were ignored, for neither had any thought for their own defense. They made the arch, the woman grabbing a fellow Sword Knight as they ran. Quickly she explained and the three youths sprinted across the chapel lawn.

The inner gate was deserted. Dimitrius slipped as they spun around the walls, his comrades dragging him forward a yard before he got his feet under him. Together they pelted down the dirt road.

The outer gate was secured, but the portcullis was up.

Two young Heaths stood uncertainly before it, unsure of what to do about the trumpet calls coming closer and closer, but unwilling to leave their post. They stared in horror at the three bloody apparitions that charged toward them. Then they went for their swords. They were too late.

Dimitrius took one with a great slash that bent him over double. The second knight dispatched the other. The first had already hurled her sword to the ground and was struggling with the huge wooden bar across the gate.

"Help me, burn you!"

The other knight joined her while Dimitrius guarded their backs, trying not to look at the Heathland boy, barely his own age, writhing in the corner.

Together the two Sword Knights got the bar up and flung it away. Dimitrius forced first one door open and then the other. For a heartbeat all was still, then the trumpet call came again, and the squire began to cheer. Up the cobblestone street came a thundering charge of cavalry. The trumpeter gave one final blast as the horsemen raced toward them.

The three youths pressed against the walls, urging them on as rescue clattered through the gate. The last three riders reined up, and one of them shouted and waved.

"Come on, then! Up you get! Don't want to miss the fun, do you?"

They were pulled up behind and the huge warhorses shot forward after their fellows, two cavalry squires remaining behind to secure the gate.

The return to the courtyard was much faster than the leaving of it. As they shot under the portcullis, a shout rang out. Before them, a handful of Heaths fled to a small opening in the battlements. The cavalry gave chase. Too late, a stout oaken door slammed behind the rebels. A rider pounded on it with one mailed shoulder to no avail.

"Go around!" their leader shouted without bothering to lift his visor. Half a dozen peeled off to obey, the rest surged forward again. They made the inner gate in seconds and headed for the courtyard.

Two abreast they entered the square in a thunder of iron-shod hooves, scattering fighters from both sides. The swords of the cavalry rose and fell and came away red. There was panic in the courtyard.

In the midst of the battle, Dimitrius saw the Crown Prince swinging his great broadsword, the Earl of Essendale at his side and knew they had heard the trumpet calls and had come out fighting. Joyously, the Royal Squire flung himself from the horse's back and drew his sword. Hurling himself at the enemy's flank, he fought toward his Lord. It was over very quickly. With the appearance of the cavalry, the fight went out of the rebels. Those still on their feet surrendered. Braxborough Castle was quiet.

Demnor leaned on the pommel of his broadsword and took in his surroundings. Dead and dying littered the courtyard, and the small group of prisoners huddled together were surrounded by cavalry.

Cavalry! Where, by the Earth, had they come from? Their leader dismounted and came toward him. Demnor recognized the quartered shield with its hawk motif and when the man knelt before him and removed his helm, the Prince smiled.

"Terion. What Aspect brought you here?"

The Earl of Linconford laughed. "I'd a feeling I'd be needed, My Prince, so Katrina said we'd better come with no delay."

"I'll have to remember to thank her. And you, old friend. I've never been so happy to see anyone."

"Nonsense, Highness. You'd have driven this rabble into the sea in no time. Still, we're glad to be of service, eh, Katrina?"

A rider turned, then saluted with one mailed fist.

Demnor nodded back, before turning to the wounded.

By noon the dead lay in rows in the Great Hall, and

the wounded lay in the barracks, tended by physicians. His Highness, the Heir of Branion, sat in Council in Gideon's Tower, debating on how to deal with the prisoners and this sudden, small Heathland rebellion. Around him sat his own people, Kelahnus, the Earls of Essendale and Linconford, Tania, and Lieutenant Grey. Warden Davies had been found in his quarters, stabbed, a garrison guard dead beside him. Katrina was in the city with her uncle Sandlin DePaula rounding up possible sympathizers and conspirators. Two of his remaining Shield Knights stood behind him, the other two guarded the door. In the castle and throughout the city, knights of the four Militant Orders based in Braxborough patrolled the streets, while their Captains sat in Council with their Prince. Standing nervously at the other end of the table were the Provost of Braxborough; a Branion, and a High Abbot of Essus; a Heath. It was to the latter the Heir now turned.

"The city is quiet?"

The older man started and wiped at his face with a lace handkerchief. "Yes, Your Highness, very quiet. We assure you, we want no trouble."

"Good. Keep it that way. You will ensure this, My Lord Provost."

The other man, as worried as the High Abbot about a vengeful Branion army in his city, nodded shakily.

The Heir turned to Terion.

"Have the messengers left for Branbridge, My Lord of Linconford?"

"Yes, My Prince."

"And the city?"

"Is secured, sir. Archpriest Belgraven's Flame Priests are even now seeking an answer to how widespread this uprising may be."

"What about that door?"

"It leads to a series of cellars, My Prince, with a rough fissure just above the lake. There's a thin path that winds around to the east. I've people searching the area in case the rebels are holed up nearby."

"Good. The fissure. Seal it."

"Yes, sir." Terion gestured to a Lieutenant and the woman left quickly.

Demnor returned his attention to the two Braxborough men. "My Lord Provost and Your Grace, I won't keep you; you have work to do and so do I. Good day."

The two men rose and bowed. On the way out the High Abbot turned.

"Yes, Your Grace?"

"Your Highness." The old man straightened his shoulders. "May I give my parishioners assurances that they will not bear the brunt of retaliation?"

Grey's expression was affronted, and he made to rise. Demnor restrained him with a light touch on his arm. The Prince smiled grimly. "If your people are innocent of conspiracy and rebellion, *and* if they remain so, they have nothing to fear from me."

"My thanks, Your Highness." The Provost and the High Abbot left, sharing a look of apprehension. When they'd gone, Demnor leaned back in his chair and sighed.

"This was a costly victory, My Lords."

He expected no answer and got none. Around the table his people reacted silently to his words. Grey ground his teeth in anger, Terion looked speculative, the four Captains grave. The Earl of Essendale cocked her head to one side and whispered to her Companion, then returned Demnor's grim frown with a questioning look. He gave a minuscule nod. They would be avenged. But they'd taken a serious beating this day and could go nowhere without reinforcements.

Of his thirty-six Guards, seven were unwounded; twelve had fallen and the death toll would rise by nightfall. Captain Hough was in the infirmary, bloodied, wounded, but alive. He'd held the door. Of the castle garrison, eleven were dead. Only two of the remainder were unscathed. How many had gone over, Demnor was unsure. He would have to speak with them, and with his own people who had fought beside and against them. The Crown Prince stood, and the others quickly rose behind him.

* * *

By the time the city bells rang two, it was done. Six Branions, members of the garrison that had aided the invaders, swung from the inner battlements, two so wounded they'd scarcely felt the scrape of hemp around their necks. Demnor watched until they were still, then turned away.

Crossing under the arch, he faced the row of Heathland prisoners. They glared back at him, grim-faced and unbowed. Those who had escaped were still at large, but they were at large without their leader. The sandy-haired woman Captain Hough had identified as the Rebel Commander lay among the dead. Her comrades refused to identify her or themselves.

"Lock them up."

"Yes, My Prince." The Captain of the Shield Knights gestured, and his people moved forward to herd the prisoners away. Demnor motioned to the Sword Knight Captain and the woman joined him and bowed.

"Assemble the Chapter in the Aspect's Chapel."

"Yes, My Prince. The entire assemblage?"

Demnor thought for a moment. "No. Just those in the castle."

"Yes, sir."

Across the courtyard, Dimitrius was speaking with Deverne Jones. He came running when Demnor called. The Prince nodded to himself. The youth was a man now, his first battle casting a mantle of maturity over his features as Demnor had known it would. A linen bandage encircled one arm and his side would be paining him, but he moved with a certainty and a new confidence. When he arrived, the Prince looked him over with approval.

"You did well in your first battle," he said. "When we were swept apart, I worried about you, but I knew you would show yourself well. You proved me right."

Dimitrius' cheeks grew hot. "Th . . . thank you, sir."

The Prince smiled. "The Earl of Linconford told me you opened the gate. Without that single act of courage we would have lost today. This victory is yours."

Dimitrius stammered, unable to speak. Finally he gulped out. "It . . . was not only I, Highness."

"I know." Looking into his squire's earnest face, Demnor struggled to remember if he had ever been so young. His memory touched on a time when he had, and gently, he put it back in the past. "Come with me."

The Lord and his squire crossed the courtyard and joined the flow of Sword Knights entering the Aspect's Chapel. Inside, the torches and candles had been lit and new cloths laid on the altars. Rose's body had been removed and placed with the other dead. The thick, familiar scent of incense filled the building and Demnor breathed it in, letting the comforting odor of peaceful sanctity settle over him. The assembled parted, saluting as he passed. Reverently he knelt before the main altar, closing his eyes in silent prayer.

Behind him, the knights convened quietly, some aiding the walking wounded. When they were all gathered together and the doors were closed, Demnor rose and turned. At his signal, the Sword Knights knelt. He spoke their ancient benediction, spreading his arms to encompass them all as they raised their heads to receive his blessing. A fierce pride seized him. These were his people, his true brothers and sisters. In their company he was whole. Going into battle with them was an honor and a joy, and worshiping with them was as close to the Essusiate paradise as he would ever wish to come. He lowered his arms and they rose.

"I won't speak of our losses here," he began. "That's for another time. The dead will be honored in their turn, but today I wish to honor the living. Maia Cowan, Lord of Guilcove come forward.

The first knight who had made the run to the gate with Dimitrius knelt before him.

"Know that your deeds will be remembered and that long after this day the minstrels will sing of them. In gratitude and honor I give into your keeping the lands of Alderbrook and Norgate, by my right as Defender of the Realm, in the name of Melesandra the Third, Aristok of Branion."

Cowan saluted and backed away, her face shining. After calling the second knight to him and rewarding him in kind, the Prince paused and allowed himself a proud smile. "Dimitrius DeLlewellynne, come before me."

When the youth faced him, the Prince began to speak. "Know that you have given good service and brought honor to your family. By rights, this ceremony should have taken place on the fields of Branbridge some time ago, but I think the Wind's Prophet held my hand until today that you might have a proper battle-field knighting. Give me your sword and kneel."

In awestruck disbelief, his squire obeyed.

The Heir laid the flat of his sword on the youth's shoulder and Dimitrius looked as if he might burst into tears as the weight settled.

"I, Demnor DeMarian, Archpriest of the Knights of the Sword and your Prince of Gwyneth, with leave of her most Regal and Sacred Majesty, the Aristok Melesandra the Third, in her name and in my own, and with the witness of your family in arms, do on this battle-field of Braxborough, knight you, Lord Dimitrius DeLlewellynne, by the Sea and Wind and by the Earth that bears us up. I name you Sword Knight, with all the privileges therein. I name you Viscount and give you the lands of Caer Aberddyn in my own principality of Gwyneth, such title and lands to pass from you to your heirs. Rise, My Lord of Caer Aberddyn and take this, your consecrated weapon, into your hands. Do it honor always in the service of the Living Flame."

Turning the sword, he held it hilt forward and rising, the newly made knight took it and reverently kissed the blade. Then he sheathed it. Unable to speak, and tears in his eyes, he seized the Prince's hand and kissed that also. Demnor smiled and turned to the assembled knights.

"And shall we greet our new brother?"

The roar that answered him rocked the chapel and when he gave them leave, the assembled converged on the youth. Dimitrius disappeared in the throng, only to

reappear on the shoulders of the Lord of Linconford.
The other two were likewise seated and the knights
spilled out of the chapel like children, chanting the
names of the three heroes. Demnor drew Captain
Secard aside.

"Take him to the chapterhouse and let him get drunk.
Tell him I give him leave."

She grinned. "Yes, My Prince. Will you be joining
us, sir?"

"Maybe later."

She saluted and departed. When the noisy crowd of
knights had left the castle, Demnor climbed the short
flight of steps to Mairi's Church and leaned against the
battlements. Two Shield Knights followed him at a discreet distance. Unable to keep a smile from his own
lips, and feeling absurdly pleased with the afternoon,
despite the morning's disaster, Demnor gazed across
the fields. The walls marched resolutely around their
perimeter, and he was reminded suddenly of another
stretch of battlements he had leaned over many years
before, though in much different circumstances. Buckdon Castle, far smaller then Braxborough, had fallen
less easily that day. As the sun sank below the city, the
Lord Demnor DeMarian, Duke of Briery, remembered
another day, and another rebellion.

Spring, 886. Prince Demnor paced the battlements of
Buckdon Castle, a small fortress overlooking the vale
it was named for in Briery County. Built in the sixth
century style, an octagonal curtain wall encircled a
small, central keep, barracks, stables, and storage
building, built on the crest of a wide hill. The wall had
recently been repaired, the garrison brought to full
strength and the stores replenished. Below, encamped
and waiting, sat the army the Crown Prince had called
to him. Five hundred strong, they would meet a force at
least twice their number. No more time remained to
gather strength. What the Heir had, he must use to
maximum effect.

A rain-soaked breeze drove chill fingers through his

clothes, and he shivered, pulling his cloak more tightly about his shoulders. In these last few days he seemed to be perpetually cold. Another guest of wind pushed him toward the archway and the warm fire below in his hall, but he hesitated. Little enough time remained to think quietly alone. In the company of others, his reasoning seemed to pale before a growing dread that all his preparation would only lead to disaster. Here, in the company of the wind and cold he could feel, although no more assured, at least less panicked.

His Council did not share his misgivings. Confident and impatient for the battle to begin, his youthful generals already boasted of the victories they would achieve. Only their leader doubted. Only he had sat in the Aristok's War Council and listened while she laid out the strategies that had won Branion the greatest empire in the world. Somehow, he must achieve the goal so many other leaders had attempted without success. He must defeat Melesandra DeMarian in the field.

A wave of dizziness hit him, and he gripped the stone parapet, waiting for it to recede. Lately the spells had been growing more frequent. Sweat beaded his face and his breathing became ragged. Vision swimming, he reached out blindly for the watchtower wall and leaning against its rough stones, he scrubbed at his face. Slowly the faintness passed. He was ill. He could not afford to be ill.

There's nothing wrong with you other than plain cowardice, he berated himself savagely. *You're just tired.*

He *was* tired. He hadn't slept well the last few nights. With a disgusted snort he amended that. He hadn't slept well in over a fortnight. Not since the night he had chosen to challenge the Aristok's hold on his life.

It had been almost three weeks since his decision to flee Branbridge, breaking his arrest and his sworn oaths of fealty to his Sovereign and his country. It had not been an easy decision to come to. And once made, it had not been an easy decision to maintain. Everything he'd been raised to be recoiled, horror-struck, at his actions. He was Heir to the Throne, pledged to uphold the law and the authority of the Aristok. He was a Triarch, highly placed in a religion that worshiped its secular ruler as divine. He was a knight of an Order whose foremost superior was the woman he now defied. He was a man of honor. And that alone stood equal to the rest. Without honor, he was not fit to rule. With honor, he could not rule. The two would not be reconciled, so three days after his first audience with the Aristok he'd written his abdication, knowing it could mean his death.

The document had left him physically ill and shaking. He'd given it all up, rights and titles to the Throne, opening a clear path for Quindara. At least on the secular level. Then he'd left.

He went immediately to the School of Companions. It was late, past two in the morning, but the Head of the Guild roused himself at the behest of the Crown Prince. After hearing Demnor's wishes, Master Klairius was respectfully apologetic. Kelahnus was not there. Fearing for the boy's life, he had sent him to their School in Bachiem. The Head Master assured the Prince that the student would return and be contracted to His Highness as soon as the present situation defused, as he was sure it would. Demnor had not disillusioned him. The Prince left the School and returned to the palace.

Several options came and went as he rode through the deserted, rain-soaked streets. Kelahnus was safe, out of Melesandra's reach, and for an instant the temptation was strong to return to his rooms and submit to her demands. Self-disgust soon drove that thought away. Whatever he chose to do, it would not involve betraying the student's trust. One thing was certain, though. The Aristok would not allow him to retire. The Living Flame passed through progenitor unless—as both his mother and his grandfather had believed—that Vessel was unworthy and then it moved on. But not until after that first choice was dead. Fifteen out of forty Vessels had proved too weak to hold the Flame, three of them worshipping a God above the Flame itself. The ultimate heresy. Each time the Realm had suffered.

The Vessel must carry the Flame with strength and total devotion, and must be the Aristok or the Realm would suffer. Melesandra DeMarian would never allow one forsworn to take on that duty after her. She would come after him with all her might, and he must be ready to meet her. He could flee to the Continent as Drusus DeMarian had done in the face of the Bastard's army, collect Kelahnus, and seek asylum in Gallia or Panishia, but he was a DeMarian and he would not turn to his country's enemies. And he was angry, hotly angry that she'd forced him to this. As the great bell of Atreus' Tower tolled three, he knew he'd come to a decision. He would defy her, and in doing so he would deliver her the hardest blow he could.

The Guard before his door had been his own. After the first day, Melesandra had allowed them to return, confident in her power over her son and over his Guard. Demnor proved her wrong. Unable to offer her victory or the adulation of the crowds, the palace garrison was ignored and slighted by the Aristok who held them in contempt and kept a company of titled Shield Knights as her personal guard. The Crown Prince, while obeying the traditions which held the Royal Guard as the rightful Protectors of the Royal Family in public, preferred the company of the untitled Palace Guard. From an early age, he'd set himself up as their patron and they'd responded in kind. Their best guarded his door and the corridors leading to his isolated suite. They kept an eye on the small collection of people he cared for and ruthlessly protected his interests. When Kassandra was born, the Prince had charged them with her safety. Recognizing the trust inherent in this honor drew the Guard even closer to their Lord. When he fled, he asked for a dozen. Fifty followed him to Briery.

Demnor was not ashamed of the choice he'd forced his people to make. He needed an army, he needed people he could trust. Of the nobility he'd gathered on the way, most were disaffected Lordlings, third and fourth children. They could bring him a few retainers, a little money, and minimal battle experience. He took what he could get, calling on whatever would bring them to his banner. Outwardly, he showed ultimate confidence. Inwardly, the voice of duty denounced him as a traitor. He ignored it and made for his Dukedom of Briery, his closest demesne of power.

He made the one hundred and ten miles in just under thirty hours. Demnor grinned darkly at the memory. The post houses, maintained on every road from Branbridge, that the Crown might stay in constant contact with the Realm, had worked against it this time. Pursuit found blown, exhausted mounts and the Prince made it safely to Buckdon Castle.

His people straggled along the road behind him, most arriving two and three days later. When they were gathered, he had the core of an army he could feel confident in.

Janet DeSharon was a hotheaded Lord of Demnor's age. Having just lost an appeal to the Aristok when her twin sister inherited their father's lands and titles, she was more than willing to throw in her lot with the Crown Prince when her cousin and husband of two months, Rathe DeSharon had told her of his intentions. They had caught up with the Heir outside Albangate.

Robert DeKathrine and Arthur DePaula, Viscounts both, had come with Demnor from Branbridge and had peeled off when they reached their own lands, promising twenty-five troops each. They'd arrived at Buckdon five days later.

Collin DePaula, at seventeen already considered to be a brilliant young tactician had laid out some rather unorthodox battle plans. After an hour's debate they had been incorporated into Demnor's less subtle strategies. Mercedes DeKathrine had brought her siblings, Marjory, Thomas, Julian, and Terilynne, good fighters all and fifty archers. Cheryl and Merle DeYvonne, Seer twins had spent the last three days searching the heavens for portents. He had Elisha DeLynne, an old friend from the continent. She offered him the twenty Sorlandy mercenaries in her pay from the spring's Continental campaign. With these and his own people from Briery sworn to take up arms in his defense, he had a force some five hundred strong. They would have to do.

Michelle DeKathrine bringing her own retainers to swell his ranks by another twenty-five told the Prince of the Aristok's fury and the growing army raised to oppose them. It would be a little over twice their number. Melesandra, confident of victory, need send no more. Michelle's father, Alexander, Earl of Cambury and Archpriest of the Knights of the Sword, would lead them. They would arrive within the week.

Finally, yesterday, as the sun dropped below the vale, two mud-soaked riders sought entrance to his hall. Gawain DeKathrine bringing his cousin Alerion.

Demnor could not have been more surprised if the Triarchy itself had answered his call. The two estranged friends had stared silently at each other while Gawain had stabbed at the tension with merry chatter. He had no troops to back him up, but what little he himself could offer he would do. Demnor had barely heard the prattle of his most gregarious kinsman. After a strangled pause he'd managed one question of Alerion: why?

His third cousin didn't answer for a long time. Then simply shrugged. When he spoke, his words were unrelated and typical of him. *You look like shit. You should get some rest.*

Rest. Nights found him staring at the walls, unable to sleep or slipping into nightmares where he knelt before the block, his grandfather and mother raising twin swords of flame above his head while the rulers of nine hundred years waited to cast him down into the Essusiate's Hall of Death. Days found him feverishly planning and replanning his strategies, sending out scouts and collecting reports on the army his mother was raising to subdue him. As battle drew nearer, his condition worsened. He hid it behind councils and inspections. He took his meals alone, tried to eat, was ill, tried to sleep, paced.

So far his weakness had gone unremarked. His generals followed his lead, his troops cheered him when he rode amongst them. They, at least, were sure of victory and believed in his cause because they believed in him. Only Alerion noticed he was unwell and after that first night, he kept his observations to himself.

The rain began to fall more heavily and finally Demnor surrendered and went inside. His Council would be gathered for another planning session. Time to stop shirking his responsibilities and join them.

Two days later a page interrupted yet another War Council to announce the arrival of Raventarian, the Aristok's private Herald. Demnor signaled that he be shown in.

The Aristok's courier was a tall, lean man, his black hair beneath the Herald's circlet, streaked with gray. He had been with Melesandra for as long as Demnor could remember, a living symbol of her authority. His words were hers, and the very sight of him hushed those gathered about her son. Raventarian approached and bowed. Teeth gritted against a sudden bout of nausea, Demnor nodded in formal greeting.

"What news do you bring me, Herald?"

"News of an army, My Most Royal Highness." Raventarian's voice was soft and well modulated, polite and respectful with no hint of the threat inherent in his words. The Council stirred and with an impatient wave, Demnor gestured for them to be silent.

"And questions from her Most Regal and Sacred Majesty," the Herald continued. "The Vessel of the Living Flame asks why are you comporting yourself thus? Why did you break your confinement? Why did you incite her Palace Guard to mutiny? Why do you gather swords to your banner and take up residence in

this place of defense, rather than remain at Her
Majesty's side where she would have you? She calls
upon you to lay down your arms, dismiss your gathered
troops, and return with me to Branbridge, else to be
returned by force by her army which even now awaits
upon your answer."

Demnor made a show of considering the Herald's
words, while inside his heart began to hammer painfully in his chest. It had begun. The room was suddenly
stiflingly hot, and he fought down the urge to bolt. But
no matter how he felt or what his Council saw, he
must allow no hint of hesitation or weakness to make
itself known to this man. Standing by the Aristok's
side in the past while the Herald had discharged
his missions, Demnor had been impressed by his
insight. Raventarian missed little and Melesandra
asked many questions. The Prince met the older man's
eyes.

"I thank you for your message, Herald. I must think
a while on Her Majesty's words and on my answer.
A page will show you to where you may refresh
yourself."

Raventarian bowed and was shown out.

Demnor motioned to another page standing by
his side and whispered something. The girl withdrew
and the Prince turned back to his Council. "Where
were we?"

There was a moment's hesitation, then Alerion
shook himself. "We were discussing the strength of
Her Majesty's army."

Gawain studied his Lord. "What will you tell her
Herald, Cousin?"

"What do you think!" Alerion snapped before Demnor could answer. "He'll tell him to scorch off!"

Despite himself, the Prince had to smile. "I doubt I'll
be that blunt. Listen and learn, Gawain. In an hour I'll
send for him, tell him, I'm sorry but I cannot oblige the
Aristok, and he'll leave."

"And then what?"

"And then we fight. Which we cannot do unless we

make some decisions today, so please, my friend, let's get back to it."

Elisha DeLynne, who'd been lounging negligently against the table, now leaned forward over the map. "My scouts report the opposing army three days' march away, My Prince, some eight hundred strong and growing."

"In two days' time they'll set foot in Briery," Alerion mused, frowning at the map. "We can either meet them here in the Vale, or sooner, near Linnchester or Oakston."

Demnor chewed at the scar on his lip. "The Vale, near Greensgate. Let them come to us. The gap in the hedgerow of the fields there is narrow. Maybe four could ride in abreast. We let a parcel of their force inside, then attack and grind them up against the hedge."

Collin coughed.

"Yes, My Lord DePaula."

"If I might suggest, Your Highness, we'll want them as weary as possible, pushing to fight before they encamp and rest."

"And how do we accomplish that?"

"Wear at them, My Lord Prince, with arrow fire and small attacks as the Heaths do, both on the road and at night. Whittle away at their strength before we engage. Slow them down with skirmishes so they arrive rattled, angry, and in confusion."

"I'll send Mercedes DeKathrine and her archers."

The page reappeared with a tray of goblets and after accepting one, the Prince motioned and she went to each of his Lords in turn.

"We are ready. My Lord DeLynne," Demnor turned to Elisha, "You will command the left flank, Alerion, the right. Gawain, you and your people will take up position in reserve in the woods to the left. I will meet the Aristok's first assault. Collin, you will ride beside me." He held up his goblet. "To victory, My Lords."

"To victory!"

The young nobility raised their cups in salute to the

Crown Prince, then drank deeply of the heavy red wine. Sipping at the camomile posset in his own goblet, Demnor grimaced, but his stomach began to slowly unknot. He motioned to the page.

"Conduct Her Majesty's Herald to our presence in one hour."

"Yes, Your Highness."

The field was ready, the sun high above. In the center of his main force, Demnor awaited the Aristok's army. Stomach knotting with tension, he clenched and unclenched his fists inside the mailed gauntlets. Where were they? He forced his hands to still. They were coming. If he strained, he could hear the faint echo of drumbeats in the distance. They would be here soon.

Beneath him, his new warhorse pranced impatiently, eager to begin. Despite himself, Demnor had to smile.

"Easy, Titan," he said, leaning down to stroke the charger's neck. "You'll get your first taste of battle soon enough."

Around him, his youthful commanders stirred as excitedly.

The drumbeats grew louder. The Crown Prince squinted up at the noon sun. Not as early as they had wished for, but nearly enough. Alexander DeKathrine had resisted the faster pace, keeping his people disciplined and together. Demnor had known his archer fire would do little to rattle seasoned troops, though the small drawing of blood would anger them and make them reckless in the field. Beneath his helm Demnor grinned mirthlessly. Let them come. He had a surprise or two in store for his second cousin Alexander.

The thought pulled his lips off his teeth, and he resisted the urge to glance at the woods to his right. To glance toward the woods which no longer concealed an enemy hidden in the trees. The enemy Merle DeYvonne had warned him about late last night.

She'd sought him out on the battlements where insomnia had driven him. Pacing from sentry box to

sentry box, searching his plans for flaws, her news had
been a welcome interruption.

She'd had a dream, she told him. There was a force
in Briery, hidden in the woods to the right of Greensgate where the Archpriest had known the Crown Prince
would meet him and why. A forced cross-country
march in secret had brought them there on the eve
of battle, to flank the Prince's force when the time
was ripe.

He'd sent Terilynne DeKathrine to verify this. She'd
returned in an hour, her face alight with excitement.

*"They're there, My Prince. And spending a cold
night without fire or hot food."*

*Merle had grinned. "It gets better, Highness. It's
going to rain.*

It *had* rained and the enemy had little fight left when
Terilynne's force had surrounded them just before
dawn. Most sat in the cellars of Buckdon Castle this
morning, their leader, Markarus DeFay, a guest in the
watchtower. With one threat negated, the Prince was
able to breathe a little easier and keep down some
breakfast.

A sudden cramp hit him. He ignored it. It would be
soon. Excitement clawed at his nerves, making his legs
tremble, and he took a deep breath to still them. If ever
he needed his full faculties, it was today. Today he
would match wits and swords against the wiliest General in the Realm. Only one of them would emerge victorious. And it must be him.

The sound of marching grew louder and with it the
bray of trumpets, the call of Triarchy Knights going
into battle in the name of the Living Flame. Alexander
DeKathrine was announcing his presence to his enemies, warning them that he approached and that they
still had time to flee before committing heresy. Even
though Demnor knew the strategy, he felt his stomach
knot in fear. Around him, his people stirred nervously,
but held. They were committed. They would not fail
him. Pulling confidence from that, Demnor straight-

ened in the saddle. Closing his visor with a snap, he drew his sword, ready to give the signal to attack.

Moments later, with a wild flurry of drumbeats and music, the enemy entered the field.

Magnificent in gleaming armor, banners snapping in the breeze, Melesandra's force cantered through the gap in the hedgerow. The sun shone off polished shields and turned the bright heraldry of surcoats and pennants into a kaleidoscope of rainbow brilliance. All four of the Militant Orders were represented; all seven of the noble families plus the Caileins of Heathland. Scanning the ranks of huge warhorses, Demnor recognized the devices of many a senior relative to those in his own force. Before them, his army seemed shabby, inexperienced, and severely outnumbered. He snorted. It was a simple tactic. The Gallians used it constantly. But the Crown Prince had fought such beautiful armies in the past and knew it wasn't how you held your sword that mattered, it was how you wielded it. Hopefully, his youthful Commanders would recognize that and not be intimidated by the array before them. Hopefully, for the Crown Prince did not have time to tell them. He would have to show them.

He waited. As the enemy steadily poured through the hedgerow, his army grew more restless. Collin leaned over to whisper something to his Prince, and Demnor waved him away. He knew what he waited for. At that moment, Alexander DeKathrine, Earl of Cambury, Archpriest of the Knights of the Sword, and Melesandra's most trusted councillor and commander entered the field.

Helmless and riding a huge, black warhorse, the Archpriest trotted to the center of his line and sat, regarding the opposing force and letting them have a good look at him. The thick auburn hair the DeKathrines shared with their DeMarian kindred, flowed loosely about his shoulders and down the jet black of his surcoat. His gray eyes showed confidence, and Demnor felt a superstitious twinge down his spine. Second cousins only, in this instant they might have been brothers, so alike did they seem. And Alexander was the older, the wiser, and the stronger. Beside him, dressed as a standard bearer, sat twelve-year-old Quindara DeMarian, come to learn the art of war from her cousin Alexander as Demnor had in his day.

Demnor felt his lips peel back from his teeth as he recognized the challenge. This was the battle the day hinged on, this and no other. Beside Alexander, Quindara held his banner aloft. A sudden breeze caught it, and the DeKathrine bear rose up, a gauntlet thrown before his adversary. Above it, the Aristok's device flashed golden fire in the sunlight. Responding without having to be told, Demnor's own standard bearer raised his Lord's colors in defiance. The rampant fire-wolf and gryphon of the Prince of Gwyneth snarled across the open field at the red and golden fire-wolf above the three oak clusters. For an instant the Royal symbols faced each other in silence, then Demnor dropped his sword and his people attacked.

The two opposing armies met with a crash. Horses and riders screamed, and the sharp crack of broken lances sounded the initial charge. On the flanks, Mercedes DeKathrine gave the first of the orders that sent the wicked goose-quilled shafts streaking into the enemy's rear ranks. There was chaos on the field.

His lance snapping against a red and black shield, Demnor flung the broken end like a spear at the knight before him. The man ducked, only to be slammed from the saddle by the Heir's sword thudding into his breastplate. Demnor did not wait to see if he rose. Screaming the DeMarian war cry, the Prince charged on.

Around him, the battle quickly formed into a struggle of politics and family rivalry. By his side, Collin hacked at an Archester DeSharon crest on the shield of an older man, one of his family's traditional antagonists, beating down his defense and laughing wildly the whole time. On the left, Demnor saw Elisha DeLynne casually dispatch a DeFay neighbor, and then move toward another. And all across the field,

DeKathrine sought DeKathrine, the green-and-black-garbed combatants forced to opposite sides by conflicting loyalties to Aristok and Prince, each side viewing the other as traitorous to their family name. The fighting between these was the most savage.

To the Crown Prince all those before him were simply obstacles on his path to Alexander DeKathrine. Quindara had withdrawn to the back with the squires, so neither had to fear for her safety. Sweeping all others aside, Demnor drove his mount toward his cousin. The Archpriest was as intent on meeting the Heir, but as they closed the space between them, Julian DeKathrine flung himself at his celebrated relative. They exchanged blows, then, as if the world had begun to turn more slowly, Alexander leaned forward and brought the edge of his sword along his nephew's unprotected jaw. Blood sprayed high into the air and Julian fell, to be caught gently by his uncle. The Archpriest drew a quick blessing on his forehead, and let him fall. Then he turned back to the Heir.

In the interim the first line of riders had charged between them and they were swept apart. One of Julian's Captains, tears of rage and grief in her eyes, hurled herself at the Archpriest, while a DeYvonne knight engaged the Prince. Soon their private war was forgotten in the midst of the greater.

Demnor dispatched his man with a savage blow that left him headless, then Titan charged toward another. This knight fell as easily. The next backed away, his eyes, behind his visor, wide with fear. The Crown Prince used the respite to take a quick tally of his people. The troops to either side of him were primarily Palace Guard. They met the Archpriest's infantry and hurled them back, chanting the Prince's name. To his right, Alerion brought his own command crashing against a line twice his number, led by his aunt, Helena DeKathrine. Combatants fell on both sides, but Alerion held.

The troops of Hamlin Cailein slammed into Rathe's people, their intent bloody. For a moment it seemed

Rathe's would break, but in the wild exchange of whirlwind blows, he succeeded in downing the other man, taking a final hack at him as he fell. Janet, fighting beside her husband, drove her warhorse into the Heath infantry. They broke and Janet gave chase. Then Demnor had no time to applaud his people's efforts for a DeLlewellynne Lord thundered toward him, lance leveled at his breast.

The Heir took the blow on his shield. As the woman passed, he hacked down at the wooden shaft, but was unable to break it. Behind her a DePaula Shield Knight swung a heavy mace, missing the Prince's head by a fraction. His next blow slammed against the Heir's shield. Demnor turned sideways to attack the Lord's more vulnerable right side, only to be blocked in return. Again they traded blows. Again the weapons thudded into shields raised just in time. Then Titan slipped on the slick grass and suddenly off balance, Demnor's shield arm dropped a fraction. The older knight caught him with a blow to the side of the head. Sparks of flame exploded before his eyes and momentarily blinded, he could only ride it out. The second blow almost unhorsed him. Unsure of where his enemy was, the Prince swung wildly and connected. When his vision cleared, the man's arm hung useless at his side, and he was backing his mount quickly from the fray. Breathing a prayer of thanksgiving to the Wind, Demnor raised his sword, quickly scanning the surrounding battle.

Beside him, Collin had lost his helm, blood matting the hair on one side of his head. Desperately he fought off two attackers, twins, Knights of the Lance, and probably Seers. Demnor charged, allowing Titan to half rear and bite, great teeth closing on an enemy mount's neck, while the Prince engaged its rider. Their swords slammed together, and Demnor felt the shock reverberate through his arm. He bore down. Even at sixteen the Heir was a big man, and his considerable strength won out. The smaller man broke first, and Demnor delivered the coup de grâce. Beside him

Collin drove off the other, and for the moment the space before them was clear.

Around them, their allies were not so fortunate. Marjory DeKathrine helmless and shieldless went down. Her brother Thomas fell moments later. Elisha DeLynne was flung from the saddle, but rose, a bloody and furious apparition to attack the mounted Sword Knight before her.

Fighting on that flank was heavy. With a curse, Demnor saw that Gawain had already been drawn out from his reserve position. Then he saw why. Foot soldiers wielding axes hacked at the hedgerow to the left, opening an ever widening gap. Through it charged a line of mounted knights intent on flanking Elisha's command. Her people met them stalwartly, even as she flung herself back into the saddle. They held.

Beside him, Collin took a blow that tore his shield from his arm. The next thudded into his side. He coughed and slumped, barely managing to avoid a strike that might have decapitated him. Weaving in the saddle, he held his sword awkwardly across his body to shield his injured side. His adversary hesitated, undecided whether to attack or wait to see if he would fall. Demnor shouted for him to withdraw. The young tactician ignored him. He raised his sword and made to strike.

An arrow took him in the throat.

Eyes wide in disbelief, he pitched backward off his horse. The animal, also pierced with sudden arrow fire, went mad, bucking and kicking out. An iron-shod hoof caught an opposing rider. Her head snapped back, the sound of her neck breaking loud despite the sounds of battle.

Demnor spun around. At first the battle obscured his vision, and then he saw the archers in the trees beyond the hedgerow. They wore the red Seer tunics of Gwynne DeLlewellynne's Champions of the Flame, the only archers who dared fire into melee. The Prince shouted even as the next rain of death fell around him, but Mercedes DeKathrine had already seen them. She

brought her archers forward, a company of Arthur
DePaula's troops to guard them. A hail of returning
fire soon drove the Seers into the cover of the leaves.
Fewer arrows fell, but enough got through, particularly
among the Guard around him.

Furious, the Prince pulled Titan in a tight half circle
and charged the line of riders between him and the
Archpriest. Alexander's death would end this battle,
that and nothing else.

The first rider had his sword swatted away almost
without effort. The Prince's second strike shattered his
shield. As Titan darted his great, black head forward to
bite at the other mount's ears, Demnor's sword struck
and came up bloody. The man went down.

Three knights remained between him and the
Archpriest.

Two.

One.

Alexander, turning from a stroke that killed a rebel
knight before him, saw the Heir and drove his mount
forward. When he got within earshot, he shouted.

"Highness! Surrender! This is madness!"

"Withdraw!" Demnor screamed in reply. "This
doesn't concern you!" His sword swept down, to be
caught on the weapon of the DeFay before him. Her
return stroke scraped along his own blade. Alexander
knocked the weapon from the hands of Robert
DeKathrine, before shouting again.

"My Prince, please! End this! I don't want to kill
you!"

This time Demnor made no answer.

"Cousin! This is treason!"

A sudden cramp nearly doubled the Prince over in
his saddle. He shuddered, and the DeFay knight took
the opportunity to swing. The Archpriest shouted. Too
late. Demnor managed to throw his arm up in time, but
the blow crashed into his shield. There was a sharp
crack and a blazoning pain in his arm. The shield splintered in three. His vision swimming, he managed to
bring his sword up in time to block his attacker's next

blow. It nearly drove the weapon from his hand. He
heard Robert scream his name, but couldn't see him.
The world spun sideways, as he fought the cramping
that threatened to double him over again. The DeFay's
sword streaked downward in a flash of steel, and helpless, unable to raise his arm to meet it, he could only
watch as death rushed toward him.

The Archpriest's sword knocked it aside.

"You fool! This is the Prince of Gwyneth! The
Aristok wants him taken alive!"

The dizziness disappeared. For a second he could
only stare at his second cousin in disbelief, then an
anger so deep it rushed over him like a boiling rain
obscured his sight and slowed everything before him.
That part of the Flame that was his birthright rose, covering his vision in a red film. He saw his sword arm
rise, saw it catch the DeFay completely unprepared.
The blow lifted her almost gently from the saddle, to
come crashing down before him. Then he reached for
Alexander DeKathrine.

The same slowing seemed to affect the Archpriest.
Demnor saw him bring up his shield to parry the
Prince's strike, then his own sword snaked out from
behind it. He heard Titan scream in challenge, and
heard the other stallion respond as if from far away. He
saw Alexander's sword descend, edge turned away and
the world was suddenly filled with fire-edged stars.
And then the stars went out.

On the battlements of Braxborough Castle, the
Prince of Gwyneth drew in a deep, shuddering breath.
So long ago, and yet sometimes it seemed only a few
days had passed. They'd all gotten older, those who
had survived the first Battle Royal in a hundred years.
He doubted many had gotten any wiser. With a tired
sigh, he rubbed at the scars on his jaw.

It was strange. Of all of those who had opposed him;
say it, he chided, *if only to yourself;* of all of those who
had defeated him that day, the only one who didn't
bring the bitter taste of failure to him was Alexander

DeKathrine. Possibly because he had outthought and outfought him, and such a victory had at least to be acknowledged, if not appreciated. Possibly because his attitude in the midst of the humiliating return to Branbridge had been honorable and straightforward. With a snort, Demnor leaned against the cool stone wall. Possibly because the Prince of Gwyneth was a perverse bastard who liked to confuse even himself. The latter was more likely.

A light sprinkling of rain misted his face, cooling his cheeks and pulling him from the past. He should go inside. He had duties to attend to, the least of which was the Sword Knight Captain's invitation to their celebrations. He really should put in an appearance. Then the reports on the city and the state of the rest of Heathland must be gathered and sent on to Branbridge, and he must decide what, if anything, to do with the dozen odd prisoners in Braxborough's cellars.

He sighed. At the moment all he wanted to do was collapse on the oversoft bed in the Royal Residence and have Kelahnus work the battle from his neck and legs. His face felt flushed, and the scars along his jaw pulsed hotly. He needed sleep.

A sound behind him made him turn to see the Companion hovering at the bottom of the stairs. The younger man's face was deathly pale, and for a second Demnor's heart slammed up into his throat with the fear that he'd suffered some injury he'd not mentioned. Then he noticed the woman standing beside him.

Covered in dust and dried mud, she weaved from side to side, obviously in the last stages of exhaustion. There were dark circles under her eyes and blood encrusted the side of her head. Demnor recognized the stance of someone who'd been in the saddle for days. With effort, she climbed the stairs, Kelahnus keeping pace behind her. At the top, she dropped to one knee and with a start, Demnor recognized Caroline DeLynne, the Earl of Buckshire, one of his mother's favorites, a Lord who'd once been her squire.

With a deep, ragged breath she began to speak.

"Most Regal and Sacred Majesty, it is my sad and solemn duty to inform you that three days ago, in the early hours of the morning, the Aristok Melesandra the Third, your mother, was most foully murdered. Hail, Demnor the Fifth, Aristok. Hail the Living Flame."

11. Alexander

In the pale light of dawn, three days before Demnor DeMarian received the news that he was Aristok, a Triarchy Page ran through the palace halls on an urgent errand from the Heirarchpriest. The eyes of the palace followed him as rumors about the night's strange events grew by the hour. Marsellus, Duke of Kempston had collapsed at three in the morning. The Hierarchpriest and the Archpriest of the Flame had been tending him for two hours when a peremptory message had summoned them to Her Majesty's presence at a time of the morning when the Aristok saw no one save her Companions and the servants who laid out her breakfast. And now a page had been sent by the head of her knights to summon the Duke of Yorbourne to this mysterious conference.

The boy whispered his instructions to the guards at Quindara's door and was shown in.

"Highness? Your Highness?"

The Duke of Yorbourne climbed sluggishly from an unpleasant dream to gaze blearily at her Companion. Nadia's expression was fearful and it swept the remnants of sleep from Quindara's mind with chill efficiency.

"What is it?"

"Something's happened. I don't know what, but you've been summoned to Her Majesty's chambers by the Hierarchpriest."

"By the . . . Help me."

Rising swiftly, Quindara began to dress. In the bed, Troy rose sleepily on one elbow. "What's the matter?"

"I don't know. I've been summoned by the Aristok. Get dressed."

She tossed his breeches at him, and he caught them with surprise.

"Me?"

She smiled tightly. "I don't know what's going on. When I do, I may need you." Looking down at the man she'd found herself growing more and more fond of, she held out her hand. "Will you come with me?"

Troy allowed her to draw him up. "Of course. I'll do what I can."

"Thank you." She pulled away and continued to dress. "Nadia, is there anything to eat?"

Her Companion passed them each a piece of bread smeared with honey before quickly braiding her Lord's hair.

Minutes later, the three of them followed the page from the room, the Royal Duke gesturing to her Guards to fall in behind

Quindara discarded a dozen explanations as they made the short journey to the Aristok's apartments. Something was wrong, very wrong for the Hierarchpriest to summon a Royal Duke to the presence of the Aristok at such an hour. Something that so totally consumed her mother's attention that she would summon her chief adviser before the Royal Cadet. Something of national, possibly empire-wide importance, then. She ticked off the possibilities while wide-eyed Palace Guards snapped to attention as they passed: treason, rebellion, or Demnor. Eyes narrowed, Quindara counted swiftly through her brother's itinerary. Depending on how long he visited with the Lord Terion, he was either in Linconford or Braxborough.

Cursing under her breath, the Royal Duke quickened her pace. That had to be it then, burn him. He'd gotten

himself killed, or worse, captured by the Heaths on the
eve of war with Gallia.

The two Champions of the Flame on guard before
the Aristok's apartments seemed to confirm her theory.
As they opened the door and stood aside, Quindara's
heart began to hammer painfully in her chest. Raised in
the shadow of the Crown Prince, every lesson she'd
ever learned from the Aristok, the Heirarchpriest,
trainers, tutors, or instructors had revolved around
Demnor; his destiny, his strengths, and most importantly, his weaknesses. He was rash, their mother had
taught her, rash, emotional, and reckless. He gave his
loyalty too quickly. He was just like his father.

Quindara had her own opinions of her celebrated
brother. He was a selfish, self-absorbed man who,
somehow, inspired admiration, even in his enemies;
even in her sometimes, she was forced to admit. If he
was dead, their mother was probably coldly and effi-
ciently plotting the revenge that would carve a bloody
path across the Northern Provinces. Quindara's sword
would likely be expected to do the carving and despite
herself, she found her sword hand clenched in wrathful
anticipation.

The Royal Duke and her entourage passed quickly
through each succeeding door with its newly appointed
guardians. Finally they stood outside the Aristok's
inner chamber. Captain Amandalynne DeFay of the
Champions of the Flame held the door, a naked
broadsword in her hands. She moved aside as the Duke
approached, only bringing up her blade as Nadia and
Troy attempted to follow their Lord.

Quindara crossed the threshold, and the door closed
behind her.

The room was somberly lit, casting shadows across
the faces of the two most powerful nobles in the
Realm. Gwynne DeLlewellynne sat by the fire, looking
old and tired, Alexander DeKathrine stood by her
side, his expression grave. There was no one else in
the room.

Quindara looked from one to the other in confusion, then her gaze turned to the great canopied bed, the form within indistinct in the shadows of the bed-curtains. Slowly, the DeMarian Cadet moved toward it.

Melesandra DeMarian, fortieth Avatar of the Living Flame, lay on her back, her head twisted sideways. Her face was swollen with angry red marks, and her expression was a frozen contortion of rage and agony. Dark vomit stained the pillows, and blood, from where her teeth had torn her lips and tongue, spattered the disheveled blankets. The fire in her eyes was out.

The Royal Duke of Yorbournc, second in line to the Sacred Throne of Branion stood frozen in shock, her own staring eyes mirroring her mother's disbelieving expression, the heightened flames which licked across her vision proclaiming the Flame's passing more accurately than any Herald, if only she had noticed.

"No."

She reached for the form in the bed, fingers drawn up into claws.

"No!"

"Quindara!"

Her grasping hands snatched up the corpse before Alexander could reach her.

"NO!"

Digging her fingers into the body's cold flesh, the DeMarian Cadet jerked it forward, snapping its head back. Vomit spewed from its mouth, spattering across her face and hands as she shook the corpse with violent desperation.

This was a lie, a trick. This *thing* couldn't be her mother. Her mother was a god, as mighty as any power on earth. Nothing could have bested her.

Hands pulled at the dead thing in her arms. Releasing it, Quindara stumbled back, then righted herself as she looked up into the face of Alexander DeKathrine.

"It's a lie."

"No, Your Highness."

"It's a lie!" Her face suffused with fury, Quindara

took one step backward, then launched herself at his
throat. Surprised, Alexander went down beneath her.

It took three Champions of the Flame to pull the
enraged Duke off the Hierarchpriest. Their Captain
helped him stumble to a chair while Quindara, green
eyes blazing fire, turned her rage upon the Archpriest.

"You!" she spat. "Where were you?"

The old woman flinched before her accusing stare.

"I was tending the Duke of Kempston, Highness.
The Flame would not reveal your mother's fate to me. I
was in the darkness, else I would have moved to stop
it."

"My mother's fate? This wasn't fate. This was
murder. Release me."

As the Champions stood back, the Heir Presumptive
turned a dark gaze on their highest priest.

"You will find who did this and you will bring them
to me, or I'll wreak such havoc upon you and yours
that you'll wish you'd shared *my mother's fate.*" She
gestured toward the bed. "Prepare that for the pyre."

As she turned, her gaze fell on Troy standing in
shock in the open doorway. Pushing past him, she
paused only long enough to order her Guards into formation about her.

Those left in the Aristok's inner chamber stood
frozen with the violence of the Duke's passing, then
after a moment the Hierarchpriest coughed, pressing
one hand gingerly against his throat. "The . . . Flame
has . . . passed."

The Archpriest nodded wearily. "Yes, but the Vessel
is not in Branbridge and the Realm remains in darkness." She turned her penetrating gaze upon him. "You
must send word to His Majesty to make haste and
return or all may be lost."

Alexander shook his head gingerly. "The Duke . . .
Yorbourne's place."

"She will not summon him. The Duke of Yorbourne
stands upon a precipice. Without the presence of the
True Vessel she may fall and extinguish the strength

of the Realm. We need him here. The Flame gives us stability."

Alexander straightened though the movement caused an involuntary hiss of pain to escape between his teeth.

"I will . . . send word."

She nodded. "Let the palace speak freely. Suppressing the gossip will only worsen matters. I'll go to Her Highness and suggest she proclaim the Flame's passing so that the Heralds' word may outgallop that of rumor."

"And . . . if she . . . will not."

"Then I will. We must face the darkness fearlessly, my friend, lest it overwhelm us."

"And . . . His Majesty?"

"Yorbourne's rage will be but a shadow of his own. We must be prepared to ride it out in safety."

He nodded and held up one arm. A Flame Champion helped him to his feet. As they left, he heard the Archpriest give the order to summon the Flame Priests to the palace. The Aristok was dead. The Living Flame had passed, but the new Vessel was not in Branbridge. The Realm was in peril.

As swiftly as he could, Alexander DeKathrine made his way to his own suite. When he arrived, he found a number of his people milling about the door. Courteously dismissing the Champion standing sentinel, he allowed one of his own Guard to help him inside. The others followed.

Once seated on the green brocade couch in his outer chamber, the Hierarchpriest waved the man away. Despite his obvious dishevelment, Alexander knew he must maintain a solid air of confidence if they were to make it through the next few days. The Archpriest's words came back to him then. *"We must be prepared to ride it out in safety."*

In safety. Very soon the Realm itself would be rocked to its foundations. They had very little time to prepare. His left side, which had cracked against the Aristok's dressing table as he'd fallen, sent a stabbing pain across his chest whenever he breathed. He tried to ignore it. "The . . . Aristok is . . . dead. Murdered," he said without preamble.

Many of those around him showed shock; others, the ones who'd been collecting rumors since early that morning merely grew grave. Alexander searched the room for his Companion Julian without success. That was not good. He gestured to his Captain.

"Summon the Guard, but deploy them cautiously. Yorbourne is powerful and may be our enemy."

Eyeing his Lord's injuries without comment, the Captain jerked his head at two guards, who took up positions inside the door, then he withdrew to do the Hierarchpriest's bidding.

Guilden, Alexander's secretary, offered him a goblet of heavy wine, then pulled a chair over beside his Lord. He leaned forward.

"Julian was gone when I arrived at six, My Lord," he whispered. "He's sent no word, although I believe he may be at the School of Companions. Rumor has it that his Guild is suspect because Alynne, the Third Royal Companion is missing. Word must have reached his ears early, and he's investigating. I do not believe him to be involved."

Alexander nodded stiffly. Julian and Guilden had taken some time to settle in together but had served him well in the past five years, and the Hierarchpriest had no reason to suspect Guilden of dissembling.

"Send a page . . . to request his . . . return . . . at his earliest . . . convenience. Ask if . . . he needs a . . . guard complement . . . to escort him."

"Yes, My Lord."

Pulling his collar away from his bruised throat, the Heirarchpriest took an experimental deep breath and winced. "Also, send for . . . a physician."

"Right away, My Lord." Guilden gestured at two youngsters hovering just out of earshot and gave them their orders. They scurried out, grateful to be doing something useful. Meanwhile the Hierarchpriest turned to the others.

"Reports?"

"The palace is anxious, My Lord," one answered. "Rumor says the Aristok was stabbed to death by a Heathland assassin."

"Poisoned."

"By whom, My Lord?"

"Unknown."

"The Champions of the Flame were summoned to secure the Royal apartments, as you know, My Lord," a woman dressed in the brown robe of a Triarchy Priest added. "If procedure is followed, the Flame Priests will be summoned to prepare the body and question those involved. The Hierarchpriest may include one of his own in these proceedings. Might I respectfully request that it be I who serves in this capacity?"

"Do so, Cousin. So far . . . only suspect, Alynne . . . missing."

"The Aristok's Third Companion," the woman murmured to herself. "And the others, My Lord?"

"First and Second . . . under guard. . . . Fourth had been sent to . . . Companion's Guild. Has not . . . returned."

"No doubt the Archpriest will have requested it. She'll have detained the Shield Knights who stood sentinel before the doors last night as well."

A soft knock interrupted their discussion. After a short conference with those outside, an acolyte in the red livery of the Order of the Flame was allowed through. She came before Alexander and bowed.

"Yes?"

"Excuse the intrusion, sir, but Her Grace, the Archpriest of the Flame, has charged me with the duty of informing Your Lordship that the palace has been sealed. Any retainer My Lord wishes to send out on such business as was discussed between the Flame and the Triarchy this morning should carry such tokens as will be recognized by the Champions of the Flame, who have orders to pass such a person."

"Give Her Grace . . . my thanks. I have . . . several

people . . . to send . . . and shall give them . . . creden-
tials."

"My thanks, sir." With another short bow, she
retired.

Sipping at his wine, Alexander considered the problem of the Shield Knights. The Guardians of the Aristok since 349, they would be chafing at the Flame
Champion's interference. The days ahead would be
explosive enough without infighting between the
Crown's Royal Guard and the Triarchy's Holy Sentinels. He turned to his Secretary.

"Guilden, send a page to . . . Head of the Shield
Knights . . . offering my support. Suggest a meeting
later today between her, the Archpriest . . . and myself.
Emilanda, behave . . . as diplomatically as possible to
. . . those detained, but bring me . . . the reports of their
questioning . . . as soon as possible."

"Yes, My Lord." The priest genuflected briefly
before rising and took three pages with her as she left.

Alexander turned to one of his guard. "Inform the
Town Watch . . . Commander, that the Aristok . . . is
dead. There may be . . . unrest, or political strife . . . in
the city. Also inform her she's . . . to keep the Coast
Road open. Tell her . . . nothing else."

"Yes, My Lord."

At that moment the door banged open, and Agrippa,
the Court Physician, stumped in, followed by the page
who'd been sent to summon him, arms laden with
medicinals. The guards outside gave a helpless, apologetic look at their Lord before the old man shoved
the door shut with one foot. Alexander looked up in
surprise.

"Thought you'd be . . . at the Royal apartments."

With a snort, the older man gestured at the girl to set
her bundle on the desk.

"Don't talk," he growled. "If you can't do it without
pain, don't do it at all. Get his tunic off."

Used to such behavior from the Court Physician,
Alexander's valet helped his Lord shrug gingerly out
of the dark green tunic and shirt while Agrippa fussed

over his supplies. When they were ready, he bent over the Hierarchpriest's throat.

"There are those more suited to tend to the dead than I," he answered finally in a mutter, as he gently turned the other man's head from side to side. "Open your mouth. Besides, scorching, snooty Flame Priests are as thick as fleas over a dog's arse right now."

He ignored the shocked expressions of some of Alexander's more pious retainers, and gestured for the page to bring a candle over.

"Does it hurt your throat to speak?"

"Yes."

"To cough?"

"Yes."

"To swallow?"

"Yes."

"But you can do it all?"

"Yes."

"Then you'll live. It's just bruised." Lightly rubbing some salve over the marks, he then handed him the jar and straightened. "Have Julian apply this every four hours or so." He gave the younger man a shrewd look from beneath his white eyebrows. "Yorbourne do this?"

Alexander nodded slowly. "She is . . . grieving."

"She is sending troops into the city to round up *potential conspirators.* I'd have a care if I were you."

Alexander smiled. "Do you suspect me, old man?"

"Don't be impertinent, Nephew. Does this hurt?" He prodded at the swelling on the other man's side.

Hissing between his teeth, the Hierarchpriest nodded.

"Thought so. Might be cracked. I'll wrap it up. *Keep* it wrapped for a few days, then I'll look at it again. Girl, bring me those bandages."

A guard put her head in the door and whispered something to her compatriot on the other side. He cleared his throat.

"Yes."

"Don't talk," Agrippa snapped.

"Um, it's the Viscount Alerion, My Lord. May he enter?"

"Yes."

Agrippa snorted.

Alerion pushed past the guards. His clothes looked as if he'd thrown on the first thing he could find. He frowned down at his uncle. "I've just heard. Are you all right?"

"Fine."

"It's true, then?"

"It's true."

"Sit up," the Court Physician ordered, "and if you've got nothing better to do than to ask stupid questions, boy, you can help me here."

Alerion obeyed his irascible great uncle, accepting the offered bandage. Together they wrapped it around the Hierarchpriest's ribs. When they were done, Alexander sat back cautiously and gave the physician a weak smile.

"It's better, thank you."

"Well, I needn't tell you what to do, you've had enough broken bones over the years. Send a page if you're in too much pain. Now, if there's nothing else, I've got to get to the Royal apartments and take the report on Her Majesty's death." He held up his hand to forestall any questions. "So far, you know all I know. When there's more I'll have you informed." He stumped out, motioning at the page to bring his things.

Alerion turned to the Hierarchpriest.

"Demnor?"

"*His Majesty* will be . . . sent for."

"So no one's been sent yet?"

Alexander sighed. "Not yet, Ler. I have to know . . . what to tell him first." He turned to the others. "Go about your business. Stay calm. Try and defuse . . . what you can, but also try . . . and stay uninvolved. Keep me informed."

His people filed out with obvious reluctance. Guilden looked from the Hierarchpriest to the Vis-

count, then quietly removed to his own office. When
the room was empty, Alerion turned back to his uncle.

"I'll go."

"No. I need you here."

"You don't."

"Ler, please. I have no idea . . . how far reaching this
is. And I can't move until I know what . . . Yorbourne
is going to do. Until then I need the family . . . to sit
tight and stay calm. There are a lot of us here right
now . . . and I don't want us drawn . . . into factionalism and violence."

"Why would we be?"

Before Alexander could answer, there was a knock at
the door. After a quick conference with their Lord, a
Guard Captain with the fire-wolf and wyvern badge of
the Duke of Yorbourne on his sleeve was ushered in.
His eyes flickered across the Hierarchpriest's injuries
with an interested expression.

Alexander gazed up at him impassively. "Yes,
Nephew?"

The man flushed. "Excuse me, My Lord, the Royal
Regent would have me ask you a few questions concerning your whereabouts last night." He looked pointedly at Alerion, who ignored him.

Alexander remained silent until the man returned his
gaze to him, then answered evenly. "I was working
here, in my office, until eleven when I retired. At three
I was summoned to attend to the Duke of Kempston,
which I did until a quarter past five when I was summoned to the Aristok's apartments."

"Were there any others with you during these times?"

"There were."

"Might I ask who?"

"Is this an official interrogation?"

The man stammered. "Well, no, not official, but . . ."
He drew himself up. "I was charged by the Royal
Regent to ascertain your whereabouts and that of your
compatriots, My Lord."

"Then you may discharge your duty by informing
Her Royal Highness, the Duke of Yorbourne, that the

Hierarchpriest of Cannonshire was in his office until eleven, involved with his Companion until three, at the bedside of Her Lordship's brother in the company of the Archpriest of the Most Sacred Order of the Flame until a quarter past the hour of five and in the inner Chamber of the late Aristok, Her Lordship's mother, until six where she found me. If My Lord Duke of Yorbourne requires more information or knowledge of the whereabouts of those who serve the Triarchy under my authority, she may summon me before the Order of the Flame where I shall be only too willing to answer any and all questions.

"Was there anything else?"

"Uh . . . no, My Lord, nothing else." The man turned to go with a subdued air.

"Turi?"

"Yes, sir?"

"Give my regards to your mother."

"Uh, yes, My Lord." He smiled somewhat sourly. "Thank you, Uncle."

As the door closed, Alerion snorted.

"Puffed up little prick."

Alexander, his head spinning slightly with the effort of making such a long speech without showing the pain in his ribs and throat, frowned at his remaining nephew.

"You were . . . asking about factionalism?"

"Never mind. You're right." The Viscount got up and strode to the window. "But we have to do something." He swung his attention back, running one hand impatiently through his dark, auburn hair. "We can't just let Demnor ride blindly into danger. He has to be told."

"The Aristok *will* be told. As for danger— Any danger that is to come from this has likely . . . already happened."

"Have you got the confessions of the conspirators, Halerion?"

The Prince Quindara sat upon her late mother's

throne in the main hall, her Guard standing at attention along the walls. Although she'd changed into a surcoat of ashen gray, her eyes were anything but grieving, and her Secretary shuffled his feet uneasily.

"Uh, yes, Highness. The Priests of the Flame report that Third Companion Alynne was the last to be seen with Her Majesty. The . . . um . . ." he licked his lips. "The Royal Companions deny all knowledge of the deed, and at this time the Flame Priests concur."

Quindara leaned forward. "Oh, they do, do they? Well, I'm not so sure the Flame Priests aren't involved in this, too, so what they report is suspect. Did you speak with these Companions yourself?"

Frightened by the accusation against the Flame Priests, the man dropped his gaze. "Uh, yes, Highness, their words were the same as to the priests."

"I'm sure, and the Guards?"

"They say Third Companion Alynne left the Royal apartments dressed for travel just after three. They didn't detain her as the Royal Companions have leave to come and go as they please at any hour."

"How convenient."

"Uh, yes, Highness. At this time, the Archpriest of the Flame believes that Alynne is our murderer and that she acted alone."

A cough interrupted him, and he gratefully moved aside as the Duke's Guard Captain bowed before his Lord.

"Yes, Turion?"

"I've just come from the Royal Stables, My Prince, they report that Third Companion Alynne left mounted, and in the company of," he paused for dramatic effect, his gaze sweeping the room, "Grant Cross of the Palace Guard."

Even those on duty along the walls cracked their precise stance to stare at their Captain. Quindara's lips peeled back from her teeth in a snarl.

"You've verified this?"

"Yes, My Prince. And there's more." His eyes glittered in anticipation. "They were met at the North

Gate by a figure in Essusiate garb and together they took the North Post Road out of Branbridge. The road to Heathland."

"What!"

Alexander DeKathrine started up, the pain in his ribs forgotten.

Stepping back hastily, Guilden ran his hand through his hair in a nervous gesture, then composed himself.

"It's true, My Lord. The Duke of Yorbourne's ordered the arrest of the Palace Guard."

"That's over a thousand people!"

"Yes, sir."

"Sir!" A Triarchy Page burst into the room, forgetting himself in his haste to discharge his message. Skidding to a halt before his Lord, he bowed quickly. "The Duke of Yorbourne's ordered the Shield Knights into the city, My Lord, to arrest the Hierarchy of Essus! Those who resist are to be taken in by force and any who defend them are to be arrested also."

"This is madness!"

Guilden shook his head worriedly. "The Essusiates won't suffer it, My Lord. They'll be rioting in the streets come evening."

"With reason, burn her. Help me up. I'll have to see her. This could destroy us all."

The Duke of Yorbourne refused to see the Hierarch-priest of Cannonshire. The Archpriest of the Flame was also refused an audience. All that day the DeMarian Regent remained closeted in the Great Hall, taking reports from her own troops and ordering the arrest of any she suspected of conspiracy.

Captain Fletcher of the Palace Guard was detained, as was every Member of the Companion's Guild found in the palace. The Head of each noble family was questioned in turn and many of their personal retainers were detained.

While not officially under suspicion, the rumors that Alexander DeKathrine was suspected by the Royal

Duke spread throughout the palace. His people were harassed and bullied by Quindara's troops as they tried to go about their business, and three were arrested. The Hierarchpriest personally saw to their release and sent them out surrounded by bodyguards, but the harassment continued. When a Triarchy Page was physically ejected from the Royal wing, his Guard swung her halberd at the offending Sentinel. Both sides suffered casualties in the ensuing battle before the fight was broken up by Champions of the Flame.

In the city, the Shield Knights dragged the Branbridge High Abbot of Essus from morning prayers, along with her priests, lay clergy, and family. When the Essusiate congregation tried to stop them, the knights attacked the crowd, driving them out of the church and sealing its doors.

Within the hour, rumors that the Aristok's death had been an Essusiate plot had spread throughout the city. Branbridge erupted in violence. The most ancient of the Essusiate churches went up in flames and two of its Clerics were murdered when they tried to put out the fire. Bands of Essusiates struck back, smashing and looting. The Town Watch was called out and then the Militant Orders, but they were unable to restore the peace.

Quindara called the Head of the Shield Knights to her and made her wishes plain. By afternoon the knights had arrested over two dozen Essusiate leaders. The word went out: Return to your homes and businesses or the prisoners will die. When the first was hanged from the City's West Gate, Alexander De-Kathrine took a contingent of his own Knights of the Sword and demanded an audience with the DeMarian Cadet. At once.

Outnumbered, her Guard Captain allowed them entry into the great hall.

Quindara's Guard immediately surrounded their Lord with drawn swords. The Hierarchpriest ignored them. He strode to within nine paces of the throne, then stood, his gray eyes hotly angry.

The Royal Duke's expression was equally dangerous. "You requested an audience with me, My Lord Duke of Cambury?"

The diminutive title was not lost on the Hierarchpriest. He drew himself up. "I did, *My Lord Duke of Yorbourne*. It is my duty as Senior Councillor to the Aristok to advise you that this course of action is illegal and will lead only to bloodshed and civil unrest."

"And what *illegal* course of action is that?"

"You may not execute the followers of Essus, especially those who hold Branion citizenship."

"I may not?" The question was polite, but the underlying steel in her voice made the Guards on both sides stir nervously.

"Political execution is the prerogative of the Aristok."

Quindara's eyes glittered dangerously.

"My Lord Councillor, take care, you overstep yourself."

At that moment she was the personification of her mother, but the Head of the Knights of the Sword met the challenge of her gaze without hesitation. "The Essusiates of Branion are under the sworn protection of the Triarctic Faith."

"So you take them under your *personal* protection, My Lord Hierarchpriest?"

"They are under the personal protection of the Living Flame, Your Highness, as promised by Atreus the Third in 675."

"The Living Flame does not allow traitors to evade the law on religious technicalities as promised by Quinton the Second in 875."

"Their involvement has not been proved. The Knights of the Sword, of which you are yourself a member, have been charged with the safety of the Essusiate minority in Branion. By pursuing this course of action, you risk the breaking of your oaths of fealty to your Order."

"And by coming before me with swords at your back you risk civil war. I would not make threats, My Lord of Cambury, unless you're prepared to back them up with steel." She leaned forward. "I remember those days. Do you?"

The room was silent for a long time as the DeMarian Regent and her DeKathrine cousin stared into each other's eyes. Finally Alexander spoke.

"Will you turn from this madness, Prince Quindara?"

The Royal Duke laughed scornfully. "I will not. My duty to the Realm supersedes any such request."

"Then I have no choice but to charge you with religious heresy and ask that you allow yourself to be taken into custody until such time as your brother, the Aristok, returns to Branbridge."

The room held its collective breath. Quindara cocked her head to one side, a faint smile on her lips.

"If this conspiracy is as widespread as I believe it is, then *my brother* may not even be alive to take up his duties. So I shall return the favor, My Lord Duke. I charge you, Alexander DeKathrine, with treason, stripping you of all religious and secular titles and ask that you give yourself up to my Guard."

"You'll split the Realm! For the Love of the Flame, Quindara, don't you see, we must be united to survive this!"

"It's in your power to bring it about then, Cousin. Lay down your arms and bow yourself to my will and we shall be united."

"United in madness!"

"United in strength. I'll ask you one more time. Will you lay down your arms?"

Again there was silence in the Great Hall. Alexander shook his head.

"No. You'll destroy the Realm, and that I cannot allow."

"Well, then we both know where we stand. You must go about your business as you see fit, My Lord of Cambury, and I shall go about mine. But heed this: What you believe is your affair and what you do about it is yours also, but if you get in my way, my people will have orders to remove you by force."

Alexander shook his head tiredly. "As you say, Highness. We shall withdraw for the moment."

He turned, and motioned his people out, following them with an air of weary resignation.

As they made their way back to the Hierarchpriest's suite, Alerion fell into step beside him.

"So much for avoiding factionalism."

"Yes, so much. It seems we're fated to bloodshed." Alexander paused. "Very well, then, we must move forward with all confidence. Rhewellynn, call the knights to order in the Tower, as many as will respond. We'll base there. Kasserion, pass the word in the city that any of Essus who wish to place themselves under our protection may come there also. Justinia, go to the Archpriest of the Flame. Make her aware of the situation and ask for her support. Alerion, go to the Shield Knight Commander and ascertain if she's thrown her lot in with Yorbourne, and how far."

"Is that wise, sir?" Caroline DeLynne interrupted. "If Sarellynne has gone over to Yorbourne, his life may be in danger. Perhaps someone not related to you, like myself, should go."

"I think I can manage the danger, My Lord of Buckshire," Alerion snapped. Alexander put a hand on his arm.

"His closeness with His Majesty should protect him from any temptation on My Lord of Kairnbrook's part, My Lord Duke of Buckshire. Besides, I need you for another task. You must find the Aristok and bring him home with all haste. You'll have to ride; the coastal winds are too strong this time of year to make a fast trip north by ship."

"And we don't exactly know where he is," she added.

Alexander thought a moment. "Head for Braxborough. Move with haste, but also with caution. If this attack is as widespread as I think, Heathland may be unsafe. When you find him, request that he come to the Sword Tower and we'll escort him into the city.

Impress on him that he must return with all speed or he may arrive too late."

"Yes, My Lord." Gesturing for her own people to fall in behind her she hurried off toward the stables.

"Glennaron, go with her and make sure she gets out of Branbridge in safety and then report to the Tower."

The Sword Knight Captain bowed and followed the Duke with half a dozen more.

When the messengers had all been sent, Alexander DeKathrine, Head of the Knights of the Sword, Leader of the Triarctic Faith and Defender of the Essusiate Church called his Order to arms. They gathered at the Tower of the Sword on the eastern border of Branbridge. Across the city's roofs they could see the tall turrets of Bran's Palace standing like giant sentinels in the west, defying any and all challengers. Turning his back on this obvious symbolism, Alexander made his plans and sent his people into the city.

Slowly the autumn sky grew dark as the sun set over the capital. The fifteenth day of Mean Damhar, 893, the day an Aristok had been murdered, was over. Across the metropolis, armed knights, both Sword and Shield patrolled the streets, carrying out the orders of their respective Lords. On the North Road a Division of Shield Knights and Flame Champions raced the setting sun in pursuit of three Branbridge fugitives, while on the Coast Road a lone figure traded one blown mount for a fresh one in her quest to return the light to the darkening Realm.

As the setting sun painted the turret tips of the palace a brilliant gold, Atreus DeMarian, Royal Duke of Lochsbridge, sat on the bed he'd shared with Marsellus all their lives, and held him while he shook. The seizures that had racked his brother's body since early that morning were no better, despite the wormroot potion Agrippa had forced down his throat. He was delirious, crying out against some invisible enemy, and cringing back from a vision that only he could see. All Atreus could do was hold him.

It was all he'd been able to do since Marsellus, caught in the throes of another prophetic nightmare, had shrieked in his sleep, snapping his brother awake at three that morning. When it had become clear that he was not going to rouse, Atreus had sent for Agrippa.

The old man could do nothing for him. He was lost in the Prophetic Realm, beyond a physician's reach. Marsellus had begun to choke, scrabbling at his throat, his breath coming in short, wheezing gasps. Then he'd begun a seizure. The Archpriest had been summoned and the Temple Herbalist, but his convulsions only grew worse. He'd begun to scream about death and the Shadow Catcher stalking the palace halls. He'd flung himself from the bed, striking his head against a trunk, and crying out when the others had tried to hold him as if their touch burned his skin. Although his eyes were open, he could not focus on anything and the one time the Archpriest had held his head, forcing him to meet her eyes, he'd screamed, a high, mewling sound, and begun to convulse again. The bond between himself and Atreus grew faint and then was lost in the torrent of his delirium. It shook his twin more than he could have imagined. Beside himself with worry, Atreus sent for the only man he knew could help them.

On their twelfth birthday the twins had returned from Lanborough to Bran's Palace. Surrounded by strangers, in a strange and bustling city, the young Princes had turned to the only familiar face they knew, their father's cousin, Alexander DeKathrine.

He had always been there when they needed him in the past. Now Atreus summoned him to his brother's bedside.

Alexander came at once. Kneeling beside the unconscious man, he'd taken Marsellus' hand in his, whispering whatever soothing words he could think of and smoothing the sweat-slicked hair from his face. Whether the comforting voice from their past had been enough to pull him a little from the grasp of the Prophetic Realm, or whether Marsellus had been able to regain some foothold in the Physical Realm on his own, Atreus didn't know and didn't care. The seizures had abated and, although his brother hadn't awakened, their bond had slowly reasserted itself. That had been enough.

But Alexander had been called away to the Aristok's quarters, and then Gwynne DeLlewellynne had gone as well. They'd not returned. Soon he was to learn why. The Aristok had been murdered in her bed, poisoned at the very moment Marsellus had begun his seizure.

Knowing the reason for his brother's condition had not helped him alleviate it and too worn out to grieve, Atreus had just taken his brother into his arms and slept.

His dreams were disjointed and chaotic, faces covered with an ashen gray mist swam in and out of his vision. The violence of war hovered just out of reach, and through it, like a thread frayed to the breaking point, his bond with Marsellus grew weaker and weaker. He'd awakened to a new outbreak of seizures, no more refreshed than when he'd first closed his eyes. He'd sent for Agrippa again.

The Physician had come and gone. There was little he could do but give Marsellus another potion and bully Atreus into eating. He hadn't much news to impart. Their mother was dead, a Companion had been accused. Their sister, the Duke of Yorbourne, had taken charge of the investigation, but had clashed with the Hierarchpriest over how that investigation was being carried out. As things now stood, Yorbourne and Cambury held opposite ends of the city. It looked like civil war. Agrippa had not been impressed. Atreus had just turned away.

As the setting sun began to paint the fields to the west of the palace, he stared sightlessly out at the pink-streaked sky. Marsellus, Alexander, Gwynne, Quindara, Melesandra—in one moment all the pieces of his life had been thrown in the air like a pack of playing cards. Grief hovered just out of reach like the violence in his dreams, and he let it remain there, grateful for its absence.

Marsellus had been right, he thought. Someone close to them had been in mortal danger. They'd just been wrong about who. He shook his head wearily. If only they could have pierced the future and seen the Shadow Catcher's hand poised over their mother's head, they might have been able to prevent it. But they hadn't. The vision they had risked the Potion of Truth for had been symbolic and vague, no different from the visions of the Flame Priests before them. Demnor's words came back to him then.

I won't run from the future. It's cowardly.

Was it? Was it any more cowardly than believing that fate was stronger than you were and just giving up? When they sought to change the vision that had so shaken his more sensitive twin, had they been running from the future? He'd thought they'd been taking action against an unseen enemy. Now he wasn't sure. He wasn't sure about anything anymore.

Better to meet the future face-to-face than have it sneak up on you when you're not expecting it.

Atreus gave a bitter laugh. Well, it'd snuck up on them all right, snuck up and thrown all their efforts to pin it down and defeat it to the Wind. It had brought them face-to-face with an uncertain future whether they liked it or not and now they had nothing left to fight it with. In the end it had proved stronger all along.

Holding tightly to Marsellus as if that alone could bring his brother back to him, Atreus closed his eyes, too fatigued to fight anymore. After a time, he slept.

In the Aristok's private office, Quindara sat going over the latest reports of the day. The door was open and a steady stream of messengers and pages came and went, giving their reports, taking new orders, and hurrying away. Sipping at a goblet of cider, Quindara pushed aside the remains of her supper and picked up the latest dispatch from the city.

Just before dusk the Knights of the Sword and Shield

had clashed over a small Essusiate church in the
Weaver's Quarters. Result: three wounded, one killed.
Both sides had withdrawn with the arrival of Gwynne
DeLlewellynne's Champions of the Flame.

Quindara's eyes narrowed as she considered the
problem of the Archpriest. Gwynne DeLlewellynne
was a powerful woman, not only ecclesiastically but
secularly as well. So far she'd remained neutral, but the
Duke knew she'd been in communication with the
Hierarchpriest and neutrality could crumble in an
instant. If the Archpriest would not aid the Throne, she
must be eliminated as a threat to it. Tapping her fingers
against the desk, the Royal Duke considered and discarded several extreme solutions. Finally she tossed
the dispatch aside in frustration. Alexander was the
key. Subdue him, and the rest would fall into line.
She picked up another missive and briefly scanned the
contents.

The Knights of the Bow had been called to their
headquarters, an ancient guardhouse built into the city's
north wall. They'd remained there, prepared for battle,
although unwilling to get personally involved. Waiting,
Quindara knew, to see to which side the Wind would
blow the advantage. They could be discounted for the
moment. Primarily a defensive Order they would not
take up arms until a victor was clearly indicated.

The Knights of the Lance had been split in two, with
the Captain staying loyal to the Throne, and the Chief
Lieutenant, seeing a chance to rise in power, following
the Hierarchpriest. Quindara summoned a page without
looking up.

"Send for my Captain."

When Turion DeKathrine arrived, she handed him
the report.

"I want two squads sent to Berius' aid," she said
when he'd read it. "Make them fifty-fifty archers and
sword arms. Add a Battle Seer if we've one to spare."

Turion, already showing the effects of the day's
pace, shook his head wearily. "Our top Seers are
engaged in the city already, Highness. The best I could

send would be young Cindana DeFay, but if any of the
Flame Priests get involved, she won't be much good."

"Send her anyway, I want the Lance secured by
morning. If the Flame interferes, have her withdraw
until they can be drawn off to flit about some other
conflict."

"Yes, Highness."

"Also, exchange the Guard at my door. They've
been on duty all day."

"Of course, Highness." The look on Turion's face
suggested he'd like to be exchanged also, but he simply
bowed and hurried off to carry out her orders.

Quindara pulled another missive from the bottom of
the growing pile, and rubbed her eyes. Burn it, but it
was growing gloomy in here. She glanced up and
caught the attention of a young page hovering before
the door.

"Bring more candles." Squinting toward the jug at
her elbow, she frowned. "And more cider."

The boy darted off and the Royal Duke leaned back
as she waited.

Alexander, Gwynne, Berius, Sarellynne, so many
factions, and so many loyalties. It seemed every time
she tried to simplify matters they just grew more entangled with family interfering with duty and duty
clashing with piety and piety becoming treason. One
thing was certain, though. The murderers must be
caught and those who had conspired with them
rounded up also. Then everything would return to
normal.

A log rolled over in the grate, sending sparks flying
up the chimney. She watched the revitalized flames
greedily devour the wood in a flowing dance of orange,
their heat echoing the heightened fire in her own gaze.
She swallowed painfully. Normal? Nothing would ever
be normal again.

Unshed tears burned behind her eyes and she blinked
them away. Tears were weak. She couldn't afford to be
weak, not now. There was far too much at stake. What

had her mother said? Tears were the refuge of a
coward.

One by one each drop of grief fought its way past her
self-control. Memories followed each one. Her mother
seated tall and stern in the saddle, silently furious, but
proud, nonetheless, of the eleven-year-old daughter
who'd followed the Hunt in disguise before the winter
storms ended her chance to be blooded that year. Her
mother bestowing on her the Cadet Badge of the
DeMarians, accepting the oaths of the fifteen-year-old
daughter to defend the family's honor at all costs. Her
mother laying her sword across the shoulders of the
sixteen-year-old daughter who'd surprised a Gallian
assassin behind the Aristok's tent before the Battle of
Wessleuvre. Her mother sprawled on a vomit-stained
coverlet, her eyes as empty as the place in her twenty-
year-old daughter's heart.

With a jerk of her head, the Duke of Yorbourne banished the last memory. She would not remember. Her
mother was strong, as strong as the Gwynethian Mountains and as strong as the wind off the sea. She could be
that strong. And she would be.

As the page returned with a large candelabrum, the
Duke of Yorbourne picked up the discarded letter and
cracked the red seal of the Order of the Flame.

A moment later she slapped it down on the desk hard
enough to make the boy start, dropping the candle in
his hand.

"Get the Captain to me immediately!"

When Turion caught up with her, Quindara was
already halfway to the stables.

"Muster as many as you can find, Captain. We're
going to war."

Skidding to a halt, he stared at her, openmouthed.
"War? Highness, what is it? What's happened?"

"The Archpriest of the Flame has taken my sister
Kassandra."

12. The *Marmoset*

Tottenham Castle. Arren Elliot Armistone sat in the late Warden's chambers staring into the fire. For the hundredth time since David Elliot Greyam had led his tiny force staggering into the safety of their newly established stronghold, the Heathland leader mulled over the Braxborough fiasco.

The attack had progressed as planned. The enemy was surprised, and the day was theirs. Then the tide had turned against them. The demon Prince had conjured up an army despite all of Sister Marie-Claire's efforts. Hilary had fallen, and Stephan had fallen, Captain Ramsen and Jock Lindie, Margaret Croser and David's own brother Peter.

Realizing they were overcome, and that word must reach her Monarch, Sister Marie-Claire had pulled David and his small force from the fray and fled. The shame of it lay on the Greyam Battle Captain still.

Arren ground his teeth. The man who'd killed Hilary still lived free, but not for long. He swore by the sword of Saint Uriel he would personally hack the De-Marian's head from his body.

When David had told Arren of his sister's death, hours after Tottenham had been secured, the larger man had backed off, his expression alarmed as his Monarch's face had gone deathly white. Choking out an order to wait for him there, Arren had left the room.

There was no Essusiate chapel at Tottenham, so alone and unobserved in the castle's tiny west garden, the cold wind cutting through his clothing, the Monarch of Heathland had fallen to his knees, tears pouring unbidden down his face, and asked his God why; why Hilary?

Hilary was lucky. Everyone knew that. She'd survived raids and battles, ambushes, retreats, and defeats. She'd been his best and most loyal Lieutenant, his most trusted Councillor, and his ablest Minister. How was he to carry on without her? There was no one to take her place.

A flash of lightning illuminated the sky as Arren wrapped his hands around his medallion, his head bowed. Why Hilary? Turning toward the rumbling clouds, he allowed the rain to beat down on his face and run in rivulets through his beard and into his clothes. Hadn't he done enough? And what could he have done to keep Essus' shining sword pointed at the enemy and not at them? Orphans by the time Hilary was eight, he'd raised her alone as best he could. Always irreverent, worshiping only her brother, she'd scorned religion, following the path only for Arren's sake. Was that it, then? In his pride had he stolen some of Essus' glory?

Squeezing his eyes shut, he'd prayed for his God's forgiveness and for his people's success. He could not win without Essus' light guiding his way, and suddenly his way seemed dark and fraught with unseen danger.

Sister Marie-Claire had found him there an hour later, soaked through and shivering with cold. She'd made him return to the warmth of the keep and remained with him until well past nightfall. She'd left him at midnight, his grief cleansed of guilt, to minister to the others mourning in the castle.

The next day he was able to meet with his councillors to discuss the change in their plans. With Braxborough still in the hands of the enemy, a new route to Branion must be found. Tantaven, securing the east was a strong possibility, as was Bothsyde on the west. Southern Threkirk had held out but would be harassed throughout the winter by the border families based in

Castle Caerockeith. The Branions there could expect no quarter and no rescue.

Despite their setbacks, they had every reason for confidence, Arren reminded them. Branion was in chaos, locked in civil war more tightly than even he had hoped for. The Essusiates of the Capital had risen against the ruling Triarchy and the city was in flames. And now, too, their empire in Gallia was toppling. Word had just come that Commlemont and Auvernais had rebelled and King Henri-Jean was sending troops against Aquilliard.

Come spring, their joint troops would hurl the invaders back to their own land, then move south to meet this new Demnor the Fifth and dispatch him as quickly and bloodily as they had the first of his name. T.en Heathland would be the conqueror and Branion, the conquered.

Arren's Council, still reeling from the loss of Hilary and Stephan were, nonetheless, staunchly behind him. Eilene, brought to Tottenham after her successful assault on Tantaven, could be counted on for the solid, traditional battle tactics and David for the brash. Now, too, Gordon was here.

Gordon. He and his lady, the Branion Companion had arrived with tales of pursuit and a country shocked and outraged, but impotent from so many years of servitude under the DeMarian yoke. Gordon had given Arren a detailed report on their new leader and after Alynne had renounced the demon ways and been taken into the arms of the Church, she, too, had joined them in Council.

Arren had listened to her impartially. Alynne had given them invaluable information on the workings of the Branion government, their battle tactics, the personalities of their leaders and what their responses were likely to be. She'd answered all their questions frankly, only reserving knowledge of her Guild.

Later, Arren had met with his four Senior Councillors to discuss this latest recruit.

"She loves Gordon, that's obvious," Colleen observed.

"But can she be trusted?"

Eilene drained her goblet. "Can you truly trust anyone who's betrayed her Monarch?"

David frowned. "She's honest enough now, but with Gordon present, she would be. I think it's too early to tell. Watch her. Her mask may slip with time."

"And her words?"

"Gordon's confirmed what he could. For now, I'd treat them like a basket of eggs, likely good, but be careful, there may be a rotten one among them."

"Eilene?"

The Duglas Head paused in the act of carving her initials into the great hall table. "They're a queer bunch, these Companions, no kin, no home. Alynne wouldn't speak of her Guild, you notice. I think they're her family, and that's where you'll find her loyalty.

"And what is this Guild?"

"Courtesans. Bedmates for hire. Branions hate to sleep alone, or are afraid to, so this keeps their decadent nobility from sowing bastards across the land." Sister Marie-Claire spat toward the fire.

"Doesn't seemed to have slowed them down much," Eilene observed dryly. The Essusiate Cleric ignored her.

Tossing a bent horseshoe nail from one hand to the other, David grunted. "She knows a fair bit for a tumble-for-hire."

With a laugh, Eilene punched him in the arm. "And don't you ever talk in bed, man?"

He grinned back at her. "No, I think it's rude not to pay attention to what you're doing."

"Still," Colleen mused. "If all the secrets spoken between the sheets were collected by one Guild . . ."

"That would be a powerful lot of secrets."

"And a right powerful Guild."

"Watch her."

"Yes, Sire."

Gordon and Alynne were to be married in the morning. The Cleric had examined them both and reported that Gordon was under no enchantment. The woman had taken the sacraments and entered the Church, so at least she was no witch or demon. Whether she was a spy remained to be seen, and love or no love, she would not be trusted so easily.

As for the other Companions captured in the fighting, they'd already been ransomed and gone and good riddance. They reminded Arren of overpampered lap dogs. Their Guild had been swift in answering his demands and hadn't quibbled over the sums. The families of the Branion nobility captured with them had not been so accommodating.

Arren shrugged. They would pay what he demanded by the date he demanded it, or the captives would die. He had neither the desire nor the stores to feed the enemy over the winter.

Already, the chill winds scythed across the fields, and whistled through Tottenham's drafty halls. The messengers came and went, shivering with frost on their clothes although their messages were warming. The country was ready. They would sit tight on their victories and prepare for spring. Meanwhile they would think and plan and grieve.

Digging his fingers into the wooden arms of his chair, Arren swallowed the heavy lump in his throat and stared at the crackling fire. Time and time again he found himself turning to ask for Hilary's thoughts or comments and pulling up short, realizing she wasn't there. Time and time again he found himself about to send for her or making a note to speak to her when she returned from ... Time and time again he found the lonely ache of grief almost too much to bear. She had been his right arm, and it had been amputated whole and healthy, and her loss left him awkward and uncertain.

A tear made its way down Arren's cheek, and he let it fall. She was with their God now, and Essus was not jealous of mourning. In the spring he would ride to battle and she would watch over him and guard his

troops and be avenged. This new Aristok would pay for
both the old blood spilled and for the new.

Arren Elliot Armistone, Monarch of Heathland
returned his hard gaze to the fire and his thoughts to
battle.

On the east coast of Branion, the frigate *Marmoset*
raced southward before an autumn storm that filled its
sails. In the bow, Demnor the Fifth stared glassy-eyed
into the distance, ignoring the wind and the spray. With
his hair whipping in all directions and his burning gaze
locked on the coast, he looked like one of the demon
titans from legend and the sailors who crept fearfully
past him made the sign of the Triarchy as they passed.
Demnor never noticed. As each rise and fall of the
ship's bow brought them closer to home, one phrase
echoed and reechoed in his mind: He should have
known.

How could he not have known? His mother had been
murdered while he stood on this very deck looking out
at the cliffs of Grimscombe. Guilt sent a corkscrew
stab of nausea through him. He had not known. He
should have known. His own brothers had warned him
and he had ignored them. He'd left the Realm when it
needed him most to walk into unnecessary danger in
Heathland. The Flame had passed and he had not been
there. He was not worthy to rule.

The red haze that had covered his vision at Braxborough came to mind. It might have been a comfort to
him, but what good was a power that only manifested
when he was personally threatened? It hadn't protected
the men and women who'd fallen all around him, the
best of his fighting force now lying dead in a Heathland castle graveyard. If only he had . . .

He pushed the budding accusation away. Doubt para-
lyzed you, made you weak. A ruler had to be strong,
had to forge ahead with all confidence in the absolute
rightness of the decision. His mother would have . . .

The mixture of grief and guilt welled up again,
threatening to overwhelm his self-control. He closed

his eyes, hands gripping the ship's railing. Finally it subsided, and he was able to open his eyes to stare at the distant cliffs once again. He should have known.

The storm drove the ship toward the jagged coast. He could just make out the distinctive rocky beach of Seal's Point at the mouth of the Brasswater River five miles north of the Mist. He gestured the Captain over. She approached him hesitantly, as nervous as her crew, but he simply pointed.

"Put in when we reach Forness Point!"

He had to shout the instructions twice to be heard over the winds, but finally the Captain nodded her understanding. Demnor turned back to the bow and the Captain gratefully withdrew. Forness Point was the final anchorage before Branbridge. The final place to pause and rest and try and pierce the fog of confusion that had surrounded him since Caroline DeLynne had knelt before him three days ago.

The stab of rock jabbing into his flesh as the ancient battlements of Braxborough Castle had cracked under his grip had been barely the shadow of pain as he'd stared down at her while his mind echoed "No," over and over again, but he couldn't deny the expression on her face or the heat of his own vision. The Aristok was dead. All hail the Aristok. For a brief moment he was catapulted back to the memory of a confused and frightened five-year-old boy standing before his murdered great uncle's tomb. Then the memory passed like a cold wind. Melesandra the Third was dead. All hail Demnor the Fifth. Somehow he'd lived through that first moment while the world dashed itself to pieces around him. When the dust cleared, he felt nothing but confusion. Distantly he'd heard himself ask how.

All she could tell him was fragmented theory and unfounded conjecture. His mother poisoned, her Companion racing for Heathland while the DeMarian Cadet and the Hierarchpriest of Cannonshire made ready to tear the Realm apart. Nothing made sense anymore. Nothing except the storm. He turned back to the spray and the wind.

Half an hour later they dropped anchor off the northern point of Forness Island at the mouth of the River Mist. Forty miles upriver Branbridge waited. Forty miles upriver his mother's death awaited. He gestured the Captain over again.

"Can you put a boat down in this?"

She looked doubtful. "It'd be risky, sire. If we were going up the Brasswater, maybe, but we'd be swamped if we tried to navigate the point for the run up the Mist."

"How long will the storm last?"

She squinted into the clouds.

"There's clear sky to the north, Sire. An hour, maybe two."

"Fine. We wait an hour."

"Very well, Sire."

An hour. An hour to try and clear his mind of guilt and grief and plan to do . . . what? He didn't know. He felt empty and hesitant in a way he never had before. He should have known.

When the dark clouds no longer dominated the sky, and the storm's end was just north of them, he went below.

The Earl of Essendale and the others were waiting for him in the Captain's cabin. Gesturing for them to be seated, he took the Captain's chair and turned to Caroline DeLynne.

"Yorbourne and Cannonshire are at odds?"

She nodded. "They were five days ago, Majesty. What's happened since, I don't know. They may have come to some understanding."

"What happened?"

Tapping nervously on the bunk, the Duke of Buckshire tried to put her thoughts in order. His Majesty had asked this of her in Braxborough, but her attempts to pull some clarity from the chaos of that day had not been very successful. If she wanted to save her political career in Branion, she'd better make sense of it now. His Majesty's dark, unfocused gaze boded ill for anyone who faltered.

"It was a confusing time, Sire," she began slowly. "How far the conspiracy extended was unknown. Her Highness . . . that is, uh . . ." She stopped, unwilling to make accusations against a member of the Royal Family. Finally she shrugged. In for a sheep, as her father used to say. "Her Highness arrested a great many people, including Captain Fletcher of the Palace Guard. She also had reason to believe the Essusiate minority was involved. She arrested some of their leadership. When the Essusiates responded by rioting, she hanged the Abbot of Charlsworth."

Demnor's eyes narrowed.

Swallowing, the Duke continued. "The Hierarch-priest challenged her right to do so, and accusations of heresy and treason were exchanged. This led to . . . well . . . when I left, the Hierarchpriest had called the Knights of the Sword to arms."

"An extreme response," Kelahnus noted.

"Hanging a clergyman is an extreme measure," Isolde countered stiffly.

"It was an extreme time for everyone, My Lord, Your Grace," the Duke of Buckshire interjected smoothly. "Nobody knew who was involved, or how many. I don't wish to cast doubts upon anyone's character. The Royal Cadet and the Hierarchpriest did have different ideas of how to handle the problem and could not reach an understanding."

"So he accuses her of heresy, and she accuses him of treason. Very helpful." The rough sarcasm in Demnor's voice made everyone stir nervously.

Unobserved by the Aristok, Kelahnus made a conciliatory gesture toward Isolde, who smiled. She then tipped her head in Demnor's direction. The Companion nodded. "What are we going to do now?" he asked.

"We wait."

"The Hierarchpriest has promised that if you put in at the Tower of the Sword, he'll escort you safely into the city, Sire," the Duke of Buckshire ventured.

"Until I know what's happening, I don't intend to be safely escorted anywhere, by anyone."

Isolde started. "You don't believe the Lord of Cannonshire to be guilty of treason, do you, Majesty?"

"No. Neither do I believe *my sister* to be guilty of heresy. What I believe is that far too many people have acted far too stupidly." The anger helped push the emptiness away and he let it build. If Quindara and Alexander were locked in a power struggle over control of the Realm, every noble in Branbridge would have lined up on one side or the other. Everyone would have a vested interest in either Yorbourne or Cannonshire. Every noble, every Order, save one.

"I'm sending Dimitrius in a skiff to Bran's Palace to bring Captain Fletcher."

Isolde and Caroline exchanged puzzled looks, although Kelahnus nodded in understanding.

"What if the Captain's still imprisoned?" he asked.

"Dimitrius will know what to do."

If Captain Fletcher was still imprisoned, then Dimitrius would go to Corporal Connie Fielding. If he couldn't reach her, any of those who wore the red badge of Gwyneth would do. All his life the only people he knew he could trust without question were the Palace Guard, the men and women who'd faced death and imprisonment by following him to Briery. If he called, they would come; with them at his back he would know what to do.

Memories of that other war so many years ago were suddenly too oppressive in the tight confines of the Captain's cabin. He rose. The others, caught off guard, quickly came to their feet.

"After I get Captain Fletcher's report, we'll continue on to Branbridge."

They bowed without comment.

Demnor nodded, turned, and left the cabin.

Isolde gave Kelahnus a questioning look. He simply shook his head. "All we can do is wait," he said in answer.

After sending Dimitrius off in the care of two veteran sailors with orders to bring Captain Fletcher as

quickly as possible, Demnor returned to his place in
the bow. Leaning against the ship's railing, he stared
into the clouds, his eyes half closed against the wind,
his mind replaying that moment on the battlements of
Braxborough Castle over and over.

Forcibly he turned his attention to the looming
problem forty miles upriver. Yorbourne and Cannonshire. If they were still at each other's throats, he
would return to a Capital torn apart by infighting,
maybe even civil war. His first priority then would
have to be the mending of Branion so it could safely
deal with Heathland. The reports he'd received before
reboarding the *Marmoset* confirmed his worst fears,
that the attack on Braxborough was not just an isolated incident bred out of his presence there, but the
beginning of yet another Heathland rebellion. At least
two of the southern garrisons had fallen. Had he
returned to Branbridge overland, he might not have
made it.

He rubbed at the stubble on his cheeks. How, in less
than a week, had everything he'd ever thought secure
been scattered like a house of cards?

A seagull fought to gain altitude over the wind, and
he watched it, sympathetic with its struggle. Heathland
had risen, the Aristok had been murdered, and the Heir
attacked. Branion, thrown into confusion and violence,
could not adequately respond. It stank of conspiracy.
Trying to make some sense of events, Demnor was
unsurprised at his sister's reaction. He, too, would have
lashed out at anyone who might have been responsible.
Better a few feathers were ruffled by a night's imprisonment than the murderers escaped. Her attack on the
Branbridge Essusiates was stupid, but again, not surprising. She was a DeMarian.

It was Alexander's response that puzzled him. The
Hierarchpriest of Cannonshire was a man loyal to the
Throne and dedicated to the peaceful preservation of
the Realm. Even his presence in Briery in 886 had been
dictated by the demands of the Crown and his own
unshakable sense of duty.

Now, however, it seemed, he was on the side of rebellion and insurrection. It didn't make sense. Demnor shook his head. He needed more information.

Unable to concentrate on the problems in the Capital, and unwilling to beat himself with his mother's death any longer, Demnor closed his eyes and sent his mind wandering elsewhere. As the sun slowly set, casting a pinkly orange glow across the clouds, the swaying of the deck became the pounding of a horse's hooves on another journey home seven years before.

As night fell on that summer day in 886 three men raced toward the Capital. They rode hard, cloaks muffling their features, trying to out-gallop rumor. Alexander DeKathrine wanted his Royal prisoner safe at home before news of the battle spread too far. The Prince was beyond caring.

Half blind from the pain in his skull, right arm strapped tightly to his chest, each movement threatened to send him tumbling from the saddle. The effort to remain astride cost him all his failing concentration. He welcomed the distraction. All too soon there would be none.

Riding between Alexander and the Earl of Snowshead, his thoughts were as unfocused as his gaze. His head was curiously light and at times he almost felt himself to be floating. Having heard of the mystic visions of the Essusiate martyrs, he wondered blearily if he hadn't already passed the veil between this world and the next. He was so cold. Ariston had said the Shadow Realm was cold, as cold as a body in death. Only the Aristok journeyed in the warmth of the Living Flame. But he was not the Aristok.

Warriors traveled to the Earth's Realm in the company of the slain, both friend and foe, and as the miles brought them closer to Branbridge, the beating of his horse's hooves became the beating of the drums before a battle. A chill breeze wove its fingers through his clothes, making the hair on the back of his neck rise. Around him the dead appeared. Devices leached of

color, ragged pennants limp in the still air, knights of
both sides gathered. A ghostly escort for a Warrior
Prince.

Marjory and Thomas DeKathrine, dead faces calm
and peaceful, rode beside their older brother Julian
who raised his arms in benediction to his Lord. Darion
DeSharon, nodding as befitted an enemy, rode within a
company of his kindred, while Rhewella DeLlewellynne
cantered in line with the two sons she'd brought to
battle.

DePaulas, DeKathrines, DeFays. All the noble families of the realm were represented, riding proudly
beside squires, archers, and foot soldiers, equal now in
honorable death. Before them all, the Palace Guards
who'd died in Demnor's service carried his banner
high above the others, heralding in whose escort they
now rode. Slowly, his company of shades grew more
substantial and his living escort faded.

Beside him, helmless and shieldless, Collin DePaula
rode as easily as he'd done the day before. Demnor felt
the bitter taste of guilt rise to his throat as he stared
into his tactician's eyes, but there was no reproach in
his friend's misty face. Collin smiled, and stretching
one hand to his Prince, he beckoned with the other. A
blanket of comfort settled over Demnor's shoulders
and he reached out, straining against some unseen barrier to take the spirit's hand. It was just beyond his
grasp. Faintly he heard Alexander's cry of alarm and
felt hands upon him. Face shadowed in grief, Collin
moved past and the ghostly company continued on
their way without him.

They entered Branbridge's northernmost gate at
dusk, the palace soon afterward. All was silent, as if
the stone walls themselves awaited word of their
Prince's fate. The stables were hushed, hands coming
forward hesitantly to take their reins, faces tight with
fear. Even used to the Hunt and its aftermath, the
whole building reverberated with the shock of the
Prince's appearance.

He was a terrible sight, he knew; helmless, hair wild

and eyes unfocused, face encrusted with blood and his clothes bloodied and torn. His escort was little better. The Earl of Snowshead's surcoat was dark with dried gore and Alexander DeKathrine's face was pale and grim.

Strangely enough, Demnor felt no resentment toward the Archpriest. He'd done his duty, fulfilled his commission, and been as polite and attentive as he was able. He'd let the Crown Prince keep his sword and had a physician see to his wounds. Had he lost, he could have expected similar treatment. The Heir and the Archpriest respected one another, it was only fate that had placed them on opposite sides of the battlefield.

With Alexander's aid, he dismounted and, supported by the two nobles, left the stables and entered the palace proper. But rather than turn right toward the Octavian Tower, the traditional hold for Royal prisoners, they went left, toward the throne room. The audience would happen immediately, then. Head still spinning from his wounds, heart still sick from his parting with his ghostly retinue, he felt no apprehension, only a resigned fatigue. A fearful-eyed page was sent ahead and soon they were moving slowly up the tiled hallway. They passed the oaken doors and entered the still and empty anteroom. Alexander knocked on the audience chamber door, then stepped inside. A moment later, he returned and held the door open. Denmor entered on his own power, the others two steps behind.

As still as the carved throne she sat upon, the Aristok awaited them, face expressionless. Dressed formally, though simply, in a black tunic and hose, she wore the Crown of Justice and held the royal scepter of the same name loosely in the crook of her arm, the fire-wolf and oak leaf clusters on her breast glinting in the torchlight. She was alone in the room.

Eyes narrowed, she watched as her son advanced, his steps the deliberate pace of one fighting to keep himself from falling. When he and his escort came to within nine paces, they knelt. The Aristok inclined her head.

"We thank you, My Lord Earl of Cambury," she began, her husky voice even. "And you also, My Lord Earl of Snowshead. You have fulfilled our hope that this matter should be resolved quickly and with little tearing to the tranquillity of our Realm. Please leave us now, for we would have words with our son, but return to our presence ere long that we might speak further of our most grateful thanks."

The two Earls rose, and bowing deeply, left them.

The world seemed very distant to Demnor as he knelt, waiting for her to speak. Head cradled on his knee, he might have fallen asleep but for the tension in the room. The silence lengthened, and he realized fuzzily that she was waiting for him to look up. Slowly, feeling as if some great weight were fighting him, he raised his head. Her face swam before his eyes. Finally she spoke.

"My Lord of Briery."

He blinked and her image grew still. "Majesty."

"Your enterprise has failed."

"Yes, Majesty."

"Do you know why it failed?"

The question was spoken in the dangerously soft tone she sometimes assumed. Ordinarily he would have hesitated, afraid of voicing the wrong answer. Today the danger was remote. His mind cast sluggishly back to the battle.

He had lost because Alexander DeKathrine had proved the better swordsman and once Demnor was down, his people had, leaderless, been swept over by the Archpriest's forces. Was that why he'd failed? And how could he have prevented it? He wasn't sure, his head ached too hard for him to concentrate. Not fallen, obviously, but how? A leader fought amongst his people. That was the way of pitched battles. Strategy and tactics only went so far. Sword and mace eventually carved the win or the loss. So what did she want to hear?

"Because I fell, Majesty."

"And why did you fall?"

The question, asked in a tone of mere curiosity, managed to clear his head somewhat and prick him into anger. Why was she playing this game with him? Surely he deserved some dignity in failure, at least.

"Because Alexander DeKathrine is the better swordsman, Majesty," he answered bitterly, clipping each word as she so often did. A raising of one copper eyebrow was her only response.

"So," she said after a time. "There is one who excels you? Are you satisfied to remain second at something?"

He snorted, reckless and uncaring what happened now. "I should be stupid to expect that at sixteen I would be better than a man almost twice my age, with twice my experience."

"And yet you felt you could battle me. Felt you could raise sword against my will and come out victorious? Is that not so?"

A neat trap, and one which would have had his heart pounding in his chest in the past. This time he merely shrugged it off. "It was on a matter of honor that I fought, Majesty. To emerge victorious was not the assumption but the necessity. In truth, I did not believe I could win."

She inclined her head, flame-filled eyes glittering. "And that, my knight, is why you failed. A stupid mistake. One I had thought you might have been intelligent enough to prevent."

He flushed as she continued, her tone businesslike.

"Of those taken with you of rank, I shall expect their families to ransom their safe return. Of the commoners taken, each Lord shall be responsible for their own. *But of my Guard,*" her voice grew dangerously low and she leaned forward slightly. "You were responsible for their defection. You shall be responsible for their return. My Herald will visit you with my monetary terms, but this I will tell you now; on your behavior rests their fate."

A worm of unease climbed his spine, but inside he felt the stirring of a faint hope that his Guard might be spared. And with them, his shattered honor. Melesandra did not realize their rescue tied so strongly to his own inner redemption, or she would never have offered him this boon. He met her eyes, struggling to mask his expression. She continued.

"You have thrown title and honors at my feet and treated your inheritance and your responsibilities like so much dross. You will not lightly retrieve them. You have broken your oaths of fealty, brought bloodshed and civil unrest to my Realm and you have proved yourself a juvenile and unready General. Many crimes, My Lord of Briery, many crimes."

His stomach churning with returning cramps, Demnor clamped his teeth on the nausea that threatened to overcome him.

"You shall go to Cannonshire to purge yourself," the Aristok continued. "From there you shall travel to Poitienne and retake the city of Poindiers so recently returned to the bosom of the Gallians. By this victory shall I know of your contrition. But for now, you shall reswear such oaths as you have broken, and return for a time to such titles as were given you. It shall be decided later if, by your actions, you have deserved their permanent reinstatement. As for the boy, the cause of all this havoc . . ."

She paused and Demnor felt the bleak despair that he'd somehow managed to keep at bay until now. it would begin again as if the battle had never occurred. She would demand Kelahnus' name. He would refuse, and the Earth alone knew what would happen then.

"Our Archpriest of the Sword has begged of us the boon that the boy be spared our wrath. It is to him you owe such thanks as are due."

Alexander?

"Our Councillor has begged that when the boy is eighteen and graduated from his Guild, and if your behavior up until that time merits such reward, your petition for his services may be brought before us once again, for the Companion's Guild has ever been a valued asset to our Realm.

"In consideration for his many years of service to the Crown, we have granted him this request."

Demnor's shock was apparent on his face. She had never given him anything he desired before in his life, and her expression said she did not do so this day. She leaned forward again, her face so twisted he almost flinched away.

"Don't think this is a victory," she hissed. "For I'll make your life so miserable that in the end, you'll not consider it worth the pain. And think on this, that even then, I can deny you. Only I rule here. Never forget that."

His eyes met hers, seeing the trap she waited to spring on him. She would dangle Kelahnus before him to make him jump, and in the meantime, poison his love with bitterness and pain. But he wasn't as stupid as his mother believed. He would humble himself before her, reswear his love and loyalty, plead for his people, and suffer any and all indignities, but he had won. He would hide his love for Kelahnus in a place she couldn't touch, and in three years time they would be together. Despite the pain in his head, he felt better than he had since their fight had driven him to armed rebellion. He would go to Cannonshire and there soothe his bleeding conscience, then wipe the last of his shame away in battle. Lowering his head in obedience to her pronouncement until his forehead touched his knee once more, he closed his eyes.

"Yes, Your Majesty."

On the deck of the frigate *Marmoset,* the Aristok Demnor the Fifth bowed his head, the ache of the past echoing the grief of the present. He'd gambled everything and almost lost, the Realm, Kelahnus, his life, but even in the midst of those terrible days, he'd been sure of his path. Honor and sacrifice had been answer enough to silence doubt and uncertainty. Now, with rebellion behind him and civil unrest before, those answers weren't good enough. Or were they? Surely he'd gained something from that time, something that had survived death and dishonor and tragedy. Something he could draw strength from today?

A noise behind him pulled him from the past, and he turned to see Kelahnus standing a few paces away, a plate of food in his hands. The Companion came forward hesitantly.

"I thought you might be hungry." He held the plate out.

The memory of the beautiful young man the Companion had been cast a hazy mantle over the beauty of the man he'd become, and suddenly Demnor wondered why he hadn't remembered. In the midst of insurrection and anarchy, of dishonor and death, the Companion had always been there, waiting, watching, comforting when the Heir allowed it, asking so little in return for so much devotion. The emptiness melted away as Demnor held out his arms, and Kelahnus folded himself into them with a sigh.

Beyond the ship's prow, the lights of the few shepherds' cottages on Forness Island shone through the darkness as the two lovers stood, waiting for Captain Fletcher with word of the future.

Just past midnight Lord Julia Fletcher, Earl of Norbrook, Captain of the Aristok's Palace Guard, knelt before her new Sovereign. In the clear moonlight her face was gaunt, and new lines had been added to the old around her eyes and mouth. She kissed his hand, lingered a moment with her head bowed, then rose.

Feeling calmer than he had for some time, Demnor smiled grimly.

"You made it."

"Yes, my P . . . My Liege." Her expression showed annoyance with her mistake, then returned to the firm confidence he knew so well.

"Things are not well in the Capital, Majesty."

"I gathered. Buckshire gave her report in Braxborough, but that was . . ." his mind cast back. "Three days ago."

The Captain nodded. "Her Highness took charge of the investigation of your mother's murder." She paused, shame darkening her features. "I have to report, Sire, that it's fairly certain one of mine, Sergeant Grant Cross, is involved."

"Grant?" The image of the tall, sandy-haired guardsman came to mind. A solid, quiet man, not one who'd followed him to Briery, but a loyal, steadfast member of the Guard nonetheless. It didn't make sense. "How do you know this?"

"He'd requested a night's leave, Majesty," she answered thickly. "The Watch on the North Gate reported him leaving with Third Royal Companion Alynne and an unknown man in Essusiate garb early that morning. The Flame Priests have sought him in vision and seen them on the road to Heathland."

Demnor shook his head. It wasn't possible.

The Captain turned back. "The Duke of Yorbourne has questioned many of the Guard, and I have also. No one else has been found guilty of conspiracy, but   " She paused. "The honor of the Guard is in doubt. You'll want to question them yourself, Majesty, before returning any of us to permanent duty. We await your orders."

Demnor studied the stiff set of the Captain's shoulders while he formulated his answer. The Palace Guard had been his protectors since he was too young to walk. This woman before him had taught him, trained him, fought beside him, and nearly died for him. She had listened when there had been no one else to hear and had sent her own into danger to take up his call to arms. What honor he knew was the honor of the Guard.

"That won't be necessary, Captain. *I trust my people.*"

The Captain's stiff stance relaxed. "I'm getting too old for this," she murmured. "Ten years ago he never would have fooled me. I should retire."

"You can't," Demnor answered bluntly. "I need you."

Squaring her shoulders, she smiled sourly. "The willing horse."

He nodded.

"The Guard have taken Grant's betrayal hard," she continued. "They want to follow him and bring him to justice. They believe his treason has stained them all."

The look on her face confirmed that their Captain believed that also. Demnor shook his head.

"The Guard is not stained. Whatever Grant's reasoning, we'll discover it soon enough. In the meantime, I need all of you here."

The Captain looked relieved. "Yes, My Liege."

"Tell me about Branbridge. What of Yorbourne and Cannonshire?"

"Her Highness commands the Shield Knights and controls the west of the city, the Hierarchpriest and the Knights of the Sword are holding the east. The night of the murder, the Royal Cadet attacked the Flame Temple."

"What!"

Stilling her first instinct to pull her sword in defense, the Captain met her Sovereign's burning gaze. "The Archpriest of the Flame sent a message to Prince Quindara in which she stated that the Duke of Clarfield was staying in the Temple under the protection of the Champions of the Flame."

"Is Kass all right?"

"Yes, Majesty. She's fine. I spoke with her this morning."

"Go on."

"Believing that the Champions were in league with the Hierarchpriest and that they had taken her by force, Prince Quindara massed her troops on the temple and demanded her sister's return. When the Archpriest refused, she attacked."

Demnor shook his head in exasperation. "And just why did the Archpriest refuse?"

"I believe she felt the grief at the Aristok's death had

made the Duke irrational and that Prince Kassandra
was in danger."

Demnor turned away for a minute. "Is there nobody sane left in Branbridge?" When the Captain said
nothing, he turned back. "What did Kass say to you?"

"Only that she was fine and would handle things herself. After the battle between the Champions and the
Shield Knights, the Prince Kassandra asked for a complement of Palace Guard to escort her and her nurse,
Auxiliary Companion Delia, back to her suite. Prince
Quindara agreed. She's there now, under the protection
of the Palace Guard."

"Were there any casualties?"

She nodded. "Two or three on either side from that
battle. There've been more between the Sword and the
Shield. The other Orders are in chaos. None have pub-
licly chosen sides because they can't agree on one."

"And the Navy?"

She shrugged. "Some have sided with the Prince,
some with the Hierarchpriest, most have remained
neutral.

"What of the Town Watch?"

"They try and keep order as best they can, but with
the nobility battling in the streets they have little
chance. Their oaths are to Branbridge, but they can't
fight the Militant Orders. Mostly they just try to protect
the citizens."

"And the Guard?"

"The Guard protects the palace, Majesty, and their
first loyalty is to yourself."

"Then summon them here."

"Sire?"

Confident now, Demnor turned toward shore. "I
want a complement of Palace Guard to escort me into
my city. Bring as many as can be gathered without
drawing too much attention. Tell the Captain of the
Town Watch to grant them passage without reporting
it, and to be ready to receive me. I shall enter Branbridge at daybreak."

"Yes, My Liege, at once." Seizing his hand, Captain Fletcher kissed it, then hurried off.

Demnor turned back to the rails, his thoughts returning to that terrible interview so many years before, a plan forming in his mind.

13. Quindara

A week after the death of the Aristok the day dawned overcast and foggy. Throughout the city, only the bold or the desperate opened their shops to the sparse morning trade. At the Tower of the Sword, one shift of guards exchanged their duty with another, while a third went armed into the market to gather provisions and make their presence known to the enemy. They were met by a company of Shield Knights and the morning's skirmishes began.

At Bran's Palace, the Aristok's office was a hub of activity even at this early hour with Guards and pages hurrying in to report and hurrying out just as quickly. A jumbled pile of blankets lay across the blue brocade couch, and a tray of untouched food sat by the growing pile of dispatches on the desk.

Squinting over a map of the city, the Duke of Yorbourne laid her finger on the outline of a warehouse to the east of the Sword Tower.

"There," she whispered. "That's where we'll make the next assault. Page!"

A girl appeared in the doorway.

"Fetch Captain Turion."

"At once, Highness, but he's gone into the city to collect the reports from the Gate Watch."

Quindara frowned. "He went himself?" Her voice, strained from the week's frenzied pace, was jagged and hoarse and the girl inched nervously toward the door.

"There, uh, there were reports of strange movements in the city last night, Highness."

The Royal Duke frowned. "Why wasn't I informed?"

The girl backed up a step. "It was near three in the morning, I believe, Highness. There were reports made."

Quindara's eyes tracked to the jumbled pile of missives the pages had brought when she'd unbolted the office door an hour ago. She shouldn't have slept, but as the bells of Bran's Tower had tolled two, she'd found herself unable to make out the words she'd been reading. A dull headache had begun to pound at her temples that no amount of rubbing had eased. She'd staggered up, determined to get some air and alarmed at how unsteady her limbs felt. Instead she'd just bolted the two office doors and collapsed onto the couch. Pulling a blanket over her, she'd dismissed the parade of ghostly writing in front of her eyes, concentrating instead on the image of a clean, wide open field with no distractions and no dangers. The next moment the bells were ringing five and there was work to be done. Now as the headache began to make itself known again, she waved the girl away.

"Send someone to find Turion and tell him we make our next assault on the Tower at eight."

"Yes, Highness."

The page withdrew.

Shuffling through the pile until she found a dispatch with Turion's seal, she rubbed at her temples as she read.

"Unknown movements away from the city . . . Skiffs taken . . . Town Watch reporting no unusual traffic." She stared into space, the red flames washing over the green of her eyes like a spray of crimson mist. "What are you up to now, Alexander? Hiding troops in the city? Stealing downriver to set up some line of defense? It won't succeed. I'll run you down and dig you out no matter where you hide. Page!"

Another youngster appeared, a boy this time, in the

green and black of the DeKathrines. The Royal Duke's
eyes narrowed, although she motioned him forward.

"Send for Captain Saralynne, I've orders for the
Shield Knights."

"Highness?"

The flames rose in her vision as the boy hesitated
uncertainly by the door.

"Well?"

The boy ran.

Minutes later there was a knock on the door.

"What?"

A DeKathrine man, his ash-blond hair tied back from
his face, stepped quietly into the room. Quindara
squinted blearily at him a moment, the throbbing in her
head sending ripples of red mist across her vision to
obscure his features. Finally, she frowned.

"Troy."

"I've been trying to see you."

"I've been busy."

He came forward. "I know. You've been working
day and night. If you don't slow down, you'll make
yourself sick."

Her frown deepened.

"What do you want?"

"To help."

She snorted. "You have no idea what's going on."

With a shrug, he seated himself in a chair. "I think I
do. You've sent people into Heathland to capture the
conspirators; you're investigating the possibility of a
widespread plot; and you plan an attack on the Sword
Tower this morning."

Her eyes narrowed. "How do you know all this?"

He gestured toward the door. "It's been open the
whole time."

"And you've been where?"

"In your outer office."

"Why?"

He spread his hands. "I wanted to help. You wouldn't
see me. So I made myself as useful as I could."

"Doing what?"

Her voice had dropped to a dangerous whisper, sending a cold chill down Troy's spine. He shrugged with careful nonchalance. "I send for food, I make people sleep. Things I would have done for you, if you'd have let me."

The slight reproach in his voice made her teeth snap together.

"I have slept, I have servants who bring me food, I'm very busy, so if there's nothing else. . . ." She glanced pointedly at the door, and he rose.

"Well, there was, actually."

"What?"

"Captain Saralynne. You sent for her?"

"What of it?"

He paused, pale brows drawn down. "She's dead, Quindara. She was killed two days ago in the first assault on the Sword Tower. You fired their outbuildings in retaliation. You remember?"

She stared at him for a long moment, then the mist over her vision cleared a little. "Oh, yes."

He came forward. Kneeling before her, he took her hand.

"You're tired. Won't you let me help?"

"I'm fine," she grated, pulling her hand free. "Why? Do you think I'm going mad?"

He dropped his eyes. "No, of course not. I think you're grieving, and I just want to help."

"Why?"

Her hard gaze tracked across his face, but he kept his expression casual. "You're good in bed."

Her eyes cleared of their glassy expression for just a moment. "What?"

He allowed himself a tiny smile. "You're good in bed, Your Most Royal Highness. I miss the sex."

Her face twisted in a grimace, then she laughed bitterly.

"You may have to continue to miss it for a good long time."

"I can wait."

"There may be nothing to wait for when this is all over."

"I'll risk it."

Her eyes narrowed again. "You'll risk it. You don't even known what *it* is. Do you think everything will be the same when this is all over? That anything could ever possibly be the same as it was ever again?"

Her voice had grown savage and she stood, upsetting her chair.

"You think you know my plans? Do you really Troyanon *DeKathrine?* Do you know that I plan to capture, try, and execute a high-ranking member of your own family? That I plan to wipe this Realm free of all the traitors and murderers who've torn it apart? Are you prepared for that much bloodshed?"

Her eyes burned into his, and he felt scared by the heat of her anger. He hadn't moved from where he knelt, but as they locked eyes, he was suddenly reminded of a time when, as a child, he'd been knocked down by one of his father's mastiffs. The dog had landed on him, and as the boy had stared into the great growling visage, he'd felt a moment's terror and then a sudden serenity. The dog had withdrawn. Now, with his heart thumping in his chest, he knew an instant's panic and then the familiar composure. The Duke of Yorbourne broke eye contact.

Sweating, he stood, trying to keep his knees from trembling. Quindara was staring past him, her wild, flame-covered eyes showing confusion, though whether it was from his response or hers, he couldn't tell.

"No," he said in answer to her last question. "I'm not prepared for that much bloodshed, but I'll risk that, too."

The fire in her eyes dimmed. "You're a fool."

"Maybe. Every ruler needs one around."

"I don't rule yet."

"How can I help in the meantime?"

Staring into his steady gaze, Quindara finally shrugged. "Send for food. Make me sleep. Try to keep out of the way. And if you like going blind, you can help me with this scorching mess."

Half an hour later, after handing two empty plates to a relieved-looking page, Troy fished a dispatch off the top of the dwindling pile. "Two more deaths in the Lance. If this keeps up, there'll be no one left to take sides."

"Anyone of consequence?"

He scanned the words. "A minor DeFay and a DeLynne Earl. It hasn't swayed the balance."

"Ignore it."

He snagged another, while Quindara sent a page out with orders to send another ten troops to Berius' aid.

"Two ships, the *Sandorion* and the *Kalandra* exchanged shots in the night, no damage. They broke off when the *Bricklin* challenged them both."

"Burn Captain Georgina, she's always interfering. Anything else?"

"Runner misses you."

"What?"

"Runner, my dog? He misses you."

Quindara sighed and rubbed at her eyes. "Troy, if you're going to be here, you have to stay on topic."

"Sorry."

When Captain Turion, his face lined with fatigue and two days' worth of stubble, entered a moment later, Troy was dutifully going over a list of projected weapons stored in the Sword Tower. The Captain glanced curiously at his younger kinsman, then saluted his Lord.

"What news, Captain?"

"It seems a large contingent of off-duty Palace Guard left the city early this morning, Highness. Their destination is unknown at this time."

Quindara's face hardened.

"And Captain Fletcher?"

"Is gone, My Prince."

"I see." Tapping her knuckles against the table for a moment, Quindara mulled over the possible consequences. When her eyes dropped to the map in front of her, she made a dismissive gesture. "One treason at a time. Pull in a few for questioning, but don't give it too much attention. It's a low priority. What's more important right now is that I've found a weakness in the Sword's defense, and I want to hit Alexander with everything we've got. I want him finished by noon today." Her fist slammed against the desk and Troy jumped and looked up. Captain Turion stilled the urge to glance at him and simply nodded wearily.

Across the city, while the Duke of Yorbourne prepared to move on the Tower of the Sword and the Duke of Cambury prepared to repel her, two muffled figures met in the ruins deep beneath the Branbridge School of Companions.

The taller of the two made a swift gesture with his right hand across his side. The feminine hand which responded had fine, long-boned fingers and curiously thickened wrists. When he returned the countersign, she bowed.

"Greetings in prosperity, Cousin."

Her voice was quiet with a faint harsh overlay that spoke of prolonged fenweed smoking. Almost on cue, she pulled a blackened pipe and pouch from the folds of her cloak. Tapping the pale-colored weed into the bowl, she waited for the other to speak.

Pushing the hood of his own cloak back to reveal black hair peppered with gray, the man indicated the stone bench beside them. His dark eyes glittered in the feeble light, and as they seated themselves, the swaying lantern cast shadows across the high arch of his cheekbones and the graceful line of his jaw.

Master Elias, Auxiliary Companion and Head of the Companion's Guild Security Force began to speak without preamble, his deep voice carefully modulated in the enclosed room.

"It's been a week since the DeMarian's death. The violence has escalated."

The woman indicated her agreement with a slight nod while she took a taper light from the lantern and laid the glowing end to the bowl of her pipe. Sucking at it a few times, she glanced over at him as the sweet odor of fenweed filled the room. "The Family is safe?"

"There've been incidents. Nothing we haven't been able to handle, but they are increasing. We may need you to pay a Visit."

"Is it to be a large party, or an intimate affair?"

"The latter."

"And the Host is . . ." Cocking her head to one side, she studied his face. "The priest or the knight?"

"That hasn't been decided yet. Possibly both. The knight is unstable and the priest is simply adding fuel to the fire."

"The knight's a dangerous Host," she noted. "All the more so because of her relation to the Aristok. What happens when he returns?"

Elias snorted. "He may not return. Word is that Heathland has risen. If he's caught in the middle, he could be dead already. But as I said, it hasn't been decided yet. If it were up to me, it would be the priest. Religious fanaticism is always more dangerous to us than secular madness."

She nodded. "I remember. The Archpriest Justinian was a cunning Host."

"Not so cunning in the end."

"True. No match for the brilliant young man who planned his downfall for a year, weaving intrigue and false plots into a web of confusion so tight his powers of prophecy were unable to pierce the future."

He smiled, although the warmth of it never reached his eyes. "And no match for the brilliant young woman who stalked him for two weeks before leaving his blood spilled on the cobblestones before the Temple of Flame."

"Those were heady times, Guild Cousin."

"They were. These times are not so bright, nor the Hosts so challenging."

"Perhaps not *before* the Visit, but afterward, I think, it will be challenging enough. Two DeMarians in one month is likely to cause more violence than is healthy.

The Family may wish to join their Cousins in an extended holiday on the Continent."

"We're considering it, but our Guild's not so retiring as your own. We'd likely be missed."

"Likely," she agreed. "You could come." Her hand stroked the inside of his thigh and he laid his own hand over it gently.

"I may when this is all over."

With a sigh, she entwined his fingers in hers. "You won't. You never do. We should have spirited you away when we had the chance; what a beautiful weapon you would have made."

"I'm flattered, Cousin." Raising her hand to his lips, he kissed it. "But I was called to a different dance."

"To fill the bed of some petty Lordling with his head up his arse?"

"I never had that honor, as you well know."

"Not silken enough?"

"Not beautiful enough."

"I find that hard to believe. No, I think you weren't coy enough. You're too arrogant, Cousin."

"Possibly. My first and only duty is to the Guild and its safety, and the Guild is in danger."

She nodded, releasing his hand and drawing at her pipe again. "Back to business, then. When shall we know the Host?"

"Today, likely. I'll send a message downriver."

"We'll be ready." They rose. "Till then." She reached up and, pulling his face down to hers, kissed him. Then she turned. "You may come out now."

There was a rustle beyond the doorway and a girl of thirteen, short black curls poking out from the hood of her cloak, stepped sheepishly into the lantern light.

Elias smiled. "How long have you been there, Elisha?"

"Not long, Master. Really."

"My apprentice," he introduced. The woman's gaze flickered from one to the other and then she nodded as the girl bowed.

"She has fine hands. An Auxiliary?"

"As I said, my apprentice."

"Of course. When can we expect her?"

"Perhaps in a month or two. What is it, Elisha?"

The girl smiled, enjoying the drama of the moment. "There's a message, Master. The Aristok has returned."

"Excuse me?"

She nodded. "An oceangoing vessel has been spotted coming up the Mist. It's flying the royal standard. When the *Bricklin* challenged it, the returning message was, *Fall in behind.* The entire fleet is obeying."

"The Aristok returns to Branbridge," the woman murmured. "This changes things somewhat."

Elias turned. "Possibly. The Aristok has returned, but he's as unstable as his sister, and a Companion has been accused. Our request remains the same. We may need the Cousins to pay a Visit. We'll let you know who the Host is to be later today or tomorrow."

"As you like." The woman stowed her pipe away and turned to go. She paused at the doorway to bend over the girl's ear.

"Some small advice, child. Never gasp when you catch someone in an intimate moment, even if it is . . . your Master. It gives your position away."

The girl blushed as the assassin moved past her.

With an uncharacteristic chuckle, the Head of the Companion's Guild Security Force allowed his apprentice to take the lantern and lead him back upstairs for a hurried conference with his superiors.

Out on the River Mist, the *Marmoset* passed the easternmost boundary of Branbridge, the rampant firewolf and golden oak leaf clusters of the Royal standard announcing its Imperial passenger. Demnor the Fifth was coming home to claim his birthright.

As word of their Sovereign's return spread throughout the city, people flooded from their homes and businesses, joined by the knights of the Militant Orders, an unofficial treaty called due to this new development. As they surged toward the riverbanks, they passed the Sentinel towers on the city walls and the Town Watch

sent up a cheer. The *Marmoset,* with the Royal Navy
following, came into view around the river bend and
the cheer was taken up by the citizens of Branbridge.

In the bow, Demnor surveyed his capital. The week
of violence had left some sectors blackened with soot,
and he could almost see the chaos and desperation
shimmering over the streets like a gossamer cloak. Far
too many guards patrolled the walls and far too many
in the crowd were armed and armored for battle. The
anger at those who'd caused this violence in his city
made his fists clench in wrath. As the ship passed the
smoking Cathedral of Essus, the crimson haze that had
formed in Braxborough rose up to cloud his vision.

Those watching from the bank saw a glowing red
nimbus of fire envelop their Sovereign. It grew,
pulsing outward to surround the ship until the vessel
resembled a brilliant red ruby floating on the water. In
its midst, the Aristok stood like the reincarnation of
Bran Bendigeid himself, pointing a crimson finger at
the beleaguered Tower of the Sword. As the people
watched in hushed awe, the battle standard of Cannonshire was lowered and the bright flag of Branion raised
in its place. The gate was thrown open and the besieged
Knights of the Sword streamed out to join their fellow
citizens on the banks of the Mist.

Sailing on, the *Marmoset* passed the eastern markets
and the merchant wharfs. Drawing abreast of the small
Essusiate dock of St. Lorenzo, the Aristok gave a
hoarse shout. The ship came about, and as the startled
crowd drew back, the *Marmoset* put in.

Sailors leaped from the side to secure the ship, and
when all was prepared, the gangplank was dropped
with a heavy boom. Captain Fletcher gave a sharp
word of command. Two by two, the Palace Guard disembarked. Those able-bodied who had served Demnor
in Braxborough came next and when his force was all
in place, the Aristok strode down the gangplank and
onto the dock. Behind him, the rest of the Royal Party
disembarked while the ruby glow about the *Marmoset*

faded away, leaving only a scarlet patina patterned into
its wooden sides.

Demnor passed through the line of Guards, the fiery
mist before his eyes rising until he could scarcely see.
He crossed the dock quickly, and as his feet touched
the soil of Branion, the red nimbus burst into flames.

The crowd jerked back, then, one by one, Triarch
and Essusiate alike, they pressed forward. Reaching
tentatively between the bodies of the Palace Guard,
they stretched out their fingers to touch their new
Avatar. Each hand that crossed the blazing barrier left
its own burden of relief or fear behind; and as each
hand withdrew, it took a little of him with it. The
Living Flame arose.

In its center, Demnor accepted the homage of his
people with uncharacteristic hesitancy. The unfamiliar
flood of other people's emotions drowned his own
senses while beneath his feet the soil of Branion pulsed
jolts of power through his limbs to make him jerk like a
puppet. Each pulse became a tiny lick of flame and as
each Flame grew, it cavorted up his body and leaped
into the crowd. As more and more people pressed forward, the Living Flame built within him until the pressure behind his eyes made him want to scream. It drove
him forward, forcing first one leg and then the other to
push him through the crowd and as his resistance
weakened, the compulsion of it grew.

It drove him down St. Lorenzo Street. Drunk and
reeling on power and need, he staggered blindly on-
ward, supported by the force of his people's communion. He reached the junction between Lorenzo and
Bank Street; reached a place where the hands of his
subjects no longer buoyed him up and fell to his knees,
the flames around his body still sucking at the emotions of the crowd like a greedy undertow. The Guard
rushed to help, but Demnor waved them off.

Free for the moment from their grasping hands, he
slowly came back to himself. The cobblestones shimmered before his eyes, undulating in time with the beat
of his own heart. The Living Flame surged within him

to the same rhythm. They merged together, blending
into one indissoluble link; the Land and the Flame and
the Aristok. As they did, the memories of forty
DeMarian Avatars paraded before his vision, their collective experiences just beyond his grasp. He reached
for them; tasted the raw potential of the link, and felt
another's presence at its edge. He turned.

Quindara DeMarian, her own eyes wild and burning,
stood just beyond the line of Palace Guard. She
remained as still as a statue while the crowd drew
back and her brother turned his flame-covered visage
upon her.

They locked eyes, the Flame rising between them.
Demnor felt the now familiar surge of power pulse up
his body; saw it emerge as a cord of flames that
reached for the DeMarian Cadet. It raised him to his
feet, stretched his arms out to his sister, and called
her name.

Quindara staggered forward, catching herself before
she fell, and a young man in the black and green of the
DeKathrines tried to leap toward her. He was blocked
by the Palace Guard.

Fighting the compulsion that dragged her inexorably
forward, the Duke of Yorbourne scrabbled for her
sword, but even as she strained toward the hilt, the
power of the Flame thrust her forward. The Aristok
met her, and as they touched there was a sudden burst
of fire.

In its midst, Demnor screamed. Pain and grieving
rushed in on him, sweeping all other senses away with
its intensity. Memories filled his mind; their mother's
face, their mother's voice, echoing over and over;
teaching, lecturing, building a daughter to protect and
defend the family against any and all danger. He tasted
the desperate need for worthiness, felt his own rise up
in recognition, and was almost lost in the gout of jealousy that responded. He fought his way through it,
forcing it down the conduit of his body and out into the
ground. The power of the Flame obeyed, sucking up

the wild emotion and leaving pure, cleansing fire in its place.

Outlined in traceries of red, the royal siblings clutched at each other while the Living Flame burned away their rivalry. Then, as quickly as it had arisen, it guttered out. Quindara collapsed, and Demnor, unable to keep his own balance, barely managed to catch her and cradle her head in his hands as they both crumpled to the ground.

People rushed forward. For a time all was confusion, and then the Duke of Yorbourne disentangled herself from the Aristok, and allowed the young DeKathrine man to support her in his arms. Coughing, she swiped weakly at a thin line of blood dribbling down her chin and met her brother's unfocused gaze.

"Burn you forever," she whispered. "Why weren't you here?"

Why weren't you here?

His sister's words echoing in his mind, Demnor took the shallow steps leading to the Royal Necropolis three at a time, pushing the words away in preparation for the trial to come. One accusation at a time.

At the bottom of the stairs, Captain Fletcher unlocked the crypt's iron gate, then stood aside to let her Sovereign pass. Above, the grotesquely carved features of the Shadow Catcher leered down at them in the lantern light. For an instant, Demnor remembered a child's terror of the grim sentinel, and then he was past. Before him a plain stone tomb waited, shadowed and still in the middle of the otherwise empty vault.

"Leave us."

"Yes, My Liege."

Placing the torch in an iron holder on the wall, the Captain withdrew. Demnor stood unmoving until her steps receded, then he came forward and laid the flat of his palms down on the cold stone.

"Mother?"

The terrible moment he'd been holding at bay for three days came and went in silence. For one irrational

second he saw himself tearing away the heavy slab
and forcing her to speak to him. Then reason returned.
She was dead, gone. He was here because tradition demanded that he come and because it gave him
some small measure of peace before facing Yorbourne,
Cannonshire, and the host of dead and wounded that
their power struggle had produced.

"Mother?"

The darkness of the Royal Necropolis gave back
only the faint drip of moisture from somewhere deep
within. The air, stale and damp, brought with it pale
memories of a child Prince venturing farther and farther from the safety of the torchlight to prove himself
worthy. Only the first of the many trials he had set for
himself. Were the trials over now?

He shook his head. The trials were only just
beginning.

Slowly he knelt and laid his forehead on the cold
slab, almost in supplication. He had come. Where was
she? Why wouldn't she speak to him? Beneath his
clutching fingers the sarcophagus spoke its answer.
Her body lay below, limbs laid out, dead hands
clutching sword and shield, dead face expressionless
and cold. Her spirit had joined with the Living Flame;
her body waited for the next Aristok, her son, to place
it on the pyre.

He closed his eyes, his sister's question repeating
over and over in his mind, her words mingling with his
own until they blended into one, long stream of guilt.
He should have been here.

His eyes stung with tears he'd forgotten how to
shed, and with an incoherent cry, he slammed his fist
against the tomb. Over and over he beat the unyielding
stone until a sharp crack brought him back to his
senses. Shakily, he raised his hand and stared at his
blood-smeared knuckles. Around him, his blows
echoed in the underground crypt, then grew faint and
disappeared.

Fool, his mind chided, *she's gone; live with it.* The
Living Flame, stirred by his grief, sent ripples of

warmth though his limbs, speaking the words louder than he could have. The warmth of it was a comfort and he laid his hand against his chest, feeling its sleeping power tingle against his fingertips. Was this how she'd felt? Had she been able to stand alone all those years because the Flame had been a constant, intimate lover? But if that was so, why had It abandoned her to death so soon? When the assassin had come, why hadn't It protected her?

He'd always believed what she'd taught him, that the Flame would not remain in a weak Vessel. That was why It had abandoned Great Uncle Amedeus, and why, when disease had weakened his grandfather Quinton's body beyond saving, It had passed to his mother. But now? Melesandra wasn't weak, had never been weak. Why had It passed to him?

He would never know. She was gone. The Flame *had* passed, and he had not been here. He swallowed hard, his eyes squeezed shut against the tomb's silent accusation.

The silence waited, and after a time he opened his eyes in weary resignation. Before him the Realm's secular regalia lay on a pall of ash-gray velvet in the center of the slab. Plaide folded neatly, Royal Seal beside it, they waited for him to take on the burdens of duty. A hysterical laugh broke the surface. She had finally deemed him worthy and delivered them up to him. And wasn't that what he'd always longed for? Wasn't it?

"WASN'T IT!"

The anguish in the cry snapped his head up and he glanced around suddenly in fear that someone had heard, but he was alone. Alone among the dead. Only the Aristok was sent to the Flame. Others, DeMarians, Consorts, faithful knights, leading citizens or loyal servants, were laid here in the cool darkness while their spirits rested in the gardens of the Shadow Catcher. He glanced around. Somewhere near, in one of the side crypts he'd never visited, lay his father, eleven years dead. And beyond him, his great uncle Amedeus who'd never worn the crown, and on down through the dusty ages. Nine hundred years of history culminating in a single instant.

His hand hovered over the heavy gold-and-silver seal, loath to touch it. Had *she* felt like this? The night she'd gone alone to stand before Quinton's tomb, had she hesitated?

No. She had never been uncertain. He was a pale reflection of her glory. He could feel another cry well up, and he clamped his teeth over it. This was stupid. She was dead. Gone, for whatever reason. His hand reached out once more, and he made a grab for the ring before his nerve broke again.

The deeply engraved signet cut into his palm, and he squeezed it, willing the pain in his hand to drive out the pain in his chest. It was no use.

"I should have been here," he said, his voice falling tonelessly in the dark crypt. "I should have known. Atreus and Marsellus warned me not to go. Why didn't I listen to them?"

"Because it wasn't meant to be, Most Holy."

Spinning around, Demnor bit back a curse as the bent form of Gwynne DeLlewellynne entered the crypt.

"I gave orders I was not to be disturbed," he grated out.

She bobbed her head, her dark eyes bright in the torchlight. "Forgive me, My Avatar, the Living Flame commands, and I obey."

His hand reaching up involuntarily to touch the new warmth in his chest, Demnor scowled.

"What do you want?"

"To give counsel, Most Holy, and to give answers."

"Fine, then give them. Why did this happen? How *could* it have happened?"

"It was meant to be."

"Horseshit! The Living Flame speaks through you. You counsel my mother. Why didn't you warn her? Why didn't you stop this?" He almost spoke the question he'd been wrestling with before her arrival, but clamped his teeth against the words, not wanting to know the answer. Turning away, his voice so low she could barely hear it, he asked the other instead. "Why did you let me go to Heathland, instead of being by her side when she needed me?"

The Archpriest of the Flame dropped her own gaze.

"I was powerless in this, Most Holy. The vision would not reveal its purpose to me. It spoke of momentous events and changes to the Realm, changes that would affect yourself, but not what those changes would be. It was your mother's command that you go north to Heathland, believing as she did that you would wrestle with your destiny there. Did you, Majesty?" She looked searchingly into his face.

Biting back the sharp retort he might have made, Demnor met her gaze. Her eyes were sunken and tired, and he suddenly saw for the first time how old she was and how much of the Realm's spiritual health had rested on her shoulders alone for so long. Gwynne DeLlewellynne was the heart of the Triarchy, of the Land itself; and the Land was grieving, searching blindly in the darkness for a presence that was no longer there. He would have to be that presence, no matter how lost he felt himself.

"Perhaps," he answered gently. "If Heathland and its struggles are my destiny.

"It always comes back to Heathland," he mused.

"It has always been so, Most Holy. Even in the days of peace when Heathland and Branion were allies of equal status, there was jealousy, each Realm coveting what the other possessed. Religion simply adds the spark to the tinder already in place."

"Well, the tinder's taken fire now. Heathland has risen, Branbridge is in confusion; I can't raise an army in time to relieve our northern forts before winter, so they'll have to hold out until spring."

The Archpriest nodded. "And before our armies can be strong, Most Holy, the Realm must be strong and united. You are the Vessel of the Living Flame. It has passed." Her thin hand touched his sleeve.

"And the Realm cried out for strength, and Brani-ana heard. She went deep into the mountains, and there she wrestled with the Living Flame. They fought for many days and nights, while her retainers waited fearfully outside. When she finally emerged she had changed."

The Archpriest's voice had taken on the singsong cadence of litany as she recited the Mystery of Flame from the Triarchy text. Demnor could feel the Flame stir within him, and he laid his hand on his chest as he'd seen his mother do so often in the past.

"Braniana made a pact with the Living Flame," the Archpriest continued in her own words now. "To be Its living Vessel and carry Its strength to the people. The Flame has passed, Most Holy. You have brought it home and given it to the people for healing. Now you must use it for unity before we are swept away by our enemies."

Demnor met her eyes and nodded. "I am the Vessel of the Living Flame, and there will be peace and unity in Branbridge.

"I have commanded Yorbourne and Cannonshire to come before me this afternoon. Afterward, we'll arrange my mother's funeral. For now, I want a report from you on the events which preceded her death. I will take it in the . . . in my audience room when I am finished here."

The Archpriest of the Flame bowed. "I am at your service always, My Avatar. May you live long in the heart of the Living Flame and may you bring peace and prosperity to our Land." She kissed his hand, then took her leave, walking straighter than she had when she'd arrived.

Demnor turned back to the tomb, rolling the Royal Seal between his fingers. It gleamed golden in the torchlight, the finely engraved fire-wolf above the three oak leaf clusters picked up by the flickering light. The ring had been made almost four centuries ago to celebrate the fiftieth year of reign of his most celebrated ancestor Atreus the Second in the year 500, the most auspicious rule in DeMarian history. Demnor frowned. Would his reign be celebrated so joyously four hundred years from now? Forty men and women had taken on the burden of the Living Flame before him, forty men and women who'd either ruled strong and well, or had been destroyed. How many of them had stood where he stood now, pledging themselves to the service of the Flame?

He snorted. "And how many of them hid in a tomb like a nervous virgin before getting down to work?"

Bringing up his hand, he placed the Seal on his smallest finger. It would have to be seized to fit his hand, as would many of the other details of his new life until they fit comfortably under his rule. Slowly, he took up the Plaide. It was time to begin.

Turning, Demnor the Fifth took his own leave of Melesandra the Third for the first time in his life.

The Aristok took possession of Branbridge in a single day. The Navy was sent back to their harbors, the Militant Orders told to stand down, and the Town Watch put in charge of the city once again. Assurances were sent to the Essusiate churches that no more mass retaliations would be forthcoming. Word that their leaders might be released soon was also cautiously offered, although His Most Regal Majesty wished to review the charges against them himself first.

At the palace, life was no less hectic than it had been under the Duke of Yorbourne. Demnor took over the Aristok's office, and with Kelahnus and Isolde, skimmed rapidly through the week's events. Messengers and pages came and went, bringing reports from their Lords and returning with orders from the Aristok. The Palace Guard were the first group completely reinstated. Leafing through the reports of their questioning, Demnor tossed the entire pile on the floor.

"Acting in concert with Third Companion Alynne, Sergeant Cross was alone guilty among the Guard. Any comments?" He turned to the others.

Isolde shook her head. "The evidence seems to suggest so, Majesty, but it still doesn't explain why."

"When we catch them, we'll both know. Page!"

A girl appeared in the doorway.

"Go to Captain Fletcher. Tell her all members of the Guard are to be returned to active service and all those still under confinement are to be released."

"Yes, Your Majesty." The girl darted away.

"Now, for the rest. I'll see the Captains of the Militant Orders tomorrow, and any of the Triarchy Orders if necessary. Who else needs an audience?"

"The most pressing *half dozen*," Kelahnus answered with a grimace, "are a delegation from the Wool Merchant's Guild, seeking damages against the Sword and Shield, the Town Watch Captain with reports of citizen looting and violence, the Lord Mayor of Branbridge and his Council, the President of the Banker's Consortium, the Ambassador Jorgenstead of Danelind, and the Directors of the Stained Glass Association. They're very angry, by the way. The Charter of 614 allows them access to any painted glass structure in the city at any time, and they were continually denied passage. Also, two of their senior members were killed trying to protect the rose window at the Essus Cathedral. There are about ten in custody, for similar reasons." He held up the list of names. "There's a host of others, I'm afraid. We'll be at this all night."

Demnor shook his head. "We haven't got time. All right. I've sent Raventarian to summon Yorbourne and Cannonshire for two; I'll see the Lord Mayor and one Councillor in the small audience hall at three, the Bankers after that. I'll take supper with the Stained Glass people at their main chapterhouse. Send Robinarden to inform them. Also see to the release of their members. The rest will have to wait until tomorrow."

"As Your Majesty commands." The Companion rose with a tired smile and headed for the door.

"Kelahnus?"

"Hm?"

"Could you stop by and see Kass as well? Tell her I'll come to her just as soon as I can?"

"Of course. Anything else? Your brothers, maybe?"

Demnor thought a moment, then glanced down at the tottering piles of missives. "No. I'm told there is no change in Marsellus' condition. Atreus can't leave his side, and I've no time to see them right now. I've sent a messenger. That will have to suffice for now. Just be back in my suite by one, I'll need you to help me dress. And, Kelahnus?"

"Hm?"

"Thank you."

Kelahnus smiled. "You can thank me at one, My Lord." They shared a brief smile, then the Companion left to the murmured admiration of the people in the outer office.

When he'd gone, Demnor turned to Isolde. "What else?"

She frowned. "The Essusiate question, Majesty."

Rubbing at the scars on his jaw, Demnor closed his eyes a moment. "It's too scorching complicated. I can believe Grant acted alone, I can believe Alynne acted alone . . . but . . . Page!

"Get me the Herald Wrenalynne."

"At once, Sire!"

"Where was I?"

"Third Companion Alynne?"

"No . . ." Tapping the edge of the Royal Seal against the desktop, Demnor frowned. "Acting alone . . . the Essusiates. Grant and Alynne met an Essusiate and fled north. That implicates the Heathland Church. Auvernais has risen with instigation from the Gallian Church, and the Gallian Church has its head up its arse, so their mandate must have come from the Continental Hierarchy."

"The Pontiff?"

"Why not? It's been seven years since her last open attempt. With all these chapters coordinated to attack within three days of each other it stinks of confederacy. The Branion Essusiates must be involved."

"These do suggest so, Majesty." Isolde indicated the pile of interrogation reports from the Flame Priests. "At the very least, the Branion leadership is guilty."

"Guilty of regicide and treason, but protected by the Treaty of 875 and their subordination to the Continental Hierarchy."

"A delicate situation, My Liege."

"Hm. And one I've no time to deal with." He studied the list and jotted down several names. "Page!"

"Take this to Captain Fletcher, have them released."

He turned back to the Earl of Essendale. "The rest will wait until I'm sure of their guilt or innocence. In the meantime I want that list of audiences settled."

By the time the Herald arrived, most had been slotted into times in the next four days.

"And the coronation, Majesty," Isolde reminded him.

Demnor rubbed at his eyes. "I think Gwynne is arranging all that."

The Captain of Heralds coughed discreetly at the door, and when acknowledged, advanced to nine paces before the desk and bowed. The Aristok waved her closer.

"One moment." He pulled a sheet of creamy yellow vellum from a side drawer and spread it out on the desk. Dipping a new quill into the ink, he began to write.

"You're to carry this to the Branbridge School of Companions."

Dripping blue wax on the bottom, he pressed the Royal Seal into it, then waited a moment. When he was sure it was dry, he folded it and sealed it shut with a black ribbon held in place by another dab of wax. He held it out.

Coming forward, the Herald dropped to one knee and accepted the dispatch.

"It will take them some time to comply," Demnor continued. "Wait there for an answer."

"Yes, Your Majesty."

When she left, Demnor rose. "Now if you'll excuse me, My Lord Earl of Essendale."

"Of course, My Liege." Having risen when the Aristok did, Isolde bowed.

"Thank you for your assistance," he acknowledged somewhat stiffly. "I'll need you again later. For now I have to get ready to meet my sister and cousin, and you'll want to relax and . . . unpack."

"Thank you, I should, My Liege. When shall I attend Your Majesty again?"

"Um . . ." Chewing a moment at the scar on his lip, Demnor frowned. "I . . . should like you to accompany me to the Stained Glass chapterhouse tonight. It would add a . . . less audiencelike air to the evening."

The Earl of Essendale smiled. "I should be only too honored, Majesty. What shall I wear?"

"Wear?" His eyes widened in alarm and Isolde suppressed a smile.

"Is it to be a formal affair, Majesty, a military function, or a casual supper?"

"Uh . . . somewhat in between formal and casual."

"Ah. The Aristok and his Betrothed dining with loyal citizens to assure them they're valuable members of the Realm?"

"Something like that."

"A peace offering."

"Yes, a bribe." They both smiled.

"I have the perfect outfit in mind. If you will excuse me, Your Majesty." Bowing, she withdrew.

Demnor remained standing in the center of the office, frowning uncertainly. Had that gone all right? Everything had run smoothly until the last. Kelahnus and Isolde were working fine together, and he'd been in perfect control. Until the last. Had he asked her to the supper properly? He'd meant it to be as unrestrained as the rest of the morning, but somehow it had come out nervously uncertain. He must have sounded like a fool. Leafing through the reports, he reviewed their conversation. Finally, he pushed the pile of papers away with a snort. However it had gone, he'd asked, she'd answered, and they were going. It was a perfectly normal function for the Aristok and the Consort to attend. It shouldn't bother Kelahnus at all. Should it? So why did he feel as though he had done something behind the Companion's back? Frowning, he turned away. He would tell Kelahnus about the decision and gauge his reaction. That would put the whole thing to rest. With a final glance around, he left, locking the office door behind him.

The bells of Bran's Tower rang two as the Duke of Yorbourne and the Hierarchpriest of Cannonshire were ushered into the Aristok's presence. Both had brought a host of retainers with them. All had been politely but firmly asked to remain in the main gardens until called for. Captain Fletcher escorted the two groups herself and the complement of Palace Guards that lined the garden walls made it plain they were to wait peaceably. Both sides eyed each other suspiciously as their Lords entered the Privy Council Chamber and the doors were closed behind them.

Once they were seated, Demnor lifted the two dispatches before him.

"I've read both your reports on last week's events," he began. "I'll comment on them later. Right now we're here to talk about the Realm, its safety, and its strength—not to try to place blame. We're at war, and I haven't got time for that kind of horseshit.

"You *will* reconcile, and that reconciliation *will* last. I don't care what you think of each other in private. In public you *will* be united. Is that understood?"

He looked from one to the other. Quindara made to say something, then simply nodded stiffly. Alexander looked away. "As Your Majesty commands."

"His Majesty does. We must spend this winter preparing to regain our northern and Continental territories as soon as spring allows. When we move, we will move purposely in one direction with no factions left behind. That being said, you, My Lord Duke of Yorbourne, overreacted and caused great turmoil and

destruction in our capital, while you, My Lord Hierarchpriest did not support my Regent and caused factionalism and more destruction in that same capital."

Alexander stiffened and stared at Demnor, his mouth
working in astonishment. Quindara simply narrowed
her eyes. Demnor glared at them both coldly.

"The Realm was in confusion, grief stricken and
lost. I was not here; you were. It was your duty to comfort the Realm and keep it safe until I returned. You
failed."

Holding up his hand to forestall a denial from both
of them, he then slammed his fist against the table.
"Mass arrests of my citizens and armed combat in my
streets does not keep the Realm safe!" He thrust an
accusing finger toward them. "Deny it!"

When they remained silent, he continued. "Branbridge is in shambles, a very costly shambles, and I'm
not paying for its restoration, you are. The Orders of
the Shield and Sword will also bear the burden, as will
the Essusiate leadership, depending on how guilty I
find them. My decision on that will be handed down
later this week and I expect nonpartisan counsel from
you both."

He glared from one to the other, and after a moment
they both nodded. Quindara's flame-washed eyes were
dark with anger. He ignored it.

"Good. All accusations of treason and heresy are
rescinded. As for the Sword; I expect you both to work
together for the good of the Realm, but I don't expect it
to be done within the Knights. My Lord Duke of Yorbourne, you are withdrawn from that Order, and I place
you in the Captaincy of the Shield." He turned his fire-
covered gaze on his sister. "The Shield Knights followed you, they are your responsibility now. I expect
the same high standard of duty from them that they've
shown in the past."

Quindara met his eyes haughtily. "The Shield Knights
have always protected the Royal Family with their lives.
That will never change. Your Majesty."

"See that it doesn't. As you're Defender of the Realm

until I raise an heir, I shall expect you to incorporate them into that duty."

He turned to Alexander DeKathrine. "My Lord Hierarchpriest of Cannonshire, you are to return to the Sword Tower and prepare your Order for the spring campaign.

Alexander rose, his gray eyes smoldering, and bowed stiffly. Demnor shook his head.

"Cousin, I know the times have been difficult and there were reasons, some both proper and necessary for your actions. I don't care how unfairly you think you've been treated this day, I want you to put your feelings aside and carry out my wishes. Later we'll meet. You may lay them on the table, and I'll hear them. For now, however, I need your support."

The Hierarchpriest nodded. "I'm at your service as always . . . Sire." He bowed and withdrew, barely controlled anger written in every movement.

Demnor turned to his sister. "There will be no more hostilities between the Shield and the Sword."

Quindara shrugged. "The Shield will not initiate violence, as *Your Majesty* commands, but if the Sword still harbors resentment against us, the Throne itself may be in danger. And the Shield Knights will protect the Throne."

Demnor's eyes narrowed, the rise of red fire washing out the gray. "You *will* obey me in this, Yorbourne. There's been enough distrust and enough bloodshed, so you move scorchingly well carefully before you put your hand to any more. Don't push me now. I am the Aristok and *my* duty is to the Land and the Flame. There *will* be peace in Branbridge before I move on Heathland, do you understand?"

"Perfectly, Your Majesty. The Shield will not be the cause of any weakness in the Realm, but what about the Essusiates?" Her own eyes grew crimson. "They killed our mother."

"I'm aware of what they have done, but I must have ironclad evidence before I move against the Essusiate

Church, or the entire Continent will face us in Gallia and Heathland. You have evidence. Let's hear it."

As Alexander DeKathrine returned to the Sword Tower, the Aristok and the Duke of Yorbourne began to examine the case of regicide against Essusiatism.

In their suite, Atreus DeMarian received Demnor's messenger politely. His words were brief. The Aristok could not see them now, but would put some time aside in the coming week. He hoped that Marsellus would soon recover as Agrippa had assured him he would.

Atreus had sent the man on his way with a dutiful response. He would wait on the Aristok's command, of course.

Now, sitting by the window, he stared out over the roofs of the palace. That Demnor could not see them was of no concern. His return to Branbridge was enough to give the Duke of Lochsbridge some hope that the violence would ease, and his Gift with it. Already he felt the tightness leaving his chest. He might even manage a decent night's sleep finally. His gaze stole to the bed and his sleeping brother.

Marsellus was still too ill to care whether Demnor came or not. Locked in the Prophetic Realm's shadowy grip, even the Vessel of the Flame's presence was not enough to help him, no matter what Agrippa had said. The crisis had still not passed. It might never pass. Closing his eyes, Atreus leaned his head back and slept.

14. First Royal Companion

The day the capital celebrated the return of its new ruler, the Branbridge School of Companions was still, its gates locked. Two of the Guild's personal guard stood sentinel before each entrance, the rest patrolled the streets along the walls. In the city there'd been violence and Guild members entered armed and escorted and remained within. In its wide, muraled classrooms its students heard their lessons fearfully, knowing the events of the times, but not their Guild's response. Today their Masters gathered to decide what that response would be.

In the Meeting Hall the Junior Members of the Guild Council rose as Master Klairius and the Senior Councillors entered. They took their accustomed seats and, after placing water and wine close at hand, the young students who usually paged at such meetings withdrew. This was no ordinary Guild Council. An Aristok had been assassinated. A Companion had been accused. Representatives from across the Realm and as far away as Nordanger were gathered, answering the Guild Head's summons, and messengers stood ready to carry their decision to the Continental Schools of Bachiem and Florenz. This meeting, complete now that Kelahnus, First Royal Companion to the new Aristok, had returned, would determine the Companion's Guild's position and future actions.

In his customary seat, Kelahnus glanced around the table, quickly assessing those gathered. Master

Klairius, looking older then his sixty-six years, sat calm
and reposed at the head of the table, showing nothing in
his posture that might indicate the seriousness of the
situation. Master Elias and Master Adell, his Seconds
sat beside him; the former as still and formal as ever,
some grim purpose in his eyes; the latter, hands laid
serenely in her lap, observing the gathering as Kelahnus
did. The Head of the School in Danelind conversed
quietly with his counterpart from Nordanger, while
beside them, Master Kerry of Eireon, Second to the
aging Master Kathlene, sipped at a glass of imported
whiskey. Gwyneth, Braxborough, Renneaux, Cannonshire, Cambury, the five Branion chapterhouses were
all in attendance as well as the Companions of the
seven ranking Dukes, Julian, Companion to the Hierarchpriest, Tania, Companion to Isolde DeKathrine, and
six of the seven Royal Companions.

Kelahnus sought Florence's hand under the table.
The three remaining Royal Companions, he amended:
Nadia, Companion to the Prince Quindara, Clarina, the
Prince Kassandra's Auxiliary Nurse, and himself.
Demnor's first act that morning had been to retire the
Royal contracts of Melesandra. Martina and Laura had
returned to the School. Florence, at Kelahnus' pan-
icked request, had remained at the palace as the Guild
Representative. Faced with his sudden elevation in
status, Kelahnus had felt as lost as the day he'd first
entered the palace as Companion to the Prince of
Gwyneth. With Florence by his side, things weren't
quite so overwhelming.

To his left, Martina took a sip of wine, composure
unruffled. Both she and the late Aristok's Second
Companion Laura seemed unaffected by their questioning at the hands of the Flame Priests. They'd
returned to the School when released and Kelahnus
didn't know how the Aristok's passing had affected
them. He didn't ask. He'd never been as close to either
woman as he was with Florence. The former Fourth
Companion was subdued, eyes pinched and shadowed,
but she returned the pressure of his hand and grinned

quirkily at him. He smiled back, then swung his attention away, embarrassed by her sadness, and his lack of it.

The highly polished cherrywood table was warm to his touch, and Kelahnus' gaze followed the smooth reddish-brown grain to its head where Master Klairius now rose. All eyes turned to the old man who'd led their Guild for fifteen years. Each person present had either served with him or had studied under him, and they arranged themselves in respectful positions of attentiveness as he began to speak.

"My brothers and sisters, as you all are aware, one week ago the Aristok Melesandra the Third was poisoned in her sleep. Some of you are in possession of more details than others, so rather than speculate, I shall simply tell you that according to Archpriest Gwynne DeLlewellynne she was murdered by Alynne, Third Companion to the Aristok."

Murmured talk broke out around the table, but the Head of the Guild raised his hand to forestall any questions.

"According to our own sources, Alynne and the Aristok took a light repast at midnight, then retired for the night. There was no business requiring the other Royal Companions to be abroad, so they also retired until five when Martina discovered the body. Alynne was nowhere to be found. It was reported that she left the palace at three in the morning in the company of a Palace Guard and met an Essusiate at the North Gate who provided them with horses.

"The Flame Priests have reported that through their ability to prophesy they've located Alynne and this guard in Heathland, which, as we all know, has risen in revolt. Our Braxborough chapter has been closed by the rebels, although I understand that we still maintain our contacts there. Is this not so, Master Magria?"

The eighty-year-old Head of the Braxborough chapter nodded as she finished her glass, then poked her aide with her elbow, signaling her desire for more whiskey. When it was placed beside her, she lifted it and eyed Master Klairius over its crystal rim. "Alynne's at Tottenham Castle," she answered evenly, her firm tone belying the fragility of her frame. "Why, we don't know." The old woman shrugged eloquently. "She hasn't tried to contact any of my people yet, although I understand she's being well treated."

"Thank you, Elder Sister." Master Klairius made her a slight bow, and Master Magria raised one suggestive eyebrow in return. "We expect to get a message to Alynne soon," the Head of the Guild continued. "And secure her release as soon as possible. Then, hopefully, we shall know the truth of this business. For the record, the Companion's Guild representatives in Branbridge were not involved in the conspiracy to murder our best client."

There was politely subdued laughter around the table as the Guild Head returned to his seat. Everyone quieted as the Eireon Second rose.

"Yes, Master Kerry?"

"The question most prevalent in the minds of the Eireon School, Eldest Brother, is why our Younger Sister is involved at all?"

Master Klairius waved one hand in a regretful gesture. "We don't know," he answered simply. "Martina?"

The former First Companion stood. "We served together as Sisters for ten years, my Masters. Never in that time did she give me any indication that she was dissatisfied or mentally unstable."

Laura nodded her agreement, and Master Adell shook her head. "A mystery, and a strange one, my Brothers and Sisters. A wholly trustworthy and loyal Guild member, head of her class, suddenly murders the Realm's Sovereign? How can we make sense of such a deed? Did Alynne go mad slowly, yet show no sign of her affliction, or so quickly that no one, not even her Sisters were aware of it? Or was she, in fact, not so loyal as we, who have raised and taught so many of our Younger Brothers and Sisters, believed? That she was able to plan and commit such a crime in total secrecy does our training no credit."

Master Adell bowed her head in sadness; Alynne had been one of her special pupils. The Guild Head touched her hand. The others exchanged glances, although no one spoke until Master Elias stood.

"One option," he began in his dark, solemn voice, "is that Alynne did not, in fact, commit any such crime. We've only the word of the Flame Priests to substantiate this and that Order has never been friendly toward us. Not two decades ago the Flame attempted to destroy the Guild because we would not place ourselves under Triarchy law. Old hatreds smolder long and spark to life again if opportunity allows."

"Are you suggesting, Master, that the Flame Priests murdered the Aristok?" Julian, Companion to Alexander DeKathrine, asked in shock.

"Are *you* suggesting that a Royal Companion betrayed her Guild and ran to the Essusiate barbarians in Heathland?" Elias turned his pale gaze on the other man. "Would you condemn your Guild Sister on the word of the *Flame,* Younger Brother?"

Julian's olive skin flushed. "No, Master, of course not," he answered hotly. "But the Living Flame murdered by the Triarchy . . . what reason would they have?"

"Who knows?"

"My Children, please." Master Klairius silenced the two younger men with one upraised hand. "This bickering is not becoming. Our Security Head's theory is a meritorious one and it will be given all due consideration. However, if I am correct, a full report has not yet come from our connections within the Flame. Is this not so, my Son?"

Master Elias inclined his head, his pale eyes hooded. "As you say, Master." He returned to his seat.

"Then let us proceed in good order and turn to the more pressing problem of the Realm's response. I have here a summons from His Majesty to a private audience tomorrow, to discuss . . . *the accusations against*

*one of your own and give you the opportunity to lay
your Guild's position before me,"* he read.

"A diplomatic message," Master Kerry noted.

"Unusually so for His Majesty," Martina added
thoughtfully. "What does he say in private, Kelahnus?"

All eyes turned to the new First Companion. Keeping the sudden nervousness from his posture, Kelahnus
straightened. "He believes the Flame Priests' reports
about Alynne," he answered. "But he also believes she
acted alone. At the moment his main suspicion is
turned toward Essusiatism."

"As it should be," Master Elias responded.

"Yes, Master."

Master Adell sipped from her wineglass and pinned
the younger Companion with a penetrating stare. "So
it's your assessment that it's safe to answer this summons without fear of surprise retaliation?"

Touching his own glass to his lips with an air of
calm assurance, Kelahnus nodded. "He's given everyone involved the opportunity to state their case freely,
Master, and as the Council knows, Demnor the Fifth is
not a man to whom dissembling and intrigue come
naturally."

"That's true, Masters," Florence added. "It's much
more in character for him to send an armed guard to
arrest us if he believed us to be guilty."

"Even Yorbourne wasn't that stupid," Master Elias
snorted, "and she believed the entire city to be guilty."

Master Klairius laid his hand gently on his Security
Head's arm. "I think it's been agreed that the Aristok's
sudden death drove the Royal Duke into temporary
madness. Whether she will recover remains to be
seen." He turned to Quindara's Companion Nadia, who
nodded her assent. "The more important question
now," the Guild Head continued, "is how has the late
Aristok's death affected His Majesty?"

Once more all eyes turned to Kelahnus. Putting his
thoughts in order, he met his Master's gaze. "He was in
shock at first," he answered carefully, the vision of
Demnor's staring eyes and bone-white complexion on

the battlements of Braxborough a frightful memory.
"And then he wanted answers. He wavers between
grief and guilt, but with so much to put right in Branbridge, he's had very little time to really dwell on it."

"And when he does have time?" Master Elias asked.
"What do you think he'll do then?"

The ominous tone of his voice gave Kelahnus pause.
What was the Security Head hinting at? That Demnor
would go on a rampage of killing once the full impact
of his mother's death hit him? Or that he would attack
the Guild, laying all the blame on them? Master Elias
was waiting for an answer, so Kelahnus made a show
of considering his question impartially.

"I think," he began, "that he blames himself more
than anyone else because he wasn't there to prevent it.
Under that, I sense a feeling of relief."

"Relief?"

"Yes, Master," Kelahnus continued cautiously. "The
hostility between them was a constant wound. Now
that she's gone, the wound's beginning to heal."

"So quickly," the Head of Guild Security murmured
sarcastically. "And you don't think his filial love will
come to the fore now that he has the power of the
Realm at his disposal?"

A warning bell began to toll in the back of Kelahnus'
mind. Had Master Elias already passed sentence on
Demnor's fitness to rule? And if he had, how was
Kelahnus to change his mind without putting his own
loyalty in question?

"I don't know, Master," he answered truthfully. "He
hasn't lashed out at anyone yet. I think it's too early to
tell."

"I agree," Master Klairius added firmly. "We will
watch and wait. You will ask the Cousins to remain on
alert a little while longer, Younger Brother."

"The Cousins?" Master Sweyn, head of the Danelind
School repeated, saving Kelahnus from his own shocked
response. "Has it been that bad in Branbridge, then?"

Master Klairius met his gaze impassively from beneath his white eyebrows. "The strife between Yorbourne

and Cannonshire was increasing, Younger Brother. Had the Aristok not arrived when he did, it might have escalated into full-scale civil war. That would have been devastating to the country, coming as it does on the eve of war to the north and east."

"And it's bad for business," Master Adell added.

"Exactly. Now that the Aristok has returned, order may reestablish itself in Branbridge. We will have to wait and see."

Master Sweyn inclined his head in acceptance of the Guild Head's words, and Kelahnus released a breath he hadn't remembered holding. The Cousins were a terrible threat, all the more so because it was one he could never have protected Demnor from. His gaze slid cautiously over Master Elias. The Head of Guild Security was frowning, unconvinced that the threat had been neutralized with the Aristok's return. He seemed eager to return to the days of his youth when the Guild had held a more bloody grip on the political strings. The threat still existed, Kelahnus told himself fearfully. Whatever grief-induced rage Demnor carried would have to be hidden from the Guild at all cost.

". . . and Kelahnus will bring us regular reports on the Aristok's mental state."

Master Klairius turned to the First Royal Companion and with a start, Kelahnus realized he'd been speaking for some time. With studied grace despite the sudden pounding of his heart, the Younger Companion bowed his head in assent.

"Very well. I shall go before the Aristok and confess our complete astonishment at this turn of events. Master Adell will accompany me, and Master Elias will provide for my safety. Now, what of this Guard; what was his name?"

"Grant Cross, Sergeant in the Palace Guard, Master."

"Thank you, Martina. It's been said they fled to Heathland together. What reasoning can there be for such actions?"

"A Guard escorting a prisoner framed for a political murder," Master Elias replied.

"Except those who saw them reported Alynne was not behaving as a prisoner." Master Adell frowned.

Talk broke out around the table, finally subsiding when Master Cosmia of the Renneaux chapter gestured and the assembled turned to her.

"Were Alynne and this guard acquainted?"

"Yes, Master," Martina answered.

"Intimately?"

"Yes, Master."

"How intimately?"

"Master?"

The older woman waved her hand impatiently. "I'm not asking you if they slept together. That much is obvious. Did they see each other at other times? Go out, stay in? Were they friends? Were they lovers in the true sense of the word?"

Martina pursed her lips. "They were certainly closer then casual bedmates, Master. As to lovers . . ." she paused, thinking as the collective waited. "Yes, I'd say they were. She had other lovers as well, though, at least two others in the Palace Guard."

"Ah. Who are still here?"

"As far as we know."

"I'd find out. And I'd question them?"

"What are you hypothesizing, Master Cosmia?" Elias asked, leaning forward.

She laughed. "That your nose is in the center of your face, Younger Brother, but because it's between your eyes and has never left before, you can't see that it's gone now."

Her eyes sparkled at his responding frown and Master Sweyn laughed. "I think what our dear Elder Sister is saying is that perhaps passion led our Younger Sister to this end."

"Passion?"

"Love, Younger Brother, love."

There was shocked silence across the room, then an explosion of babbling voices.

"Love!" Master Elias spat. "What are you talking about?"

"Are you suggesting that Alynne was so obsessed with this one man she was willing to betray her Guild?" Master Kerry stared at the Danelind Master.

"Absurd!" Master Elias banged his fist furiously against the table as the Eireon Second burst out laughing. Around them arguments broke out across the table, voices rising. Finally Master Klairius stood.

"Please, my children, please!"

It was several minutes before the assembled were calmed enough to turn to the Head of their Guild, but finally order prevailed.

"I think we should pause a moment for refreshments."

Sternly he reaching behind him and pulled a long purple cord. Sooner then expected, a breathless Junior entered and bowed. Master Klairius gave his order, then sat down, staring levelly around the table from under his eyebrows. By the time the student returned with a tray laden with cider and fruit cakes, the Council had mended its shattered dignity and they were conversing quietly on other subjects. The student left with obvious reluctance, closing the door behind her.

Master Klairius sipped at his glass. After the polite silence had lasted some moments, he turned his gaze to Master Cosmia and Master Sweyn.

"Your suggestion merits deeper thought, Younger Sister, Younger Brother. It is ... unusual to say the least, but I will give it all due consideration. Now, however, I think we should leave discussion of Alynne's motives until she is safely within our care once more."

Master Sweyn bowed and Master Cosmia inclined her head regally, touching her wineglass to her lips.

"We shall continue, I think, with the Realm's response and that of the Continent. Kethra, how has this affected the Household of Exenworth?"

The stately First Companion to Isabelle DeKathrine smoothed an invisible wrinkle from her robe before responding.

Sitting quietly beside Florence, Kelahnus allowed himself a faint, inaudible sigh of relief. The subject of love was a dangerous one, all the more so today, but with the discussion now turned to more prosaic topics he was able to calm down and mull over this latest development while Kethra reported what he already knew.

The news that Alynne might have betrayed the Guild for love of another had not shocked him as much as it had the more orthodox members of the Council. Elias, Kerry, Kethra, Adell, most had lived structured, uncompromised lives within the Guild Hierarchy. Companioned at eighteen, in most cases retired by thirty to fill other positions within the Family. Lovers came and went; more permanent relationships invariably grew between Guild Siblings. They would not see what they did not wish to see. And that was all to the good.

Master Sweyn maintained a permanent relationship with his final contract while running the Danelind School in Bryholm. Master Cosmia had a score of noble lovers both male and female whom she was more fond of than true propriety demanded. Arthur, Companion to the Duke Amedeus DePaula of Dunmouth had had his contract renegotiated with the Duke every two years for the last thirty. The less cloistered Companions were far more dangerous to his secret.

Alynne. The First Royal Companion reached out for her in his thoughts. *What was this Palace Guard to you? Did you love him? Love him enough to throw your life away on a single, desperate gamble and become a hunted fugitive?*

Beside him, Florence sat, listening intently to her Sister Companion. Years ago, she'd come to the School to comfort a Younger Brother near the breaking point from the necessity of hiding his feelings. Instinctively, she'd searched for him and, in the quiet of a solitary tower room, he'd fallen apart in her arms.

Demnor had run to Briery, an army at his back. He'd sent his lover a message via the grubby urchin who would one day become one of Kelahnus' most trusted people. *There's been some trouble. Hide. Tell no one about us. Be ready to run.*

Master Klairius would never have agreed to his student's first instinct: to fly to his outlawed Prince; to stand at his side and meet their fate together. Kelahnus had not even suggested it. But as the days passed and news of the growing army raised to defeat the Prince of Gwyneth came in daily, it became harder and harder to maintain his self-control. Nightly he dreamed of the Heir's death, alone and without him. Daily he longed to break the stifling duty to his Guild and go to him. *To throw his life away on a single, desperate gamble and become a hunted fugitive.*

The older Kelahnus smiled inwardly, although his expression quickly became serious.

Yes.

The day Florence had come to him, somehow knowing her Little Brother was poised on the brink of a crisis between opposing loyalties, he'd made up his mind to leave. She'd held him, soothed him, and kept him in the bosom of the Family, but the damage was done. He'd broken with the Guild in his heart that day. He'd never seen anything quite the same way since.

The day Florence had stood by his side to hear the news—that the Heir to the Throne had been defeated, captured, and returned to face his Sovereign's wrath had been the hardest day of his life. By that time there was no turning back. Hiding had become second nature. Master Klairius had not suspected, and Florence had not informed him. In a way, she, too, had broken with the Guild for love of another. It made Kelahnus suspect it happened more frequently than any of them were willing to believe.

The more orthodox members of the Guild would only see what they wished to see. That was all to the good for him, but very bad for the Guild. He was unsure of how he should feel about that.

One thing he was certain of: he loved Demnor and would do whatever was necessary to protect him, and if that meant breaking openly with the Guild, defying Master Elias, and thus making an enemy far more dangerous than Melesandra the Third could ever have

been, then so be it. He would do no less for love than
Alynne had. In the meantime, he must get Demnor
moved to the more defensible apartments in the Royal
wing. Tonight. It couldn't wait a day longer.

Returning his attention to his Guild Sister's words,
First Royal Companion Kelahnus schooled his expression to one of polite interest. Inwardly, however, his
mind carefully began to lay plans for the future.

That night, with pressure from his Companion and
the Captain of the Palace Guard, Demnor the Fifth,
forty-first Aristok of Branion, moved from his isolated
west wing suite to the grand Royal apartments in the
central palace. His belongings were moved during his
inspection of the Palace Guard and, knowing his dis-
taste for populated areas, they assumed this was the
cause of his stiff preoccupation. None suspected he
would have rather moved to occupied Tottenham than
the rooms that had been his mother's private domain
all twenty-four years of his life.

As darkness fell, unable to put it off any longer, the
Aristok turned his steps toward the Royal apartments,
two Guards keeping pace behind him.

As he strode down the blue and black tiled hall, the
pairs of formally armored Palace Guard snapped to
attention, their spear butts ringing against the marble
floor. Each one had been personally chosen by Captain
Fletcher, and each one wore the red badge of Gwyneth.
As Demnor made his way past, his mind recalled
their names and deeds with perfect clarity. Daniel
Carrington had nearly died leading a charge into
Alexander DeKathrine's flank, Flewellynne Wren had
lost an eye by a Seer's arrow in the same charge.
Jennet Hawthorne had stood over the unconscious
body of her Guard Sergeant, holding off three Knights
of the Sword, while her brother Denion had braved a
hail of archer fire to come to her aid. Each one had a
story of bravery and honor. Each one stood before his
door now in reward for their loyalty so many years
before and Demnor could feel their pride wrap around

him like a protective cloak. It comforted him, but all too soon, the door opened and he left them, stepping into the hushed anteroom of the Royal wing.

Little had changed. The Chief Clerk's desk sat where it had always sat, the ornate candelabra and blue divan inviting guests to take their ease as they had always done. However, the great picture of the late Aristok was gone and the two Guards who came to attention before the inner door were not ones who had ever stood there before. Demnor smiled.

"Captain."

"My Liege!"

"A cold night to be standing watch."

Captain Fletcher allowed the faintest of smiles to touch her lips. "It's just for the first hour of darkness, Sire. So many of your Guard wanted the honor of standing watch on your first night that we're taking it in hourly turns."

Demnor felt his face grow hot. He opened his mouth, and found himself unable to speak around the sudden lump in his throat. Instead, he merely nodded and turned to her comrade.

"Connie."

"My Liege."

"All is secured?"

"Yes, Sire. His Grace, Kelahnus, awaits you within."

She opened the office door at his gesture, and with one last nod, Demnor passed inside.

The Companion was sitting in one of the thick leather armchairs reading a document. He rose when the Aristok entered. Demnor walked to the cupboard behind the desk and poured himself a drink before speaking.

"Have you been waiting long?"

"Not really. I thought I'd catch up on my politicking while you were away."

Glancing down at the document, Demnor grunted. "Royal Pardons?"

"Well, you did ask me to arrange to have that Fellows boy returned from Fenland."

"Oh, yes."

"You need another Secretary," the Companion admonished. "Dernian will be swamped with new work and I can't run all your special errands for you, you know."

Demnor turned. "You're right." Watching the candlelight dance over the other man's smooth features, he found himself growing aroused. "It's been just the two of us for so long."

Kelahnus came around the desk. Wrapping his arms about the other man's waist, he breathed in the scent of leather and musk, as familiar as his own, and sighed in contentment. "I wish it could be just us, but you have to get another Secretary. Shall I make an appointment with Master Klairius for an Auxiliary Companion? It's going to be terribly lonely in those great big rooms off the Royal suites."

"If you like, but not until after the Guild is clear of all suspicion."

"Of course. I'll go next week. We'll also need an assistant."

"Another Auxiliary?" Demnor asked, unable to be anything but amused at the greedy expansion of Kelahnus' retinue.

"No, actually, I had in mind a promising young fellow I'd like to steal from the Court Historian."

"Terence."

"Yes."

"Ariston won't thank you for it."

"Maybe not, but he won't stand in the way of the boy's advancement."

"Likely not. Anything else while I'm handing out golden coins?"

The Companion smiled at the sarcastic tone. "Well now that you mention it, you could get a valet."

"Why do I need a valet?"

"To promote employment."

"Employment?"

"I've a young fellow in mind . . ."

"We're stalling," Demnor interrupted abruptly.

Kelahnus lay his head against the other man's chest, listening to the overloaded beating of his heart. "We are, aren't we?" he agreed. "But there's really no need. Everything's prepared. All your furniture's in place, the fire's built and the bed's made and ready to unmake."

He gave an overacted leer and Demnor found himself smiling despite his apprehension. Unwinding himself from the other man's embrace, he turned to the small, wooden door he'd never been through.

"I wouldn't even know which passageway to take," he said, bitterness sharpening his words.

The Companion took his hand. "Then let me lead you."

Opening the door, Kelahnus drew his lover inside. He raised his face to Demnor's and as their lips met, the Companion closed the door on the late Aristok's ghost.

They passed quickly through the wide outer chamber, the high, arched ceiling in shadows above them. Portraits of men and women in the changing regalia of nine centuries watched their progress from the walls, the flickering candles touching the crimson dabs in their painted eyes. Demnor averted his own gaze and tried not to feel like a trespassing five-year-old.

The inner chamber was as dark as the outer; windowless, like all the rooms in the Aristok's wing. Here, too, candles cast a flickering light against the walls, illuminating the tapestries which gave the room a false air of open meadows home to happy, wandering couples. The ceiling was a gilt-edged mural by Simon of Branbridge, depicting a vast expanse of stylized green and golden trees. Here and there a bulky shadow hinted at a lurking dragon waiting for the hunting party above the door to drive it into the tapestried fields. Demnor shivered involuntarily, his jaw aching at the memory of his last Hunt. Dropping his gaze, he studied the chamber's furnishings, stilling the superstitious chill that had worked its way up his spine.

Much of the room was empty, depressions in the

lush Ekeptland carpets betraying where cabinets and trunks had recently been removed, but the few pieces of furniture arranged before the fire were his own and the candelabrum standing by the old worn chair was the same one he'd stared at as a child, tracing the leaf-covered branches with his fingers. It was his room and not his room, but maybe, he told himself, as the golden-haired man before him took his hand and led him toward the next doorway, maybe there was enough here to make it his.

Opening the door, Kelahnus drew his lover inside the bedroom beyond. This room was smaller than the others, made for warmth and comfort rather than for show. The fireplace was on the wrong wall, and the wide bay window with its blue velvet window seat was missing, but the bed was the same one they'd shared for five years. Demnor walked to the center of the room and turned in a slow circle. His wardrobe, trunk, and chairs were in the same places as they'd been before. Even the small portrait of himself and the one of his first hounds, Tuffy and Figgy, were hanging in their accustomed places on either side of his arms stand. He touched the painted dogs' memory-familiar muzzles, then turned the picture around to find the locks of brittle fur still tied to the handling wire at the back. Replacing it gently, he turned.

"Thank you."

Kelahnus came to him, his eyes overly bright. "You're welcome," he whispered, the golden cloud of his hair enveloping them both. "Dressing room and bathing room are past that door there, the midden's beyond it. My rooms are to your right."

"Do you like them?"

The Companion smiled. "They're adequately grand and huge. I'll cope."

"Good." Closing his eyes, Demnor breathed in the clean scent of the other man's hair, laying his cheek against his head. Finally Kelahnus gave an impatient wiggle.

"Come to bed."

With a chuckle, Demnor allowed himself to be pulled across the room.

The fire, crackling in the hearth sent different shadows across the blankets, but the lovemaking was the same, and when it was over, the familiar touch and scent of the man he loved lulled the new Sovereign to sleep.

Draped across his chest, Kelahnus listened to Demnor's heartbeat and slowly fell asleep himself to dream of another night in another new bed long ago.

Mean Luchar, high summer 889 DR. Graduation Day at the School of Companions.

Dressed in blue and gold, Kelahnus stood before his mirror while Gabriel brushed his hair for him. Around them, pandemonium reigned, as the Senior Session made ready.

It had been a heady week. The ceremony had taken place that morning, many of his classmates as groggy as he from the revelry the night before. Kelahnus had graduated first in his class, Senior Session Head, and destined to be Companion to Demnor, Prince of Gwyneth, Heir to the Throne of Branion. Kelahnus clenched fists suddenly damp.

They'd seen each other regularly over the last three years. In the company of Master Klairius and Ariston DeLynne, they'd held their courtship to a stilted and formal friendship, frustrating to them both. In between, the Heir had been fighting on the Continent and Kelahnus had been immersed in classes.

His studies had doubled. Politics, diplomacy, espionage, and the killing arts had been drummed into him ever since that first day when he had caught the heart of the Crown Prince and lost his in return. It had been a hard three years, but Kelahnus had never faltered. He *would* win Demnor, and they *would* live happily ever after. All that remained were the formalities.

Gabriel pulled at a tangle, and Kelahnus jumped. His best friend laughed. The Senior Session Second was already in negotiation with the Earl of Richford, so this was to be their last day together. They'd spent an emotional hour in each other's arms last night, before their classmates, jealous of their absence, had found them and pulled them apart. There were many friendships to honor that night.

This morning, sore and tired, he caught Gabriel's eye, and smiled. The School would always be here, like an immortal parent, willing to shelter them again when age had tarnished their luster and blunted their ambition. Then old friends would be together again and new friends made. It was a comfort.

But this morning they stood on the brink of desire. One step and they would be swept into the world of pageants and ceremony, riches and fine living. They were young and beautiful, and life beckoned with all its splendor spread out before them. Gabriel put down the brush, and together they swept from their rooms and down to parade before the assembled nobility in the Audience Hall.

Kelahnus felt as if he danced in a dream, the dream of a fifteen-year-old boy hidden behind a sea of green cry, and far beyond in the bed of an Aristok, the older Companion smiled in his sleep. Demnor sat in the same place beside his mother, and the graduate's heart pounded in his chest as much from fear as from anticipation. The Heir had grown in three years, hardened. The look of bored impatience had been replaced by stony control. He held himself as stiff as a statue, but his eyes were dark fire, seething with a mixture of determination and desire.

Melesandra looked no different, as severe and unbending as she had that day three years before. But behind her, Ariston smiled at him and Kelahnus relaxed. He had come to think of the older man as a friend and he knew that with him there, all would go smoothly.

Too quickly the parade ended and Kelahnus

followed Master Klairius and the Royal Party to the
Guild Head's study for the final negotiations. Behind
him, his classmates filed from the dais to meet with
their prospective Lords and a Guild representative in
the small studies off the Audience Hall.

The negotiations followed with strict formality. Neither Kelahnus nor Demnor spoke much. The Aristok
did little more than nod her agreement, but her presence filled the room, and when she turned her gaze full
on the new Companion, Kelahnus nearly flinched away
from the menace of it. Reminded of a giant snake, the
young man recognized the threat before him and kept
his stance as neutrally respectful as possible. She
would do him no harm, his contract and the influence
of the School protected him, but at that moment the
battle lines were drawn. Melesandra DeMarian, Her
Most Regal and Sacred Majesty and Kelahnus of the
Branion School of Companions became very personal
enemies in a very personal war. It dampened what
should have been a joyful moment.

An hour later he took leave of the place he'd called
home since he was three years old and of the father
who'd loved, trained, and lost him.

He entered a foreign world of three rooms off the
Heir's suite in the west wing of the huge Royal palace.
His teachers had molded him well and his training had
readied him for everything save the loneliness, but Florence was there and Demnor was there, and slowly he
made his life over to his designs.

That first night, the Prince and his Companion had
stood and stared at each other, not believing that they
were finally alone with no secrecy or chaperon between
them. They touched, tentative, then frantic. The past
made them awkward and uncertain in each other's
arms but, when they finally came together, it was good.
The three years of determined struggling and fearful
hoping could not be melted away so quickly, but they
had time. The contract was signed and sealed, and the
Aristok would hold to its statutes.

As Kelahnus lay in a new bed with a new lover and

stared out the window at the night sky, he carefully took stock of the day's events. This was a turning point in his life, and he wanted to remember it. From now on everything would be different, new and frightening, each step made alone without the comfort of a classroom full of friends. But he would take this foreign world and make it his, and he would take the hard and angry man he'd won and work him as one worked stiff clay until he softened and revealed the reckless and loving boy Kelahnus had fallen in love with on that other graduation day.

As dawn dimmed the stars and turned the horizon a pale pink hue, the Prince of Gwyneth's Companion snuggled down beside his Lord and planned the future.

The morning after Demnor moved into the Aristok's suite the first full Privy Council met with trepidation, but there was less upheaval than expected. Demnor's Herald had visited the three ministers he was dismissing and the two whose dismissal was imminent if they didn't show some obvious sign of obeisance. They quickly complied, happy this was the only move taken against them. There was one addition to the Senior Council, Viscount Alerion DeKathrine, and one member whose continued participation was a surprise, Caroline DeLynne, Earl of Buckshire, once favorite of the late Aristok. Demnor did not explain. The assembled did not ask.

The meeting was as short and direct as it had been under Melesandra. Demnor's demands were few. He wanted an army to fight the Heaths and then the Gallians come spring. He wanted funding for that army. Parliament would be held after his coronation. He would have this Parliament's cooperation. Other than that, he was content for the moment to leave things as they were. Having expected far more drastic demands and far more wide-sweeping dismissals, the Privy Council threw their support behind him.

That afternoon the Companion's guild was likewise told that the new Aristok was willing to believe that

Third Companion Alynne had acted alone, but the Head of the Guild was warned that any move to shelter her, if found, would bring the wrath of the Crown down upon their heads.

At Master Klairius' order, Master Elias reluctantly asked the Cousins to stand down. Privately, he counseled his old friend to remain alert, and waited.

Two more Branion Essusiates were released, but they were told not to expect the return of any more. The evidence against them was far too great. The Aristok had not decided their sentence, but the word went out—on the behavior of their congregations rested their fate. The Essusiate community held their breath, praying that the spring fighting would ease the pressure.

Meanwhile the ruling Triarchy prepared to crown the forty-first Vessel of the Living Flame, and the Aristok prepared to send his mother's corpse to the pyre and with it, he hoped, the achingly unfinished feeling in his heart.

15. The Living Flame

The drums beat a solemn march as the funeral procession of Melesandra the Third wove its way through the streets of Branbridge. Nine Senior Priests of the Flame, carrying fifteen red doves, one for every year of Melesandra's reign, followed the casket on its gilded carriage. Nine Knights of the Shield rode in front, nine rode behind. The secular mourners stretched the column for over a mile, and more swelled its ranks at every junction. At its head, the Herald Raventarian carried a scroll from which he proclaimed the long roll of Melesandra's deeds. It was an impressive list.

Branion had never been so strong, its sphere of influence so wide. Melesandra had enlarged its territory, made strong alliances, and opened new trade routes that had brought wealth and prosperity to her island Realm. Reformist Fenland had turned from its Orthodox Essusiate allies with aid from Branion's armies, and bonded strongly with their neighbors Triarctic Danelind and Nordanger with aid from Branion's diplomats. Gallia was beaten, Panisha in confusion; Branion's enemies were weak, and so Branion's people were strong.

Riding just before the casket with its royal burden, Demnor contemplated Raventarian's words. Branion was strong, but for how long? They were at war on two fronts. Once again Heathland had allied with Gallia and Essusiatism to try to tear the Realm in three. In the spring, Gallia's ships would set up a blockade of

Branion's merchant fleet, and Demnor would have to
send the Navy to protect it. Ships would be lost; cargos
of wool would be sent to the bottom of the sea, and the
merchants would begin to howl. The fighting to the
north and east would pull the people from the land and
the crops would suffer and so would the harvest. The
nobility, soundly behind him now, would start to
grumble as the war sucked more and more money from
their pockets. The year 894 would be a hard one.

Squinting through his helm's narrow eye-slit, Demnor surveyed the rain-drenched crowds. Dressed completely in heavy gray wool, helm and cloak muffling
his features, at least he was warm and more or less dry.
Some of his people had been waiting since early morning to see them pass, and there'd been heavy downpours all day. Now, just before dusk, everyone was
soaked. Many wept openly, and the sight of their grief
made his throat ache. The year would be hard, but if
the war were prosecuted smoothly and quickly, 895
would see prosperity again.

Stilling the urge to stretch the cramped muscles in
his legs, a gesture which would have interrupted the
slow rhythm of Challenger's hoofs, Demnor straightened. "We'll win," he whispered to the crowd. "We'll
win, and she'll be laid to rest, and there'll be peace
again."

Blinking away the rain that had somehow managed
to enter his closed helm, the new Aristok swallowed
thickly. *This is a stupid time to become grief stricken,*
he chided himself. *Get a grip on yourself.* The feeling
remained. *If only . . .* He pushed away the thought. The
time for that kind of self-indulgence was past.

Flexing cramped fingers inside gauntlets long gone
stiff from the wet and the cold, he winced as the
knuckle he'd broken in the necropolis scraped against
the leather.

Squinting through the helm's eye-slit again, he
watched Carolania DeFay, the young page who held
the reins of the Funerary Horse, march proudly ahead
of him with a seven-year-old's fierce concentration.

Traditionally the riderless horse was led by the youngest page of the Knights of the Shield, the horse then being gifted to the child. Melesandra's warhorse towered over the girl, but she showed no fear as she led it through the crowded streets.

Before her, in the honorary company of Shield Knights, rode Fionn DeLlewellynne, his grandfather's Funerary Page. Twenty-one years old now, riding beside Jennet DeKathrine who was twenty-four; page for Kalandra the Great only three years before him. Three Funerary Pages in one procession. It reminded Demnor of an old rhyme he'd learned as a child.

One time fate, two times chance, three times more than circumstance.

It told the story of the early years of DeMarian rule where three Aristoks in a row had come to the throne in their minority. It spoke of weakness, instability, and ill omens and made him uneasy that he'd thought of it today of all days.

As the procession turned ponderously south down Harbor Road, he pushed that fear aside also. There would be plenty of time to worry in the winter months ahead.

The torches sputtered in the rain, although they continued to burn as the street opened up to the banks of the Mist River. Before them stood their destination, the Shrine of Flame, the sacred site of renewal.

An unimposing little stone chapel, the Shrine sat alone on a rocky outcropping. The Mist, lapping at its stone base, had left a thick line of green algae behind. Years of smoke had patterned its outside walls in a mottling of gray and black soot. Visitors used to the great cathedrals in Branbridge could not believe that this tiny building represented the heart of Branion's faith. However, for the people gathered at its door, it held an awesome power; the Living Flame, symbol of the Realm's prosperity. As long as it burned, Branion would remain strong.

Braniana DeMarian had brought the Flame down from the mountains of Gwyneth and Gabriel DeMarian, her son, had founded the Order of the Flame to guard it. Through war and famine and four Essusiate Aristoks, the Flame Priests had kept that duty.

Now as the funeral procession made its way toward the site, it was brought to a halt by the upraised palm of Gwynne DeLlewellynne, fifty-third Archpriest and Guardian of the Flame. At her back, twenty-seven Champions of the Order, armored in red enameled plate and wielding the traditional double-bladed axes barred the door. The Champions were Seers as well as the militant arm of the Flame, and their combined power created an almost physical wall between the Shrine and the throng. Their Archpriest raised her voice in challenge.

"Who are you that comes thus accompanied to this sacred place?"

A ripple of disquiet passed through the crowd as Demnor urged Challenger forward to stand before the old woman. To those watching it seemed as if a great shade bent toward the Archpriest, voice booming though an empty helm.

"It is I, Vessel of the Living Flame."

The Archpriest drew herself up, the power of her office giving her a presence as formidable as the spirit she faced.

"And what do you require of us, Vessel?" she asked clearly.

"That you discharge your sacred duty. The Flame has passed, and the rites must be observed."

"By what right do you demand this duty?"

"By right of birth."

"How do you claim this?"

"As the firstborn of the Vessel just passed."

"This right is recognized."

"By right of strength."

"How do you claim this?"

"With a sound body and a clear mind."

"This right is recognized."

"By right of honor."

"How do you claim this?"

"With deeds done by the sword and by the open hand, in Branion and in lands across the sea."

"This right is recognized." She stood aside. "You may pass within our boundaries. Those you brought with you must remain behind as those who followed Braniana were constrained to do."

The Vessel nodded and dismounted. Challenger stood quietly while the Champions opened a path to the Shrine and the Vessel and its Archpriest passed within.

Crossing the threshold was the single most difficult task Demnor had ever performed. Up until now he could pretend that life would continue on unchanged, but here the future could not be denied. To enter and take on the religious mantle of the Living Flame was to accept the awesome responsibility of the Realm's spiritual needs. He felt a second's panic, then crossed over and the familiar peacefulness of centuries of faith settled over him.

Removing his helm, he took a deep breath of the warm, incense tinged air as the Archpriest closed the door. A hush fell over the sanctuary.

It was not a large room. The whitewashed walls held three tiny stained glass windows outlining the deeds of Gabriel DeMarian; a door to the west led to the tower stairs, and one to the east led to the meditation chamber. Walking carefully so his footsteps would not disturb the silence, Demnor crossed to the stone fireplace which dominated the south wall.

High enough to allow a man to stand erect beneath it—had the hearth ever been cold—the Living Flame blazed in its center, the scent of burning yew filling the room. On any other day the fire would have been small. Today, the day of Its rebirth, it slapped against the mantel, throwing cascades of sparks across the hearth and bright orange shadows against the walls. It seemed to beckon to him with ethereal fingers, and Demnor obeyed the compulsion, stripping off his sodden gauntlets and stretching out his hands toward the comforting warmth.

This was the center of the faith he'd strived to be worthy of all his life. The deep symbolism before him pushed him to his knees and he stared into the fire's depths, feeling its power call to him, and his own rise up to meet it. It was a giddy sensation. He felt drunk on it, filled with it, and poised on the brink of some mystical understanding. Somewhere, hidden deep in the dancing spirals lay the answers to all the doubts and questions he'd ever had. They were just beyond his grasp, like Collin's hand eight years ago, but this time he would not allow them to pass. This time he would take them. He stretched out his hand. The firelight danced over his fingers as the flames seemed to take the form of the forty Aristoks before him. Once more he tasted the power of his link with the past. The heat of the flames touched his fingertips and the pain drove him closer to his goal. He could almost reach . . .

A log rolled over in the grate, sending a shower of sparks up the flue. The sparks became his mother's face and he jerked back in alarm the compulsion broken.

"The flames call to the fire in your blood, My Avatar."

Demnor turned a fierce, unfocused gaze on the old woman, the shameful taste of fear in his mouth making him scowl. She met his eyes gravely, her head tipped to one side.

"What do you see in the fire, Most Holy?"

My unworthiness. The unspoken words hung in the air like tendrils of crimson mist. Demnor shrugged carefully, knowing he should confide in her, lay this burden to rest before taking on the greater burden of the Realm, but hesitant to voice the pain that had plagued him all his life. *Say it,* his mind chided, *if only to yourself.* Hesitant to let go of the pain that had been a familiar presence all his life.

The moment to speak came, and then passed.

"What do *you* see?" he asked instead.

The old woman squatted down beside him, her black eyes wide. For a moment it seemed she would pursue her question, then she turned her own gaze to the fire. "I have drunk from the Potion of Truth, as the ritual requires," she answered, "and the prophecy will do your bidding. Ask."

"Tell me, Seer, what do you see?"

The aged priest swayed and slowly her eyes grew cloudy as the trance took her. "War," she answered in a distant voice. "The Thistle and the Dragon fighting the forces of the Triarchy. High overhead the Living Flame stands upon a pinnacle, swaying first this way and then the other. At its back is a mighty army, and in its fiery hands it carries two many-faceted gems, the color of blood. It throws them high into the air. One gem takes wing, becomes a bird of red and white plumage soaring into the sky, and the army transforms into a vast green field as far as the eye can see.

"The other gem falls, spinning down into the abyss to shatter upon the rocks below. The army flows down the mountainside like a mighty avalanche and lays waste to everything in its path." She fell silent.

Eyes narrowed, Demnor waited for her to continue. When she remained silent, he turned his own gaze to the beckoning fire.

"Two gems," he mused. "Two countries, two provinces, two . . . people?"

The Archpriest shook her head. "Two futures." The thick, drug-induced tone of her voice made the hair on the back of his neck stand on end.

"Two futures? You mean two outcomes to the war?"

Dark eyes almost painfully wide, the Archpriest shook her head again. "I can't . . . There is a fork in the road, and each path is clouded by fire. The Living Flame controls which path we shall take, and the gem is the key. Throw it in the air, and it will either transform or shatter."

Demnor frowned. "How do I know which one it will be?"

"You will know, Most Holy, when the time comes."

She sagged suddenly as the vision left her, and without thinking, Demnor caught her before she fell. A

single image of a fiery vortex spinning above two
armies locked in combat, streaked through his mind as
their hands met, and then it faded away.

The Archpriest coughed, her head lolling back and
Demnor stroked her hair absently, feeling the Living
Flame tingle through his fingertips as it responded to
the need of Its highest priest. Staring into the fire
again, he waited for her to recover her strength. The
flames still beckoned, reaching out to the reflected heat
within him, but the strength of the compulsion had subsided. He felt strangely at peace. When she was ready,
he helped her to her feet.

"Are we finished here?"

"Yes, Most Holy."

"Then let the ritual continue."

A murmur went up from the crowd as the new Avatar
appeared in the Shrine's doorway. Dressed now in
scarlet, he faced his people, then turned and strode to
the huge pyre by the riverbank, the late Aristok's casket
secured to the top. He stood for a long time, staring at
the sky, and then knelt by the flat stone at its base.

The Flame Priests began to chant, and as one their
torches were doused. In the sudden darkness, the collective held its breath. For the Realm to remain strong,
the new Avatar must replenish the Living Flame by his
own hand. Most remembered Melesandra's Flaming.
That night had been hot and dry, the fire catching
easily. Tonight the rain had fallen steadily all day and
the wood was soaked. Many closed their eyes, adding
their own will and need to that of their Sovereign's.

One strike, two, and a feeble flame stabbed upward,
faltered, and was caught in the clinging arms of the
tiny pile of moss. Slowly the Avatar added to the
Flame, twig by twig, shielding the vulnerable tongues
of fire with his hands. Finally, when it burned with a
steady strength, he gestured, and the Archpriest passed
him a torch.

It caught easily, and Demnor stood, the burning knot
of hemp at its top reflecting the fiery glow in his eyes.

The crowd remained deathly silent as their new Aristok held the torch high overhead. He stood unmoving for the space of one heartbeat, then turned and hurled it into the pyre. For a moment it seemed to disappear and then the pitch-soaked wood sprang alight. At the same instant the doves were released.

A roar of triumph went up from the gathered as the birds took flight over the bonfire. The Flame was renewed. As the crowd began its noisy celebration, Demnor watched the flames roar around the oaken casket. An hour passed while he stood there, eyes locked on the last moment of Melesandra's earthly presence until, with a great gout of fire and sparks, the center collapsed and the casket fell. Then he turned away. Challenger was brought forward, and he mounted swiftly, stilling the urge to glance over his shoulder at the burning pyre. The past was dead, the future uncertain, and the present concern enough for the moment.

An honorary guard of Shield Knights took their positions around him and, at his signal, they moved out, pushing their way through the pressing crowd to the Sword Tower, and the beginnings of the coronation ritual.

You will know, Most Holy, when the time comes.

As the bells of Bran's Tower tolled twelve, Demnor's head jerked up. He'd been dozing, his head pillowed on his arms, the warmth and quiet of the Sword Tower's inner chapel lulling him to sleep. Shaking his head to clear it, he rose with a groan from before the small altar and glanced around for something to take the stale taste from his mouth. A jug sat on a table by the door and he padded over to it, his bare feet sinking into the fur rug before the fire. The cider was weak and warm, but it helped keep the sleep at bay, so he poured himself a second cupful.

Dressed only in a scarlet tunic, a coronet in the shape of a band of oak leaves on his head, he might have been cold, but the fire kept the closed room warm and stuffy, and all he wanted to do was curl up on the rug and fall asleep.

When you should be praying and meditating on the future, he told himself sternly, *instead of falling asleep like some green acolyte and setting your hair on fire.* A yawn broke through his self-control and he stretched, shaking out the stiffness in his limbs. He needed a distraction. Glancing around the room, his eyes fell on the ancient crest of the Priests of the Sea.

Their Order had built the round inner sanctuary in 543 over the burial site of Bran Bendigeid to guard his remains from the weak Dorian the Priest and his Essusiate Court. The outer tower and fortifications had been finished with monies provided by Kassandra the Fifth and the Knights of the Sword in 700, as part of the celebrations for seven centuries of DeMarian rule.

Demnor's duties as the Defender of the Realm had brought him here often, and in the hushed sanctity of its inner chapel, he'd always felt safe. He'd studied in its libraries, trained in its courtyards, been knighted in its grand hall, and had stood on its topmost battlements, staring out across the city that would one day be his. That today would be his.

A sudden need to see that city again before the final ceremony seized him, and he followed the compulsion. Tonight was the night he communed with the Spirit of the Land, and the Archpriest had told him that wherever his thoughts took him, he should follow.

The two Shield Knights at the door jumped in surprise as their Aristok emerged, but quickly regained their composure when he outlined his wishes. The junior knight raced up the stairs, then returned to announce all was safe above. She moved aside as Demnor climbed the narrow staircase to the upper battlements.

The sky was cloudless, the Mist sparkling magically in the moonlight, and the cool breeze that swept the last vestige of sleep from his mind almost made up for the cold stone against the soles of his feet. Crossing to

the railed turret, he leaned out and stared down at the
Royal City of Branbridge.

All was dark, the revelers and mourners long since
gone to bed. Demnor's gaze swept across the ancient
metropolis, from the farms which butted up against the
east wall, to the rambling citadel of the Knights of the
Bow built into the north; from the very center of town
with its great Cathedral of the Wind where Alexius the
Fair had signed Branbridge's charter in 271, to the
west wall with its permanently opened gate, the grand
merchant homes and residences of the nobility having
long since passed beyond its boundary. Beyond them,
barely visible, stood Bran's Palace itself.

The dark turrets of his home stood out against the
moonlit sky, and Demnor let his mind wander the
familiar rooms and corridors, snatches of the past over-
laying the reality of the present. He passed the training
yards and stables where he'd spent so many happy
hours. He passed the west wing, his for almost a
decade, empty now. His mind traveled the familiar corridors effortlessly, flew unseen down the wide, marble-
tiled hallway in the Royal wing, to alight on the
sleeping face of the young man who lay waiting for all
the pageantry and ceremony to give him back the man
he loved.

The Companion's face would be peaceful, Demnor
imagined, looking as smooth and young as the night
they'd first lain together on a cloak spread over the
crumbling stones of a forgotten tower. In his mind's
eye Kelahnus awoke, smiling the sleepy, seductive
smile that Demnor knew so well; the smile that always
slept behind the Companion's every move, behind the
insightful and always diplomatically phrased commen-
tary on the day's events, behind the subtle manipulations and the not so subtle proddings; a gentle smile,
one that was ready to slip forward after every victory to
make you forget he'd just arranged your life as surely
as a general arranges a campaign. Demnor laughed quietly. He wondered what Kelahnus would make of the

Archpriest's vision and what response he would suggest to his Lord.

Demnor's mind supplied the answer from a hundred such conversations. The Companion would grow
thoughtful, his face assuming that careful look he
always wore when their conversation touched on the
religious. He would ask for the Archpriest's exact
words and frown when Demnor answered carelessly
that he could not remember them, but he would wait,
more or less patiently, for his Lord to drag them up
from memory and then examine each detail, one by
one. The Thistle and the Dragon, easy enough. Heathland and Gallia. And the Flame with two gems, one
destined for glory, the other for disaster. Demnor
cocked his head to one side in unconscious imitation of
his youngest sister, imagining some cryptic, slightly
sarcastic remark Kelahnus would not have been able to
help making. And there would be that smile again,
appearing for just a moment before the younger man
became serious once more. The war, the army poised
on some dramatic errand, a crucial decision involving
the risk of something precious. Demnor would suggest Heathland, for if the Heathland Provinces weren't
precious, what was, and the Companion would frown
again and answer caustically, his life maybe, and the
smile would dim and he would press him to take care,
his expression young and vulnerable. Demnor sighed.

You will know, Most Holy, when the time comes.

Kissing his lover gently in his thoughts, Demnor set
this line of musing aside and returned his gaze to the
darkened city below. To the south, on the banks of
the River Mist the funeral pyre still glowed sullenly.
He wondered if his mother's corpse had been fully
consumed yet, or if some lingering spirit remained,
unburned, like a statue's leaden heart in a children's
story; some unseeable, half-felt presence lurking just
beyond his vision that would have him looking over his
shoulder for the rest of his life.

He shivered, imagining that presence rising from the
ashes of the pyre, a wraithlike specter weaving its way

through the empty streets to scale the Sword Tower's ancient walls.

Leaning over the edge, he squinted into the darkness, the red glow of the pyre burning a faint afterglow before his eyes. He could almost see something moving just beyond his vision. He leaned farther out. The railing shifted suddenly under the pressure of his hands and he drew back with a curse.

The only specter you face is the specter of plunging to your death, idiot, he told himself sharply. *Time to go back.*

Descending the stairs more quickly than he'd gone up them, he nodded distractedly to his guards and reentered the chapel. Pouring himself another cupful of cider, he carried it back to the altar, sinking his feet into the rug with a sigh, and calling himself a fool while he waited for his heartbeat to return to normal. The embarrassment of jumping at night shadows finally eased, and he knelt once more, staring ruefully into the depths of the small candle on the altar top. In less than one hour they would come for him, and the day he had dreamed of all his life would finally arrive. So why did he feel so . . . he studied the emotion curiously . . . sad?

Because you're a contrary fool.

Most probably. With a sigh, he returned his attention to prayer, laying his head on his clasped hands. Fighting off the drowsiness which seemed to rise up as soon as his head was bent, he concentrated on the Living Flame.

An hour later there was a knock at the door, and Alerion, dressed in the traditional cream-colored coronation livery, entered the sanctuary. The communal ritual required one bodyguard trusted beyond all doubt, and the Viscount's surprise had quickly changed to embarrassment when Demnor had made his request the day before, but he'd accepted. Now the two cousins stared at each other, uncertain of how to begin. Finally, Alerion shook himself.

"It's time," he said simply. Demnor nodded.

Breakfast was hard bread made with raisins and spices, and cold water tasting of some bitter herb. Demnor ate what he could, but his stomach was too tight in anticipation of the ritual to come to make much of a meal of it. Alerion made no comment, simply wrapped the last of the bread in a handkerchief to take with them.

The tower was quiet as the new Sovereign and his bodyguard descended the worn steps to the vault deep beneath the cellars. It was cool and dark, the centuries of sanctity hovering in the air like a veil of mist. Demnor breathed deeply, letting it sink in through his pores and settle over his mind. At the bottom of the stairs Gwynne DeLlewellynne and Alexander DeKathrine awaited.

The Hierarchpriest showed no sign of the tensions between them, merely bowed and indicated the steaming bath in the center of the room. With Alerion's aid, Demnor stripped quickly and eased in until the water covered him to the neck.

The deep warmth and soothing scent of herbs relaxed him as it was meant to. Closing his eyes, he cleared his mind, moving down into a state of peace as was required. It wasn't a state he was much familiar with, and it was some time before his churning thoughts stilled. Finally, when his fingers were beginning to wrinkle, he rose and allowed Alerion to help him from the water.

The second bath, an open well in the center of the vault, was some paces away and the cold, moist air pulled wisps of steam from his body as he walked. The first bath was supposed to bring peace of mind, the second, receptiveness to the Spirit of Sovereignty. Sitting on its crumbling, moss-covered side, Demnor glanced down into its murky depths, then dropped in.

Sharp, icy water crackled along his limbs, like a great hand had smacked him hard. It tore an involuntary gasp from his lips as his head broke the surface, aching from the sudden cold. Nothing in the ritual

demanded he remain long in the well and as quickly as
he'd entered, he left. Alerion wrapped him in a heavy
woolen blanket and drew him into a small room where
a fire awaited.

Numbly, Demnor allowed his cousin to dry, shave,
and dress him, his perception knocked askew by his icy
plunge. The ritual garb was warm and soft, however,
and soon a haze as peaceful as before settled over him
as he ran his hands down the unfamiliar clothing.

Soft cream-colored undertunic and breeches, tan kid
boots, laced high with strips of hide and a heavy,
cream-colored sheepskin surcoat, cloak, and heavy kid
gloves. Demnor stared at his reflection in the mirror
Alerion held out, his expression wondering. His face
swam above the cloak's mantle, strangely innocent in
its cream-colored halo. He'd never worn such a color
before and it stripped the years from his face, leaving
him young and unmarked by the world. His eyes
widened as a boy, his broad face open and trusting,
stared back at him, gray, fire-touched eyes filled with
curiosity. A memory surfaced for an instant, bringing a
sense of joyful discovery with it. He felt the ghost of a
man's hand on his shoulder, and then it was gone,
leaving such an ache of loneliness behind that he
almost sobbed aloud.

When he turned, Alerion was moving away to accept
a heavy, metal bowl from the Archpriest. Kneeling
before the Aristok, his cousin held it out.

Demnor accepted it.

A sharp, narcotic scent wafted up to him, and the
deep breath he took over the bowl made his head spin.
The Potion of Sovereignty. Only the Herbalists of the
Flame knew the secret of its brewing, although Ariston
had made some shrewd guesses, based on information
gleaned from three previous Aristoks.

*"It's distilled in part from holly juice and birch sap,
I believe, Majesty, with possibly hemlock or mistletoe
added, maybe even some belladonna, that sort of
thing."*

"Aren't they poisonous?"

"Oh, yes. In minute doses, however, they produce a state most receptive to visions and hallucinations, without actually causing death."

"All together, they must pack quite a punch."

"Indeed, Majesty. The Potion of Sovereignty is supposed to draw you into communion with the Land so that you might rule wisely and well. Your mother, the late Aristok, spoke of her visions with me afterward, though you needn't."

Ariston's thin face had been alight with hopeful curiosity, and the new Aristok had promised to consider it after the ceremony. The Historian had accepted this concession with easy grace. Like Kassandra, he knew Demnor usually gave in to his requests and was content to wait.

Alerion stirred beside him. It was time. Raising the bowl to his lips, Demnor allowed himself an instant's hesitation, to mark the ritual in his memory, then drank.

The brew was bitter and hot and filled with tiny bits of bark and leaves. His first reaction was to choke and spit the vile stuff out, but he forced himself to swallow it, mouthful by mouthful, until the bowl was empty.

When he lowered it, his limbs felt heavy, as if the entire potion had filled his body with lead. He found himself unsteady on his feet and would have fallen if Alerion had not thrown out a hand to catch him. After a minute, his cousin took his arm and led him through the vault and back up the stairs.

By the time they reached a small inner courtyard, Demnor was reeling. Putting his Sovereign's hand on the trunk of the young oak tree in its center, Alerion withdrew.

One arm wrapped around the tree to keep upright, Demnor gazed blearily around him. His eyes swept right, left, and up into the great canopy of branches above his head. They spun sideways and he fell to land heavily on a gnarled root. After a minute, he struggled to sit until his back was pressed against the tree. That

was better. The world stayed in its place more easily
from down here. He looked up again.

With their leaves the color of worn copper, the great
oaken branches resembled a huge basket turned upside
down. Demnor twisted his head, imagining lying in
their protective arms, swaying back and forth in the
wind's embrace. Long ago, he'd climbed a tree in
Collin's Park and pretended he was a wood spirit,
soaring through the air to alight on the great limbs and
build a nest of branches and leaves. It was a happy
memory and it made him smile drowsily, only the cold,
late night air on his cheeks keeping him from falling asleep. But he couldn't sleep. He had to meditate,
or communicate or . . . something. With a sigh, he
dropped his gaze.

The courtyard was small, shrubs and flowers planted
about the walls to give it a gardenlike feel. Shadows
danced around him in the moonlight, figures merging
and changing into other figures until they converged
into the shape of a great, red fire-wolf. Demnor
watched it, uncomprehendingly, for a long time. The
creature sat as still as stone until it raised its shaggy
head and its flaming eyes stared into his. The beast
rose and slowly padded forward.

A surge of panic took hold of him, and he tried to
scramble to his feet, groping for a sword that wasn't
there, but the potion held his limbs immobile and he
could only watch as the animal approached.

It passed through the shrubbery like a ghost. With
each step it grew larger until the twin suns of its eyes
blotted out all other sights. Unable to look away,
Demnor found himself falling into their depths.

The wind stirred, whipping at his clothing. Hair
slapped against his face bringing tears to his eyes and
dimming the brilliant, crimson light. Around him
voices rose in a confused cacophony of sounds like the
shrieking of banshees in a storm. He pressed his hands
to his ears and squeezed his eyes shut, but the terrible
howling drove through his fingers and made his head

ache. Finally he rose, leaving the security of his bed to drive away the voices himself. He would make them stop. He was a Prince. He would get Randolf, the guard before his door, to help him, now that his nurse Marri was gone.

He left his rooms, opening the door quietly so as not to startle the man. The alcove before him was empty.

The storm lifted the edges of the tapestries from the walls of Migard Castle, sending icy wafts of air swirling about him, as he stood, uncertain of what to do. Randolf was supposed to be there. Randolf was *always* there. But Marri had always been there, too. Maybe the storm had taken them both away. His heart began to pound in his chest. Maybe it had killed them, like someone had killed Great Uncle Amedeus. That had been . . . yesterday. Yesterday when everyone had screamed and wept and Grandfather had flown into such a terrible rage that Randolf had come and taken him away.

Demnor didn't really understand what killed meant, but when Randolf had said that Great Uncle was gone and would never, ever come back, he had cried, too. A lot of people had gone away—Her Majesty, and Great Uncle and Marri and now Randolf.

Hopping from foot to foot, he thought about going back to bed, but shook his head. Randolf was *his* guard, like Snowfoot was *his* pony. You took care of what was yours; Great Uncle had said so. Pulling his robe more tightly around him, the five-year-old Heir Apparent set off determinedly down the corridor, heading for the stairs and the main floor of the Gallian Castle.

The halls were empty and quiet. He didn't dare go to his mother's apartments, so he made for the more populated south wing. Chewing at his lower lip uncertainly, he finally paused before Alexander DeKathrine's door. His second cousin had spent a lot of time with him lately and had told him he could come to him whenever he needed him.

There was no answer to his knock.

Maybe *everyone* had gone away, the young Prince thought suddenly. But no, he was sure he could hear voices screaming over the noise of the storm, so he made himself turn and walk toward the noise, the slap of his bare feet muffled by the howling of the wind.

The screaming grew louder, and just before he turned into a wide junction he heard the clash of steel. Creeping forward, he peered around the corner.

People battled up and down the corridors, a group of light blue-and-gray-clad nobles charging into his company of Palace Guard. The Guard fought them off with pike and halberd and Demnor saw one man skewered, the point of the weapon plunging out through his back. He fell, blood spilling from his mouth and onto the floor already soaked with gore.

The Prince's eyes went wide with shock. He began to tremble, and when a Guard he knew skidded on the slippery stone and a mace crashed down on her head to split her face into a pulpy mash, he screamed and ran forward.

The world took on a fuzzy, dreamlike quality. People stopped and stared, some made a grab for him as he ran, others cried out in surprise, some with voices he recognized.

"The Heir Apparent!"

"By the Flames, Prince Demnor!"

"Catch him someone, before he gets killed!"

That stopped him in midflight. Killed, like Her Majesty Kalandra and Great Uncle Amedeus. He gazed about him in confusion, then looked down at the ruined visage of the dead woman. He screamed. And kept on screaming, even after Randolf, ordered to the castle's defense against the attacking DeSandras with the rest of the Guard, caught him up in his arms.

The man held him while he thrashed and cried out hysterically. The others moved to flank their fellow and his precious cargo as the DeSandras, seeing an advantage, made a wild charge toward them. One of his protectors went down, a great wound in his neck spurting blood into the air. An angry roar rose up from

the ranks of Palace Guards and they flung themselves
into the fray. Unable to pass, Randolf crouched amid
the legs of those before him, arms wrapped protectively around the boy. Demnor watched, mesmerized,
as his Guard slaughtered every enemy in the junction,
running through those that fled down the halls. When it
was over, Randolf rose, Demnor's arms wrapped
tightly around his neck.

He whispered soothing phrases to the little Prince as
the others, gore splattered and wild-eyed, crowded
around him to assure themselves that their Royal charge
was safe. They seemed so frightened that Demnor
found himself reaching out, patting the smooth and
rough cheeks alike, reassuring them in his piping voice
that all was well.

When the madness left their eyes, they moved away.
Then a tremor ran through them.

"The Heir, Prince Melesandra!"

"Quick, Randi, get the boy away, or she'll hang us
all!"

Demnor felt the fear take his heart and squeeze. Her
Highness would be angry, and she would punish him.
He struggled to free himself from Randolf's grip and
run, just as the guard turned, as terrified as he, and
dived down a side passageway. The boy could feel the
man's own fear and he ceased his struggles and
remained still as Randolf hurried along.

They were a long time getting back to his rooms
through the cold, dark corridors. Often Randolf would
pause, glancing fearfully around the corner before
moving on. Demnor said nothing, merely held tight to
his protector and closed his eyes. Finally they reached
his rooms.

Randolf searched them carefully, and it was only
when he was certain they were empty that he put the
sleepy-eyed child back into bed. Bending down, he
kissed the tiny, bloodstained fingers, then slipped out.
Demnor stared into the darkness for a long time,
straining to catch the sounds that meant Her Highness
or the DeSandras were approaching. Finally at dawn,

worn out, he slept, the image of his Guard standing like a protecting wall around him.

The fire-wolf's crimson eyes receded and its visage twisted until it became the Royal symbol embroidered into the curtains of his grandfather's inner chamber. He stared at it, willing himself not to see the man who lay, dying and diseased on the bed before him. But his mother held his shoulder in a death grip and forced the reluctant boy to the bedside. Breathing shallowly through his mouth, the eight-year-old Prince looked down.

Quinton the Second lay thrashing deliriously, his head beating on the silk pillows. Blood crusted on his lips where his teeth had torn them and his eyes were glassy and unfocused. His neck was horribly swollen and bruised and the ear on his left side was black and scabrous, clear ooze seeping out from cracks in the skin. Demnor swallowed convulsively, unable now to take his eyes from the man who had filled his young life with fear and nightmares ever since he could remember.

Quinton DeMarian had ruled the land with an iron hand for just over three years when an infection in his ear had achieved what no enemy or weapon could have done. Within a fortnight he was bedridden, racked by pain and delirium. His condition deteriorated rapidly. Holding its collective breath the country waited for its second Aristok in a decade to die.

Melesandra split her time between Council and her father's bedside. Still ill herself from the birth of Demnor's twin brothers, her face was gray with fatigue, but her fire-filled green eyes glittered with mad resolve. If her father was to fight this final battle, he would not fight it alone. She had called in the greatest physicians in the Realm, but his fate was written. When the Archpriest of the Flame told her he would die before the dawn, she took her firstborn to his bedside and remained there.

The hours ticked by. Demnor and Melesandra stood, unmoving, while, howling and raving, Quinton wrestled with the Shadow Catcher. As the bells tolled four, he suddenly screamed his brother's name and bolted upright. One desiccated hand shot out and, grabbing Demnor by the tunic, he dragged his head down. The dying Aristok stared into his grandson's face, expression contorted with mad terror.

"Amedeus! Amedeus, you traitorous hound! Why do you stand there so, like a statue, waiting for me to die? Answer me, burn you! Come to take me, have you? Come to drag me down to death with you? Well, I won't go! Do you hear me, you betraying weakling? I won't go!"

Spittle sprayed the young Prince across the face, and he cringed back from the shouted words, but Quinton's grip never slackened.

"You died! You! You left me and ran to death with our mother! The throne is mine now, and I'll never give it back. Do you hear me, Brother? You'll never take it back! I'll give it to Anda in my sweet time! My issue, not yours, mine! Mine was the strongest seed! Yours withered on the vine!

"Take your face away, boy! Take it away! Why do you mock at me with that face, with his face! You're not mine! You're his!

"How could you do this to me, Anda? How could you take the ghost of my brother in your arms and bear a boy with his face! I won't have it! *My* seed shall rule!"

His grip suddenly slackened and Demnor had to throw his hand out to keep from falling onto the wasted figure below. His fingers came away red. Stumbling away, he barely heard his mother hiss at the dying Aristok.

"*He* is your issue, old man. *My* son. His face means nothing. He has your strength, your power, as I do."

Her father thrashed about, tearing at his lips again. "No! He has my brother in him! Amedeus wants my throne, and he'll take it through him!"

"Then I'll deny it to him! I've killed the ghost of him

in the boy! I drove out the weakness and kept him strong. *I* have done this. He *shall* be strong!"

Quinton screamed once more, then grew still. The smell of feces filled the room and Demnor saw his mother's face twitch, then harden. She turned and left, looking neither left nor right.

The eyes of the embroidered fire-wolf blazed and Demnor, the man, stood over his grandfather's death-bed. He looked down at the wasted form dispassion-ately. Beside him, Demnor the child stood shaking his head from side to side and then turned away. The two seemed to stare at each other for a long time. Demnor saw the terror he'd felt all those years ago, saw a spin ning vortex of power pass like a ghostly shadow between them, and then he stood alone in the royal chamber.

It looked much as it had before, although something told him it was not the same. The shadowed figure in the bed was not his grandfather, and with growing horror, he realized he was drawing inexorably nearer. Panic seized him and he cried out, fighting the vision with all his strength. He would not look, he would not see the poison-tortured features below him.

Pressure built behind his eyes as the Living Flame rose with the struggle. The scene began to shift and voices began to scream and babble all around him. He heard his brother Marsellus cry out in pain, heard his sister's raging howl of denial. Someone, somewhere was crying in deep, grief-stricken sobs, and beneath it all he heard his mother's voice, ragged and harsh with dying, raging in fury.

He clapped his hands to his ears, much as he'd done all those years ago, but the voices continued to rise and he realized they were in his mind. One voice he almost knew whispered one short word, and the voices sud-denly went silent. The voice spoke again. It whispered, "Die," and he saw a form bend over the bed.

"No!"

He tried to jerk forward, but now the vision held him frozen in place while Melesandra's murder played out before him. He saw her fight to breathe, fight to spew the poison from her system. He saw the final recognition of defeat in her eyes, and the stark terror of it nearly made him faint. Finally the murderer withdrew and Demnor stood alone, staring down at a dying woman.

The Aristok's eyes were wide, her lips torn and bloody. She coughed suddenly, spewing vomit across the pillow, and then grew still. Demnor choked, tried to turn away, but was unable to move. Slowly the fire in his mother's eyes dimmed and his own vision grew hot. When he thought it was finally over, she stirred again, her eyes widening impossibly. They seemed to stare into his, recognition widening them still further. Her lips moved, whispered his name, and the vision blurred.

Demnor cried out, reached for her, and found himself crouched beside the oak tree, his fingers digging into the bark. Releasing it, he buried his face in his hand and wept.

Some time later, his back pressed against its trunk once more, he scrubbed at his face and coughed. The vestige of his visions hovered at the back of his mind, making him shiver, but he knew this was not the time to question them. He coughed again. By all the hearths in the Realm, he was tired. He felt like he'd been tired all his life. He glanced around the courtyard.

Dew covered the plants, sparkling in the early morning sun. As he watched, a late starling alighted on the ground before him, pulled something from the grass, and flew away. He smiled sadly, wishing he could fly away, too, but knowing he could not, and would not, even if he was able to.

Long live Demnor the Fifth, he thought. Long and happily ever after? He nodded to himself. The morning was bright and cool, and everything seemed possible all of a sudden, despite the goulish character of his visions. Using the tree for support, he got carefully to his feet.

"Alerion."

His cousin emerged from the courtyard doorway, his face drawn and tired, a testament to his own sleepless night. When the Aristok gestured, he came forward. Something in Demnor's face made him bow his head, and when he looked up, his Royal cousin had reached out his hand. Alerion took it.

They didn't speak, but a new understanding passed between them as the years of misunderstanding melted and faded away.

The crowd roared its approval as its new Aristok, flanked by the eight Archpriests of the Land, stepped from the pavilion wearing only a circlet of mistletoe. As his bare feet touched the first of the boughs strewn along his path, the trumpets sounded and Gwynne DeLlewellynne called out, "Behold, your Sovereign comes! Let all see that he is whole and strong!"

The crowd cheered as the Royal Procession began the Walk of Recognition, a twisting, three-hundred-yard journey on the grounds of the Holy Triarchy Cathedral; through the Branion multitude, to the open altar and the gathered Rulers of the Triarctic nations.

At the Head of the Procession, The Archpriest of the Flame marched, carrying Tre-Macha, the Sword of Justice. Behind her came the Archpriests of the Sea and Wind, bearing across their open palms, the Scepters of Truth and Wisdom. Demnor walked in the center, with Quindara, as the new Archpriest of the Shield, following, carrying Badb-Dwynwed, the blunt-bladed Sword of Mercy. Behind marched the Archpriests of the Lance and Bow with the Royal Regalia and Insignia. Finally, Alexander DeKathrine, Hierarch-priest of Cannonshire, dressed in formal enlaquered armor, carried Coir-Cairenn-Nemain, the great two-handed Sword of Sovereignty, point held high above his head and Ariston DeLynne, Archpriest of the Oaks, bore the carved DeMarian Crown upon a blue satin cushion.

The crowd chanted Demnor's name, threw seeds and nuts in his wake, and stretched out their hands to touch him as he passed. This time the Living Flame was content to ride the crest of their worship, only the flame-washed eyes of its Avatar betraying its presence.

Standing in a crowd of nobility, First Royal Companion Kelahnus sighed in appreciation as Tania leaned over to whisper in his ear.

"My, he is a perfect specimen, isn't he?"

"Yes," he agreed, "in every respect."

"Hm. He does seem a trifle . . . small though."

"You try walking naked in the middle of Mean Damhar and see what shrivels up on you." Kelahnus' voice was indignant and Tania laughed.

"If you joined me, I might take you up on that challenge." Her breath was warm on his neck as she pressed herself against him. Already excited by the sight of his Lord, Kelahnus swallowed. "Later," he murmured, his voice slightly ragged.

Tania laughed.

The crowd roared. Demnor was halfway to the altar now, surrounded by people on all sides. Hands reached out, touched, then passed him on to new hands. The new Aristok carried himself easily this time, allowing the crowd to dictate his movements and his speed. The cold wind raised goose bumps across his body though he didn't shiver. The people murmured their appreciation. Only Kelahnus saw the spark of fear in Demnor's eyes, and realized how much control it took for his reticent Lord to allow so many unfamiliar people to get so close to him.

The Companion felt a twinge of fear in his own belly. So many hands. Any one of which could be holding a dagger.

Demnor left the crowd, his relief only obvious to his Companion, and began the last few yards to the altar. Here there were less people, but the danger was no less great. The highest nobility of the land bowed before their Aristok, then they, too, reached out to touch him on the arm or wrist.

He paused before Kelahnus. Lifting his hand slowly, the Royal Companion brushed his fingertip along the other man's face, caressing the haggard line of his cheek, then raised them to his own lips. Demnor smiled and a sigh went through the crowd. He moved on.

Standing beside King Brand of Eireon and Queen Hildegard of Danelind, Isolde caught her breath as Demnor approached them. This was the first time she'd seen him fully naked in the light of day and she had to admit, she liked what she saw.

The Aristok was a big man, six feet four inches tall, and heavily muscled. His auburn hair, spreading across his shoulders, flashed in the sunlight. Her eyes dropped down, past the wisps of flame on his chest, to his manhood in its wreath of ruddy curls. Demnor paused before her and with an evil twinkle in her eye, Isolde reached down for a light touch of intimacy. The only blush of the day spreading across Demnor's face brought a whoop of laughter from the Eireon King and a shout of appreciation from the nearby throng. He moved on quickly, only stopping when he faced the altar.

The coronation stone was a wide, natural rock formation, thrusting some four feet up from the ground. In its center, a small cavity held a pool of water, collected that night. The eight Archpriests of the Land took their places and Demnor turned to face them. The crowd grew still.

Three pages came forward to clothe the Aristok in red and turn him toward the north. The Archpriests of the Flame and Shield moved to flank him, holding Badb-Dwynwed and Tre-Macha above his head.

"May you reign with justice and mercy."

The swords were then presented to him and Demnor laid his left hand on the flat of Tre-Macha while brushing the Blade of Mercy with his lips.

When he straightened, they stepped aside and the pages turned him to the west. The Archpriests of the Sea and Wind copied the others' stance, holding the scepters high, the ends crossed above their Sovereign's head.

"May knowledge and wisdom guide your footsteps always."

Grasping each polished, wooden stave above their leather bound grips, Demnor raised his head. After a moment he released them, and the two Archpriests also moved aside.

The pages then turned him to the south and Alexander DeKathrine knelt and held out Coir-Cairenn-Nemain in its sheath. Demnor accepted it and allowed the pages to buckle it around his waist.

"May your reign see an abundance of prosperity and victory," the Hierarchpriest intoned. Demnor caught his eye and held it. Alexander bowed and withdrew.

Again the pages turned the Aristok until he faced the east and the Archpriests of the Bow and Lance. The one placed the great Seal of Branion and the Ruby of Flame on his fingers, rings he'd worn already, but had relinquished into the Archpriest's keeping for this ceremony. The other wrapped him in the DeMarian Plaide and pinned it at the shoulder. Then she held out the Dagger of Divine Right.

Demnor accepted it. He held it up in the air so that the blade caught the light, then dropped the point and drew a thin line along the back of his right hand. Catching the few drops of blood in a tiny cup, the Archpriest of the Lance mingled it with the water of the altar. She then dipped in the cup and presented it to Demnor. As he drank, they spoke.

"May you live in harmony with the needs of the Land."

When he faced the altar once more, Ariston approached and removing the crown of mistletoe from his brow, he dipped it in the altar's cavity and shook the droplets out onto his Sovereign's head and across his face and chest.

"May you reign in truth, in law, and in victory. May you reign in prosperity, in righteousness, and in peace. May you reign in strength, in wisdom, and in knowledge."

He then held out the Crown of Sovereignty. The new Aristok accepted the carved wooden helm of flames and oak leaves and raised it above his head.

Before him, the crowd was as silent as stone.

"I, Demnor the Fifth of the House of DeMarian, forty-first Aristok of Branion, Heathland, Kormandeaux and Aquilliard, Gaspellier, Poitenne, Roland, and the Columbas do swear to defend, uphold and preserve the faith, to ensure peace and order in the land and to assure mercy and justice in all my judgments, and may the Living Flame abandon me if I break these my sacred oaths."

He placed the crown upon his head, stilling the superstitious chill the words caused to play down his spine.

The throng began to cheer, but quickly grew silent as the DeKathrine family, led by the Hierarchpriest, gathered and knelt as a group before their ruler. Demnor held out his hand, and Isolde, also dressed in red, rose and took it. They turned to face the crowd.

"Here, on the day of my Recognition and Acceptance by the Land, I do accept Isolde, of the House DeKathrine, Earl of Essendale, as my wife and Consort, and do name her Duke of Aquilliard.

Isolde bowed. "I, Isolde, Duke of Aquilliard, Earl of Essendale, do accept Demnor of the House of DeMarian as my husband. And as a Knight of the Bow, I do pledge my loyalty to his name and my arm to his service."

With a beaming smile, Ariston placed the Consort's Crown on Isolde's head, then clasped their joined hands in his.

"May you find happiness and love in your union and pass your good fortune on to the Land."

The crowd went wild. With the Archpriests in front, the royal couple passed through the cheering mass of people to the twin thrones at the eastern end of the clearing. Here they were served cider and cakes as Demnor prepared to accept the homage of the Peers of the Realm.

The first to kneel before him to swear the public oath of loyalty was his sister, the Duke of Yorbourne, her face an unreadable mask. She swore her oath of fealty to the new ruler, kissed the flat of the Sword of Sovereignty, then rose.

Demnor stood.

"As next in line, Prince Quindara, Duke of Yorbourne and Archpriest of the Shield, we name you Defender of the Realm, until such time as we produce an Heir and it is old enough to take on such duties." He handed her Defender with only a small twinge of loss and Quindara kissed the pommel before sheathing it.

She rose and met the Aristok's eye. The look that passed between them was formal, but nonconfrontational. "I will do my duty always to the Land and to the Crown," she whispered, her green eyes blazing.

"I never doubted it," Demnor returned as just quietly.

The Duke of Yorbourne bowed stiffly, then moved aside to allow her brothers Atreus and Marsellus to come before the Aristok.

They came together as they always had, the one supporting the other. The Duke of Kempston's eyes were deeply sunken, his voice ragged and slurred. He whispered his oath after his twin's, unable to meet his Sovereign's eyes and Demnor gestured to Agrippa, hovering in the wings, to help him rise.

The next to come before him was his sister Kassandra.

Dressed in formal court attire, the young Duke of Clarfield's face was wondering as she knelt before her brother. Too young to take the oath of fealty, she'd been both surprised and suspicious when Ariston had told her she was to follow the twins at the oath swearing. Now, as she knelt, she looked trustingly up at her beloved older brother as he smiled down at her. The twinkle in his eyes made her frown for just an instant, and then he was standing, reaching out to place his hand upon her head.

"On this day we take our sister Kassandra as our squire, calling upon her to serve us and learn the art of war under our care. Will you do so?"

"I swear it!" she answered loudly, causing King Brand to grin widely and poke his own squire in the ribs.

Demnor nodded solemnly. "Then rise, My Duke of
Clarfield, and be entered into the annals of the Sword
Knights as an initiate."

She obeyed, her young face aglow. As she left the
dais, she stripped off her golden belt and flung it into
the crowd. Smiling, Demnor then turned his attention
to the waiting throng.

One by one the nobility of the Realm swore their
oaths and received such positions as they were entitled
to from the hands of their new patron. Then the Triarctic Rulers of Nordanger, Storvicholm and Sorlandy
came forward to pledge their covenant to their High
Avatar.

Finally, King Brand approached, and Demnor rose to
meet him. The two Island Rulers exchanged the kiss of
friendship, pledging their alliance once more and then
parted. Queen Hildegard came forward next to seal the
friendship of Branion and its ancient parent, Danelind,
offering service under Triarchy law and accepting it for
the DeMarian held Dukedom of the Columbas Islands.

When they drew apart, the trumpets sounded and the
people began to cheer. Demnor took Isolde's hand, and
the two of them led the way inside the cathedral.

Holy Triarchy was the religious center of the Triarctic Faith, where the three minor Aspects joined in
one nexus of potential. It was said that when the active
Aspect, Flame joined with them on holy days, miracles
happened. Begun by Atreus III in 657, and finished by
Kassandra VI one hundred years later, it rivaled Bran's
Palace in beauty. The great, painted ceiling in the main
sanctuary, masterpiece of Essusiate born, Simon of
Branbridge, was considered one of the greatest works
of art in the world. After seating Isolde in the front
pew, Demnor strode down the wide center aisle to the
huge Pillar of Flame.

Sculpted of multihued marble, the pillar reached to
the top of the roof and its base was as wide as nine
people stretched hand to hand. The stone floor around
it was worn smooth and dipped in parts from the years

of kneeling worshipers seeking healing. Demnor also knelt a moment in silent reflection while the cathedral filled with people.

As the bells of the city rang twelve, Demnor sang the High Sabat Mass before a crowd of three thousand; more than he'd ever seen gathered together for worship before in his life. Hundreds more crowded into the courtyard outside. The charged potential was so strong, it sizzled through his nerves like fire.

At the final blessing nine Seer Flame Priests channeled the people's raw belief through themselves and into their Avatar. The Living Flame caught the power of their faith and exploded upward toward a great copper dish high above the altar. As the Sacred Oil took fire and leaped toward the ceiling, three of the priests collapsed and Demnor had to grab his head to keep it from splitting apart. A murmur of appreciation went through the crowd of worshipers. It was a good sign.

When Demnor was able, the Royal Procession formed once more, the Aristok leading the way out. The Royal carriage was waiting and Demnor and Isolde were ushered inside for the ride back to Bran's Palace for the banquet. Quickly the Procession formed around them.

Demnor's personal Herald rode in front, carrying the Royal standard. Half the Order of the Shield rode next, surrounding the Aristok's carriage. The rest guarded the carriage of the Royal Dukes of Lochsbridge, Kempston, and Clarfield. The coaches of the Great Orders of Branion followed, and behind them came the nobility of the Realm.

As the sun climbed high over the capital city, the streets along the route were jammed with people come to see their new Sovereign. The same people who'd reveled through the streets last night, the crowd was somewhat subdued this afternoon, although the roar of their approval still ebbed and flowed as the Procession left the cathedral grounds. As it passed beyond the gates of Bran's Palace, the crowd surged behind them, cheering and shouting out "All Hail the Aristok! Long Live Demnor the Fifth!"

When the feasting and dancing were finally over, the newly married couple retired to the Royal suite. Exhausted, Demnor let Isolde take the initiative and as soon as he was able, he collapsed into sleep. When his breathing deepened, she slipped from under the blankets and returned to her own rooms.

Kelahnus and Tania were sitting in their outer chamber by the fire, sipping hot rum punch and talking quietly. They rose when the Consort entered. Yawning, Isolde accepted the chair Tania relinquished for her. The other woman took her usual place at her Lord's feet and as Kelahnus made to leave, the Consort waved him back.

"Stay a while, Your Grace," she said. "His Majesty is asleep, and I would spend a quiet hour with you both."

"As you wish, My Lord." The Companion returned to his chair and, stretching out his toes toward the hearth, studied the Consort casually from beneath his lashes. She carried her new position well, and he'd been curious about what her first consolidating move would be. Him. How nice. After a few minutes' silence in which they all grew comfortable before the fire, he looked up.

"Do you find your new apartments pleasing, Your Highness," he asked, willing to make the opening move in the mutual wooing of their positions.

"They're very lovely, thank you, Your Grace."

"Kelahnus, please, Highness."

Accepting the offered obeisance, she smiled.

"Kelahnus." Glancing at the table, she shook her head. "Did you have food sent up *after* the banquet?"

"Well, we had to do something while Your Highness was closeted with His Majesty," Tania answered with a laugh.

"I don't want to know. Is there any left?"

"A bit of chicken, I think, I'll get you a plate."

Tania rose, and after passing over a plate heaped with food, resumed her place at her Lord's feet. Picking up her mandolin, she began a quiet tune.

After listening for a time, the Consort turned back to Kelahnus. "I haven't had much chance to explore my new home, Kelahnus. Perhaps you might guide me on a tour of it tomorrow. The history of its construction makes fascinating reading."

The Companion's expression remained polite while a tiny warning bell began to ting in his head.

"Certainly, Your Highness," he answered smoothly. "However Bran's Palace is a vast and somewhat confusing place. It would take more than one day to see it all. Is there any particular wing or area you would like to . . . explore first."

"Those which surround the Royal apartments and the Meeting and Council areas both private and public will do for now," she answered.

"Of course, Highness. I should be only too glad to conduct you." And only too glad to set Tania to finding out just how much the Consort knew about palace construction and where she'd gotten that information. Of course, he mused, she might be making a subtle suggestion that the Guild tread carefully when traversing such areas in a political sense. He had the sudden feeling that Isolde DeKathrine, Duke of Aquilliard, would not be so easily maneuvered around as the rest of her family. The thought excited him.

"Have you had a chance to see the full Royal wing itself, Highness?" he asked, casually changing the subject slightly.

"Not yet. Why don't you describe the rooms for me, while I finish my chicken."

With a smile, he cocked his head to one side as he arranged his thoughts.

"They're much like these," he began. "Large, sumptuous, filled with candlelight and dark, ornate furniture. There's a fireplace in every room and deep rugs on every floor." He smiled. "The bedrooms have huge wardrobes and great, floor length gilt-framed mirrors.

All the walls are covered with beautiful tapestries and paintings and the ceilings are decorated with lovely forest and pastoral scenes of people eating and laughing and making love."

That they were also riddled with spy holes and blocked and subsequently unblocked passageways, caused by centuries of renovations, was another subject entirely and one he would enjoy exploring and exploiting later with Tania, alone.

"There's an immense walled garden in the center," he continued, "filled with roses and other flowers which surround a great fountain in the shape of a charging horse. Birds fill the air with music and just enough wind enters to keep you cool and comfortable. All the apartments have doors leading to a pillared walkway around the garden so in bad weather you can circle it away from the elements if you don't wish to traverse the rooms indoors.

"The Aristok resides in the west wing, as you know, the Consort, yourself, Highness, in the east, and the Companions, myself and Her most beautiful Grace in the north."

"How cozy," Tania murmured and Kelahnus smiled invitingly.

"And what of the children?" Isolde asked.

The first Royal Companion frowned, chosing his words with studied care. The reports on the Consort warned that his response here would set the stage for any relationship yet to be. "The Late Aristok's children did not reside in the Royal apartments, Highness, but one floor up," he said after a time, his voice registering his own disapproval. "They were not . . . a close family."

"I see." Isolde's expression was cold and she tapped her fingers stiffly against the arm of her chair, eyes hooded in thought.

Kelahnus found himself warming to her and allowed it to show on his features as he leaned forward. "The rooms above are quite comfortable, Highness and easily renovated to include a stairwell between, or you might knock a passageway through the wall to link to the rooms surrounding instead."

Isolde studied him a moment, then smiled, the expression reaching her eyes. "A meritorious suggestion, Kelahnus. I shall speak with the Royal Architect when we complete our tour. Perhaps you might do me the pleasure of joining in our plans to change the palace . . . topography."

He bowed, "I shall be only too honored, Highness."

"Thank you." The Consort covered a yawn with her hand. "And now the night grows long. We'll continue this conversation tomorrow. Would you be so kind as to pour me a rum punch before you retire, Kelahnus?"

"Of course, Highness."

The Royal Companion rose, realizing he'd just been politely dismissed and finding his respect for the new Consort growing with each passing moment. At her Lord's feet, Tania continue to play, a smile on her lips.

16. Branbridge

In Tottenham Castle's main courtyard the crowd jeered as Jasper DeSharon, Earl of Westonborough and Priest of the Wind walked proudly toward the scaffold. The bruising on his face and neck showed he'd not been taken easily, but now that death was inevitable, he displayed no emotion. He'd made his peace with the Shadow Catcher earlier that morning. His only regret was that he wouldn't live to see the Branion army sweep through this land in the springtime, but his spirit would greet the victorious dead when it was all over.

Taking his place without prompting, he ignored the two corpses already swinging from the makeshift structure. A Heathland man bound his arms behind him, then secured the noose about his neck. The Earl's face remained impassive.

Before him, in the reviewing stand, the man who claimed to be the Monarch of Heathland stood. The two men studied each other, then the Earl turned his head and spat onto the ground. The Heath smiled faintly, then nodded. Two men leaned on the rope and the Earl was hauled into the air. He struggled finally, the need for breath outweighing his courage, but before long he grew still. The crowd cheered.

Arren turned to the Branion man kneeling beside him.

"A life for a life. Three Triarchy Priests for three Essusiate Clerics."

His face a sickly white, the man nodded.

"I'm sending the rest of you home," Arren continued. "You're of no consequence to me, but I want you to take this message to the Living Flame." He bent forward. "Burn this into your memory: I'll have the head of the one who murdered my Clerics in Branbridge, either on the battlefield or on streets of Branbridge itself. Tell him that."

"Y . . . Yes, Your Majesty."

Arren turned away, a look of disgust on his face. His eyes fell on the Earl of Westonborough's corpse. "He was worth ten of you," he said contemptuously. "It's always better to hang a brave man than a coward."

The Branion said nothing.

"Take him from my sight."

While the guards dragged the man away, Arren gestured and Gordon appeared at his elbow.

"There's an empty Branion merchant ship being held at Kirkrail. Put them on it."

"Yes, Sire." Scratching at his new growth of beard, Gordon made to go, then turned back. "Oh, Bridget's arrived from Branbridge with news of the DeMarian crowning."

I'll see her now."

His cousin bowed, and after gesturing a young woman forward, took his leave. The woman dropped to one knee before her Monarch.

"What news from Branbridge, Cousin?"

She rose. "More pomp and fawning I've never seen," she snarled, "and I'm sorry to say it went without a hitch. Two of my brothers tried to enter the tower where the DeMarian was in seclusion, but the rotting security was too tight. We couldn't get near him at the Cathedral either. Duncan sends his apologies."

"There's no need for that. It was merely important to have someone ready should Essus take a hand.

"And Yorbourne?"

Bridget frowned. "She's surrounded by guards day and night, but we'll get her, Sire, I promise you, we'll get her."

"I have no fears on that account."

"As to the rest of the DeMarian get," she continued, "the Duke of Kempston had some kind of breakdown, and his twin's not much better. They'll probably miss the war come spring, and may not recover even after that."

"Good. Two less to contend with."

"The youngest one's a child and no threat as yet. She's as reckless as the rest, so she may not live the war through anyway, and when we rid the world of her thrice-damned brother, the Branion line will be snuffed out like a candle." Bridget snapped her fingers.

Arren smiled. "I would it were that simple. But keep the faith and with Essus' blessing it just might be. Meanwhile . . ." He motioned a servant over. "You'll need to eat and rest before I send you back. Come to see me in two hours. I'll have orders for you then."

"Yes, Sire." Bridget followed the servant back into the keep.

Returning his attention to the scaffold, Arren stood a moment. The three corpses swung gently back and forth, taking his thoughts with them. Yorbourne, Kempston, Lochsbridge, Clarfield, Branion. Could they really get them all, extinguish the entire cursed line in one blow? He shook his head. He was getting ahead of himself. One move at a time. Yorbourne and then the war. Yorbourne and the war.

"The day some Essusiate sheep-fucker takes *my* head is the day I don't deserve to keep it."

Quindara's scoffing reply to the Viscount Jonnarin DeSharon's report brought a laugh from the Privy Council and even a smile from the Hierarchpriest.

Demnor frowned.

"You're to take precautions, regardless, My Lord Defender. Heathland assassins have penetrated the palace before."

"I'll be ever vigilant, Majesty," Quindara answered dismissively. "It's Mars and Tray I worry about, and Kass."

"I can take care of myself," Kassandra piped up

indignantly. Demnor shot her a stern look, and she subsided.

"The guards about Kassandra have been hand-picked," he replied. "She'll be fine. However, our brothers *are* vulnerable."

He frowned, his thoughts sifting back to the audience he'd had with Atreus just the day before. Weakened by his attendance at the coronation, Marsellus had not been able to obey his brother's summons, so Demnor had seen the more outgoing twin alone. The audience had begun awkwardly, Marsellus' unusual absence making both men unsure of how to begin. Finally Demnor had simply asked:

"How's Mars?"

Atreus glanced down at his hands before answering.

"He's recovering slowly, Majesty, but he doesn't speak much, and he can't stand visitors. His Sight's still so raw that even one or two people overwhelms him terribly."

"His Sight? I thought he had a physical collapse."

Atreus gave him a startled look, "I . . . I thought Gwynne, I mean, the Archpriest of the Flame would have told you."

"It seems not."

"On the morning of our . . . of the late Aristok's death Mars had a vision followed by a violent seizure."

"Her Grace did mention that. I thought that sort of thing was common among Seers."

"It is, but not with us. The magnitude of the convulsions is linked to the degree of ability, and our ability was always small. Until now." He bowed his head.

Demnor waited for his brother to collect himself and after a moment Atreus continued. "We think he linked with her at the moment of death. The struggle to break free rent a great hole in his mind and tore the protective caul around his Sight. It's left him vulnerable and weak, unable to build new protections."

"So he's vulnerable to attack by other Seers?"

Demnor asked, thinking of his experience at the Holy
Triarchy.

"No, not exactly." Shaking his head in frustration,
Atreus struggled to find the words that explained their
Gift to the uninitiated. "The Sight is split between
Mars and myself. Gwynne believes it was because we
were tied by flesh in the womb." Unconsciously his left
hand dropped to brush against the scar on his hip.
"For Mars the prescient visions come when he sleeps;
for me, they come more often when I'm awake, but they
were never so strong that we couldn't control them, or
needed very strong protections against them. Now
that's changed, for Mars, at least."

Demnor could hear the grief in his brother's voice.
For the first time in his life he didn't share something
with his twin. It would be like he'd lost the use of half
his body, or half his mind. The Aristok had often wondered what it must be like to look at another and see
his own face mirrored back at him. To have someone
who knew you so intimately that he could sense your
thoughts and dreams almost before you did. To never
be alone.

He shook his head. That intimacy had its price and
its price sat before him. Atreus had lost a stone and
looked ready to collapse. Worry had aged him, edged
his face with fine wrinkles and dulled the bright copper
of his hair.

"The Sight's running rampant through his mind,"
his brother continued. "He can't stem it." Turning the
Ducal signet on his finger, he looked almost ready to
cry. "He says he can see the future in people's faces
and it terrifies him, that he can read the hour of their
death when he looks at them.

"Gwynne wants him to go to a cloister, but he won't.
He says he's afraid to be alone. He keeps reliving . . .
our mother's death."

"Our mother's death." Demnor shuddered, remembering his vision in the Sword Tower. If Marsellus kept
reliving that, it was a wonder he was still sane.

*   *   *

"Your Majesty?"

Demnor turned to Alexander and blinked.

"What? Oh. I was thinking. Where were we?"

"Palace security, Sire."

"Yes. Captain Fletcher, double the Guard on the palace entrances and the Royal wing. Also, the Consort is to have a full complement."

"My thanks, Majesty," Isolde interrupted smoothly, "but I have my own people. Any more and we shall seem an army moving about the halls."

There was polite laughter, and Demnor inclined his head.

"Very well, My Lord Consort. If you need any more, tell the Captain."

"Thank you, Sire, I shall."

"As to my brothers," Demnor continued. "They're moving to the cloisters in the Temple of the Flame tomorrow. The Archpriest will see to their safety.

"Was there anything else?"

"Just our response to the murder of the Triarchy Priests in Tottenham, Your Majesty," Quindara answered.

Demnor met and held her eye. "There will be no response just yet, My Lord Defender."

"So we allow this Heathland rebel to go about his business murdering our people as he pleases?"

"Enough."

The word was spoken quietly, but the steel in it made the Duke of Yorbourne subside.

"They'll have our response come spring. In the meantime, I want no more violence in my capital, is that clear?"

Quindara's eyes were dark fire, but she nodded stiffly. "Crystal clear, Majesty," she answered through gritted teeth.

"Good. Council is dismissed.

"Kassandra tell Metellus we're going pheasant hunting. He's to bring two spaniels. My Lord Consort, if you'd care to join us, we'd be pleased to have you."

"Of course, My Liege, I'd be honored." Isolde

smiled, and without thinking Demnor returned it. They left together, the Council filing out behind them.

Slowly the days grew shorter on the sun's journey toward the winter festival of Calan Dudlach, and the cold settled in to stay. Palace activity ebbed as the nobility returned to their own lands. Stag hunting took the place of dragon hunting, and mead took the place of beer. The Dukes of Lochsbridge and Kempston remained cloistered. The Duke of Yorbourne, busy preparing the Knights of the Shield for war, was rarely seen. The Duke of Clarfield continued her training with her Royal brother and this brought the Aristok into closer contact with his DeKathrine cousins, invited to join the fray. As the cold winds danced across the palace roofs and around the turret spirals, he found himself relying on their counsel more and more often. During these times the ghost of his mother seemed far distant in the wake of their easy company.

"Get up, burn you! How can you be bested so easily by your little sister?" Demnor roared at the man lying prone below Isolde's sword.

Alerion grunted, and tried to twist away. The Consort's point followed him. "With ease, Majesty. She cheats."

"Liar." Isolde laughed. "Now, Your Grace, Duke of Clarfield, pay close attention. The ways to defeat a larger opponent . . ."

With a grin and a quick flick of her braid, Kassandra leaned on her sword to listen. The Consort and she had become fast friends, and the new squire welcomed the chance to rest and watch her tease Alerion.

Isolde placed her right foot on her brother's chest, ignoring his pained expression. "Rule one: Allow your opponent to underestimate you."

"And when have I *ever* done that?"

"Rule two: Use his bulk against him."

"Bulk!"

"Rule three, shut up, please. Rule three: Make use of all terrain and distractions."

"Zold, are you going to let me up sometime this week? There's water seeping into my breeches."

"Rule four: Be gracious in victory and accept his *surrender*." She looked pointedly down at him.

"I yield, already."

The Consort moved her weapon aside and held out her hand. With a sour look, Alerion took it and allowed her to help him rise. Futilely, he brushed at the seat of his pants.

One hand resting on the pommel of his own sword, Demnor smiled. "Rule five: Ransom his safe return, paying ten percent to the Aristok."

"I like that rule," Kassandra piped up.

"I thought you might."

"So when I capture a dozen Heathland Captains, I shall buy a gigantic warhorse and you can buy a new saddle."

"Yes, well, that won't be for some time yet."

"Why?" she demanded suspiciously. "We're going to war this spring."

"But you won't be in it."

Her young face darkened. "You promised!"

"I promised only to *take* you to war, not to let you get killed in it. As my squire, you'll perform your duties and remain in camp with the others."

"But, Dem, it's not fair! I'm a Prince! *You* never had to wait behind when *you* were twelve!"

"Eleven, and, yes, I did." Kneeling down, Demnor took her hand. "Kass, you will go to war with me. You'll clean my armor and feed Titan and do all the other tedious, horrid work that squires do."

"Did you?"

"No, and I always wished I could. I was never a squire, I was always the Heir. You'll get the chance."

"But, Dem . . ."

"Let me finish. Don't think that time will hang heavy on your hands. As squire to the Aristok, you'll take my messages, fetch my Generals to me, find the best loca-

tion for my tent and stand behind me in Command
Council. And you'll be the leader of the other squires.
Some of them will be younger than you and less expe-
rienced. I'll look to you to guide them and keep them
safe."

"So how'm I 'sposed to get that experience, if you
won't let me fight?"

"You'll fight in time."

She sighed. "In time, in time! I'm so tired of waiting
to do *everything!*"

With a laugh, Demnor rose. "One day you'll wonder
how *everything* came and went so fast."

"Sure, but then I'll be old like you, so it won't
matter."

"Brat." Leaning down, he kissed the top of her head,
then rubbed his cheek against hers.

She laughed and skipped away. "Don't, you're all
scratchy." Leaning her head to one side, she studied
him. "I like your hair braided like that. You look like
King Brand."

"Without so much bulk I hope."

"Not quite so much. But then, you arc both awfully
old."

"Thank you, Your Grace. And if you don't stop
chewing on yours, you'll have none left by the time
you get old."

With a peeved expression, she flicked her braid
behind her. "Well, then I'll just have a beautiful wig
from Jehalabad made, like the Viscount Alessanda."

"Until then we'd best do something about your
shield work, or you'll never capture those twelve
Heathland Captains to afford it."

Tossing her a practice shield, he raised his sword in
salute before he attacked.

It had rained later that day, heavy globs of half
frozen water covering the palace grounds in a slippery
glaze of ice. Today, the winter cold had relinquished its
grip on the city a little and Demnor breathed in the
crisp air with pleasure. The heavy sadness that had

hovered over him these last few days lifted with the breeze, and he whistled as he stepped from the west tower.

He'd crammed in as much time with Kassandra as possible, using it as a means to unwind from the demands of Royal obligation. They'd enjoyed the time spent together, but sometimes when the fighting was over and they sat side by side on the rails, her elfin face would grow still and sad. Three days ago, she'd come to him and asked to visit their brothers.

Demnor had been surprised. He hadn't known Kassandra was close with her other siblings. His face had grown dark, but she'd stood her ground. Finally, recognizing his ire for jealousy, he'd granted her request. She'd thrown her arms around him, and, as usual, he'd been unable to maintain a bad mood in the face of her joy.

Today, it was unable to maintain against the beauty of the day and his anticipation of the morning's training.

Alerion had begged off, citing other duties and with Kassandra gone, it would be only he and the Consort. He found himself eager to begin. They'd had little private time together since the coronation. He enjoyed her company and was looking forward to spending time with her without the chaperoning of their respective siblings.

The only fly in the day's ointment had been Kelahnus. The Companion had been off on some errand before dawn and had returned more subdued than usual. Worried, Demnor had attempted to discover the problem and had met with frustrating defeat. Running over the conversation in his mind, the Aristok frowned.

"Are you feeling all right?"
The Companion's face was pale, and he nodded vaguely without looking up. "I'm fine. I'm just tired."
"Are you sure? Has something happened?"
"No. No, everything's fine. Everything's perfect."
Demnor was unimpressed. "The Wind help us when

things are poor. Are you going to the School this morning."

"What? Oh, yes, yes, I must." Kelahnus tried a weak smile. "I'll be back before supper."

"Good."

The silence stretched between them. Chewing pensively at the scar on his lower lip, Demnor cast about for something to say. What would the Companion do in this instance?

"You look unwell. Maybe you should put off your visit until tomorrow and rest."

Kelahnus glanced at him in surprise, then gave a small laugh. "I can't. I'm expected."

"So cancel. We could spend the morning resting together." He tried an experimental leer.

"Companions can't do that. Besides, you're expected too."

"I'll cancel. Aristoks can do that."

"I'm fine. Really. This business with Alynne has just kept me very busy. I'll rest tonight."

"Is there anything I should know about this business with Alynne?"

"Not yet. When there's something to tell I'll tell you." The Companion shrugged.

Unsure of how to draw the younger man out if he didn't want to be drawn, Demnor frowned. "If you're really all right?"

Rising, Kelahnus smoothed his hair and managed a more cheerful smile. "Of course, I'm really all right. Now go on, you'll be late for your leaping about. I'll help you dress."

Brows drawn down, the Aristok strode across the training yards. He wished Kelahnus would confide in him. Stopping in mid stride, a very uncomfortable thought made him wince. Not so very long ago, he and the Companion'd had the very same conversation, only the roles had been reversed. Kelahnus, anxious and ready to help, to listen. Demnor unresponsive and, he realized suddenly, untrusting, refusing to admit he needed help, or that the other man could. Had Kelahnus felt the same frustration and hurt that he had? With a sigh he continued on his way.

"I am such a fool."

The Consort was waiting for him in the practice circle. She'd discarded her leathers and sweat damped her shirt in patches. That and the condition of the practice dummy she was hacking at told him she'd been there for some time. Her movements were short and jerky, anger written in every line.

Demnor entered the circle. At the sound of his footsteps, the Consort left off her attack and turned. She bowed sharply. Demnor nodded with a slight frown.

"Aquilliard."

"Majesty." Her tone fought to be civil, though her chest heaved with barely suppressed fury. She approached him and, before he could think, drove the point of her sword into the ground before his feet. Then, spinning on her heel, she stalked off toward the rack of weapons beside the circle. Hefting a backsword, she tested it, then swung it at the dummy with enough force to decapitate it. After slipping into a breastplate and helm, she came forward and stood in the center of the circle.

"Whenever you're ready, Your Majesty."

With one raised eyebrow, Demnor plucked the weapon from the ground and advanced. Why everyone was in such a strange mood today, he had no idea, but he assumed that Aquilliard at least, might tell her Sovereign after she'd worked off the edge of her anger.

They saluted with their weapons and began.

An hour later, spent, but no less incensed, she looked up at him and told him bluntly the reason for her ire. There was a roaring in his ears as the world rushed at him with all the force of a thunderstorm. All he could think to say was, "No."

That didn't help the situation at all.

* * *

"Pregnant." Pausing, Master Klairius pursed his lips, but before he could voice an appropriate response, there was a soft knock at the door.

"Come in."

Carrying a silver tray of hot chocolate and fruit tarts, his page maneuvered through the door and set the tray on the ornate table by her Master's elbow. Klairius accepted a china cup and sipped at it until the child left. Then he set it carefully down and looked at Kelahnus. "And you're sure the conception occurred in Linconford?"

Taking a drink from his own cup, the Royal Companion helped himself to a tart before answering. "Yes, Master, quite sure. As you remember, Tania's report mentioned there was a possibility. She didn't know for certain until this morning."

"Why this morning?"

"The Consort threw up. Apparently she also threw a fit, involving the destruction of her breakfast crockery and several expensive pieces of furniture. Then she stormed off to confront His Majesty."

"To confront His Majesty," Master Klairius repeated. "One might imagine that would go down like a mouth ful of sea water. How did he react?"

Kelahnus frowned, considering his answer. "Like his horse had kicked him in the head. It was certainly a surprise."

The Head of the School of Companions snorted. "I'm sure. What did he say?"

"Tania and I were watching them from the west tower, so we couldn't make out their words, but it was fairly obvious what they were discussing. He just stared at her and kept shaking his head. The Consort, it seemed, had some heated words for him after that."

"Heated words. For the Aristok."

Despite himself, Kelahnus had to laugh. "Yes. She can be quite blunt when she wishes to be, though one wouldn't know it from her court persona. She was lividly furious. The army marches in the spring, and I doubt they'll let her fight. Not with the Heir to the throne seven months in the womb."

"Hm. Well, that solves one problem, at least. Has the Aristok spoken of how he plans to announce this . . . premature event?"

"We haven't had time to discuss the matter yet, Master." In truth, Kelahnus had been waiting all day for Demnor to broach the subject with no success. "He'll likely simply announce it as conceived and let the populace wonder about the date when it's born."

Master Klairius shook his head. "Better to have him speak openly of their tryst in Linconford. The population will see it as romantic and there'll be no doubt about the child's father."

"But it will carry the Flame, Master. Proof enough isn't it?"

Master Klairius frowned from under his bushy eyebrows.

"The Flame passed while the infant was only days in the womb. What if this passing has damaged it and it's stillborn?" he asked. "Suspicion of infidelity may still fall upon the mother, souring the DeMarian-DeKathrine alliance."

"Do you think that might be possible?"

"Who can say? It may have been protected by the mother, but the Flame is a powerful force, and when it passes to a child it is always dangerous."

"Of course, Master. I'll speak with him directly."

"Good. Now, this leads to the most awkward question. Are *you* completely sure that it's his?"

Kelahnus tucked his feet up under him and poured himself another cup of chocolate. "Oh, yes. The Consort is far too politically astute to have had an affair that close to their marriage. Besides, if she *had* dallied with anyone on our journey, Tania would have included that in her report."

"Well, *he* might not realize that. Keep an eye on their relationship and glean his thoughts on the subject.

The last thing we need right now is another altercation between the Crown and the DeKathrines."

"Yes, Master."

The old man's fingers hovered over the tray of tarts, then with a sigh, he picked up his cup again.

"As to the subject of a Nurse," he continued. "I'll make up a list of available Auxiliary Companions that you may discuss with both he and the Consort at the appropriate time."

Kelahnus nodded.

"Do you know if she's chosen a midwife?"

The Royal Companion shook his head.

"Yes, a bit premature, I expect. I'll speak with Tania. The Consort will likely employ the same woman as her mother, although Tania should have a list of our other affiliated Sisters just in case. Have her come to me tomorrow."

"Yes, Master."

Lifting his cup, the Head of the Guild sipped at it in silence. After a moment, he set it down again. "The political ramifications of this will be slight, I think. The DeKathrine family will be mollified and it may bring a note of cheerfulness back into the city. Those who benefit financially from such news, like ourselves, will prosper.

"As to the personal ramifications, it may create a bond between the Aristok and his Consort. Then again, it may not. Keep me informed."

"Of course, Master."

Rain began to patter against the window, and the two men sat quietly for a time.

Rolling the chocolate around his tongue, Kelahnus relaxed. The fire in the grate sent a pleasant warmth through his bones, fighting the weather's chill, and the chair was comfortable and soft. Helping himself to another tart, he allowed his mind to sort out the events of the day.

Tania had come to him in a panic after Isolde had left for training, spilling out the morning's news in one frenzied burst. Certain she should have done something to prevent it, the younger Companion had point blank refused to tell their Guild Head. Kelahnus was the Senior Companion. He could tell him.

After spending some time convincing her that this was not a terrible situation, nor even an unfortunate one, Kelahnus finally managed to calm her. The Aristok must have an Heir, he explained. The Consort and he were now wed, so what difference did it make when the child was born. Finally reassured, Tania had returned to her own suite.

Alone in the unused dining hall he practiced in every morning, Kelahnus had leaned against the window-sill and stared unseeing at the overgrown, walled garden beyond. Demnor was going to have an Heir, have a child. Demnor and Isolde were going to have a child.

Gnawing at a lock of hair, he examined the ache this produced. He'd known they would wed, sleep together, have children, grow closer, possibly even grow to love each other. So why this feeling of betrayal?

He tossed it from one mental hand to the other. They would wed. *In the future.* Sleep together. *Unwillingly.* Have children. *Through duty.* Grow closer. *As friends.* Possibly even grow to love each other. *No.*

There it was. He didn't want Demnor to grow to love her or anyone else. He wanted him all to himself, much as he'd accused the other man of wanting him. He sighed.

"I've known him for almost a decade. Loved him for as long. So why does it surprise me that some of his less endearing qualities have rubbed off on me?"

Suddenly cold, he hugged himself. "I won't lose him," he told the silent hall. "His love for her won't lessen his love for me."

Deep inside, a tiny part of him remained unconvinced.

Sitting in Master Klairius' study, the Royal Companion was careful to keep the insecurity from his features. So far, Master Klairius was content to wait for Demnor's thoughts. Kelahnus was still uncertain of what to tell him.

After his initial shock had worn off, Demnor had smiled. A tender, happy smile of anticipation the Companion hadn't seen on his face since the early days of their courting. It frightened him, that smile. It made him wonder if he now had two rivals for his Lord's affection, and what, if anything, he could do about it.

The days passed. Demnor told Kelahnus of the child's existence with all the unwillingness and apprehension of a confession of murder. Fear of the younger man's reaction made him angry and defensive and he was unable to meet his eyes except as one might meet an executioner's.

Unable to penetrate the tangle of emotions, both the Aristok's and his own, the Companion backed off, his response light and superficial. Demnor dropped the subject, his new-found resolve to share his feelings with the other man shaken. Kelahnus couldn't help him. The wall had grown suddenly higher, and the Companion had no idea how to scale it.

The city was ecstatic. Ariston DeLynne insisted on ringing the bells of Holy Trinity after the public announcement and an unofficial holiday was declared as the people flocked to the palace grounds. Alerion teased his sister with undisguised awe and Isolde beamed at the attention. Quindara paid Troy one hundred crowns with a disgusted snort.

Demnor drew back from it all in embarrassed hesitancy. He avoided the Consort as much as he could, but as stag hunting season entered full swing, it became impossible. Finally he pushed it aside as he had always done to problems with no answers. It would work itself out, somehow.

Days passed. Spring sent its skirmishers out to do battle against entrenched winter, sending rain to awaken the fields and meadows, while in Branbridge the populace prepared for war.

* * *

"One month until the roads are passable."

The Aristok leaned against the north tower railing and studied the fields below. The evening was warm and damp, a fine misting of rain coating the ground. To the west, the sun was setting, pale pink fingers caressing the clouds. To the east, the lamps of Branbridge were still dark.

Demnor closed his eyes and breathed in the heavy scent of wet earth. In one hour he would meet with his War Council, the first of many such meetings before the roads were dry enough to begin the march north. But the time was coming. He could smell it on the wind. One month until the roads were passable.

His thoughts followed their own path, moving from Heathland and the possible strengths and weaknesses of its army to Branion with its barely healed unity. Turning the Triarchy ring on his finger he stared down at the square cut ruby, his mind setting on the Archpriest's prophecy.

. . . in its fiery hands it carries two many faceted gems the color of blood . . .

Two gems, two provinces, two countries, two people?

Two futures.

"Two futures."

The ruby was the symbol of the Triarchy, a gem holding the Flame in its crystal heart. If the vision spoke of blood-colored gems, it spoke of the Triarchy. So the answer to the vision must lie in religion. But then how did it tie in to his visions in the Sword Tower? Two deaths? But there had been many more than that. Chewing at the scar on his lip, Demnor stared unseeingly down at the ring until a noise behind him made him turn.

Kelahnus stood by the tower door, a mug of mulled wine in his hand. He held it out, and Demnor accepted it with an awkward word of thanks. Much of their discomfort over the Consort's pregnancy had eased during the winter, but it still raised its head now and then, like an itch over a partially healed wound.

The Companion leaned against the other man with a sigh, and Demnor instinctively put his arm around him. Breathing in the younger man's faintly perfumed scent, he made himself relax.

"It's a beautiful evening," he commented, distinctly aware of the soft rise and fall of the Companion's breathing.

"Hm. It reminds me of a night years ago, do you remember?"

"Which one?"

"The one where you convinced me to climb Dorian's Tower to that rickety old balcony just to see Collin's Park in the sunset."

Demnor smiled. "I remember."

Kelahnus put his own arm around the other man. "I was scared to death. I thought we'd crash through the boards and kill ourselves."

'We didn't, though."

"No, we made it safely down, and I swore I'd never climb that high again."

"And here you are again."

"Yes." *Here I am again.*

Leaning his head against the other man, the Companion closed his eyes. How much had he accomplished since that night eight years ago when they'd stood on that old platform, staring out across an unknown future? How many wounds had they healed? How many stones had they torn down, and how many had they set in their place? The strain on their relationship was caused more by their own fears of confronting the Aristok's and Consort's tryst than by the actual deed.

Kelahnus shivered. War was barely a month away. Anything could happen. If they didn't mend the rift now, they might never get the chance.

Well, get on with it, then, a voice chided in his head. Demnor had never learned to bridge such a gap. It would have to be him.

"You will be careful, won't you?" he began.

Hearing the childlike fear in the other's voice,

Demnor pulled himself from his own thoughts and
looked down.

"Yes."

"You won't . . . get killed or anything."

"No."

"I wish you wouldn't go. Why does the Aristok
have to fight with the army anyway? If you got killed,
it would tear the Realm apart. You should stay
behind."

Stroking Kelahnus' soft mane of hair, Demnor laid
his cheek on the top of the younger man's head. The
Companion was usually more subtle than this. He wondered what was on his mind that could ruffle his composure so. "If I stay behind, my cowardice will tear
the Realm apart just as quickly," he answered, sure the
real purpose behind the younger man's words would
reveal itself shortly. "Besides, I have to fight. I've
always fought. It's more than what I was trained to be,
it's what I am. I never made a secret of it. You've
always known it."

Kelahnus nodded with resignation. "I've always
known it," he echoed. "But I've never liked it. Still, I
understand why you chose a warrior's life. And . . ."
the younger man took a deep breath. "I understand why
you chose the Lord Isolde."

"Chose?" Demnor made to pull away, to look the
Companion in the face, but Kelahnus held him tightly
close.

"Yes, chose. Chose her as a friend and as the mother
of your child before your marriage."

"But Kelahnus I wasn't . . . I was drunk!"

The Companion smiled sadly. "No. Not that drunk.
Shall I tell you how it went, how I saw it go?" he
asked, looking up into the other man's face.

Unable to speak beyond a choke, Demnor nodded.

"You grew to like her, and she is very beautiful, and
you thought, why not, we'll be wed soon enough, why
not fall to temptation? No one believes it will happen
anyway, so throw it in their teeth, you thought."

"I did not!"

Kelahnus touched his finger to the other man's lips. "You were attracted to her and you wanted to sleep with her ever since Leiston, but you felt guilty because of me. So you got drunk for the first time in your life and you forgot the whole incident afterward until the appearance of the child. Not very honorable, my love."

Demnor said nothing, although a muscle jumped in his jaw.

Kelahnus smiled a little sheepishly. "Shall I tell you a secret? I was jealous. With all my lovers and all my freedom, I was jealous and a little bit hurt."

"Why didn't you tell me?"

"I couldn't. I don't know why. Maybe I've lived with a mute for too long, hm? But I'm telling you now because after this spring everything may be different. I want you to know that I'm more afraid of losing you to your new life than I ever was of losing you in battle. And the battles filled my life with fear every time you fought in them. When you have your court and your wars and your wife and your children, I want to know if in the midst of all that, you'll still have time for me."

"How can you doubt it?"

"Because I'm just a man. I'm not a Seer or a Prophet and I need to hear you say it."

"Of course I'll have time for you. You're . . ." He paused awkwardly. "I love you."

With a sigh, Kelahnus leaned against him again. "You know, you haven't said that to me since before we were contracted."

Demnor shifted uncomfortably. "I thought it."

"Yes, my love, but I can't pluck it from your mind like a newly blooming rose."

"Nice analogy. I . . . what's that?"

Demnor straightened, squinting down at the fields below. Kelahnus turned.

"Four riders? No four horses. There's a body across one of them."

"A body." Demnor's eyes widened. "Kass and Quindara went hunting this afternoon."

By the time they reached the north courtyard there was already a sizable crowd gathered. The people moved aside as the Aristok and his Companion made their way to the gates. The riders were already visible and Demnor breathed a sigh of relief as the last of the day's sun shone off the dark auburn of Kassandra's hair. Her clothes were muddy and torn, but she was unhurt. Beside her, the Duke of Yorbourne rode, one arm bound in a rough piece of cloth, her face a dark mask of rage. A Shield Knight, supporting another before him in the saddle, rode behind them. Last in this parade was a horse, its reins tied to the Shield Knight's pommel, an unfamiliar, rough-clad man tied across the saddle.

The wounded knight weaved drunkenly, clutching at his abdomen where the blood had stained the blue of his uniform an ugly black. His face was white, and his eyes rolled up in their sockets as he was handed down to the waiting arms of the Guard. He was rushed into the palace.

Leaping from her own mount, Quindara scowled as the movement pulled at her bound arm. After sketching a quick, jerky bow in Demnor's direction, she dumped the contents of a bag at his feet. The crowd gasped as a bloody, bearded head rolled out onto the ground. Then the Duke of Yorbourne strode to the body, and cutting it free, let it slide off onto the ground with an audible thump. The body groaned.

"Kassandra put an arrow in his eye, or I'd probably be dead right now." Quindara winced as Agrippa prodded at the knife slash in her arm.

"Hold still," he snapped. "If you demand medical attention in the council chamber, you get what you deserve. Drink that."

Demnor pushed the goblet in question toward her

and she accepted it absently. The Aristok then turned
to his youngest sister.

"Are you all right"

Kassandra nodded. "Turion was killed, though. Protecting me."

"Turion?"

"My Guard Captain," Quindara answered, her voice
harsh. "Turion DeKathrine. He was also a Shield
Knight."

"I see." Agrippa had brought the news that the man
had died en route to the infirmary, but had neglected to
mention his name.

"It was his job, Kass," Demnor said gently.

"I know that." The Duke of Clarfield rubbed a grimy
sleeve across her eyes. "but I don't have to like it."

"No, you don't." Pulling her to him, Demnor hugged
her tightly, then kissed her cheek. "I think I'll make
you a priest. That way I'll never have to worry about
you like that again."

"Don't you dare!"

He smiled to show that he was joking, and she
grinned back only a little shakily. "Very funny," she
muttered.

With a slightly forced laugh, he turned back to
Quindara.

"Essusiates?"

"Yes."

"Heaths?"

She shrugged and Agrippa growled a warning as he
began washing out the wound. "We left one alive," she
answered simply.

Demnor nodded. "The Flame Priests are questioning
him now. We should know soon enough."

Laying the bowl and cloth aside, Agrippa picked up
a needle.

"Do you want to leave?" he asked Kassandra.

She glared at him, her flame-tinged eyes flashing.

"Then don't faint."

Ignoring her indignant protest, he began to sew.

* * *

An hour later they were joined by Captain Fletcher and Alexander DeKathrine as the Archpriest of the Flame made her report.

"The attackers were Branion Essusiates, My Avatar. And their orders came from Tottenham."

"Who brought these orders."

"A Heathland woman. Our man didn't know her name, but he's given us the names and whereabouts of others party to the attack, including . . ." she paused, "a palace servant who told them My Lords of Yorbourne and Clarfield were going hunting in the north fields today."

"They're like rats!" Quindara snarled. "They slink into everything!"

Demnor motioned to Captain Fletcher.

"Arrest them," he said darkly.

"And our assassin, Majesty?"

"Keep him until his story checks out, then hang him."

"At once, My Liege." After consulting quietly with the Archpriest, the Captain withdrew.

"Your Grace, inform me when your priests have all they need from their prisoners. Then they will hang as well."

"Of course, Most Holy."

His flame-covered eyes glowing hotly, Demnor turned to Alexander.

"Do you have any counsel, My Lord Hierarch-priest?"

His second cousin met his Sovereign's gaze, his own expression sad. "No, Majesty. I ask only that I may be dismissed now to see to my nephew Turion's burial."

"Of course. Inform us when the service will be held, and we will attend."

"Thank you, sir."

He and the Archpriest left together. When the three DeMarians were alone in the Council Chamber, Demnor turned to Quindara.

"Are you all right?"

She nodded, flexing the arm with a grimace. "The cut's shallow. It'll heal by Mean Ebril."

"Have Agrippa check it regularly. I need you healthy come spring."

"I will be, Majesty, unshakably healthy."

Her flame-filled DeMarian eyes mirrored the fire in her brother's vision as they both turned and stared northward. Kassandra watched her siblings quietly, wondering how high the flames in her own eyes might have to grow by the end of the summer.

At Tottenham Castle, Arren heard the news of the executions with little visible reaction.

"And Bridget?"

"She's at our church in Larmouth," the messenger, Jamie Elliot Croser, Stephan's son, answered. "She wants to return and kill Yorbourne herself. I've offered to go with her, if Your Majesty agrees."

Arren made a negative gesture with one hand. "They'll be expecting it now. Tell her to follow her orders and wait. Come spring, she'll have her chance. So will you."

"How have the Essusiate Branions reacted to the deaths?"

"Not a whimper, Sire," the messenger said disgustedly. "Neither side's initiated violence. Some of our people tried to stir up the Essusiate population. It didn't catch. No disrespect intended, but these Branions can't be relied on, Essusiate or not."

"They share our religion, Jamie," Arren said quietly.

The younger man made to answer and then dropped his gaze sullenly.

Placing his hand on his shoulder, Arren walked him to the door.

"Have faith. Essus is with us, Heath, Branion, and Gallian alike. If we keep our oaths, we cannot fail."

Staring darkly forward, Jamie clenched and re-clenched his fists. "I'll tell Bridget to wait, Sire."

"You do that."

Bowing, Jamie took his leave. Arren returned to his chair and sat staring into the Hall's fire.

"Have faith," he whispered. "All my people, have faith, and wait."

17. Falmarnnock

Sunset, Late spring, 894 DR

Removing her sword from its sheath, the Duke of Aquilliard kissed the blade, then laid it on the small altar in Braniana's Chapel, the most ancient place of worship in the palace. After a moment's reflection, she knelt awkwardly. Before her, carved from a great block of polished stone, the first Branion ruler held the newborn baby, Gabriel DeMarian, aloft. A trick of the moonlight through the windows cast a reddish glow about the marble figures, brining a sense of warmth to their shared smiles.

Touching her abdomen below the loosely fastened sword belt, Isolde sighed. Bran Bendigeid had built this chapel for his Royal half sister in the year of Gabriel's birth. It was said that the figures spoke prophesy when the light caressed their upturned faces. The Consort hoped the unusually gleeful expressions meant that this child would be born healthy and whole, and as quickly as possible. It could just as easily mean it would be colicky for three straight years. She grimaced.

Her earlier anger at her condition had been replaced by the sullen belief that fate had an unpleasant sense of humor. The hour-long talk with her mother, newborn twins howling in their cradle near at hand, had not helped.

Isolde ground her teeth together. The child was due

in high summer, early Mean Lunasa, so in the best days
of battle, she would be the size of a small whale. For
his Most Regal, Sacred, and too torchingly fertile
Majesty's sake, it had better be a long war.

The Aristok and Consort had spent many hours that
winter preparing for Isolde's stewardship of Branion,
but as the days of war drew nearer, she'd found herself
wanting him gone. She had work to do, and he was in
her way ... fussing. They were all fussing, Demnor
and Ler and Kelahnus and even Uncle Alex. The
bigger she got, the more they fussed. They were like a
flock of old hens.

Returning her gaze to the figures of Branion's first
and second rulers, the Consort sighed.

They meant well. They were afraid that the Flame's
passing might have damaged the child, but Constance,
her midwife had assured her that it had not. The mother
protects the child in the womb, especially in this case
where the mother did not herself carry the Flame.
Ariston, too, had dug through his histories and come to
the same conclusion.

Isolde was not so much worried about physical
damage as she was about the child's mental state.
Tania's words in Leiston had made an impression on
her and she had mulled them over often since that day.

*"Quinton DeMarian was an unstable man and his
mother and brother's untimely death and the passing
of the Flame was too much for him. It broke his mind."*

Shocked at first by the Companion's almost heretical
comments, the Duke of Aquilliard now agreed with
them. Quinton II had been violent, suspicious, and
prone to fits of what could only be called madness. So
had his daughter. The history of the DeMarians was
filled with such rulers.

Studying the face of the woman who'd carried the
Living Flame from the mountains in the Vessel of her
own body, Isolde wondered if Braniana had known
what a price her descendants were going to pay and if it
would have given her pause if she had.

Isolde sighed. These were not the sorts of thoughts she'd expected to have after her wedding day.

They'll have a proper DeKathrine family life whether they're DeMarians or not and we'll see what Flame and Throne can do against that."

Easy enough to say, but would she be able to carry it out? And would Demnor, raised to view the world along the harsh lines of strength or weakness, be an ally or an enemy in this raising?

Isolde hugged herself, suddenly cold. The Aristok would never believe the history of his family was the history of pain and madness, of rulers unable to withstand the burden of the Flame that they had no choice but to carry. He wouldn't see it, or couldn't. Would it then consume him, and his children after him? And could she stop it if it tried?

She closed her eyes. Kelahnus had said that his Lord was softer than he let on, and in truth, Isolde had seen that side of him herself. Perhaps between them they could bring it to the surface. But first he must survive the war, and she had duties of her own to worry about. Pushing her fears to one side for now, she brought her mind firmly back to business.

Now that the army had finally left, she'd had a little peace to set things in order. Her first priority had been the mending of the rift between the Triarctic and Essusiate faiths. It was a momentous task, but one she had confidence in. The Essusiate Cathedral should be repaired and the new Religious Philosophy section of the Branbridge University finished before Demnor returned. It was a good start. Quindara had written that they were almost at Falmarnnock, the war was going well and they should be back at home before the birthing.

Isolde narrowed her eyes, her worry for Demnor's safety momentarily replaced by her earlier ire. Demnor had burning well better be back before the birthing. It was all his fault to begin with.

Her bladder twinged, pulling her from her thoughts. *You'd think,* she muttered to herself with a disgusted snort, *that a chapel dedicated to childbirth would have provided a pot.* The creature was six months in the womb, and she had to pee all the Earth-shaking time. She rose with an annoyed groan. If she hurried, she'd have time to empty her bladder and consult with Tania before she met with the Fenish and Bachiemen Ambassadors to talk trade, another task she wanted completed before Demnor returned to Branbridge. If the child kept to its schedule and the Aristok to his, she should have the Realm under control by autumn. If fate had no more surprises in store.

She saluted the statue ironically, and replaced her sword in its sheath. The two figures continued to smile, unperturbed.

Squaring her shoulders, Isolde DeKathrine, Consort of the Aristok, decided to accept their prophecy as one of happiness, and woe to the force, metaphysical or otherwise that got in her way. Then, feeling better at least in spirit, she left Braniana's Chapel to face the future and mold the present.

That same night, Demnor stood on the innermost battlements of Cairnhaven Castle, south of Braxborough, gazing past the outer curtain wall to the fields beyond. Small fires winked in the dusk and the sounds of horses and soldiers making camp drifted up to him. Above, storm clouds cast a foggy pall over the landscape, although with a little imagining he could clear the mist before his eyes and see his people preparing for sleep.

Foot soldiers, archers, cooks, squires, blacksmiths, and camp followers, the bulk of his army made ready for war; building small cooking fires from brush and what wood they could scrounge from the nearby birch copse; seeing to their weapons; eating and drinking. A comfortingly familiar scene that had played out before him, season after season, for as long as he could remember.

And season after season he'd marched in their midst, sharing their rocky camp except when some castle or keep had provided a separate, more secure bed for the army's Royal charge. And each night that he was able, he'd walked the upper battlements of those keeps, looking down on his people and ruminating on the battle to come. Only one night in all his life had this ritual failed him.

Chewing at the scar on his lip, the Aristok remembered the cold and rain slicked stones of Buckdon Castle and the disastrous battle in the Vale. He shook himself. This march was different. No heavy questions of loyalty or treason battled inside him; no fear of failure sapped his judgment or his strength. This time the young knights who'd followed him stood side by side with the elder Lords who'd taught them their first lessons about power and arms. This time, they would win.

The wild, scratchy cry of a gryphon in the distance jolted him from his thoughts. The battlefield scavengers had been following the army since they'd crossed into Heathland, sensing blood. They'd feasted already and would do so again before the season was done. Branion was on the move.

The day after the Spring Festival of Calan Mai had seen four thousand take ship for Gallia under Captain Hough with orders to build the remainder of his force on the Continent. The rest, some twenty thousand strong went north in three great Battles, to resecure the Crown's Heathland territories.

The Main, under Demnor's own banner and that of Elisha DeLynne, had pushed through the center of the land, crossing the Gildarrock Hills that marked the borderlands. The inhabitants of the tiny villages they passed fled at their approach, and the Aristok let them run. The army outfitted itself with what supplies were left and carried on.

Just east of the county town of Arrenburgh they had their first skirmish on the banks of the Glaviot River. The Heaths under the Armistone banner stood well, but finally retreated at the deployment of Demnor's

Gwynethian archers. The Aristok forbade pursuit and
continued north.

He had no need to pursue at this stage and face a
possible ambush around the river bend; the main
Heathland force was not here. He was making for Laurwich where he would join forces with Quindara, and
then press on into the heartland of the country, to
Tottenham, where the Heathland leadership had head-
quartered. Through a constant relay of messengers, he
knew his other two forces were making steady progress
through the countryside.

The Vanguard, under the Duke of Yorbourne's command, had gone northeast through Rossbury Forest and
from there had crossed the Gildarrock Hills east of the
Main, to Abberstream. On the ancient battlefield of
Falkeith, after ambushing her scouts, a force of some
three thousand Heathland infantry met her eight thousand with a determined surprise attack. Banking on
DeMarian impatience, the Heaths almost carried the
day, but the Duke of Yorbourne kept her head and
brought up her archers, carefully holding her mounted
troops in reserve until the Heathland infantry was deci-
mated by arrow fire. Then her mounted knights swept
in with murderous intent.

The Branions won the day, but their old foes had
struck a telling blow, with many casualties on each
side. Quindara advanced through Heathland, bent on
revenge. Raids on her supplies were met with raids on
the villages, her people rounding up cattle and livestock and whatever supplies they could carry. Essusiate
abbeys were stripped of their valuables, the Triarchy
Knights entering in force. Riding in the center of her
army, she sent word ahead of her presence, daring the
Heaths who lusted after her blood to come to her. The
army left the bodies of those who tried hanging from
the gates of each town they passed. Her progress was
slow, but she continued to push toward Laurwich.

The Rear Battle, under the command of Alexander
DeKathrine, swung northwest from Carisley, won a
small skirmish on Branion soil at Banngate, then

crossed the border to lay siege to Caerockeith Castle,
and bring relief to beleaguered Threkirk. He left a
force of one thousand for Davin Hughes, commander
of the Branion-held fortress, to carry on the siege, and
then turned north. He met little organized resistance
until Dunley Vale. There he had his first serious check
as the border Heaths, including many younger Caileins, halted his progress on the banks of the Nyth
River with a force of three thousand.

The two armies held off at first, each gauging the
strength of the other and its relative position. Night
fell. In the darkness, the Borderers swept down on
Alexander's flank, inflicting light casualties on a company of Arthur DePaula's. The young Viscount was
furious and set out early that morning intent on teaching his foe a lesson. The lesson was taught, though not
the way he expected.

Sweeping around the curve of the town, he met a
hidden force more than twice his number. Arthur's
people were cut to ribbons and the Viscount badly
wounded. His escapade cost the Hierarchpriest a Commander and host and opened his flank for an attack
later that morning. The Heaths got away with several
wagons of supplies and arms and wreaked havoc with
the surprised and awakening soldiers before Michelle
DeKathrine and her mounted troops managed to drive
them off.

Demnor met these reports with an even temper.

"This sort of thing's inevitable," he told his Command Council, meeting some days later, two miles
south of Arrenburgh. "You know their style of
fighting. Many of you've witnessed it firsthand. Attack
in small numbers, then melt into the hills. But you also
know it doesn't last. The Heathland leaders want my
head as badly as I want theirs, and sooner or later,
they'll fight, all together, their main force against
mine. When that happens, *we* will carry the day."

Elisha DeLynne nodded. "In truth, we've lost very

little and inflicted comparable losses they could ill afford to lose."

"Could we afford to lose Arthur?" Robert DeKathrine, asked, turning on her angrily.

"Yes. Your partner's a hothead, Robert. Everyone knows this, including the Heaths. It was his own rash actions that led to his defeat."

"And should he have sat by and watched these half-naked hill savages attack his flank?"

"Enough."

Demnor held up one head and the two nobles subsided. "Arthur's still alive, My Lord of Carisley. He walked into a trap. Next time, he'll be more cautious." The Aristok turned to the others. "We can afford to let them win a skirmish or two. It will make them over-confident and reckless. Eventually their leadership will fall apart, as it always does. Have patience. That's all for tonight."

Eventually their leadership will fall apart ... It wasn't until four days later on Ballcrum Moor, that they discovered it wouldn't be so easy this time. A Herald, dressed in the old colors of the Royal Elliots of Heathland entered the camp at dawn. Glancing disdainfully at the gathered host, she weaved her mount slowly through the camp toward the Royal banner.

Demnor stood before his tent, bare-chested and dripping from a bucket of water brought to him by Kassandra, when the Herald reined in before him.

"I bear a message for the Branion Monarch. Where is he?"

Her voice was imperious, and Demnor smiled slightly.

"He stands before you, Herald."

She inclined her head, eyes flicking quickly over him. "I am sent to warn you that you tread on the sacred soil of Heathland, Your Majesty; that you were not invited and that you must leave with all haste or it shall be seen as an act of aggression to which the entire country will respond."

A murmur went through the gathering crowd, and Demnor raised his hand for silence. "You find me just awakening, Herald, or I'd greet you more appropriately." Reaching for a towel, he scrubbed at his hair a moment before continuing.

"In whose name do you come with this warning?"

"In the name of Arren Elliot, descended from David Elliot, Monarch of all Heathland."

Demnor showed no surprise at her words though the knights around them glanced questioningly at each other. "I see. Well, I and my hosts are here to keep the ancient pact of Unity, made by my ancestor Kassandra the Fourth and Stephan, fifth Steward of the North."

"This pact was made without the consent of the true Monarch of Heathland, nor of its people, sir," the Herald answered evenly. "And as such, holds no legal power in this land. My Monarch, Heir of David, and rightful ruler of Heathland, demands that you withdraw this unlawful host beyond the borders of his domain, or be expelled by force. Also that you return the Elliot Plaide, stolen from David Elliot on the battlefield of Kilburnen."

The assembled murmured in indignation and drew closer. The Herald gave no notice and Demnor only smiled faintly.

"The *DeMarian* Plaide is in my tent, Herald," he answered. "I shall wear it into battle. If the Elliot has the courage to joust for it, he may consider it the prize in our struggle."

"It shall be so, Your Majesty."

With a nod, she turned her mount and made her way sedately through the crowd. Demnor reached for his tunic. After dismissing those who had gathered around, he handed the towel to Kassandra.

"Find us some breakfast, then assemble my Commanders."

"Arren Elliot?" Alerion scratched at the stubble on his chin and looked questioningly at Demnor. The Aristok shook his head.

"Never heard of him."

Elisha DeLynne tapped her pipe on the edge of her boot before grunting in disbelief. "The Elliots are all dead."

"Then who is he?"

She shrugged. "Some pretender making use of the Elliot name to raise support. It's happened before."

"Not this time." Demnor paced across the tent, pausing to accept a chicken leg from Kassandra. Eyes narrowed, he chewed at it in silence for a moment, then continued to pace. "There's something, something I can't remember."

His Council glanced at each other.

"The name," Demnor continued, pausing again to stare into space. "The name sounds familiar, but not, not Elliot . . ."

"Arren Armistone."

He turned to Kassandra. Her own face was screwed up with the effort to remember as she chewed pensively at her braid, then smiled.

"He led the Armistones in the West Border Wars. Ariston taught me about them last winter."

Demnor slowly nodded his head. "I remember now. I faced him at Falkeith. He's a charismatic leader and an Essusiate fanatic. It would be in character for him to take on the Royal name. If he could carry it off, it would give him an edge over any rivals."

"It seems to have worked," Elisha commented.

"For now."

"Is he the Heir of David, My Liege?"

Demnor shrugged. "As long as his people believe he is, it doesn't matter."

Alerion frowned. "How good a General is he?"

The Aristok smiled coldly. "Good, but I'm better."

The Main Battle continued due north, meeting up with Quindara at Laurwich two days later. The Heaths continued to throw small forces against them, taking what opportunities came their way to harass the wagons and supplies. The great Branion army, secure in its

numbers, posted extra guards and ignored their attempts
to lure them into the hills. A week later, they reached
the small fortress of Cairnhaven. The Earl of Linconford and his daughter joined them from Braxborough,
and two days later Alexander DeKathrine marched the
Rear Battle into camp.

That night, Demnor found himself, once more,
walking the cold, quiet battlements, contemplating the
violence to come.

Elliot. It had been a long time since that name had
been thrown down in challenge. A name from the history books, as tied to his family's destiny as his own.
The Elliots and Demnor the First, the Elliots and Kassandra the Third, the Elliots and Marsellus the Black.
Demnor had thought it was a name long laid to rest in
the bloody killing ground of his mad ancestor's rage,
but here it was risen like a ghost to challenge them
again. It was fitting. If ever there were two families
locked in immortal combat it was the Royal Houses of
DeMarian and Elliot.

Nodding absently to his guard, Demnor continued to
pace the length of the battlements.

"*. . . that you return the Elliot Plaide, stolen from
David Elliot on the battlefield of Kilburnen . . .*"

The gray DeMarian Plaide shot with dark red and
black had been worn by Branion's Aristok since Kassandra the Fourth, though it had been in the family far
longer. A battlefield trophy won on the field of Kilburnen in the year 506 by the Crown Prince Marsellus,
it had become the symbol of Branion supremacy in
Heathland.

And now Arren Elliot wanted it back.

Demnor smiled. It mattered little whether the man's
claim was true or false. All that mattered was that
Arren Armistone was a foe worthy of the name. A
large enemy force was said to be gathering at Falmarnnock, south of Tottenham, and Demnor was sure the
Elliot claimant would be there to plant his flag. It was a
fitting place to recreate the battle of Kilburnen where

the DeMarian Champion had slain the Elliot Monarch
with his own hands.

The next day the Branion army was on the move to
meet the Heath. Demnor rode eagerly, knowing in his
bones that this was it, the final place where battle
would be joined. They swung slightly southwest and
came within sight of the town of Falmarnnock two
days later in the pouring rain. A large Heathland force
had been spotted in the hills to the north. Demnor made
camp to the south and deployed his scouts. They were
not long returning.

Night had fallen and the final Command Council
was under way when his Scout Captain, Terrilynne
DeKathrine, entered the Aristok's tent. Stripping off
her sodden gauntlets, she accepted a goblet of mulled
wine from a squire before crossing to the map-strewn
table where Demnor and his nobility were gathered.
She saluted.

"What news, My Lord of Salchester?"

"My Liege, a force some eight thousand strong is
encamped north of town. More arrive at every hour."

"Show me."

Leaning over the map, she pointed. "They're gathered here, My Liege, behind this marsh, the hills at
their back. My scouts report nominal mounted warriors, but many archers armed with short bows. If the
flood of those coming in continues at this pace, there
may be eleven or twelve thousand arrayed against us,
well entrenched by dawn.

"Many Heathland family banners may be seen,
including the ancient Royal standard. I believe their
central leadership is there."

"Your Grace?" Demnor turned to Gwynne
DeLlewellynne.

She frowned.

"The Sight has been cloudy today, Most Holy,
although I've sensed a great resolve and high morale
within their ranks. Their forces are disciplined and
eager for the dawn. It would be safe to assume they've

drawn the line and that their self-proclaimed Ruler will take up arms in their midst tomorrow.

"My priests are even now in meditation to penetrate the thoughts of their Council and their Essusiate clergy."

"My Liege, will they have Seers attempting the same with us?" Robert DeKathrine's squire burst out, before his Lord sent him flying for his presumption.

Demnor held up his hand to restrain Kassandra's angry reply and motioned the boy to stand. He obeyed, casting a fearful look at Robert. The Aristok eyed him sternly.

"The Heaths are Essusiates. Those with the Sight among them are branded as heretics and put to death."

The youth swallowed.

"There will be clergy attempting to call up the power of Essus to aid them in the battle," the Aristok continued in a lecturing tone. "That's why the Order of the Flame rides beside us. Are you afraid of the power of Essus?"

"N . . . no, Your Majesty."

"Good." When Demnor returned his attention to the map, Robert jerked his head at the tent flap. The squire fled.

"My apologies for my cousin's actions, My Liege. He'll be punished."

"No need, my Lord, I think we've frightened him enough for one day."

"Thank you, sir."

Smoothing the map, the Aristok motioned his Generals closer. "We outnumber them at all points, My Lords, but they're sitting in a defensible position. It would be folly to attack through a marsh, so we'll go around.

"The ground is still firm at the edge of our range so the archers of the Main and one in three from both the Rear and Vanguard will concentrate on their center. Once they've taken their toll, the Main will sweep in from the left.

"My Lord of Yorbourne, I want you to deploy your

people in an all out assault on the right. Set your archers on this hill to soften up that flank, but sweep in without hesitation. The main thrust will be to the left. I want the enemy believing it's to the right. Do as much damage as you possibly can as quickly as you can. I want their leadership off-guard and in confusion."

Eyes alight with anticipation of an attack much to her liking, the Duke of Yorbourne nodded.

Demnor turned to his Marshal of the Rear.

"My Lord of Cannonshire, you I will hold in reserve for the left. If the Main can't take them alone, I count on your good judgment to know when to arrive."

"Thank you, My Liege." The Hierarchpriest bowed and Demnor returned his gaze to the rest.

"That's all for now, My Lords. We'll prepare at first light. At this stage and with our numbers, I think it will only aid us for the enemy to see us at full strength. Good night."

The Council bowed as one and filed slowly out. The Archpriest of the Flame remained and when the tent was empty, Demnor turned to her.

"How many Essusiate clergy are arrayed against us, Your Grace?"

She pursed her lips. "A dozen of consequence, Most Holy, a few more that may be ignored. They'll likely build a Circle of Twelve during the battle to block the Flame from taking the field. They may even attempt to call their God to the fray. Essus is a God of both music and warfare, and may manifest."

Demnor grew thoughtful. "In all the battles I fought alongside the late Aristok, I never saw Essus take form."

"It requires a very powerful Avatar, Most Holy. The need and blood lust of your army will be enough to call the power of the Flame to you. It will make you stronger, more terrible in battle, but to manifest the full potential takes a combination of events and powers that is rare. This is also true with the Essusiates. Casting a mantle over the battlefield to dampen the Flame is easier than calling Essus to fight at their side," her toothless mouth drew open in a grin, "and less fatal to the clerics involved."

"Essus doesn't like being inconvenienced for petty reasons?"

"No more than does Your Holiness."

Demnor gave a short laugh. "And this dampening mantle, how does it manifest?"

"The Flame will not be so easy to call up or control and you may begin to feel fatigued more quickly than usual. Your own priests will be on the field to combat these effects, however, so there will be periods of complete freedom. You understand, Most Holy, that with just one person to focus on, yourself, they have a slight advantage. Once their circle is in effect, it battles our attempts to halt their powers."

"So what you're telling me is essentially only I will likely be affected by these clergy, and that, slightly."

"Yes, Most Holy."

"Then there will be no effect. Thank you, Your Grace."

She bowed stiffly and withdrew.

Demnor found himself alone with Kassandra. Tipping her head to one side to see if he wanted her to follow the Archpriest, she then turned to roll up the map. Demnor sighed and lowered himself to the single camp stool.

"Kassandra, when the troops are deployed, you will retire to the back and remain with the other squires."

"Yes, My Liege."

Her answer was too quick and the Aristok's eyes narrowed. "Kass?" he said warningly.

"I said I would! But I don't have to like it."

"True enough, so long as you do it. Now go find yourself something to eat, then get some sleep. I won't need you again till dawn."

She bowed, her expression dark, and left to go in search of Robert DeKathrine's squire. A few minutes later, the tent flap parted and Kelahnus entered.

He was dressed for travel in nondescript browns and tans and his hair was bound in a thick braid behind him. Crossing the tent, he knelt and laid his head in Demnor's lap. The older man stroked his hair, then put his hand under his chin, lifting his face to his.

"You're going, then?"

"Yes."

"I wish you wouldn't."

"Worried?"

"Yes."

"Now you what it feels like." The Companion smiled gently to remove the sting from his words.

Demnor shook his head. "Feels like? I knew it every time you left the palace grounds until ... just recently."

Until my mother died and I didn't have to fear she'd never let you come back. Kelahnus heard the unspoken words and laid his head on his lover's chest listening to the thump, thump of his heart beat.

"You never told me."

A dozen answers came and went. Finally Demnor lifted his hand to resume stroking the other man's hair. "I couldn't."

"I know. I couldn't tell you either. Not really. I couldn't say, please don't get killed; I love you."

Demnor closed his eyes, feeling his throat constrict. They stayed that way for a long time, and then the Companion sighed and looked up.

"I have to go. Florence and I have Guild business in Tottenham and we have to be there before dawn."

"Guild business."

"Yes."

"It's State business, too."

"Perhaps, but any Guard or Commander of yours would only slow us down, and they wouldn't have a hope of getting into the castle undetected."

"And you would?"

"You know I would. Please. We've been arguing about this for days. You know I'm right."

Chewing at the scar on his lip, Demnor looked uncertainly down at him. "I don't know what I'd do if you ... if you were ..." Unable to voice the words, he simply dropped his hand and continued to stroke the other's hair.

Kelahnus sighed and closed his eyes, allowing the smooth touch to settle a kind of lazy peace over him but, after a time, he shook himself and rose.

"I'll be fine. You're more likely to come to some hurt tomorrow than I am."

With a snort, Demnor caught his hand in his. "You're going after a woman who murdered the Aristok in cold blood and a Palace Guard with ten years experience, with no weapon bigger than a dagger."

"And you're going after a force of ten thousand, every one of which would rather see your blood spilled than any other in your army."

"I have an army to protect me."

"I have Florence." The Companion stilled his lover's next protest by bending down and touching his lips to his in a long, drawn out kiss. Finally, when they drew apart, he smiled. "You will be victorious tomorrow, and so will I."

"You've Seen this, have you."

"Of course. Now I really have to go."

The younger man straightened.

"Kelahnus?"

One hand on the tent flap, the Companion paused.

"Be careful. I'd . . ." Demnor looked away. "If any thing happened to you I'd die."

"I'll be careful. You be careful, too."

"I will."

With one final glance, the Companion slipped away. Outside, Demnor could hear him speak softly to the Shield Knight on guard before the tent, and then there was silence. The Aristok was left alone with his thoughts on the eve of battle.

Darkness settled over the Heathland camp. Back against an old stump, Arren stretched his hands toward the fire while around him, his Battle Captains lounged, confident and unafraid of the enemy host encamped to the south.

Filling a tankard with ale, Colleen passed it to her Monarch. Arren took a deep drink. They were ready. Let the twice-damned DeMarian try his best on the morrow. He was doomed to failure. Arren had two thousand archers, the same number of mounted warriors and four times that of individuals on foot willing to raise swords against the Branions. He had familiar ground, a defensible position and more than a dozen clerics ready to hurl the DeMarian's heretical fire-wizardry back in his face. With their prayers, Essus would take the field and send the apostate army to the demon-kind where they belonged, and Hilary and Stephan would be avenged.

Across the fire, Sister Marie Claire knelt in whispered conversation with a handful of Arren's people. She and the other clerics, one from as far off as Tiberia, were busy about the camp, handing out the sacraments of Essus' Grace and giving comfort and reassurance.

Arren had received her blessing at dusk, kneeling with Colleen, his sole heir now that Hilary was gone. As the Gallian cleric had sung the benediction above his head, the setting sun had cast a mantle of golden light about her shoulders. Arren had bowed his head in recognition of the sign and when he'd stood, his heart was light. Essus was with them. They could not fail.

Now that battle was only a few hours away, the Heathland Monarch swept his gaze over his commanders, mentally reviewing each one's readiness.

To his left, David traded laughing insults with a group of Greyam kin. Through the night they had continually tried to lure him away from the fire, but their wily Battle Captain had stayed put so whatever mischief they were planning remained unsprung. Untroubled by fear of death or the worry of strategies, they were eager for battle. They would be in the thick of the fray, fighting alongside the Armistones and Ramsens in the main thrust of Arren's attack.

Next to David, Eilene, Arren's left flank Commander, lent a spare pipe to Ross Elliot Armistone, the Captain of the archers who would be deployed on the hillsides above the field. Ross borrowed some tobacco from the Kerr Battle Captain, lighting it from a burning twig passed to him by Jock Elliot Ramsen, Head of the north-land Ramsens, and thus managing as usual to have a smoke without effort or expense.

Arren watched him fondly, remembering happier times when he and Hilary had visited their third cousin at his keep in Dunleyshire.

The thought of his sister cast a darkness over the fire and he drew his cloak more tightly about his shoulders. *Ah, Hilary,* he thought, *you should be here.*

To his left, Jamie Elliot Croser, the family's Battle Captain now that his father, Stephan, lay dead in an unmarked grave in Braxborough, sat mirroring his Monarch's expression.

Nursing a tankard, Jamie fanned the slow fire of his vengeance. Sister Marie-Claire had gone to Braxborough to ensure their success. They had failed. She had helped plan the attack on the Duke of Yorbourne. That had also failed, so she had failed. Essus was not with her.

He downed the contents of his tankard in one quick swallow and coughed. She'd failed them deliberately. Gallians. They promised aid and at the last minute they always betrayed you. Like the Branions. Not one of them could be trusted any more than the other. His father had told him that. He blinked drunkenly at the fire. Essus' Grace did not shine upon the Gallians, so they could be killed as righteously as the Triarchs. And they would be.

His dark gaze passed the cleric to the other Gallians in the camp as he waited for dawn.

Arren watched him with a frown. Jamie was consumed with hatred for the Branions who'd killed his father. He prayed the young man's passion would not cloud his judgment tomorrow, but had little hope. He had seen it too often in the past. The dawn would bring an ocean of blood spilled in the name of centuries of wrong, but when the sun set it would set on a new Realm, a Realm free and self determinant. That was worth the price; worth the price of Stephan and Hilary and Jamie. His pale gaze passed over his commanders to the camp beyond.

Douglases, Ramsens, Greyams, Armistones and more; the strongest of Heathland's families were gathered here under his banner to battle the Branion army; the army that was twice the size of his. Arren dismissed the thought.

The Branions outnumbered them, but their leadership was uncertain and their ruler unstable. They had a great many archers, the majority bearing the infamous Gwynethian longbow with its deadly range and accuracy, but archers were useless in melee and Arren planned to bring the DeMarian to combat as quickly as possible.

He knew his own folk, knew they wouldn't stand watching the enemy parade before them for long. So he would attack, use all the pent-up rage and battle fury his people could muster.

To accomplish his goal, he'd laid his force out in a semicircle, archers on the hills protectively cupped around them. The DeMarian's army would have to come within their range to reach him, so they would run the gauntlet of determined fire for as long as his archers would stand. Then it would be hand-to-hand with the Branion heavy cavalry at a disadvantage in the sodden, marshy ground. And the Heaths would carry the day.

To his right, Gordon began a quiet tune on an old, wooden flute. It was a love song, and Arren could see the faces of his Battle Captains grow soft as their minds were drawn to loved ones at home or elsewhere in camp, preparing to meet the morrow and their own allocation of glory. Gordon's face was far away, too, no doubt thinking of Alynne, safe in Tottenham Castle. Arren had no love save Heathland, so he let his mind wander over the hills and moors of his homeland as the fire burnt low. The night passed.

Dawn came slowly with misty tendrils of fog creeping along the ground and swirling about the knees of the horses and the foot soldiers as the Branion army moved forward. The colors and devices of the noble families and the Dukedoms and Earldoms they represented rubbed shoulders with the brilliant green of the Gwynethian archers and with the dull browns and tans of the Continental mercenary companies and the plain trappings of the infantry. Steadily, the huge army of the Living Flame, some nineteen thousand in all, moved toward the entrenched Heathland lines, then paused. Beneath the royal standard, Demnor the Fifth rose in his saddle, hair bright fire in the early morning sun, and gazed at his enemy.

Beside him, Elisha DeLynne turned to her Sovereign. "The Elliot banner's in their midst, My Liege, as are the devices of Touleuvre and Champsailles."

"I see them."

The Aristok turned and, sweeping his gaze past his own lines, marked the wolf and wyvern pennant of the Duke of Yorbourne and the bear, hippogriff, and phoenix of the Hierarchpriest of Cannonshire. Within their ranks knights from across Branion were represented; Terion and Katrina DePaula of Linconford and Robert DeKathrine of Carisley. Dimitrius DeLlewellynne, his new crest with the device of Caer Aberddyn on the green-and-white DeLlewellynne field waving proudly beside those of his Gwynethian kindred; Gawain DeKathrine of Wilshire, helmless and shield held negligently by one strap, laughing aloud at some joke told by one of his many cousins. Gawain had been the first to ask his new Sovereign for the honor of wearing the red badge of Gwyneth, and the others who had followed him to Briery had been quick to follow suit. Now they made up a small army within the army, each one ready to prove their loyalty again. Demnor smiled as he continued his inspection.

Proud beside the pennant of the Duke of Yorbourne, the rampant fire-wolf and Lochbridge's statant enfield crest of his brother Atreus caught his attention. Marsellus, better, though still too ill to fight, remained in the rear, safe within the ranks of the Priests of the Flame, where the Archpriest had counseled Demnor to place him. Atreus was on the field at his royal brother's request. Fighting for the first time without his twin beside him, the DeMarian Seer looked vulnerable but determined, and Demnor felt a sudden fondness for his younger brother that seemed to reach out and embrace him. Atreus looked startled for a moment then turned, his face less pale. He smiled and saluted.

With a lighter heart Demnor turned his attention to the warriors in the Main Battle, to the faces who'd protected and followed him for so long. Elisha DeLynne, wearing the newly added red gryphon of Gwyneth as well as her own device; Grey, Benger, Jones, and Glicksohn, who'd been with him in the chapel at Braxborough and the host of Palace Guard who'd requested the honor of accompanying him. Finally his gaze fell on the black and green standard of Alerion DeKathrine.

Their gazes locked, gray eyes staring into gray eyes, then Alerion smiled and raised one mailed fist high, the red badge of Gwyneth on his own sleeve flashing in the sunlight.

"Long live Demnor the Fifth!"

"ALL HAIL THE ARISTOK!"

The army's roared response was almost deafening, and Demnor could feel their desire to do battle in his name lift him up and fill him with Fire. His mind, opened to the Flame, throbbed in time with their chanting. As he raised his sword, scarlet flames chased each other down his arm, and flashed off the sword point as it caught the sun. He held it high for half a heartbeat, then swept it down. The trumpets sounded and the Duke of Yorbourne began the Battle of Falmarnnock, 894.

*   *   *

Across the miles two figures crouched in the shadows in Tottenham Castle. A week before the army had moved on Heathland, Master Klairius had sent for Kelahnus and Florence. Master Adell and Master Elias had also attended the meeting, but the lack of others had been an ominous sign. Kelahnus had briefly sought Florence's hand under the table, before turning his full attention to his Guild Master. The Head of the Companions had come quickly to the point.

"Alynne has not responded to any of our messages. It is time to send a delegation to find out why. As it is no longer safe to send an unaccompanied delegation into Heathland, I have decided to send this delegation within the Branion army. It will consist of you both."

Only the widening of her eyes betrayed Florence's surprise. Kelahnus, equally taken aback, schooled his expression to one of polite interest, but immediately his mind began to race through the arguments he was going to have to use to convince Demnor of the need for his presence.

Master Klairius allowed them a moment to collect themselves before continuing.

"As the Royal Companion and the Guild Representative, it will raise no suspicions to have you traveling with the army. Once you near Tottenham, you are to move out on your own. You both have field experience, so I trust that you will reach your destination without difficulty." He turned to Master Elias.

"The Cousins have provided us with information on Tottenham Castle," the Security Head continued. "We have an entranceway mapped out for you. Once in, it will be up to you to stay out of sight until you locate our Sister."

"And then what, Master?" Florence asked, a strange light in her eyes.

"And then you discover why she's there in the first place."

"You are to gather information only," Master Klairius said evenly. "You are not to make accusations or attempt to force her to come home with you, merely find out the truth about the Aristok's death and her subsequent flight from Branbridge, then return. I will decide what course of action is warranted after you deliver your report."

Kelahnus had risked one glance at Florence. Her face had been smooth and unreadable, but the line of her jaw suggested she had her own ideas about a course of action. Kelahnus had stilled a sudden shiver.

There'd been more; advice and warnings, but essentially only details. Eventually Kelahnus and Florence were able to return to the palace to make their own plans. They rode in silence, each busy with their own concerns: Florence, already rehearsing her words to the renegade Companion, Kelahnus rehearsing his to the Aristok.

As it turned out, Demnor had been too distracted with the coming campaign to put up much of an argument. That had come later.

Now, before the sun had touched the sky with its pale fingers, the two Companions made their way along the embankment beside the main gateway of Tottenham Castle. Skirting the walls to the right, they followed the curve of the outer battlements, clambering over the rough stone of the embankment and creeping through the bracken. It became progressively steeper and more entangled, but with patience, they made their way through until they came to a small, barred window in the south tower.

Florence peered through, then motioned Kelahnus forward. They began to work at the bars. They were old and rusted, just as the Cousins had said they'd be and, in less time than expected, the iron was removed and, one after another, the Companions wriggled through.

The room, a kitchen, was dark, the fire, banked coals. Moving carefully so as not to rustle the rushes on the floor, they passed out the door and into the lower square. A quick dash across the open flagstones and they fetched up against the Great Hall. Pressed into the shadows, Florence gave the all clear, and Kelahnus crept into a recessed corner between the hall and inner battlements. Squinting in the moonlight, he jumped. His fingers found purchase on the rough stone and he hoisted himself up to eye level. The wall walk was empty of guards.

Silently, he pulled himself up. He gestured. Florence joined him seconds later.

Together they made their way along the walkway, then swarmed over the edge and into the inner gardens. An archway led to the upper square and the old royal residence where they knew their quarry to be. Cautiously, they made their way to a small door, and after a moment's pause, slipped inside.

As the sun began its climb to the horizon, the castle slowly awakened, shrugging off its blanket of sleep. Servants began to hurry back and forth, not so quickly as on other days, their new Lord of the Manor was away at war, but still at a quickened pace, for the Lady of Gordon Elliot Croser was in residence and would soon require their attention.

Unaware of the intruders hidden in its ancient recesses, the castle moved about its day, and it wasn't until almost noon that Alynne Croser heard a soft footfall behind her as she sat in a window seat in her inner chamber. She rose, her expression unsurprised.

"Welcome to Heathland, Younger Sister."

Standing just inside the partially open door, Florence made no response. Quickly scanning the room, she took in the two closed doors to her right which the Cousin's map had indicated led to a midden and private solar respectively, the tapestries which hid at least two other window seats, and the woman who stood before her.

Alynne looked older, more regal in the old-fashioned, red velvet gown she was wearing. Her blonde hair was bound loosely in a fine, gem-covered snood, and she wore an Essusiate wedding band on her finger. A golden medallion, etched with the figure of Merrone, dragon of Essus, lay on the swell of her bosom, but the bodice beneath was stiff with embroidery: a hidden sheath for the dagger that would match the tiny knives concealed in the gown's voluminous sleeves. Alynne had been one of the School's most promising assassins and the younger Companion moved warily beyond the safety of the door. Behind her, Kelahnus hovered uncertainly.

An hour of eavesdropping on the castle servants had told them where the former Companion resided, although it wasn't until some time later that they'd heard Alynne dismiss her maid. Now, the two Guild Representatives stood staring at Melesandra the Third's murderer, neither one willing to break the silence first.

Finally, Alynne gave a brittle laugh. "Well, don't stand there hesitating by the door, Younger Brother," she said, peering around the other woman. "You were bred better than that. Pee or get off the pot, as they say."

Seating herself at a small table, she poured three glasses of wine from a crystal decanter and glanced inquiringly at the others. Florence moved cautiously forward, declining the wine with a sharp jerk of her head.

"Afraid I've poisoned it, Younger Sister? Well, you always were a cautious one. Don't worry, I've no need to do you in. You're little or no threat to me." She touched the red liquid to her lips and smiled coldly.

Florence was expressionless as she took the seat across from the renegade Companion. Behind her, Kelahnus came to stand, one hand on the back of her chair.

"Quite confident of that, are you?" Florence asked, her tone only mildly curious.

"Of course, Younger Sister. You're young and fit, however, I think you'll find me both wilier and more skillful."

"We are two."

"You are, indeed." Alynne turned her full attention

on Kelahnus, who returned her gaze evenly. She smiled. "I think you forget, however, that this is a Heathland-held fortress," she continued. "You're the ones in need of silence, not I. All I have to do is call out and a host of guards will arrive to add to my odds."

"Then why don't you?"

"Because I don't wish to." She leaned forward suddenly, her eyes sharp. Cutting off the urge to jerk backward, the younger woman allowed her fingers to brush the handle of her dagger, but remained expressionless. Alynne relaxed and sat back with an air of amusement. "Why don't we just say, I missed you," she replied. "Missed hearing news from home and what passes for family among us. How is the Guild?"

"As it has always been."

"Coy. And the late Aristok's funeral? I was so disappointed that I was unable to attend."

"So were many others. They had a special place all prepared for you."

"I'm sure they did. But they seemed to have managed without me. Found another to wear the crown fairly quickly it seems."

"Yes."

"He'll be some time filling it. Let's hope he lives at least as long as his predecessor. Long enough to pass on his seed at any rate. But then, I'm remiss. He has, hasn't he? Give him my congratulations on his marriage and his upcoming family, will you, Kelahnus?"

With a studied air of nonchalance, he shrugged. "You might tell him yourself when he arrives," he said, speaking for the first time.

"I might. If the war goes as my hosts plan, that could be quite soon. I doubt he'd be in a position to converse at that time, however."

Kelahnus felt himself growing very still, although he returned her false smile with one of his own, and changed the subject.

"I hear you've recently been married also. And had a change of religion. Pray, then, if you've learned how, that your new Contract doesn't fall under my Lord's sword. He doesn't take kindly to treason."

Alynne smoothed the red velvet of her sleeve before answering. "There's a nasty streak in you, Younger Brother. I never noticed it before. Although you needn't fear for *my* man. *He's* not so stupid as to make himself a target for the enemy.

"But this bantering is becoming boring. You're not really very good at it, you know. You're too easily read. Let us move on to a more interesting topic. You didn't, I'm sure, come here to offer me your hopes for a long and happy life with many children."

"Is that why you did it?" Kelahnus asked gently.

She shot him a strange look before answering.

"Perhaps. Perhaps I got tired of living life for other people."

"You could have retired," Florence snapped.

"It's more complicated than that."

"Really? Then why don't you explain it to me."

"Perhaps another time.

"I understand that our two armies are at Falmarn-nock," she said, changing the subject. "We shall play *Give and Take* while we await the outcome.

"How did Master Klairius take my sudden retirement?"

"I couldn't say," Florence answered coldly. "But Master Adell was hurt."

Alynne's face softened and just for an instant she looked sad. "Yes. I'm sorry about that. It was unavoidable."

"Was it?" Kelahnus asked.

"I'm afraid so. The motives of our Guild are obscure enough to outsiders, though less to those of us raised within its philosophy. Power and loyalty to the Guild are its only passions. And they are cold passions, aren't they, Younger Brother? I think you've found that out yourself."

Her tone was quietly sympathetic and Kelahnus found himself remembering his musing at the Guild Council meeting.

What was this Palace Guard to you? This man who
was in reality a Heathland spy. *Did you love him?* Love
him enough to flee from your life and marry him in a
foreign religion. To embrace his cause and lie night
after night, waiting to carry out a desperate plan?

His own years of deception welled up with a strength
that surprised him. He'd thought he'd gotten used to
being alone, but here in a hostile land in the midst of
war, it seemed, he'd found an ally who knew exactly
how he felt; who had shared the knowledge that their
love would never be accepted, and who had finally
dared do what he had only dreamed of.

*To throw her life away on a single desperate gamble
and become a hunted fugitive.*

He shook himself. What was he thinking? This
woman had betrayed the Guild, left them open for
reprisals by the government, by the Aristok, and
endangered every one of her siblings. He looked up at
her, his struggle plain.

"Not so as murder and betrayal become pleasing
alternatives," he answered finally, but even he could
hear the weakness in his tone.

"No? Well, your love hasn't been put to such a harsh
test, then. Mine was. Some day, you may understand
my reasoning."

"Enough." Florence stood. "I don't need to understand your reasoning, and I don't care to try. We've
come to return you to Branbridge."

Having expected something like this, Kelahnus was
not taken by surprise. He simply moved a step so that
he stood beside his fellow Companion.

Alynne gazed up at them impassively. "By force?"

"If necessary."

"I see. Well, I'm hardly dressed for travel, whether I
accompany you willingly or not." She rose. Upon
seeing Florence's eyes narrowed suspiciously, she
laughed. "I've no desire to see expensive velvet ruined
due to your paranoia, justified or otherwise, Younger
Sister. I plan to change. You may wait where you
chose."

Stripping off the dress, she paused, unafraid by the vulnerability of her nakedness. She gazed sadly at the other woman.

"Do you remember the day you came to the palace, Florence?" she asked. "The day you first tasted the coldness of the Aristok and heard the echoing of the stone walls? I held you that night, like the mother you'd lost. I held you until your fears had been soothed. Then I took you to such heights as you had never known. And when it was over, and your head lay cradled on my breast, I told you I loved you."

"You lied."

"No."

"You betrayed me."

"Yes. Yours is the only betrayal I regret."

"Just get changed."

Alynne was ready in a few moments. Dressed now in a simple tunic and hose, she gestured politely toward the door. Florence made the same motion. Smiling, the former Companion swept by them with regal disregard. As she passed Kelahnus, she suddenly turned and struck out.

The morning passed in violence. The Duke of Yorbourne met the defensive fire from the Heath's left flank by charging headlong into it. Suffering heavy losses, but momentum carrying them forward, when they reached the row of stakes protecting the archers, they barely paused. Throwing herself from the saddle, Quindara led the charge. The enemy broke and ran to the ranks of the entrenched. When her foot soldiers caught up, it was already hand-to-hand on the right flank. They held there most of the day.

Demnor's mounted troops kept back at first, watching while his archers rained death upon the enemy's center. Much sooner than expected the Heaths broke from cover and charged the field, sweeping around to his left. So much the better. The foe was now split and much less capable of maintaining it than he. He gave

the signal and the row of Sword Knights before him
surged forward to meet them.

Noon saw no abatement in the fighting. The Duke of
Yorbourne was still mired on the right, and the Rear
had quickly plugged a hole left by the Main and stayed
there.

Most of the archers from both sides, unable to fire
into combat, had swarmed onto the field, attacking the
fallen combatants with ax and knife, and robbing the
bodies. Only the Gallian relief force, some five hundred strong, waited in reserve, held by the personal
agenda of their leader. Slowly, the battle swung in the
direction of Branion's superior numbers.

Demnor brought his arm sweeping around and
crashed his sword down on the helm of the man before
him. The blade destroyed the helmet, sinking into bone
with a sickening crunch, crushing the skull below. The
man toppled, and the Aristok wrenched his sword free,
sending pieces of bone and blood flying. He turned on
another, the flames crackling along his sword blade,
illuminating his face with a eerie red light.

Early in the fighting the force of the Flame had
caught him up and swept him forward, a beacon of
light for his people. Moments later a misty web of
power had risen up from behind the Heathland ranks to
cover him in a sheet of ice. Prepared by the Archpriest,
Demnor was ready, but the sensation was so reminis-
cent of his plunge into the well beneath the Sword
Tower that he'd jerked back, Titan starting nervously
at the unfamiliar motion. As the hours passed and his
priests battled with the Essusiate clergy, he grew used
to the ebb and flow of power, using it when it rose up
in him, fighting the fatigue that rushed in when it
receded. He knew now why his mother had always
been so absorbed in battle.

The day wore on, and the dead and dying soon littered the field. One of the first to fall was Arthur
DePaula, still weak from his wounds, though determined to fight. Exchanging blows with a Heath man

twice his size, he took a strike to the head that drove him to his knees. One more blow and he was dead. By the time Robert reached his partner's side, the burly Heath had been swallowed up by the battle.

Phillip DeKathrine, mired in his first true combat, charged forward with the line of Sword Knights from the Main. He took an arrow under the arm, above where his breast and back plate joined and was dead before he hit the ground.

Rathe DeSharon, too, took an arrow and fell, to be trampled by the son of Hamlin Cailein, here to avenge his father's death eight years ago on the field of Buckdon Vale, and bring the Caileins back into the fold of Heathland. The boy himself died at the hands of Janet DeSharon who, in her rage, was then an easy target for Eilene Elliot Duglas.

As morning passed into afternoon, the two armies swayed back and forth, neither able to gain the upper hand and drive the other from the field.

Gawain DeKathrine found himself on foot like many of his company, trading blows on the slippery field with a older Heathland man. The ground was uneven and thick with mud, churned into deep pits and slippery trenches. The uncertain footing, coupled with the unfamiliarity of fighting against ax and mace, lent the other the advantage. After losing his shield and then his sword, the young Branion Lord made one, final reckless charge. Throwing himself at the other man, his sheer weight bowled him over. One blow with a gauntlet covered forearm knocked his enemy senseless, and Gawain sat on him a time, catching his breath. Then he moved on.

When Ross Elliot Armistone came to, he found himself facedown in a muddy trench, alive. Rage driving him to his feet, he leaped up to attack the nearest Branion. Surprised, the woman fell quickly, and Ross came face-to-face with the Duke of Yorbourne. Quindara caught Ross' ax with the side of her sword and jerked it away. One blow and he was flung to the ground. This time to remain there.

Gathering her foot soldiers for a countercharge against Eilene's people, Quindara barely noticed. They slammed into the tightly packed, pike-wielding Heaths, and were driven back. Three times they tried to break the enemy's lines and failed. Her face grim, the DeMarian Marshal brought up her Gwynethian archers.

In the center of the fray, David Elliot Greyam traded blows with a Branion woman for the third time before the battle swept them apart. Bashing in the skull of the foot soldier before him, the burly Heath fought to keep her in sight.

They'd squared off early in the day, David taking the first wound. The woman, dressed in vibrant red and purple had easily slapped his shield aside, dealing him a blow to the head with her mace that had set his ears to ringing. Incredulous, he was not long in returning the blow, but even with her helm knocked off, she seemed no worse for wear. She returned his attack, strike for strike, a smile on her face. Laughing with the joy of it, David swung his ax, chanting his ancient songs to the whistle of his weapon. Here was an adversary worth killing.

As the morning wore on, his groin ached from the saddle and the pleasure of fighting a beautiful woman. Visions of what she must be like in bed kept distracting him and at one point he had to withdraw to bring his mind back to business. But they soon came together once again. Although others came between them throughout the day, interrupting their strange courtship, they always returned to test each other's resolve.

Impressed by his abilities, and intrigued by the fate that kept bringing them together, Caroline DeLynne eagerly pursued the bearded Heathland man with the burly forearms and the lust in his eye. If they lived through this battle, the Earl of Buckshire thought, she'd have him, enemy or no.

Nearby, another pair of adversaries were fighting to reach each other. Demnor, exhausted by the constant slamming of power through his mind, nonetheless urged Titan toward the Elliot banner. Arren, too, was struggling to reach his Royal adversary. His people were badly outnumbered on the field and only the death of the DeMarian would end this quickly in their favor. But so far the tides of battle, or the determination of their people to protect their leaders had prevailed. Soon it would be just a question of who succumbed to exhaustion first.

Wearily the Heir of David Elliot raised his sword, and pushing his mount forward, swung again.

Florence thrust with her knife, then swept her legs sideways. Alynne, caught by the sudden feint, fell. Her arm flew out, a tiny throwing dagger whipped past Florence's left ear, carving a thin line of blood across it. While the Guild Representative jerked from its path, Alynne recovered into a defensive crouch.

"First blood, Younger Sister."

Teeth gritted, Florence ignored her and attacked again. Neatly avoiding the strike, the former Royal Companion left another line of crimson across the other's forearm.

Huddled in a corner, Kelahnus cradled his left arm and watched fuzzily through a haze of pain.

Alynne's attack against him had been lightening fast. Her first blow had snapped his arm just below the elbow; her second had hit him in the temple and the darkness had rushed over him. He'd fallen senseless as she turned to face her other enemy.

When he'd come groggily to consciousness, he'd crawled into a corner, his arm held tightly to his chest, his head spinning. Before him, the two former Royal Companions fought and, despite the pain that threatened to make him faint, he watched, unable to turn away.

Florence was angry, hurt by Alynne's betrayal, and it showed in her fighting style. Her attacks were aggressive and unplanned; her reactions wild. At this rate, she wouldn't stand long against Alynne. The former Com-

panion was cold, fighting with the grace and economy
of movement they'd all been taught. She'd already
scored first and second blood, and the light of victory
was in her eyes.

The thought of facing her, injured and unsteady on
his feet, made his testicles draw up. She would make
short work of him for certain.

With a lightning move, Alynne shot her dagger to
within an inch of Florence's right eye. The other
woman threw herself backward, then sideways to tear a
rip across Alynne's sleeve. But it missed the arm.

Panting, they circled each other warily.

Florence stumbled and, like a cat, Alynne was on
her. The two women struggled, the Guild Companion
throwing up her good hand to halt the other woman's
strike. Alynne's left hand clamped down on Florence's
injured wrist and for a moment they paused, frozen in
stalemate. The former Companion's knife dropped a
fraction of an inch toward the other's throat and she
smiled, knowing she'd won.

Florence grimaced in pain and then, as she stared
into Alynne's eyes, her expression grew bleak with
defeat. She closed her eyes. Alynne's arm loosened for
an instant as she prepared to strike. At that moment the
Guild Companion surged upward. Her wrist was slick
with blood, and using it as a lubricant, she jerked it
from Alynne's grasp. Ignoring the fresh gout as the
knife wound tore open, she thrust a stiffened, blood-
coated finger into the other woman's eye. With a cry,
Alynne fell back.

Florence flipped to her feet, knife ready.

One eye streaming tears, the former Companion
backed away.

"Tricky, Younger Sister. You seem to have regained
your composure."

She was expecting an attack, but instead of leading
with her blade, Florence feinted a strike to the left, then
dove forward, catching the other woman about the
knees. They fell together.

Rolling along the ground, each struggled to steady

herself for an instant and return to the attack. They reached the point simultaneously. Florence's blade sank into Alynne's thigh while the former Companion's knife caught the wound in the other's forearm and chewed upward. Florence cried out, losing her grip on her knife and jerking back.

Ignoring the wound spreading blood down her leg, Alynne dove forward. Her knife stopped half an inch from the Guild Representative's throat.

Kelahnus cried out and lurched forward.

Steel touched flesh.

"Not another step, Younger Brother."

He stumbled to a halt. His legs gave out and he fell, to land heavily against the wall.

"Alynne, don't," he gasped, as the pain made the room spin in sickening circles.

"I have to, Little One. It's her or me."

Florence said nothing. Her knife, a foot away from the arm pinned by Alynne's knee, lay unreachable.

"Alynne, please," Kelahnus begged. "It doesn't have to end this way."

"Doesn't it?"

"No, you've won." Pressing his back against the wall, he tucked his arm against his chest with a hiss. "We . . . we were just supposed to get a report, not bring you back. You can just leave."

"Don't be naive, Younger Brother. The Guild would never stop searching for me."

"But if you kill Florence, they'll send the Cousins. Even you can't defeat them."

"It will add to my lead."

Florence met her eye. "Master Elias will come after you himself," she croaked, "and then you'll pay." The movement sank the tip of Alynne's dagger a fraction into flesh, bringing a tiny welling of blood to the surface. She ignored it. "What are you waiting for? Do it. You've murdered once, what's twice?"

"Florence, shut up!" Kelahnus shouted. The effort made his head jerk in pain, but when his vision cleared, the two women had not moved. It gave him some hope.

"Alynne," he said urgently. "You said life was ... more complicated then I thought. You're wrong. I know. It gets all tangled up by love. Sometimes you have to choose. You chose love the first time. Please, choose it again."

"You're such a fool," she replied scornfully, but her knife eased back a fraction of an inch. "How did Klairius raise such a fool?"

"He didn't. His Majesty did."

"You're well matched, then. He's a fool, too."

"Maybe. But I love him. I broke from the Guild in my heart because of him. And Florence broke because of me."

Under Alynne's weight, Florence stirred, and the knife returned to its place. Alynne smiled in faint amusement.

"Oh? The loyal Companion of the Guild and the Crown has broken from them? Do tell me another faerie story, Younger Brother."

"It's true. She knew I loved him ... would do anything to protect him. She kept the Guild from ... from finding out how flawed he'd made me."

"Touching. What's your point?"

He could feel himself weakening, the darkness nibbling at the edge of his control. Taking a deep breath, he rushed on before it could claim him again. "That love can compromise us all. It should compromise us all. You said you loved her. Spare her for love's sake."

"And for love's sake, should I allow her to hunt me down?"

He could hear the softening in her voice. Just a few minutes more, and he was sure he could convince her. The throbbing of his arm made him feel nauseous, but he pushed on. "She won't," he panted. "She loves you, too, or she wouldn't have been so hurt. But even if she did, better to be hunted by someone you've already bested, than hunted by someone you haven't."

Florence's eyes shot daggers at the Royal Companion.

He ignored her. "And you won't be hunted at all if we convince the Guild you're already dead."

"And just how would we accomplish that?"

"I'd tell Master Klairius we killed you."

Once said, his strength seemed to ebb away. He leaned his head back, the pain in his arm pulsing up his shoulder to join the pain in his head.

Alynne laughed harshly. "You argue like a priest, with as much subtlety as a idiot child! Why, by all the flames in the world, should I believe you? And even if I did, what will you do, call down a miracle? I'm not planning on providing you with my corpse for added realism. Or will you simply lie straight-faced to the Head of the Companion's Guild and believe you could convince him! You've lost your reason, little man!"

Kelahnus groaned as he raised his head to meet her gaze. "I've been lying to him for years. So have you. You must have been. You know he doesn't see love for anyone but a Guild member. It's his weak spot. Please, Alynne. It will work. I know it . . ."

A sound behind him made him stop. Florence surged upward but, with a crack by her elbow, the former Companion subdued her again.

By the door, Alynne's maid stood, frozen in shock, staring at the blood-splattered carpet and the three figures frozen in a tableau of violence.

"My Lady," she breathed.

"It's all right, Maggie, just some old friends come for an impromptu visit." Alynne rose carefully, her knife still pointed at the other woman. Florence remained still.

Entering the room hesitantly, the maid made her way as far from the two strangers as possible.

"Shall I call the guards, My Lady?"

"Not quite yet. You may sit up, Younger Sister, and tend to your wounds. For now."

Pushing herself up with her good arm, Florence leaned against the wall and wrapped her other in the bottom of her tunic. Her black eyes stared uncompromisingly into Alynne's.

The former Companion turned to her maid. "Was there something you wished of me, Maggie?"

Glancing at the others, the woman rolled her eyes.

Alynne waved a dismissive hand. "They're no danger. You may speak freely in front of them."

"It's, ah, bad news, My Lady. Our forces have been routed at Falmarnnock and this fortress is no longer safe. We have to leave at once."

Alynne paled. "Gordon."

The maid shook her head. "I don't know, My Lady."

Alynne chewed at one knuckle, her thumb turning the golden band on her finger, then her face grew resolute. "Don't be afraid, Maggie. Gordon and I planned for every contingency. If he's alive, and I shall believe he is, he'll make for the place we agreed upon." She turned and began to stuff items into a small valise.

"What of the rest of our leadership?" she asked as she packed.

"Many have fallen. I don't know if . . ." The other woman choked, "I don't know if our Monarch is alive or taken."

"Then believe he's alive and free. To think otherwise is counterproductive. We'll meet up with them, regroup and plan for the next assault."

"Yes, My Lady."

"And of the enemy?"

"They took the field, but there've been some strange rumors. I heard they're now leaderless, that our Monarch slew the DeMarian in single combat with the aid of Essus. How true that rumor is, I don't know."

The world seemed to slow for Kelahnus, the only sound being his own heartbeat, growing louder and louder. Gray fog rushed in to blind him, and he would have fainted, but for a strong arm around him. As a paralyzing numbness began to creep over his limbs, he looked up into Alynne's face.

She shook him, her expression stern. "Don't believe

it until you see it, Little Brother. Be strong. Fly to him."

He nodded thickly.

"I don't know whether you're the fool, or I am," she continued. "But you're right. Love compromises us all, and we must live with our choices. I will tell the castle guards that you're under my protection. They'll let you leave." Her voice softened. "Take care of Florence. When her heart has healed, explain my reasoning to her. You can make her understand."

Dumbly he nodded again. Bending down, she kissed him softly, her lips salty with sweat. Then she turned to her maid, all business once again.

"Come."

"But, My Lady, you're injured."

"It's nothing. We'll tend to it on the trail."

They hurried from the room, leaving Kelahnus and Florence alone, staring at each other.

In the main Council Chamber of Bran's Palace a sudden jolting pain in her abdomen tore an involuntary scream from Isolde as she spoke with the Archpriest of the Sea. She fell.

Her guards rushed forward. Her midwife was summoned immediately as they carried the fainting Consort to her own rooms.

An hour passed. The Court hovered uncertainly about the entrance to the Royal wing. Rumors abounded. Blood had been seen spattered on the floor of the council chamber. There were whispers of poisoning, of miscarriage, of a new Essusiate plot to kill the Heir to the Living Flame.

The Temple Herbalist was summoned and came with a flock of priests and Flame Champions. Whispers of last fall began to be passed about the halls. These quickly abated when Isabelle DeKathrine, Duke of Exenworth, arrived on the scene. The area was quickly emptied of people and Isolde's mother swept inside to tend to her daughter.

Meanwhile, in the Consort's outer chamber, the most

senior priest left in Branbridge gulped down the potion of truth. Those hovering about him waited impatiently while the vision took him. Finally he spat out, "The Aristok!"

As one, they turned to the north, toward Heathland.

18. Demnor V

The fighting had gone on unabated most of the day. As the late afternoon sun beat down on his head, Demnor wearily raised his sword. Suddenly a face illuminated by a white light surged into his vision. Above it, a blade swung into the air. It hung balanced for an instant, then came whistling down. Crashing through surcoat and breastplate, it hit bone with an exploding crack.

Blood spurted up from the great wound and Demnor's hands flew up to clutch at it. He leaned forward, almost slowly, and fell, his lifeless body hitting the ground at Titan's feet.

The Aristok was dead.

The warhorse reared, its scream of pain echoed by the Duke of Kempston's.

The vision passed and Marsellus found himself kneeling, staring horror-struck at the ground an inch before his face. Shakily, he rose and wiped the saliva from his lips as the Flame Priests around him held back, waiting for the seizure to pass.

The Royal Seer clutched his head. His mind, numbed by the bulk of the violence around him, now throbbed with pain and the realization that he had stared death in the face.

Atreus, he thought. *Help me!*

But he was alone, his twin was in the fighting without him, and now his eldest brother was going to die. Soon.

He could see it. Smoky gray tendrils stretched across the battlefield, branching out like some great, evil tree, the tip of each one touching a friend or comrade destined to die. The thickest followed a blood link out to the very center of the fighting and the Royal standard.

The emotional cacophony of pain and blood lust crashed over him and he fell to his knees once more.

He couldn't face it, not again. Their mother's death, muted by years of disregard, had nearly destroyed him. This would kill him for sure.

Digging his fists into his eyes, he willed the visions away. For so many years they'd come at night, creeping in when he slept and slipping away just as quickly when he awoke. Now they seemed to have a life of their own, attacking when he least expected them.

Hands touched him on the shoulder, bringing the faint tingle of a Seer's touch that only another Seer could feel. He shrugged them off. Their comfort was shadow. Their Archpriest had made him come, taken the protective presence of his twin away and forced him to stand on the very edge of violence and slaughter where every death ripped great holes in his mind. She'd said she'd Seen him face his destiny on the battlefield of Falmarnnock. Years ago, he would simply have obeyed, trusting in her great prophecy, but his experience with his mother's death had made him hesitant and afraid. It'd taken an order by the Aristok to force him here and now that Aristok would die and he would be made to live through it all again.

Already he could feel the vision retake control. Scenes of violence and death swam before his eyes as the emotions of another man, a brother fighting for his life, swept over him. He fought them, struggled to retain his own thoughts, to push his own fear of death between himself and the growing doom of the other. The vision built and on its heels came the other. He saw a thrashing form, saw a murderer stand silently by and felt the achingly cold presence of the Shadow Catcher in the wings.

Marsellus screamed as his mother's death snatched

him up once again. He felt the poison on his lips, felt the fear and rage and the longing to speak just once more to the boy-child left behind to carry the burden. The veins in his neck standing out in painfully sharp relief, the Duke of Kempston fought his mother's presence as it struggled to find voice, to reach the man who carried the Flame. Within him, his own link to the Living Flame surged into life. In desperation, his Gift snapped out like a crossbow quarrel, racing toward his twin; the other half of his identity.

The violence of the sudden contact threw Atreus to the ground. All his brother's terror, all the unfiltered hate and pain of the battlefield, all of Melesandra's death throes slammed into the Duke of Lochsbridge's mind with the power of a hurricane. It tore a cry from his lips as it sucked him into the maelstrom. For an instant, he spun out of control, then with one surge of will, his mind caught hold of the storm and flung it outward. It burst forth with a great crack of psychic thunder that deafened all with even the faintest sensitivity on both sides.

Twisting above them, the vision took the form of a giant scarlet tornado. People on both sides stopped and stared, the battle forgotten, as its twisting form hurtled toward them. It sucked up the pain of the wounded and the blood lust of the fighters, adding each raw emotion to its bulk like a greedy child. Where it touched down, people died, their minds blown apart by its chaotic power.

Mary Elliot Ramsen was the first to fall. The vortex caught her up like a rag doll, carried her fifteen feet in the air and flung her into the line of stakes protecting the Heathland archers. Her only brother, fighting alongside her, died moments later, his neck snapped by the force of the psychic blast.

The vortex tore through the Heathland ranks, churning up mud and people alike in its destructive path. It caught up a retainer in the party of the Marquis de Touleuvre and scattered the others like chaff. Then it turned and struck into the very heart of the battlefield.

Deverne Jones, fighting beside the Duke of Yorbourne, saw it bear down on them. Without thinking he leaped between it and the Royal Duke. He took the full force of the maelstrom in the chest. It whipped around him, catching the Duke a glancing blow. The Flame that was her heritage surged up to meet it and she was flung forward by the force of it. The Sword Knight's last sight was of dark red blood staining the bright copper of her hair and he died without knowing if his sacrifice had been worthwhile.

On the edge of the battle, Kassandra DeMarian suddenly screamed as Fire burned a path through her mind and she collapsed into the arms of Robert DePaula's squire.

People began to flee the battlefield as the vortex grew bigger, eclipsing the sun.

A single command froze it in its path.

Another called it home.

The maelstrom churned, fighting for control, then streaked down into the waiting mind of Gwynne DeLlewellynne. She caught it, absorbed its wild power and forming it into a great spear of fire, the Living Flame's Archpriest spat it with all her strength at her Avatar. Then she crumpled to the ground.

Deep in combat that had seen no abatement despite the maelstrom's sudden appearance, Demnor had little time to react when his form suddenly exploded in Fire. Titan shrieked, reared and slashed out with his forehooves, while Demnor's enemies fell back, crying out in terror.

The conflagration streaked toward the sky, crackling against the clouds above. Drowning in the blaze, Demnor screamed, his head thrown back, flames pouring from his eyes and mouth. Fire roared through his body, tracing a raging pattern down his limbs and bursting out through his fingertips. The force of it drove him up in the saddle as Titan reared. His sword, blood-red, sent a bolt of lightning into the air as the Living Flame took the field.

The specter opened its mouth to scream again, and

the unearthly shriek bounced across the sky. A great
gout of blood-red flames spewed from its mouth and
shot into the air, taking the form of a giant, crimson
fire-wolf. The enemy broke, but before they could flee
there was a deafening crack of thunder and a white
light so pure that it blinded all who looked at it, illuminated the sky.

Arren felt the power of Essus slam into his body.
Around him the air grew bitterly cold as the God's rage
built into a towering cone of power. It raced through
him and burst from his lips with a shriek that destroyed
his throat. Streaking toward the clouds it twisted and
changed until Merrone, the colossal white dragon of
Essus, rose up to challenge the fiery wolf.

Those left standing on the field gaped as their
leaders came together with sword and shield, mirroring
the immortal combat surging above them. The specters
on horseback, almost as terrible as the manifestations
of their Gods, savaged each other, hacking at the bands
of protective light, both red and white, while the wolf
and dragon tore at each other with tooth and claw.

Below, the Priests of the Flame and the Clerics of
Essus threw their support behind their Avatars but,
without the control of their Archpriest, the Triarctic
powers began to fold.

Inundated by fire, Demnor gave himself up to the
Living Flame. It moved his limbs with unearthly speed,
hacking and slashing at the Avatar of Essus with mania-
cal fury. The pressure build behind his eyes until he
feared his head might blow apart. His surroundings
blurred and suddenly he stood atop a rocky pinnacle
overlooking the battle. He held two, multifaceted gems,
the color of blood in his hands and an ethereal army
gathered at his back. Above him the dragon and fire-
wolf savaged each other with desperate fury. Below, his
body fought on while the priests of the Triarchy began
to fall.

The dragon screamed in triumph.

"No!" His vision in the Sword Tower streaked
through his mind, demanding an answer, a decision.

Two gems, one leading to victory, the other to destruction. But which was which, and what was the decision he was supposed to make? He stood, frozen with uncertainty, on the very edge of the pinnacle while the dragon tore a mouthful of fur and meat from the fire-wolf's flank and a Triarchy Priest crumbled to the ground.

"Two gems."

Gwynne DeLlewelynne's voice echoed in his mind.

"Two futures."

"You will know, Most Holy, when the time comes."

"I don't know!"

"You will know." Her voice began to fade.

"Wait!"

"You will . . . know ."

Demnor fell to his knees. Above, the dragon ripped a great slash across the fire-wolf's back, as below another Triarchy Priest collapsed, and Arren's sword cracked against the Aristok's shield.

"I don't know! Please, don't go!"

"Demnor!"

The harshly spat word jerked his head up and he cried out in surprise as Melesandra's ghostly form appeared before him.

"Demnor!"

Her hands reached out blindly searching, and her agonizing cry sent the hairs on the back of his neck rising in horror. Death had turned her skin a sickly gray, and, limbs thrashing convulsively, she cried out again.

"Demnor!"

"No! Get away!"

"My son!"

Arms wrapped around his eyes to block out the ghastly sight, Demnor curled himself up, the gems clutched to his chest.

"I can't!"

"You must!" Her words were imperative, and when he looked up, she glared at him through flaming, poison-glazed eyes.

The Living Flame stirred in response, pulsing up from the ground to throb through his body. Demnor tasted the now familiar link with the past, felt another's presence and looked past Melesandra into his grandfather's dying eyes.

The scream that tore from his lips as he jerked back, convulsed the spectral fire-wolf and the dragon took the opportunity to slash at it once again. Below, his body took another blow.

On the pinnacle, behind his mother and grandfather, thirty-eight DeMarian rulers took form, stretching out their hands toward their descendant. On their heels came the Shadow Catcher.

Its face was misty and expressionless and, when it breathed, a chilling wind stirred all around him. The Avatars stepped back in supplication and it drew nearer.

High in the sky, the two spectral combatants paused as a great cloud drifted toward the fire-wolf, but unseen, the ghostly presence of a gentle man touched his niece's arm, offering a kind of strength she had never known in life.

"Get back!"

The shouted command halted the Shadow Catcher and it turned its blank features on the form of Melesandra DeMarian, now standing over her Heir, spectral sword in hand.

"You'll not have him before his time!"

It reached forward, and again she commanded it to halt. Again it obeyed. The fortieth Avatar of the Living Flame then turned, her own hand outstretched toward her son. Demnor flinched away.

On the battlefield, consumed by opalescent energy, Arren raised his sword, icy waves of power pulsing down his arm. His eyes, no longer pale blue, were marble orbs of white light, tracked across the faltering bands of fire about his adversary. The bands faded and Essus struck.

Demnor's shield, red hot, exploded into a burst of flying metal and burning wood.

On the pinnacle the Aristok cried out as pain blazoned up his right arm. He almost lost the gem in that hand but, at the last minute, he kept his grip.

Above, the fire-wolf shrieked as the dragon caught its throat up in its jaws.

"Demnor!"

Melesandra reached for him again and again he flinched away.

"My son!" Her voice ragged with desperation, her face an agony of grief, his mother's ghost fell to her knees beside him. *"Please, you must let me help you!"*

The dragon bit down.

Demnor's scream mirrored the fire-wolf's cry. Pain ripped through him, snapping his body into convulsions. The Shadow Catcher reached for him and he saw tears streaming down his mother's face. With his last ounce of strength, he flung his good arm out, the gem forgotten, and caught her hand. The gem spun into the air and disappeared from his sight.

Arren's sword caught Demnor across the chest. An explosion of pure, clear energy shattered the breastplate and both men were flung to the ground from the force of it. Demnor, almost unconscious, was jerked to his feet, the power of forty DeMarian Avatars snapping his body forward. His sword swept down and was caught by Arren's blade as Essus threw the other man's arm up in defense. The two powers strained against each other, the faces of their Avatars drawn into masks of animal rage, then the white light was suddenly extinguished. Demnor's weapon crashed down on the skull of the Heathland leader. Arren fell, the dragon disappeared with a final discharge of energy, and the fire-wolf slowly melted into the clouds as Demnor collapsed.

Behind the Heathland lines, the Clerics of Essus beat Jamie Elliot Croser to death with their bare hands, but the deed was done. Sister Marie-Claire of Gallia, the focal point of the Circle of Twelve that had called up a God, lay dead, Jamie's ax buried in her back.

* * *

The sun was setting as Eilene Elliot Duglas picked at a congealed mass of blood on her chin and grimaced. They were defeated; defeated and routed. Shaking her head, white hair standing up in stiff spikes of gore, she spat onto the ground. Defeated.

Arren was dead. Most of his army was also. Of the four hundred Duglas kin Eilene had brought to Falmarnnock maybe three dozen had escaped, and a dozen more were captives like herself, held in a commandeered coral outside the village.

Pulling at the encrusted blood in her hair with blunt fingers, she spat again. It'd been a good fight, until the end. At the back of the corral the four clerics who'd been taken alive glared at the small collection of Crosers. Eilene shook her head.

Ah, Jamie, she thought. *Why? Why did you do it?*

They were winning, they'd all seen it. The DeMarian was weakening; one more blow would have finished him. *Why?*

Had the Branion God found some traitorous weakness in his heart to exploit? They would never know, but the Croser family would never be the same. Her gaze swept over the small group of men and women standing defensively alone in one corner of the corral, shunned by their fellow prisoners. There would be war in Heathland again, family against family. Branion and Yorbourne would be forgotten in this smaller, older battle, as if Arren's dream had never existed.

Eilene was too tired to be bitter. Never especially devout, the Head of the Duglas family decided maybe it was time to become so. Essus had manifested, fought at their side, and then abandoned them. They hadn't been worthy, hadn't been truly unified, but maybe they would be next time.

She straightened. They would regroup and try to hold Heathland together despite the defeat. She hadn't seen Gordon among the prisoners or the dead. His historic deed might keep the Croser name clean and free from dishonor until they could reorganize. Whether he had the will to continue the battle with so many taken remained to be seen. Eilene shrugged. They weren't her problem now. Her problem was to protect the youth who stood, shaking and wide-eyed beside her; Colleen Elliot Armistone, last of the royal House of Elliot, symbol of Heathland sovereignty, an anonymous prisoner in Branion hands.

As unobtrusively as she could, Eilene had stripped the Elliot badge from Colleen's arm when they were taken, whispering fiercely in the girl's ear not to reveal her heritage. Then she'd quietly grouped her kindred around them. Relying on Colleen's training not to do anything that would make the enemy suspicious, she made ready to grab at whatever straw Essus might throw them. She doubted they'd be hanged, the DeMarian had shown no love of that kind of sport, but languishing in some filthy Branion prison wasn't to her liking either. She waited.

Beside her, David Elliot Greyam stared scornfully at the opposing forces. His eyes fell on one face in the crowd, the face of the woman he'd fought to a standstill. And, until that last bit of mummery had distracted him, almost gained the upper hand over. But the flash and fire had given her enough room to land one lucky blow and he'd gone arse over tip. Damned but she was a spirited lass. Pity she was a Branion.

Feeling his gaze on her, Caroline DeLynne turned and met his eyes. She ached in a hundred places, although the look she shot him showed none of this. He grinned at her, white teeth flashing in the dark, bearded face, and she smiled haughtily in return. It'd been a good fight, and you never knew. Once the country was subdued, she might return and take him up on the invitation in his eyes. But first the Aristok had to decide his fate, and the Aristok was not here. Her eyes tracked across the camp to the small orchard where they'd carried His Majesty. If the Aristok survived to decide his fate.

At the base of a gnarled apple tree, Demnor turned in the Hierarchpriest's arms and retched. His back against the trunk, Alexander waited until the spell passed, then gathered up his Sovereign again, careful not to jar the broken arm lashed to the other man's chest. As Demnor's body began to jerk with renewed convulsions, Alexander closed his eyes.

He'd carried his second cousin, semiconscious and raving, from the battlefield after the Living Flame had guttered out. Others had raced to assist him with his Royal burden, but when the seizures had threatened to spill him from their arms, they'd been forced to stop in the orchard. They'd laid him on the ground and the Hierarchpriest had dismissed them, cradling the younger man in his arms. An hour later they were still there.

Retching and choking, Demnor slipped in and out of consciousness, the visions still gripping his mind. Something held his limbs immobile and he fought its constraint, crying out as movement sent fresh pain sweeping up his arm. Dimly he heard a familiar voice whispering comfort and he groped for it, as a man in the dark reaches for a faint light in the distance.

His hand pressed against the fevered brow of his Sovereign, Alexander rocked him gently, whispering that everything would be all right. The Aristok calmed for a moment and the Hierarchpriest was remembered of a day, many years ago when he'd held a young Prince on the field of Kormandeux, where his mother had insisted he come. Demnor had been . . . he thought a moment . . . only four. The boy had looked out across the corpse-filled field, then turned and gazed into his cousin's face. His grave, fire-tinged gray eyes had been sad, and Alexander wondered now at the madness of bringing so young a child to a place of such carnage. He hadn't questioned it then.

Closing his eyes, the Hierarchpriest bowed his head, ashamed. Melesandra's word had been law. He'd never contested it, even in his heart. He'd stood by her side, giving safe counsel and following her orders, secure in his loyalty to the Crown. Until now.

Melesandra had died, and the Realm had all but been

lost because of Yorbourne's madness. Then Demnor
had returned, expecting his loyalty as the Aristok had
the right to do, and he had turned away. Why? Because
he'd always seen the young DeMarian as a boy?

*"He's a bright and affectionate child, and I'm afraid
of what might happen to his nature should anything
befall me . . ."*

The words of Amedeus DeMarian, so many years
ago, echoed in his mind. Alexander looked down at his
Royal cousin, seeking the boy he had known.

Demnor's face was cracked and sunburned from the
power of the Flame. His eyes, gazing inward, were red,
his face bathed in sweat, and his body taut with
renewed convulsions. No hint of the open and loving
boy he'd been remained in the tortured features. He
was a man and the Avatar of a God, lost in the throes of
his vision. No Flame Priests remained on the field to
help him, only the Leader of their Faith who had never
been a Seer.

*". . . so I want you to promise that you'll watch over
him and protect him."*

"You have my vow, of course, My Prince . . ."

Stroking his ruler's forehead, the Hierarchpriest of
Cannonshire closed his eyes in recognition of his
failure.

Finally, as the setting sun cast deep shadows about
them, Demnor coughed and looked up into the face of
his second cousin. The fire had subsided, returning the
gray to his eyes, although they were still dark and
bloodshot.

"The gem," he whispered so quietly that Alexander
had to bend to hear him.

"My Liege?"

Demnor dropped his head, then glanced around him
wearily.

"Kass?"

"She's here, Sire."

Gesturing for the Duke of Clarfield to approach,
Alexander shifted so she could take her brother's hand.

"Kass?"

Kassandra's face was gray, blood drying on her mouth and nose. She moved stiffly, but nodded at her brother's word, wiping the sudden tears from her face with a violent swipe of her sleeve. "I'm here," she said. "I'm all right."

"Where am I?"

"Under a tree."

He frowned in confusion, then sighed.

"Did we win?"

"Uh-huh. It's all done."

"Done?"

"The battle, My Liege," Alexander answered. "We hold the field and the Heaths are all fled or captured. Elisha DeLynne has given chase, and the word is that Tottenham has surrendered."

"But the gem . . ."

"Sire?"

Demnor coughed again. "The gem didn't change," he whispered almost inaudibly. "I don't . . ."

His slumped. After a minute his eyes opened again and he turned with a groan. Pulling his fingers from his sister's grip, he made a faint gesture toward his mouth. She nodded and repeated the gesture at the crowd of watchers waiting beyond the orchard.

Leaping the fence that separated them from their ruler, Alerion approached at a run. Kneeing before them, he pulled out his pipe. Alexander glared at him.

"Don't you think that water might be a better choice?" he asked caustically.

Alerion shrugged. "He asked for a pipe." Filling it, he then struck a flint. When the pipe was lit, he passed it over.

Demnor accepted it, gripping the bowl tightly to still the shaking of his fingers, and sucked in one, long lungful. The thick narcotic acted quickly, dampening the pain in his arm and chest.

"Thank you . . . Ler."

His oldest friend nodded without speaking. Touching Demnor lightly on the shoulder, he glanced away, searching for some light-hearted topic. He smiled.

"Zold'll never to forgive you for getting yourself covered in glory without her," he said casually.

"Make it . . . up to her in Gallia."

"Well, you better, or you'll never hear the end of it. She can scald the ears off an iron gargoyle when she gets going."

Alexander shot a cold look at the younger DeKathrine.

"The Consort will naturally be worried about her husband's well-being and not give herself over to petty jealousy, Nephew," he admonished.

Alerion bowed his head in mock contrition, although the smile remained on his face. Demnor found himself smiling weakly back.

"The Aristok has recovered himself," the Hierarch-priest continued. "We'll be moving him shortly. Tell the others."

Alerion nodded. Staring into Demnor's face for a long moment, he grinned crookedly, then rose. After sketching a quick bow, ne moved off.

Slowly the crowd around the fence began to disperse.

Demnor looked up at Alexander. "How many . . . have we lost?" he asked thickly.

"Not many, My Liege."

"Who?"

Alexander looked away. "We don't have a complete list yet, sir . . ." he began.

"Cousin."

The Hierarchpriest met Demnor's eyes, then sighed. "Gwynne."

"Dead?"

He nodded. "The Flame was too much for her. Ten other priests fell also, and the seven remaining are unconscious."

"Mars? I felt him . . . is he. . . ?"

"No, Sire. He's not dead, though I couldn't say if he'll recover."

"He and Tray are with the priests," Kassandra interrupted. "It doesn't look good."

"And . . . Quindara?"

Kassandra glanced quickly at the Hierarchpriest.

"She's injured," Alexander answered hesitantly. "But Agrippa is confident that she'll recover."

"Who else?"

Alexander hesitated. "Sire, don't you think maybe you should . . ."

"Who . . . else, My Lord of Cannonshire."

Alexander bowed his head. Wordlessly, Kassandra held out a list and, shifting so he had a hand free, the Hierarchpriest accepted it and began to read.

"Arthur DePaula, Earl of Bethwich, Rath DeSharon, Viscount of Surbrook, Janet DeSharon, Earl of Woolstan, Deverne Jones, Knight of the Sword, Phillip DeKathrine . . ."

Demnor closed his eyes as the list went on and on. Finally Alexander paused.

"In all six hundred dead, and over one thousand wounded, My Liege."

Demnor absorbed the numbers silently.

After a moment, the Hierarchpriest gave the Heathland tally. Twice that number. The Aristok shook his head painfully.

By the Flame, it'd been a bloodbath.

"Their leader?"

"Dead, Your Majesty. You slew him in single combat."

Demnor frowned. "No. The light . . . went out. I think . . . he was dead before I hit him."

"Perhaps, Sire," Alexander agreed noncommittally.

The Aristok was quiet for a long time, and just as Alexander began to think he had drifted away again, he looked up.

"Cousin?" His voice was childlike with fatigue and pain, and Alexander felt a sudden thickening in his throat.

"Yes, Demi?" he answered, using Demnor's boyhood name without thinking.

"My . . . arm hurts."

"I know." Alexander resumed stroking the younger

man's forehead gently. "It's broken. Will you take a draught for it?"

After a moment Demnor nodded, and the Hierarch-priest gestured Agrippa over.

Sometime later they were able to get him groggily to his feet and out of the orchard. With Alexander on one side, and Agrippa on the other, he managed to walk to his own tent.

The crowds of warriors and camp followers bowed silently as he passed until a bloody Palace Guard, the red badge of Gwyneth on his sleeve, lifted one fist in the air.

"Long live Demnor the Fifth!"

The cheering spread until the entire victorious army was chanting. "ALL HAIL THE ARISTOK!"

Demnor paused before his tent, gave his people a weary nod, then disappeared inside. Alexander helped him to his cot and Kassandra removed his boots, while Agrippa finally set his arm properly. When they left, the forty-first Avatar of the Living Flame slept.

In the prison compound, Eilene Elliot Duglas scowled, as she listened to the crowd, and drew her cloak more fully about her Royal charge.

Early the next morning, Demnor stood on a high out-cropping, staring out across the silent battlefield. The warriors were gone now. The only movement on the blackened landscape were the camp followers fighting their own skirmishes with the eagles and gryphons, come to devour the dead. He looked away.

Rubbing at the sunburned flesh on his face, he sagged against a scraggy tree, then jerked back as the movement pulled at his broken arm. The pain made him sick and he gagged, just managing to hold onto his breakfast. Dizzily he groped for a seat, then sank down on a pile of rocks.

He was ill yet. Agrippa had asked him to remain in his tent for one more day, but there was work to be done and Demnor had refused. Now, sitting above the battlefield where the Heathland archers had deployed the day before, his gaze swept across the field.

The enemy had fought well, but then they always did. They'd held his superior forces, met charge with countercharge over and over, until he'd begun to fear the battle would never end. And in some ways it still hadn't.

His people had carried the day, won on the field and driven the enemy into the hills. Those castles that still held out would soon fall, but it was far from over. He had only to look into the faces of the Heathland prisoners to see that as long as one of them remained alive, they would fight on. Maybe not today, but tomorrow, and next year and the year after that, and on down through the ages. Essus had taken the field. Their struggle had their God's divine blessing.

He was suddenly very tired.

A noise made him turn and he saw Terion DePaula climbing up the hill behind him. The older man's graying hair was damp as if he'd just come from bathing and he smiled shyly at his Sovereign as he ascended the last few feet.

"My Lord of Linconford."

Demnor's voice was ragged, torn by the shrieking of the Living Flame, and his throat ached when he tried to form words.

Terion bowed. "I hope I'm not interrupting your thoughts, My Liege . . ."

"No."

The Earl smiled happily and, with Demnor's permission, took a seat beside him. Pulling out his pipe, he absently stroked his fingers over the bowl. "That was quite the battle, sir, wasn't it?"

"Hm."

"Young Phillip got himself killed, you know."

"I heard. I'm sorry."

"So is Katrina." Terion shook his head. "So young," he mused. "They get younger every year."

"Hm."

"Oh, I'm forgetting my errand." Brushing a hand

through his hair, Terion frowned. "Your Generals await your decision on the prisoners, and on the occupation of Tottenham Castle, and Agrippa fears that you'll topple off from here and kill yourself. He's asked if you will remove yourself to a less dangerous vantage point."

"Presently."

Terion nodded. Lighting his pipe, he drew on it then stared out across the battlefield.

"You know, it's a funny thing, Majesty," he noted after a moment. "I had a feeling you might have something on your mind. I looked up at you, sitting here all alone and thought to myself, he wants you Terri, so get up there. Isn't that funny?"

"No. You said much the same thing to me after Troysailles."

"That was a terrible battle."

"Hm." Demnor stared into space for a long time. Finally he turned to his old friend. "How long have you had the prescient feelings, Terri?"

"All my life, Sire."

"Have you ever had actual visions?"

"One or two."

"I never had them, until I took the Throne.

"I always thought they were supposed to unveil the future. What happens when they confuse more than they clarify?"

The Earl rubbed at the stubble on his chin before answering. "You keep searching for the answer until you find it, I believe, Sire. What did you see?"

Briefly Demnor sketched out the visions, the gems, the replaying of his mother's death in the garden, and her ghostly form above the battlefield. Terion frowned in concentration.

"I've found, Majesty, that there's seldom one meaning, or message if you will. This seems to be twofold, one choice for yourself, and one for the Realm. For yourself, you accepted your mother's death, and her love as it was given, as flawed and raw as it may have been. Just as you accepted it so many years ago, even though you didn't know it, and now you're ready to grow green and healthy." He chuckled at the image his words invoked.

Demnor blinked at him. "Excuse me?"

Terion looked confused. "Sire?"

"I accepted what years ago?"

"Her love. When she gave you the Palace Guard. When she set your crest upon their sleeves."

"That was a punishment, for them and for me."

"No offense, My Liege, but you're wrong. No Ruler would allow such a large martial body to wear another's crest unless she's given them that body. The late Aristok gave the Palace Guard to you in reward for bravery and honor on the field of Briery, sir."

Demnor was shaking his head, but the more Terion spoke the more it made sense.

"She wasn't able to come right out and say it," the Earl continued sadly. "Her training forbade it, as yours does, but she felt it, I'm sure she did. She was proud of your strength."

Demnor turned away, his eyes burning. After a moment, he asked thickly, "And the choice for the Realm?"

"Well, sir, it's a mystery." Terion brushed his hand through his hair again, then stopped. "What does Your Majesty think? I mean, if you were to simply answer me without thinking, what would you say the meaning was?"

Demnor stared out across the field and suddenly it seemed to become the field of his vision, the rocky outcropping, the precipice and the army encamped below, the same army that awaited his decision. He held his left hand out, envisioning a red multifaceted gem glittering in the sunlight.

"Heathland." He blinked. "I remember thinking it represented the risk of something precious, and if Heathland wasn't precious, what was?"

"Perhaps that's your answer, then, sir. Heathland."

"The Archpriest disagreed."

Terion observed his Sovereign shrewdly. "No offense

to the fallen, My Liege, but *you* are the Vessel of the Living Flame."

"I am that." Demnor dropped his hand, the seeds of an idea tugging at his mind. He let it grow, turning it this way and that, searching for flaws. He never noticed when the Earl of Linconford slipped away.

An hour later, Demnor the Fifth stood, looking over the rows of Heathland prisoners. They glared back at him, undaunted and unafraid of the power he held. They were defeated in the flesh, though not in spirit; never in spirit. He smiled inwardly.

Their two countries had been tied by battle and conquest for centuries, but a great gulf separated them in culture, in national pride and most importantly, in religion. Heathland had been staunchly Essusiate since the defeat of the Triarctic King Maelbeatha in 357. Five hundred years. And Essus had taken the field in defense of Heath independence this very day. Religion was the greatest barrier to peace on the island. Or was it?

Branion was allied with Eireon, a one-time enemy But a Triarctic nation also, his mind supplied. Well, then, with Essusiate Fenland, fast becoming Reformist, a much more flexible form of worship than its orthodox parent. They were even trading partners with the Free Cities of Florenz, whose capital Tiberia was the birthplace of Essusiatism. Stranger bedfellows had been made before. But . . .

But to accomplish anything Heathland's tie with Gallia must first be weakened. To do it would take time, maybe years and an abundance of patience he wasn't sure he had. And why would Heathland turn then to Branion, their traditional enemy?

Heathland would have to be wooed. For that wooing to have any merit, Heathland must be seen as an independent nation of power and wealth equal to that of its southern neighbor. The shadow of freedom was not enough. Heathland must be released to its own destiny,

and then offered a partnership with Branion. The
audacity of the idea had left him gaping.

It would be seen as a weakness, as the DeMarians'
reign losing its centuries-old grip. It would lead to a
greater resolve to fight them on the Continent. It would
lead to absolute ruin, rebellion and chaos in his own
lands. Wouldn't it? Would it?

He scratched at a patch of peeling skin by his ear.
Unused to subtlety and guile, his mind had carried
him this far, then met a stubbornly blank wall. How do
you gain without force? It was still the unanswered
question.

He caught sight of Caroline DeLynne, staring with
open lust at a huge, bearded Heathland man. The man
seemed equally enthralled. Well, that was one way. He
would have an Heir come spring. And he had Councillors used to diplomatic intrigue. It could be done.

The image of a multifaceted gem transforming into a
white-and-red-plumed bird crossed his mind.

*The risk of something precious, and if Heathland
wasn't precious, what was?*

Letting go was not weakness, he thought suddenly. It
was strength; an act of faith and courage. Uncle
Amedeus had told him that years ago. He had only just
now remembered it.

The image of his grandfather and mother fighting the
Shadow Catcher with their last scrap of will echoed in
his mind. They had not known it. He may have been
the first DeMarian ruler in history to know it.

He made his decision.

He would do it and to the Flames with the consequences.

He would do it bluntly and suddenly, with no
warning and no discussion. He stepped forward, gesturing for the corral gate to be opened wide.

The prisoners tensed, ever so imperceptibly leaning
toward a white-haired woman wearing a Duglas clan
badge and her squire. The Aristok spoke.

"I would speak my terms with one of you. Choose
someone."

After a moment, the Duglas woman stepped past the guards and stood facing him. Her stance was aggressive, arms crossed over her chest, yielding nothing.

Demnor almost smiled in response. By the Flame, he loved these people and he would have them as his allies if took a thousand years. They held each other's gaze for a long time, then the Aristok stirred.

Reaching up, he undid the great sapphire clasp that held the ragged DeMarian Plaide to his shoulder. The Branions around him stirred in confusion and the Heaths grew very still. The Plaide slid down into his arms; an untidy bundle of gray and red wool, shot with black and spattered with blood. Symbol of Heathland's Sovereignty; symbol of Branion's supremacy; part of the DeMarian royal regalia for four centuries; Demnor the Fifth held it out, cloth spilling out past his fingers.

Desire winning over suspicion, Eilene's hands darted out to catch it. She drew back a step, the bloody sash cradled protectively in her arms, then passed it to her squire.

Demnor grunted his approval and raised his voice so those around could hear.

"I would have an end to this pointless aggression between us. I *will* have it. If there are any left who carry the Royal blood of Heathland in their veins, have them send ambassadors to me and we'll talk. Heathland is an independent nation from this moment. You're all free to go." He spun on his heel. "My Lord of Yorbourne!"

Caught off guard by the sudden announcement and the sudden summons, Quindara jerked forward. Her face was gaunt and gray beneath the bandage about her brow. She, like Demnor, was up and about against Agrippa's wishes. She saluted automatically.

"Have our dead borne from the field. The Heaths may go likewise without hindrance. Then we're going home."

"Your Majesty. . . ?" Staring at her older brother as if he'd gone mad, her face mirrored the shocked expressions of his host. Finally the Duke of Yorbourne managed to choke out a strangled, "Why?"

"Because I wish it!"

"Because . . . By the Flame!" She stood, shaking her head, and Demnor sighed.

"Sister, I know what I'm doing. Trust me."

Green eyes stared uncertainly into gray, saw the new strength of purpose there, and then cleared. She turned, her own decision made. Waving at her people, she moved off to carry out his orders.

The prisoners, equally dumbfounded, stood silent and unbelieving. After a long while, the white-haired woman started cautiously away, her squire behind her. As if awakening from a dream, the others quickly moved to surround them and their precious cargo. An honor guard of warriors escorted the Elliot Plaide from the camp of the Aristok.

Demnor turned to Alexander DeKathrine. "Your thoughts, my Lord of Cannonshire?"

Alexander shook his head. "I confess they're in a state of confusion, Sire," he answered after a time. "As I don't know what My Liege intends, I can't comment." His voice held a faint touch of reproach. "It will lower the Crown's income, that much is certain."

With a sudden predatory gleam in his eye, the Aristok smiled. "Nonsense, Cousin. We have all of Gallia to conquer. We'll leave within the month."

"Yes, Majesty." Alexander made to add something, then stopped. "Shall I ready the camp to depart then, My Liege?" he asked simply.

"Tomorrow. For tonight, rest and recover. Set guards . . . just in case. I'll speak to the troops later this afternoon. You'll understand my reasoning then." He paused.

"I have an idea, Cousin," he said after a moment's silence. "It's risky, and it may not work. I have to think on it a while. Then I'll call a Council and listen to the thoughts of my Ministers. For now, tell any who ask that they fought well, and that I'm proud of them.

I'll be in my tent. My arm pains me, and I want some rest."

"Yes, My Liege."

As the Hierarchpriest moved off, Demnor turned and reentered his tent.

You'll understand my reasoning then.

Stretched out on his cot, Demnor studied the canvas above his head. Better come up with some pretty convincing words, his mind warned, or the gem might still fall.

He nodded to himself. There was time. The army would be a buzzing swarm of bees when he emerged, but Yorbourne and Cannonshire would keep order. This time he knew they would work together.

Content to let the muted sounds of camp life drift over him, Demnor dozed.

Some time later a familiar touch brought him abruptly up from sleep. Opening his eyes, he gazed at a golden-haired vision.

Kelahnus, dust covered, gaunt with fatigue, and dried blood encrusted on his temple, knelt beside him, gazing worriedly down with eyes wide and dark. When he saw his lover awaken, he tried a smile though tears began to spill down his face. He made no attempt to stop them, just stared at the other man with a starved, frightened expression that caused a lump in Demnor's throat.

Chewing uncertainly at his lower lip, the older man held out his good arm and Kelahnus folded into his embrace. Only then did Demnor notice the sling about the Companion's own arm. His eyes widened in alarm, but he had no chance to speak of it as sobs shook the other man's slender frame. Finally he calmed.

"I thought you'd been killed," Kelahnus choked out, his voice muffled by Demnor's leather jerkin. "I'm so *tired* of thinking you've been killed."

Undone, all Demnor could do was hold him, wincing as Kelahnus pushed his head against his bruised chest.

Leaning his chest against the Companion's head, he closed his eyes.

"I'm sorry."

Swiping futilely at his nose, Kelahnus straightened, looking rumpled and embarrassed. "You should be," he sniffed, attempting to wipe the tears from Demnor's tunic. "look what you did to me. My eyes are red and my face is all blotchy.

Demnor met his eyes. "I think you're beautiful."

"What do you know."

"Not much.

"Your arm?"

"It's broken," the Companion shrugged. "A woman in Tottenham set it. She says it'll be fine. Are you all right?" Kelahnus's voice was childlike with weary worrying. "Someone said you caught fire and burned to death and someone else said a giant white dragon ate you and someone *else* said he had no *idea* what happened to you, he just hoped it was something awful, and Florence said I couldn't kill him for it, and I *wish* you were a scholar or a priest or something because I don't think I can take much more of this."

"You won't have to. We're going home."

The Companion searched his face. "Promise?"

"I promise."

"No more wars?"

Demnor hesitated. "Well, not right at this moment. I have to go to Gallia, but . . . later."

The Companion sighed. "Sometimes I hate you, you know. I never come first in your life."

With a helpless gesture, Demnor touched the younger man's cheek. "You come first in my heart. It's all that's mine to give you."

With a tired smile, Kelahnus nodded. "I know. I do really. I'm just tired. It was a long ride." He looked up at the older man again. "You look terrible."

"I feel worse. Are *you* all right? I mean besides . . . the arm?"

"I'm fine. Why, don't I look all right?"

The warning tone in the Companion's voice made

Demnor smile. "You look perfect." He stroked the other man's cheek. "But the blood?" He gestured at the other man's head. "What happened?"

"Alynne."

Demnor grew very still. "Where is she?"

Kelahnus looked away. After a long moment he turned back and met his lover's gaze.

"We let her go," he answered simply.

Demnor's eyes went wide and the red flames rose as his expression hardened. Propping himself up on one elbow, he stared in disbelief at the other man.

"You what? Why?" he croaked, unable to trust his voice above a whisper.

"Why did you let Heathland go?"

"Answer my question."

Touching the older man lightly on the chest, Kelahnus smiled weakly. "I am answering it. Why did you let Heathland go?"

Demnor shook his head. "The reasons are complicated."

"So are mine."

"She murdered the Sovereign of Branion."

"I know." The Companion dropped his gaze. "To be honest, I had very little choice. We were only supposed to talk to her. Things got out of hand."

Demnor nodded his sudden understanding. "She was ready for you."

"Yes."

"By the Flame, you could have been killed!"

"I know. Florence and I both. She's a better fighter, and a better strategist." *The best the School had to offer,* his mind added.

Rubbing at his temples, Demnor shuddered. "You fool," he whispered. Looking up, his eyes were wet. "What would I have done if you'd been killed."

"I wasn't," the Companion answered in a low tone. "She couldn't do it. She had Florence at her mercy and couldn't do it. It's . . . complicated."

"I'm sure. What am I supposed to do now? I'll have

to send troops searching through a country I've just freed to its own destiny."

Kelahnus looked up. "That mightn't be very politic, My Lord," he said carefully.

"Politic?"

"If you're planning on building an island alliance, it might shake the foundations."

"What makes you think I'm planning an island alliance."

Kelahnus raised one eyebrow. Demnor smiled a moment, and then his expression grew serious once more."

"What would you suggest I do, then?"

Kelahnus sighed. "Let it go?"

"Let it go? Let a Heathland spy and a Branion traitor who murdered the Aristok go? You're not serious."

The Companion gestured helplessly. "I don't know. What I am is tired. I'm tired of lying. I'm tired of conflicting loyalties and I'm tired of conflicting love. I'm tired of pleading and praying for other people's lives and I'm tired of following other people's orders. I just want to live, I want you to live, and I want Florence and Alynne and even Grant to live, because she loves him and *I want a happy ending!*"

The Companion was smacking his fist into the bed by the end of this speech, and Demnor winced as the movement jarred his arm, although he didn't interrupt. Finally when Kelahnus sat, staring stiffly into space, he reached up and tucked the wisps of golden hair back from the other man's face.

"I love you," he said simply. "You'll have your happy ending. I don't know how yet, but I'll get it for you."

They're probably halfway to Tiberia by now, anyway, his mind added.

"Do you want some sleep?"

Kelahnus nodded. "Maybe a little. Move over a bit?"

Demnor shifted with a groan and the Companion frowned.

"You're stiff. I thought only your arm was wounded?"

"My chest's a bit bruised. It's nothing."

"Let me see."

"It's nothing."

The look Kelahnus shot him made Demnor shake his head. "Very well, if it makes you happy to fuss."

He went to lift the edge of his tunic and the Companion brushed his hand aside. "I'll do it."

The older man's ribs were black and blue where Arren's sword had hit and Kelahnus ran his fingers feather soft along the ridge of muscle.

"DeMarian colors," he whispered.

Demnor grunted. "I'm getting too old for this sort of nonsense."

"Good."

Lowering the tunic, Kelahnus lay down beside him, his good hand resting proprietorially on his chest. For a long time they lay, just breathing in each other's company and then they slept.

North of Gerrenloch Town, a small, ragged band of Heathland warriors led by Gordon Elliot Croser stumbled into Murdoune Castle, the Greyam family's south-land keep. Margaret Elliot Greyam and Alynne Elliot Croser were waiting for them. Their news of Heathland's defeat was only an hour ahead of the news of Heathland's emancipation. It was met with disbelief and suspicion.

The head of the Greyam family cut the discussion short. No matter what the DeMarian had in mind, Gordon and Alynne were still wanted fugitives and the older woman was certain whatever terms were discussed, their return would be part of the negotiations. Plans must be made to get them to safety.

An hour later saw the two lovers supplied and escorted on the road, heading for the Ross family's north-land holding. They would remain there until the political situation shook down. Whatever was to come after was unimportant. They had each other, and that was all the world. For now, the war was over.

High summer, Mean Mehefin, 894 DR

The bells of Branbridge rang out as they had every hour since four o'clock that morning, but no one was awakened by it. The streets were teeming with people decked out in their holiday finest. Most had been celebrating since the wee hours of the night and the Town Watch had had its hands full with drunken revelers. Royal births were few and far between and the city planned to welcome its new Prince of Gwyneth in style. It had no care for politics or power, the war still raging in Gallia, or the Aristok's strange victory gift to the Heathland barbarians. The Royal line was secured. That was enough for a holiday.

Branbridge had had an anxious few months of it. The Consort had been bedridden for weeks after her collapse, the priests and physicians tending her daily. For a time it looked as if she would lose the baby. News from Heathland of the manifestation of the Living Flame had come, explaining her condition, and the herbalists went to work. Finally the word was given that mother and child had stabilized.

Isolde met the returning Aristok from a pillow-laden carriage and allowed his fussing with only a minimum of ill humor.

As the birthing day drew nearer, the inns, ale houses and private homes were filled to bursting with visitors from across the Realm. Those that couldn't pay, beg, or wheedle a room had set up camp in Collin's Park, to the very edge of the palace gates.

Finally the day arrived. Vendors moved among the growing crowd before the north balcony, hawking everything from provender and bedding to little cloth-and-wood commemorative dolls. The people waited. Each time some faint stirring showed behind the balcony's glass doors, they ebbed forward, then back again, disappointed.

Finally when the sun was well placed in the sky, the trumpets sounded from the battlements. The people began to cheer and the balcony doors were flung open.

The first to emerge were the three religious leaders of the Land; Alexander DeKathrine, the Hierarchpriest of Cannonshire, Deborah the DeFay, Archpriest of the Oaks, and Cheryl DeYvonne, the new Archpriest of the Flame. Dressed in the red ceremonial robes of her office, she flung her arms wide, and a great sheet of crimson flew out above the crowd. It transformed itself into a shower of rose petals which drifted down to land on their upturned faces. The crowd cheered.

The members of the Royal family then stepped onto the balcony: Quindara, Duke of Yorbourne with her Companion and young Troyanon DeKathrine whom it was rumored might soon become her husband; Atreus, Duke of Lochsbridge and Marsellus, Duke of Kempston, still very ill, but slowly recovering from their sacred vision on the battlefield of Falmarnnock; and Kassandra, Duke of Clarfield, proudly carrying her regal brother's banner. Alerion DeKathrine, now Earl of Patenford, and the Duke of Exenworth, Isolde's mother, followed their DeMarian cousins.

The trumpets sounded again. The Duke of Yorbourne drew her sword and shouted one word of command. The great blue-and-black DeMarian flag was raised into the warm, summer air, the crimson-eyed fire-wolf and three golden oak leaf clusters snapping in the wind. The trumpets sounded once more and the crowds broke into wild cheering as His Most Regal and Sacred Majesty, Demnor the Fifth, Aristok of Branion, Kormandeaux and Aquilliard, Gaspellier, Poitienne, Roland, Hereditary Earl of the Danelind Islands of Columba, Gracious Sovereign of the Triarchy, Most High Patron of the Knights of the Sword, Vessel of the Living Flame, strode onto the balcony.

Isolde DeKathrine, Duke of Aquilliard, Consort of the Aristok, mother of the Heir, pale, but proudly erect,

walked beside him. And to her left, holding the
squirming bundle they had all come to see, walked
Kelahnus, First Royal Companion to the Aristok. He
smiled and passed over the child to Isolde, almost
shouting to make himself heard over the crowd.

"She's not wet . . . yet!"

Isolde laughed as she took the child in her arms.

"Of course she isn't," she crooned to the newborn
infant. "She's saving that honor for her Papa's arms,
aren't you, my darling?"

The Companion laughed.

Then the Duke of Aquilliard turned. "My husband,
may I present you with our firstborn daughter? Healthy
and whole."

Demnor looked into her eyes, then down. His face
softened and Kelahnus nearly choked back a sob of joy
as the boy he'd known shone fully from the eyes of the
man he loved. Taking the bundled child in his arms, the
new father folded the blanket aside to reveal a furious
little face, gray eyes sparkling with indignant fire. He
laughed.

His laughter reached out to the crowd as he held her
high in the air for them all to see.

"I give you, Amedea, Prince of Gwyneth!"

The trumpets sounded one more time and Alexander
DeKathrine shouted, "Long live Demnor the Fifth!"

"ALL HAIL THE ARISTOK!"

The crowd's answering roar drowned out the infant's
howl of indignation.

"Your people, Amedea," the forty-first Ruler of
Branion whispered into the damp, auburn hair of his
daughter. "Yours and mine. I love you."

Catching Kelahnus' eye, the two men shared a soft
smile of past memories and future promises, before
turning back to the adulation of the crowd.

FIONA PATTON

"Rousing adventure, full of color and spectacular magic"—*Locus*

In the kingdom of Branion, the hereditary royal line is blessed—or cursed—with the power of the Flame, a magic against which no one can stand. But when used by one not strong enough to control it, the power of the Flame can just as easily consume its human vessel, as destroy whatever foe it had been unleased against. . . .

☐ **THE STONE PRINCE**   UE2735—$6.99

☐ **THE PAINTER KNIGHT**   UE2780—$6.99

☐ **THE GRANITE SHIELD**   UE2842—$6.99

TANYA HUFF
VALOR'S CHOICE

"Readers who enjoy military SF will love Tanya Huff's
VALOR'S CHOICE. Howlingly funny and very
suspenseful. I enjoyed every word."
—*scifi.com*

Staff Sergeant Torin Kerr was a battle-hardened professional.
So when she and those in her platoon who'd survived the last
deadly encounter with the Others were yanked from a well-
deserved leave for what was supposed to be "easy" duty as
the honor guard for a diplomatic mission to the non-Confedera-
tion world of the Silsviss, she was ready for anything. Sure,
there'd been rumors of the Others being spotted in this sector
of space. But there were always rumors. Everything seemed
to be going perfectly. Maybe too perfectly. . . .

0-88677-896-4 $6.99